MW01264862

First Printing 2007 by Tongue Untied Publishing
ISBN 0-9745783-2-0

For more information regarding special discounts for bulk purchases, please contact Tongue Untied Publishing at (678)576-2768 or www.maseyree.com

Cover Design by www.mariondesigns.com

Edited By- Jessica Tilles- XYP Publishing
www.xpressyourselfpublishing.org

Printed in USA

ACKNOWLEDGMENTS

First of all I'd like to thank God for blessing me with a second chance for the world to see my light shine.

To my mother, whom, I love with all my heart. I am blessed to have you in my life to share this monumental moment with me. Keep on holding on because this is still just the beginning. In the future there will me many more celebratory moments for you to go and brag to your friends about.

To my husband, McKinley, my silent partner, and best friend, thanks for supporting all of my spontaneous endeavors no matter how crazy they may seem. Just keep on having my back because *we're gonna be rich one day. Watch!*

To all my family, Granny, Granddad, my aunts and uncles, Ann, Danny, Bob, Michael, Webbie, Gail, Kelvin, Puddin, Cyn, Demetra, Linda, Monica, Tasha, Jake , Orlando and Andrew. My sisters Yatanya and Angel, and sisters-in-law Yolanda and Annette, my brothers, Cortez, Willie, Milton, all my nieces and nephews, Javon, Corneisha, Destiny, Jalil, Najha, Marcus Jr., Kennedy, and Ate. To all my cousins, whom I have to many to name, I love you all too. To all my in-laws, especially Sandra Mitchell, my mother-in-law, thanks for supporting me.

To my cousin, Eleanor Patterson, aka, "Shug", who was like a grandmother to me, I will never forget all the things you taught me as a child that helped to mold me into the woman I am. Your words of wisdom will always be with me. RIP

To my father, Willie Lee Richardson whose time here was a short one, I will always love you.

SHOUTS OUTS!!
To my homegirl's, Ronda Horton, Danne Johnson, Jewel Richardson, Carla Noyles, and Tink, What it do Chanique & Dramani. Hold it down, Cory & Heather Buford, my web designers. Keep on striving to be a good girl, Chalsea Lynn Tucker aka "My Pretty Cousin." Make us proud of you, Devonnte Tucker, aka "Game 2". Hey Gayla Shivers! Hold it down in Durham, Chris. Hi Margaret Marria. To my bestis male friend, Darien Mason, put it on chill for a minute. Stay strong, Angel White! What up all my family, friends and supporters in Grand Rapids, Michigan. And to all my family and friends in East St. Louis, me nuv u too.
To everyone who had a part in making this book a success, thank you. And last but not least a special thanks goes out to the South River Baptist Church Choir, in Jackson Georgia for teaching me to harmonize. *"A whew, whew, whew……..umph, umph,"* back to what I was doing. Oh Yeah, Peace and Love to everyone and stay blessed.

Mari Anna

Thanks for Supporting

Masey Lee

ONLY TIME WILL TELL

www.maseyree.com

CHAPTER 1

It was Tuesday, August 13, the last day of Andrea's jail sentence. As she packed up her belongings and looked around the fourteen-by-fourteen-foot room, she smiled. The day that she'd been praying for was finally here. She smiled as she watched her roommate, Ilene, who was lying across the top bunk reading a book that one of her family members had sent her. Ilene busied herself by scanning the book, not really reading it. She was dreading their final goodbye. Andrea would miss her too, she thought as she stood in the middle of the room staring up at her friend. Although it was time to part from someone she'd grown to love, Andrea was thrilled that it was her time to go. Now, she'd be able to sleep in a real bed. The one that she'd been provided with was a hard, cement block, topped with a two-inch thick pad. Andrea shook her head, as she looked in the direction of the vacated bed. She remembered how cold it used to be during the fall and winter months. That cell would be freezing. Most nights, in order to stay warm, she had to double up her clothing while she slept. She was only provided with a cheap throw blanket as thin as the ones offered on airplanes. She never knew how hard some people had it until she served her residency in the county jail. Now, she sympathized on a higher level with the homeless people she sometimes saw sleeping outside during the winter. A couple of years ago, she could never have been convinced that she would see days like these. The sixteen months that she'd spent in jail had really given her time to heal, both spiritually and mentally. She had gone into jail a little girl, but was leaving, a woman.

It was the immature, disobedient little girl in her that landed her in the place where she was. Her trip to nowhere commenced with her refusal to obey and follow the rules of her parents' home. At some point, Andrea felt like she was the smartest fifteen-year-old of her time, and her parents didn't know shit, especially her mother, whom she despised. During that phase of her life, Andrea was going through some things, and wanted her parents to allow her to do what she wanted to do, when she wanted to do it. She started a pattern of lying and staying out late to avoid being at home and following their orders. As the months passed, she and her mother's relationship became more estranged. Andrea searched for excuses to justify why her mother got on her nerves so bad. Those days, Andrea had ulterior motives. She would do anything she could to get others to see how inattentive and inadequate her mother was.

Her mother, Caroline, was a high maintenance diva, who put all her time and efforts into material things, to avoid facing the facts of her life, which was that she had never been crowned heiress to someone's billion-dollar fortune. Her reality was that she was a blue-collar employee who ran the safety belt assembly line at one the leading automobile plants in Michigan. To fill the void of what she saw as an empty, meaningless life, Caroline indulged in expensive shopping trips and splurged money on personalized pampering sessions, expensive furniture, or anything that she could brag about to her friends, who were as shallow and as phony as she. If only her budget matched her pocketbook.

In Andrea's opinion, Caroline didn't pay enough attention to her children, and spent too much time clocking her husband's income, rather than focusing on being a good wife and mother. If Caroline hadn't spent so much time tending to everyone else's business, she would have known that Andrea wasn't doing the right thing. Since Andrea had a close relationship with her father, she grew to hate her mother for the way she mistreated him. Seeing the evil, conniving ways of her mother early on, led to Andrea's being unappreciative of the woman who'd given her life.

Even though she could practically ask her parents for anything she wanted and get it, Andrea developed a thrill for shoplifting. For some strange reason, shoplifting made her feel powerful, and grown-up. It was absolutely fulfilling for Andrea to know that she could get what she wanted without having to go to her parents for the money to purchase it. At the time, Andrea thought that misbehaving would make her mother more attentive to her, but now she knew better. It was her behavior and disobedience that caused all the chaos that followed.

Things got out of control after she met her baby's father, Tim. He was a white boy she attended school with; he was also the person who introduced her to smoking marijuana. One day, after coming from the mall with Tim, her cousin, and some of her friends, Andrea had her first experience with weed. She remembered the day very well because it was also the same day she found out that Tim had a crush on her. He serviced the majority of the potheads at their school and one day, Tim invited Andrea and her friends to smoke with him. The four of them sat, parked in a vacant lot of an abandoned building, and smoked the weed together. From that point on, there was no turning back for Andrea. She and Tim were hanging out more frequently, and Andrea was coming home later and later. Her grades suffered, reflecting her lack of participation in school.

The latter of her problems came when Andrea became acquainted with cocaine. A couple of Tim's friends convinced Andrea to snort the drug one night at a party, and from that point on, her life would never be the same. Tim's parents found out that he was seeing her, and gave Tim an ultimatum. He was to end the relationship or risk being put out of their home. By this time, Tim had stopped attending school on a regular basis, and his attitude had become more aggressive. He came and went as he pleased, and suddenly, he became Mr. Popularity. He got himself a cellular phone that seemed to be glued to the side of his face every time his parents saw him. That's when the Dobersons knew that Tim was using drugs. It was obvious. When Tim was on the drugs, they noticed he'd become enraged and ill tempered. He was like a totally different person, even verbally abusing his mother to the point where she was afraid to say anything to him. The Dobersons insisted that their son's behavior was directly relating to his hanging out with Andrea, and their insinuations would really send Tim into a rage. He loved Andrea, and refused to let them say one bad thing about her. They insisted that their disdain for Andrea was not at all racially motivated. The Dobersons didn't want Tim to see her because they felt that he'd become disconnected with everything since the beginning of his relationship with Andrea. She was simply a bad influence. When Tim refused their order to disassociate himself from her, he had to go. His refusal to follow their rules earned him a one-way ticket out of his parents' home.

Andrea was still allowed to live in her parents' home until her insubordination became constant. Andrea's drug habit had gotten so far out of control that she was stealing from her mother. One day, Caroline let her borrow a very expensive purse and Andrea sold it to get some powder. When her mother confronted her about it, the two of them got into a physical altercation. As a result, Andrea was put out of her parents' home, too. Shortly afterwards, she and Tim dropped out of high school and started living in hotels so they could be together. They shoplifted and sold the items in order to buy drugs to support their habits, and to pay hotel room fees. Months afterwards, Tim was arrested and sentenced, leaving Andrea alone on the streets.

Since she didn't want to go back to her parents' home, Andrea became disheartened. She was so depressed after Tim left that she starting doing anything she had to in order to survive. She met a couple of older females, Stephanie and Flo, who turned her toward prostitution while she shared their home. The three of them would go to the mall and boost all day, and then turn tricks and get high all night. Andrea had done so many things that she now regretted and wished she could undo. If she could do it all over again, or if she had one wish to change at least one thing about her past, it would be getting pregnant while she was on the drugs, which resulted in her having a drug addicted, premature baby. Not even a week after giving birth, Andrea was sent to jail for violating probation, and cruelty to children. At the time, her daughter, Timya, was in the hospital fighting for her life. Her daughter had been taken from her so quickly that Andrea barely had time to name her. She'd turned so many tricks before her pregnancy, that Andrea had no clue who fathered the baby until Timya was born obviously bi-racial. Then being institutionalized so soon after having the baby, Andrea never even had the opportunity to tell Tim that he was the father. For sixteen long months, Andrea remained locked away from the child that she never got the chance to know, and Tim never knew existed.

Andrea detached the picture of her daughter from the wall near her bedside, and placed it in the pile of her things she was preparing to leave with. Andrea felt bad about missing out on the most important months of her daughter's life. She couldn't wait to hold Timya in her arms. Andrea wanted to make sure that her child knew how much she loved her. She had so much to make up for. She hadn't been able to hold and caress her daughter since the day she was born, but she'd never forget that moment. It was as if it was photographically taped to her memory. Holding Timya momentarily after her birth was the only memory Andrea had of her daughter. She hadn't seen the child once since being placed behind bars, but she hadn't gone one day without thinking about her. Andrea wondered if her daughter was being told how much her mother loved her. She wondered if Timya slept well at night and wanted to know if she experienced the same separation anxieties that Andrea felt being away from her.

Andrea's mother felt that jail was no place for a child to see her mother, so she never brought Timya to visit Andrea, nor would she allow anyone else to take her. Caroline hadn't even bothered to pay Andrea a visit. Thomas had visited so many times, Andrea lost count. Her dad was sweet, loving and considerate, the complete opposite of her mother. Why he chose to marry Caroline, Andrea would never know.

Whenever Andrea got a money order, she knew it had been sent from her father or her Aunt Dorothy. Caroline would have probably preferred that Andrea sat in her cell and suffered for all the changes she'd taken her through. That was what made today so important to Andrea. It marked the start of her new life. It wasn't merely a day to re-experience the world, but a time to practice being a good mother. It was also a time to try to be an obedient daughter and a responsible adult.

Andrea was extremely nervous when the guard approached her cell and called out her last name. "Smith."

Andrea turned and hugged Ilene one last time, and told her that she loved and would miss her. As tears fell from both their eyes, the cell door slid open. Andrea broke their embrace, and turned to exit. She took a deep breath and stepped into the hall. Her crying eyes looked toward the ceiling as she thanked Him for the opportunity to do it all again. She had used the time she'd spent in jail wisely; acquiring her GED and preparing to enroll in a junior college or technical school as soon as she could. Unlike before, Andrea had plans for the direction in which she wanted her life to go. She wanted to get a degree to practice as a substance abuse counselor. Since she'd had hands on experience, she felt she could use her knowledge as a means of inspiration for others who wanted to clean up their lives.

Andrea stepped into the lobby and immediately noticed her father. She quickly ran and jumped into his arms. There was no real expectation to see her mother waiting there alongside him, but it would have been nice to see her face. Thomas was thrilled to see his daughter, and they both wept as he held her in his arms for a lengthy embrace before finally releasing her. As tears continued to run down her face, Andrea looked straight into her father's eyes. "I love you, Daddy."

"I love you too, daughter, and I've missed you very much." He hesitated briefly. "Are you all right?"

"I'll be fine as soon as I get out of here. Daddy, I want to see my baby."

"Okay, hon, let's go." Thomas and his daughter left the jailhouse wrapped in each other's arms.

Once inside the car, Andrea interrogated her father. "So what happened to Mom? Did she have something else to do?"

Sadly, Thomas answered, "Well you know how she feels about bringing the baby up here, and she didn't want to get a sitter for the hour it takes to make the round trip. Your mother, Timya, and even Taylor, played hookie from school to see you. They're all at home waiting for us."

"I can't wait to see my baby," Andrea repeated. "I bet she is as big as she is spoiled."

"You know right then," her dad validated. "Your mother is too over protective, and she lets Timya have her way all the time. Timya gets away with murder in that house."

"Daddy, do you know what it feels like to have a child that's been in the world for nearly two years, that you've only seen once?"

"I don't, honey, but I'm sure that when you see your daughter, that void will be filled. Try not to focus on what you've missed, but more so on what you have to look forward to."

Andrea smiled. That was exactly the reason why she loved her father so much. He was always positive and supportive. His refusal to give up on her is what kept her strong.

As they neared the house, Andrea thought about Tim; especially when the car rolled past the street on which his parents lived. She wondered if her baby's father was again living with his parents. Surely, Tim couldn't still be in jail.

"Have you all heard anything from Tim?" she quizzed.

"I can't say that I have. If your mother has, she hasn't mentioned it to me."

Andrea was silent again. Once she was settled, she could go by the Doberson's to find out Tim's whereabouts. She needed to let him and his parents know about Timya. It didn't matter how Tim's family felt about Andrea, Timya was their blood relative and she needed to know her family, on both sides. Andrea knew that once Tim found out about his first-born child, there was no way he would deny her existence. As they pulled into the driveway of her parents' home, Andrea felt nervous, her hands suddenly trembling. Tiny beads of perspiration burst through her skin and soon, her face was covered in sweat. She was afraid that her daughter wouldn't recognize her.

Before getting out of the vehicle, Thomas looked over at his daughter. He sensed her uneasiness. He reached over and patted her leg. "Relax, honey; you're home now."

Tears welled in Andrea's eyes as her mind replayed her father's words. *She was home now.* Those words terrified her. Home was where all her issues had evolved. At home was where her mother was. At home was where she felt the issues of abandonment and resentment. Andrea never knew why she and Caroline didn't get along. Maybe it was because Andrea absolutely hated the person her mother portrayed herself to be. Caroline had always been so caught up in trying to be someone she was not, that she never had much time to be a mother, or a wife. She never took the time to see that her children needed her. Caroline was always trying to keep up with the Joneses.

Andrea climbed out of the vehicle and took a deep breath. She was scared of facing an unknown reality, so she walked behind her father like a frightened child. Upon entering the house, she noticed that her mother had re-decorated. From room to room, all the décor and furniture seemed to be different than it was before Andrea went away.

As soon as Taylor heard someone entering the house, she ran into the kitchen to see if it was her father returning with Andrea. When she noticed her sister, Taylor ran to her, giving her a warm and welcoming hug. "I missed you so much, big sis," she remarked.

"I missed you too," Andrea muffled through tears. Taylor was hugging her so tight she couldn't help but to cry.

Caroline pranced into the kitchen with Timya attached to her hand. Thomas stood off to the side and an eerie silence filled the room. As soon as Andrea set eyes on her child walking into the kitchen, she wept even more. When she left, her daughter was a little over a week old, and now, Timya was walking. Andrea bawled with guilt. Timya was so beautiful. She had light, golden skin and golden brown hair that fell in big curls. It was apparent that Tim's genes were more dominant than Andrea's because besides the slight hint of color in her skin, Timya was the spitting image of her father. She even had Tim's oval-shaped eyes. The only difference was Timya's eyes were a dark, greenish-gray, and Tim's were ocean blue.

Before even acknowledging her mother, Andrea ran to Timya and whisked her into her arms. Her embrace was so sudden that she scared the baby, causing Timya to burst into tears. She had no idea who Andrea was, and she wanted the stranger to release her back to the familiar arms of her grandmother. Caroline grabbed the baby and quickly propped her on her hip. After Timya quieted down, Caroline reached out to hug her daughter.

"Good to see you," her mother remarked. "The baby doesn't know you, Andrea, but give her some time; she'll come around."

Andrea continued to stare at her child. She felt like a stranger.

"Here, Thomas, take your grandchild since she doesn't want to go to her mother. I was waiting on you all to come back so that I could run to the mall and pick up a few things. They have a sale at Parisians and I want to go and get some new bedding for Andrea's bedroom." She looked toward her daughter. "I've placed all the old linen in the attic. I also need to pick up some crystal serving dishes, for the welcome home party I'm throwing you on Sunday. I'm having it catered and I'd like everything to be set up really fancy. Everyone will be meeting up here after church."

Thomas looked disgustingly at his wife, as he reached for his granddaughter. Timya was full of smiles. She loved her "Pa Pa." Finally, Caroline kissed Andrea on the cheek and said she was glad for her to be home. "We can talk and get caught up on things as soon as I return. You know that if I take a day off work, and miss my money, I have to make it worth while."

Andrea looked at her father, and shook her head. It was obvious that this was not going to be easy. She knew that she had to hurry up and get on her feet so she could move out, and get her own place. Unfortunately, her mother had not changed from being her pompous, cynical self. Andrea knew that it was only a matter of time before she and Caroline would be at each other's throats.

Thomas walked over and gave his daughter a hug. "It's alright, sweetie, your mom's right. It's going to take some time for Timya to get used to you. In the meantime, let's get you up to your room so you can get situated."

Taylor was right behind them. Caroline had her purse on her shoulder, and was on her way toward the garage.

CHAPTER 2

Sullivan walked through the front door, entering behind his wife, Dorothy. They had gone out to see an afternoon matinee and had also stopped by the grocery store for Dorothy to get a few things to complete her dinner. As she followed her husband down the hallway toward the kitchen, Dorothy could hear their two daughters upstairs arguing. The girls were screaming at the top of their lungs. Dorothy yelled for them to be quiet, and for them to go into their own rooms, but her voice could not be heard over their ruckus. After placing her grocery bags on the counter, Dorothy headed upstairs to see what the fuss was all about.

Lately, Keisha and Tonya had been getting on her last nerves with their constant bickering and fussing. Dorothy walked straight into Keisha's bedroom, unnoticed by the arguing siblings. The room was decorated in red and black, Keisha's two favorite colors. Both the windows in her bedroom were covered with black mini blinds, which made the room very dark and dreary. Draped over the blinds were homemade valences that Keisha made at school in her sewing class. A large, plush area rug was sprawled across her already carpeted bedroom floor, and every area of her wall was covered with pictures of the rapper, Ludacris. Keisha loved him so much that she had posters, of all sizes, of him everywhere.

Tonya, Dorothy's youngest daughter, noticed Dorothy before Keisha did, so she immediately became silent. Her sister's sudden calm was suspicious, prompting Keisha to turn toward the door and notice her mother standing there. She yelled, "Mom, can you please tell Tonya to get out of my room? I am trying not to hurt her, but she is pressing her luck. I was in my own room, sitting on my own bed, watching music videos, and minding my own business, when Tonya came in here talking about the devil is in me."

Dorothy looked at Tonya, and then back at Keisha, as she continued talking. Not only were the girls loud, but the volume of their television was also turned up.

"She must think that she's a preacher or something, Mama, and she's getting on my nerves."

"Tonya, why are you even in here?"

"Mom, I was in my room, lying down on my bed, reading the Bible when all of a sudden, Keisha turns up that stupid television. All I hear is, 'shake yo bootie this, pop that bootie that,' like I want to hear that junk. So, I kindly walked in here and asked her if she could cut down her television some and she started getting all loud and in my face and acting crazy. That's when I said she must have the devil in her or something."

"No, what you did," Keisha interrupted, "was come in here talking about you don't want to hear no devil music while you're reading your Bible. I don't know how you think you are about to come up in my room regulating something. All you had to do was close your door."

Dorothy couldn't help but laugh at her feuding children. The two of them were always at each other's throats about something. When her oldest daughter, Monet, was living at home, Keisha and Tonya would always team up and rival with Monet. Now that their big sister was gone, the two of them had become each other's enemy. Dorothy thought they would get along better since Keisha and Tonya each had their own rooms, but that didn't seem to be the case. Dorothy disguised her smile with a serious expression before she chastised the two of them.

"Tonya, why don't you just go into your own room? If you don't want to hear what's going on in Keisha's room, then simply close your bedroom door. And, Keisha, you can be courteous and try to keep your television at a reasonable volume. There, problem solved," Dorothy concluded as she turned to walk away.

The girls rolled their eyes at each other, and then Tonya stomped her way out of her sister's bedroom. Dorothy shook her as she exited. Before Tonya entered her messy room, Dorothy said, "Tonya, I don't think you have the right to say who has the devil in them, and who doesn't. Keep your comments to yourself and let God be the judge, okay?"

"Yes, ma'am," Tonya answered as she walked across the hall to her bedroom.

Dorothy waited until Tonya was back in her room before she headed downstairs to the kitchen. She wanted to make sure that the girls didn't start arguing again. She didn't know what had gotten into Tonya. Since she'd been appointed assistant to the teacher in the junior Bible study class, she'd been acting like her name was Reverend Tonya.

When Dorothy made it back to the kitchen, her husband had put away all the items from the store, and was sitting in the living room. She could hear him and Dwayne, their son, debating about who was going to win the next round of football on the PlayStation 3.

Dorothy smiled as she washed her hands to prepare her family's dinner. As soon as she had everything on the stove, she was going to call her sister's house to see if Andrea had awakened. When she called earlier, Thomas told Dorothy that Andrea was sleeping, and Caroline was gone shopping somewhere. She couldn't wait to talk to her niece, and was even more excited about seeing her.

Her thoughts were broken by the ringing telephone. "Shoot," Dorothy griped. She hated being interrupted when she was trying to do something. After the third ring, Dorothy headed to the telephone. She was trying to avoid leaving her workstation, hoping that one of her family members would answer the phone; but since no one had jumped at the opportunity, she dried her hands and walked over to the cordless phone that sat on the table.

"Hello," she huffed into the phone. It was her sister Caroline. She was calling to remind Dorothy of the party she was throwing for Andrea after church on Sunday. Dorothy told her sister that she hadn't forgotten about Sunday. "You could have saved yourself a call though, because we'll all be over there tonight to see Andrea when we finish eating dinner. Where are you, anyways? I called your house earlier and you weren't there. Thomas said that you were out shopping somewhere."

I'm at a bakery downtown, taste-testing frostings for the cake that's going to be served at the party. I think I'm going to go with the butter cream. It's heavenly."

Dorothy rolled her eyes, while asking, "Are you going to be at home by the time we get over there?"

"I hope so. I just have one more stop to make after I leave here. Call me on my cell when you finish eating, just to make sure."

"Okay," Dorothy said before hanging up. She sucked her teeth and headed back to her kitchen counter where she was chopping onions. Caroline's priorities were definitely out of order. *She needs to be at home spending some time with her daughter.* Dorothy shook her head in disgust as she picked up her knife.

Later on that night, Dorothy and her family drove to her sister's place for a visit. Andrea ran into Dorothy's arms as soon as she stepped foot through the door. After their embrace, Dorothy took a good look at her eldest niece and said, "You still look the same, although I see that you have gained a few pounds."

As Andrea smiled and invited them into the family room, Dorothy added, "Monet said that she's sorry she couldn't make it over here today, but she will definitely see you on Sunday."

When Timya heard Dorothy's voice, she immediately turned and ran to her. Andrea's smile dropped. She wished that Timya had given her half the response, when she showed up. Dorothy hoisted Timya in her arms and carried her into the living room. Everyone else soon joined them and for the next hour or so, they sat around exchanging conversation.

Dorothy didn't stay as long as she would have liked because her sister eventually aggravated her. Caroline kept interrupting Dorothy and Andrea's conversation to add a comment about the party she was planning. The way she was carrying on, one would swear that she was a planning for her dream wedding or something. Dorothy eventually stood to leave, saying that she needed to get her rest since she had to get up early in the morning.

Andrea wished Dorothy could stay longer, but she didn't mention it. She knew that after her Auntie left, she'd be stuck all night listening to her mom talk about the party that Andrea felt was stupid and unnecessary. If it were up to her, they would have a normal Sunday dinner after church and call it a day. After all, Andrea had no desire to stand around telling a bunch of her mother's friends, who were strangers to her, about her life behind bars. *What a celebration.* Andrea thought.

"Okay, Auntie, thank you for coming." Andrea watched Dorothy leave. "I guess you and I will have plenty of time tomorrow to catch up on small talk."

"Okay," Dorothy said as she and her niece embraced in another hug. "Just take it one day at a time," she whispered to Andrea. "You need to focus on taking care of that baby, and getting back on your feet. None of that other stuff is important. And, don't let anybody fool you. That baby knows who her mother is." Dorothy then looked over at her sister. "God is gone work everything out, just be patient." Afterwards, Dorothy and her family said their goodbyes and left.

The next day, Andrea decided that after visiting her probation officer, she would stop by Tim's parents' place to see if they knew of his whereabouts, and to let them know that they had a grandchild. The last time Andrea had seen Tim, was two years ago, when he was arrested for shoplifting. At that time, Andrea was really strung out. She was such a different person now. The life of drugs and prostitution was behind her, and she was ready to rebuild her life and take care of her child. Although her parents knew about her drug problem and living on the streets, they had no idea that Andrea had slept with various men to get the money she needed to support her drug habit, and Andrea never planned to tell them. If she could take it all back, it would have never been her choice to have Timya; but it was all too late now. If her daughter hadn't come out an obviously bi-racial baby, Andrea wouldn't have known who her father was. Fortunately, Tim was the only white guy she'd slept with. If he had not gone to jail, he'd have been the only guy she would have slept with. He was her high school sweetheart, and even after so much time had passed, he was still the person she wanted to spend the rest of her life with. Andrea missed Tim desperately. She thought about him everyday and dreamt of the day she'd finally introduce him to their child.

Dorothy didn't go inside with Andrea to see her probation officer. Instead, she and Timya sat in the car outside and waited for her. The weather outside was pleasant, so Dorothy preferred to sit in the car with the baby, rather than sitting inside the air-conditioned building. Besides, she and Timya were used to being in one another's company. Dorothy had been caring for Timya since she was about six months old. Since she'd quit working as a manager at Kentucky Fried Chicken, Dorothy found that sitting around the house all day didn't suit her. She needed to have something to do. There was only so much cleaning that needed to be done on a daily basis. So, when Caroline mentioned that she was looking for a sitter who would come to her house everyday and watch Timya, Dorothy jumped at the job opportunity. Although her husband made enough money to take care of their family, Dorothy was accustomed to earning her own money.

After Timya was released from the hospital, she had to have the assistance of an oxygen tank twenty-four hours a day; and with all her other health issues, Caroline was skeptical about the person she would hire to tend to the child. With Dorothy being family, she proved to be the ideal person for the job. Timya ended up being on the oxygen machine for eleven months before her lungs were fully developed. It took Dorothy a minute, but she eventually got used to the maneuvering process of the baby. However, getting used to Timya's constant crying spells was hard. Timya was about eighteen months old when Dorothy finally managed to control the baby's constant outbursts. Caring for Timya had proven to be a more difficult task than when she babysat her grandson, Deshawn.

As soon as Andrea stepped out of the Probate Court building, she jumped into her aunt's car, smiling. Looking in the backseat at her daughter, Andrea thought of how happy she was to be in her presence. Timya's deep dimples appeared when her cheeks puckered up to a smile. "I think she looks like me when she smiles."

Dorothy smiled, and closed the magazine she'd been reading. After placing it to the side, she started the engine to her Chevy Malibu. The car had been a wedding gift from her husband.

"So, how did it go, Andrea?"

"Everything is fine. Mr. Watson wants me to find a job right away. He gave me a few leads to some different places that are hiring, but I told him I wanted to spend a few weeks with my daughter before I go out to look for work. He said he'd give me two weeks."

"That sounds good to me," her aunt told her as the car turned out of the parking lot and into traffic.

"Aunt Dorothy, do you mind taking me by Tim's parents' place? They live over on Stephens Road. It's a couple of blocks away from my house."

Dorothy didn't speak immediately, but she did address Andrea's request. "Are you sure you want to go over there without calling first? I mean, these people haven't seen you for a long time. You don't want to scare them. You know how timid those folks can be."

"I don't have the telephone number, so I have no choice but to stop by. Besides, I doubt if I will be able to get my mother to take me. She probably doesn't care if Timya never meets the other side of her family," Andrea sadly announced.

"All right, then," Dorothy said as the car continued down the street.

When Dorothy's car turned onto Stephen's Road, Andrea suddenly became panicky. She told her aunt that she was happy that she'd decided to come with her instead of her mother. "I know her. If my mother would have come over here, she would have immediately lashed out and tried to control the entire situation." Andrea knew that Caroline would walk into the Dobersons' home, trying to tell them what was going to be done whether they liked it or not.

When they parked in front of Tim's parents' lovely, four-sided, brick home, Dorothy shut off the car's engine and turned to Andrea. "I will stay in the car with the baby until you give me the cue to bring her in."

"Okay," Andrea agreed as she climbed out.

Dorothy sat motionless and observed while her niece slowly walked toward the house. She watched Andrea ring the doorbell and then glance back at her as she waited with Timya.

This was it, Andrea thought. She had waited a long time for this moment, and although her palms were sweaty, she continued waiting. When she heard the front door open, Andrea turned toward it. She had prepared a speech in case Tim's mother answered, but Andrea was astonished to see Tim standing in the open doorway. She peered into Tim's wide blue eyes and was instantly mesmerized. Her mouth moved, but no words came out.

Andrea's first thought was to jump into his arms, but still uncertain of where things stood with them, she decided against it. She hadn't seen Tim in two years, and had no idea what was going on in his life. For all she knew, he could be married with children. A lot could have happened in the two years they'd been apart.

"Andrea," Tim finally mouthed. "What are you doing here?"

"I came here to check on you," she answered.

Tim busily shook his head back and forth as he stepped onto the porch and closed the door behind him. He quickly pulled Andrea into his arms and held on to her for what seemed like minutes. After he released her, his lips collided with hers. Andrea threw her head back and closed her eyes. She felt like she was dreaming. It was as if her fantasy had come true. She knew that there was still hope for their relationship. After their embrace, Tim stood back and took a long, good look at his estranged girlfriend.

"Baby, you look good," he commented.

"Thanks," she smiled. She looked out toward the car, wondering if she should come right out and tell Tim about their daughter. But what popped out of her mouth was, "So when did you get out?"

Tim smiled. "One year, and four months ago. Where have you been?" When Andrea hesitated, Tim continued. "I've been taking it easy since I got out. I did almost eight months in the county, but I've been walking the straight and narrow ever since."

"I know what you mean," Andrea huffed. "I'm trying to walk that line myself."

"You wanna come inside?"

Andrea quickly shook her head no. She wasn't ready to deal with his parents until she spoke with him.

"Dang, I missed you," he reminded her again as he gave her another hug. His embrace felt so good Andrea wanted to cry. Before he'd gotten locked up, Tim was her all, her everything. She really wished that their relationship could start where it left off, because she was still very much in love with him. Apparently, he felt the same way.

"I stopped by your parents' house after I got out of jail, and I asked your mother if she knew where I could find you, but she said that she hadn't seen you."

Andrea gawked in surprise. That was purely like her mother to say something like that when she knew very well where Andrea was. Since Carolyn didn't tell Tim Andrea's whereabouts, she definitely hadn't informed him on the existence of their daughter. Andrea was sure of that. Sometimes, her mother could be down right dirty.

"Look, Tim, we need to talk." She looked out toward her aunt's car once more. "My aunt gave me a ride over here and I didn't come to stay, but we definitely need to talk, in private, and soon, it's very important."

"Okay, that's cool," Tim answered. "I attend Davenport, three days a week. Tomorrow, I get out at one. I can meet you somewhere around two o'clock, or do you need me to pick you up?"

"No," Andrea quickly responded. There was no way she would have him pick her up and she come running out of the house with Timya in her arms talking about, "This is your daughter." That was not the way she intended on breaking the news to him. If she agreed to meet him somewhere at a certain time, she would show up early with the baby, and tell him then.

"I can meet you at McDonald's at around two."

She briefly thought about it. "That's cool."

"Cool."

"I'll see you tomorrow, then," she yelled as she rushed off the porch, toward the car. She could still see Tim standing on the porch after Dorothy navigated the car out of the driveway and they were driving down the street. Andrea couldn't wait to see Tim's reaction after she'd introduced him to Timya.

CHAPTER 3

Monet picked up her telephone after the second ring. "Hello," she chanted in a friendly voice.

"Is Monet there?" came through the phone.

Monet didn't recognize the voice, but could sense that this was not about to be a friendly conversation. "This is Monet," she finally confessed.

"Monet, this is Kim."

Monet sat thinking, *Kim*; the name didn't ring a bell. "Kim, who?"

The female huffed into the phone as if she were irritated with the question. "I'm Derrick's woman. You know, your baby's daddy, Derrick."

Monet had absolutely no idea where this conversation was heading, but she remained on the line anyway.

"Well, Monet, to make a long story short, I was calling to let you know that Derrick and I have been living together for the last year, and I am four months pregnant with *his* child."

Monet held her peace while thinking, *why would I care about them having a baby, or about their relationship? I don't want Derrick.*

"Well, Monet, up until the last few days, Derrick and I were supposed to be engaged, but since he hasn't come home since yesterday, I can't see myself marrying him, so he can play me like no fool. I don't know what has got him trippin' like this." Kim paused before continuing to vent about her dysfunctional relationship, but eventually got to the matter in which she'd called about. "I was just wondering if you could come and pick up your son. Derrick left him here yesterday, and I have my own two kids to watch," she griped.

Monet was baffled. She could not believe what she was hearing. Derrick had come to pick up Deshawn to keep him for the weekend, while she studied. She could not believe that fool had left her child with some hussy for two days. If he didn't feel like being bothered with Deshawn, then Derrick should have brought him back home.

Monet tried to compose herself, but she remained frantic. "Where do you live?"

"On Franklin and Neland, by Ms. Tracy's," she muffled.

Monet knew the area, so as soon as Kim gave her the address, Monet told her that she was on her way. Hanging up the phone, she rushed out of the house. She jumped into her car and sped off, all the while dialing Derrick's telephone number. Monet couldn't wait to speak with him but she tried to remain calm. When his voicemail picked up, she damn near listened to the entire song, "Drop It Like It's Hot," by Snoop Dogg, while waiting for the beep. Frustrated, she eventually hung up without leaving a message. She would try again later. Monet preferred to talk directly to him instead of his voicemail anyway. Right now, she needed to focus on getting her child from the stranger his daddy had left him with.

In less than ten minutes, Monet was parking in front of Kim's apartment. She jumped out of her Cavalier and rushed up to the door that displayed apartment two. Frantically, Monet knocked on the door and waited for an answer. The yellow, two-family, apartment building was freshly painted, and the lawn looked as if it had recently been cut.

Kim opened the door without a welcome smile or a hello. She surveyed Monet up and down, and then turned to walk back up the stairs. Monet entered, closed the front door behind her and followed Kim. She would have felt more comfortable if Kim would have come to the front door with Deshawn because she preferred not to go inside her apartment.

At the top of the stairs was another door that was the entrance to Kim's apartment. Right away, Monet could see that Kim was not the cleanest female. The first room they entered was the living room. In that space sat a honey wood-colored couch covered with a sheet, blanket and pillow. Someone must have been using the couch for a bed. There were toys and clothes all over the floor. A couple of rolled up, dirty pampers, candy wrappers, and a plate with old food were sitting on the edge of the end table. On the recliner was a bag of opened chips, surrounded by crumbs, and an empty plastic cup that had tipped over into the chair.

Kim told Monet to hold on while she got Deshawn who was in the bedroom. Kim's pregnant belly poked out as she wobbled into the back bedroom with her left hand on her hip. She was walking as if her back was hurting. Monet looked around the place as the word, *"Trifling"* slipped out of her mouth. One, she could not believe that Derrick had left her son with this girl, and two, she couldn't understand how he could be living with someone who was so filthy. What was even worse, Kim was pregnant again, and already had two children. She couldn't have been any older than Monet and Monet wondered if either of Kim's children belonged to Derrick. He was such a whore that Monet still couldn't figure out what she'd seen in him. Maybe it was her naiveté. When she got pregnant with Deshawn, she was only sixteen. Derrick had caught her during her young and dumb phase of life. She was happy that her days of playing the fool for Derrick were long gone.

Deshawn came running up to his mother as soon as he set eyes on her. "Mommy, Mommy," he shouted.

"Hey, baby," Monet said, as she bent over to pick up her child. She checked his appearance to see if he had any obvious scars or bruises. She wanted to make sure her son hadn't been abused before she took him home. That way, if anything were wrong with him, she would deal with Kim before she left. "Did you miss your mother?"

"Yes," Deshawn happily answered.

Monet stood and looked at Kim. "Did Derrick bring his bag over here?"

"Yeah. I was back there looking for it, but them kids got stuff all over the place. I will have to gather his things later and give them to Derrick."

Monet was totally outdone. *Now, this hoe is Queen of Trifling. Derrick's whoreish ass will lay up with anything.* Monet looked at Kim sternly. Kim was not the least bit embarrassed. Instead, she tossed a look at Monet that said, *What else are you waiting for?* Monet rolled her eyes at the girl and prepared to leave. At the door, she thanked Kim for keeping her son. Monet couldn't wait to get her baby home so she could put him in the bathtub. There was no telling what germs he'd picked up at Kim's place.

As soon as Monet got Deshawn strapped into his car seat, she jumped into the front seat and took out her cell. She dialed Derrick's number and pulled out onto the street. As soon as the telephone rung, she prayed that Derrick would answer. She couldn't wait to curse him out. Again, there was no answer. How dare he leave their son with a strange female? While waiting to leave a message for him, her line beeped.

"Hello," she answered. It was Derrick and she instantly went off. "Derrick, why in the hell did you leave my son with some tramp, who I don't even know? What kind of father are you? I can't depend on you for shit, Derrick." Her voice was cracking. "If you didn't feel like being bothered with your son, then you should have brought him back to me."

A car honked at her because Monet's car was veering into the other lane. Realizing that she was in no frame of mind to be driving right now, she put on her turn signal and pulled her car over to the curb. She looked in the backseat at Deshawn. He had already fallen asleep. Monet was happy because she didn't want him to hear some of the things that were about to come out of her mouth.

"Monet ain't nothing wrong with Deshawn. He a'ight."

"He's not alright Derrick. How would you know if he's alright or not, when he's not even with you? I left him with *you*," she yelled.

"Monet, quit trippin'. I just told yo–"

"The only thing I want to know is why your irresponsible ass left my son with that ole nasty trick."

"What are you talking about, Monet? Did Kim call you? Don't believe nothing she says. My son is okay; he's with his daddy."

Monet abruptly hung up the telephone and cried. All sorts of thoughts were running through her head. As she looked back at her son, the tears fell heavier. Derrick was such an idiot. How could she have been so stupid to have had a child with him? Monet couldn't believe that he was going to try and talk her into believing that he had Deshawn with him, when Deshawn was in the car with her. He wasn't even aware that she'd picked him up from Kim's house.

"Oh, God," she cried. "Thank you for waking me up to see that Derrick's a fool." How could she have been in love with such a worthless individual? Deshawn would never be left with Derrick again. Monet made a mental note to call the child support office the following day to give them Derrick's new address.

CHAPTER 4

Punkin rocked in the La-Z-Boy rocker in the family room of the group home where she worked as an In-Home Aide, smacking on her Juicy Fruit gum. Her eyes were glued to the television set as she watched her favorite soap opera, *All My Children*. She was working the first shift, and needed to be in the kitchen preparing lunch, but her butt would not part from the chair until the secret about the baby girl was revealed to Bianca. Punkin simply knew that she was about to find out that Bianca's friend's baby was really her daughter, but of course, the news wouldn't be revealed until the next day.

"Damn," she cursed as the credits rolled. With her mind full of anticipation, she got up and walked into the kitchen to prepare lunch.

After lunch was served, Punkin walked into the food pantry to grab the items she needed in order to restock the kitchen, for the next shift. She worked in a private, four-bedroom group home that housed three elderly residents. The job was divided into three eight-hour shifts, and whenever she wanted, Punkin could easily alternate days with the other two women who worked there and she loved the flexibility. Although it was her week to work the morning shift, that would not stop Punkin from going out somewhere to get her groove on later that night. Since her hangout buddy, Niecy, whom she'd met through her best friend, Dorothy, found a man, she didn't get out much; but Punkin still partied every chance that she got. Punkin discovered that going out solo was rather cool. That way, if she wanted to leave the club with someone, she wouldn't have to worry about making sure that the person she came with had alternate available transportation.

As Punkin exited one of the resident's bedrooms, a bell alarmed. It was the bell that rang every time someone entered the front door of the home. She stood, waiting for the person entering to appear in sight. An aroma of a sensual masculine cologne told Punkin that the stranger was a gentlemen. When the tall, dark-skinned brother appeared within her eyesight, her smile grew. The gentleman was rather short in statue, a little over five feet tall. He wasn't a very attractive man, but his charming smile was probably what he used to attract the opposite sex. As he approached her, the man extended his hand, introducing himself as Alan Bell. He was the son of Mrs. Nola Mae Bell, one of their residents. Of the four years that Punkin had worked at the assisted living home, this was her first time meeting Mrs. Bell's son.

"Hello," Punkin said to the stranger as she shook his hand. As was the home's standard procedure, when their hands parted, she walked to the desk and asked Mr. Bell if he would sign their visitor's register and show some identification.

"Of course," Alan answered, joining her at the desk.

"Your mother just had her afternoon medication. She is either sleeping, or watching T.V, but you can go right in."

"Well, thank you," he spoke in a southern drawl, while glancing at her nametag with his flirting eyes. He read it aloud. "Nice to meet you, Ms. Charlotte–"

"Oh, please call me Punkin," she interrupted with a smile. "I can't stand the name, Charlotte. I don't know what my mother was thinking about when she named me that."

"Whatever you like, Ms. Punkin," Alan winked at her and said, before proceeding on toward his mother's private bedroom suite.

"Ooh, don't say it like that. You might make a sista wanna do something to ya," Punkin whispered to herself, while heading back into the kitchen.

Alan visited with his mother for about an hour or so before Punkin heard him closing the door, and then his footsteps trotting down the hall. By that time, Emily, the second shift employee, had arrived. Coincidentally, Punkin was leaving at the same time as Alan. In reality, her shift had ended about ten minutes earlier, but she planned to speak with Alan before he left. They nearly bumped into each other in the hallway as she exited the kitchen, two feet in front of him.

"I'm so sorry," Punkin apologized. "I guess I wasn't paying attention to where I was going. You know how it is when it's time to go home."

Alan also apologized as they walked toward the exit. "So what does one do in this city, for entertainment?"

"It depends on what you like to get into."

"Well, I just recently arrived in town from North Carolina. I'd like to go somewhere where I can get my dance on."

"Well, tonight, is singles' night at the Lenox Room. You might like that."

"Oh, yeah?" Alan smiled while staring at Punkin. When she wasn't looking, he marveled at her well-rounded behind that followed her. He couldn't seem to keep his eyes from staring at her backside.

"Yeah, that's right."

"Well, if you're free tonight, I'd love to have you show me how y'all get down in Grand Rapids."

Punkin stopped walking and turned to face him. "Are you asking me out?"

"Only if you're considering my offer," he smiled with a flirtatious smirk.. "If it'll make you feel more comfortable, you can give me directions to the place, and I can meet you there."

"That'll work," Punkin happily answered.

After they exchanged phone numbers, she recited the directions for Alan to get to the Lenox Room. Subsequently, they each said goodbye and went their separate ways.

That night, Punkin and Alan met up outside the Lenox Room at ten o'clock. Punkin made sure she dressed in her most impressive attire. Since Alan was new in town, she wanted to make a lasting impression on him. She noticed Alan right away, as his Silver Maxima with the Carolina license plate pulled into an empty parking space. She'd been sitting in her car listening to music and watching people go in. Once Alan climbed out of his car, Punkin did the same and stood beside her vehicle, hoping Alan would notice her. She was wearing a pair of red, fitted bell-bottom slacks that snuggly wrapped around her curves. Her red top was short sleeved with fringes hanging from the bottom, and around the sleeves. With all that red she was wearing, it would be hard for Alan not to notice her.

As soon as Alan spotted Punkin standing by her car in the bright outfit, he smiled and walked toward her. He was looking scrumptious in his black slacks and casual shirt, Punkin thought. When he approached, she greeted him with open arms. Alan was totally mesmerized once he got up close to see how different she looked outside her work uniform.

After their embrace, he remarked, "Um, um, um, Punkin. You really know how to get a brotha's attention, don't you? Every man in the place is going to have his eyes on you."

Punkin blushed as she turned and looked toward the door, and then back at Alan.

"You clean up nicely yourself," she purred. Alan couldn't help but to blush. "Shall we?" Punkin exclaimed, insinuating that she was ready to go inside.

"After you," Alan replied as he waited for her to start walking. He followed closely.

The club didn't get as packed as Punkin had expected, but it was a nice crowd. The D.J kept spinning the right cuts and Punkin and Alan stayed on the dance floor all night. Since she was originally from Chicago, she was trying to show Alan how to do the bop, and the four-step. He seemed to be impressed by her moves. On the last slow song of the night, Alan was rubbing up against her and grinding on her as they danced. Punkin could feel him growing between his legs, and she was impressed. They both had been drinking all night and Punkin, like Alan, was ready to take it to the house.

When the D.J announced that closing was in fifteen minutes, Punkin could hardly believe the night with Alan was about to be over. Neither of them seemed ready to part, so Punkin invited Alan back to her place. They headed straight to her bedroom where they began undressing each other without so much as turning on the lights. Alan laid her down and licked her erect nipples. Punkin moaned as she rubbed her hands through his hair. He kissed her lips, and pulled her to the edge of the bed, before removing her pants. She threw her legs straight into the air and smiled. He was excited to see how flexible she was.

Alan smiled devilishly and stood to his feet. "I'm gon' tear that thing up, baby," he howled, as he stepped out of his underwear. Alan got back on his knees and licked around the lining of her panties. It sent shivers through her. Heat ravished through her body, causing tiny beads of sweat to form. He then removed her underwear, dropping them to the floor. His tongue immediately flickered across her clit and Punkin screamed out with satisfaction. She purred and moved her body to the motion of his tongue. His mouth was full of her, and she was begging for more.

"You want some more? Well, let me see if you want some of this." He climbed into the bed and drove himself deep inside her. Alan was panting and breathing heavily as he rocked his body back and forth. He was sexing her as if it was his job to make sure that she was satisfied, and she loved it. Alan was packing, and knew how to work with the seven inches of thickness he'd been blessed with. He pulled himself out of her and turned her over on her stomach, as her round bottom jutted upward. Without delay, his searing penis slid back inside. He grabbed her breasts and massaged them, his thumb teasing her nipples. She moaned gratifyingly. The fire grew within them, and fulfillment was moments away. Alan's thrusts became more powerful. Punkin couldn't get enough. He was loving her hard, and she pleasingly received it. Her lover grasped on to her hips, and pulled her closer into him. Alan was calling her name and asking her if it was good. She screamed out yes, as he pulled out and waited for her to beg for more.

"More, Daddy," she begged as he soared back inside her. Afterwards, Punkin and her exhausted lover lie side by side on the bed. He wrapped his arm around her and let her know how much he enjoyed being with her. She loved the way he felt. His body was so strong and comforting. After they had rested some, they continued lying in bed, talking. Punkin finally asked what brought him to Michigan.

"I had to come and get things settled with my mother's house. I had previously been renting it out, but when the last tenants moved out, they left the house a mess. I had to pay for major renovations over there. I will only be in town until the work is finished and I get the place rented again."

"Oh, no," Punkin responded in a disappointed tone. "I thought you were here to stay."

"No, I wish I could, but I have a fiancé back at home who is seven months pregnant. She would never forgive me if I wasn't there for the arrival of our first little one. I hope to be heading back home within a month."

Punkin pulled away from his embrace. "You have a fiancé and a baby on the way?"

"Yeah," he answered, unashamed.

Punkin was silent. Her euphoria was gone. Prior to Alan breaking the news about having a fiancé, she felt a bond with him. He'd made good love to her, and until his announcement, she'd even contemplated doing it again.

"If you are engaged to someone and you have a baby on the way, then why are you here with me?"

He laughed. "Come on now, Punkin. If you really cared that I had a woman or not, you would have asked before you invited me to your house to put this big ole thing up in you."

His words were so stunning that Punkin didn't have a response. Before she could say anything else, Alan jumped up from the bed, saying he had to go. He dressed as Punkin laid there, feeling like a fool.

Alan couldn't have put it any simpler than he had. As a matter of fact, he'd shed light on something Punkin already knew. *A man is only going to do to you, what you allow him to,* she mouthed silently. With feelings of embarrassment and shame, she thought, *I should have never even invited Alan back here.* She felt used. How could she have been so stupid? If Alan cared anything about her at all, he would have at least spared her the details about the fiancé and baby on the way, or maybe it was nice of him to come out and tell her. It only saved her the heartache of finding out later.

"Um, um, um," Punkin sighed. Maybe God was trying to tell her something. Maybe it was time for her to stop jumping into bed with every Tom, Dick, or Harry who proved to have interest in her because of her fat backside. She was getting too old for this. What she needed was her own man, a husband.

CHAPTER 5

Thursday morning, Sullivan drove down the street, in his Cadillac Seville, while listening to a newly purchased jazz CD. He was on his way back to work from lunch. He felt so content that he sang along with the Queen as she hummed the lyrics to *Simply Beautiful*, the third track on the Dana Owens CD. The song seemed to be metaphorically symbolic for how his life was unfolding. He had recently been promoted to vice president of the juvenile detention center where he worked, and he was happy to be in love and to have a family. He and Dorothy shared such a genuine affection. She was his number one supporter and always had his back. She was his everything, his true soul mate, and he'd told her so earlier that morning after she removed his empty breakfast plate from in front of him.

To show his appreciation for her, Sullivan had a very special surprise weekend planned for the two of them. He had purchased two tickets for the new Tyler Perry play, *Madea Goes to Jail*, which was being performed downtown Friday evening. Dorothy loved Madea. Sullivan bought all of Tyler Perry's DVDs for his wife so that she and the children could watch them. They enjoyed those DVDs so much, they'd watch them back to back, all day long, and would be laughing all throughout. Dorothy had never seen Madea live, and Sullivan knew that she would be thrilled to go. Afterwards, he had dinner reservations for the two of them at a fancy, downtown Japanese restaurant. To work off their dinner, they could stroll down the waterfront, which was less than a mile away. The children were going to spend the weekend with their father, Delvin so after their walk, Sullivan and Dorothy could go back home and have the entire house to themselves.

As he parked his car into a space near the building, Sullivan waited until after the song went off before he got out of the car. It was a cool afternoon, but the temperatures were expected to reach nearly sixty degrees by late day. For Michigan, that was more than to be expected in August.

Sullivan stepped toward the building when suddenly, he heard someone from behind, calling his name.

"Mr. Edwards, can I speak with you for a minute?" The female voice was one that Sullivan didn't recognize right away. Once he turned around, he was surprised to see the woman sitting in the car that was now parked directly behind his. It was his ex-wife, Rhenee.

Sullivan stood in a cold stance staring at her head on. The look on his face told Rhenee that she was the last person that he'd expected to see at his job. Rhenee smiled at Sullivan, turned off her car engine, jumped out of her car and walked toward him. Rhenee appeared to be dressed for work, so Sullivan figured whatever it was she wanted, it wasn't going to take long for her to tell him. He would keep the conversation short so that she could keep it moving. Sullivan's eyes scanned her from head to toe. Her hair had grown past her shoulders and Rhenee looked as if she'd lost about fifteen pounds, but she was still as fine as Sullivan could remember her being. Her caramel brown skin was still flawless and her smile was curiously bright. Uneasily, Sullivan glanced in all directions to see if anyone else was in the parking lot besides the two of them.

"So, what's up?" He hadn't seen or talked to Rhenee in three years.

Rhenee's demeanor was peculiar. She busied herself, sizing Sullivan up before she answered. "So, how has life been treating you, Mr. Vice President? I see you're still looking good."

He smiled. "You look nice yourself." The moment fell still for a short while before Sullivan broke the silence. "How did you know about my promotion?"

"It was in the newspaper," Rhenee answered. "You know I read the paper religiously."

"I must say," Sullivan, feeling a bit more relaxed, smiles, "I'm enjoying the accolades, as well as the new position. So, what's up with you? How has life been treating you?"

"You know me...working real hard, putting in way too many hours as usual."

"You always did dedicate yourself solely to your job."

Rhenee wasn't sure how to receive his comment, being that they'd divorced because of her infidelity. Sullivan caught her and a co-worker, Ray, in bed together. Three days later, he filed for a divorce. Unsure whether Sullivan was complimenting or ridiculing her, Rhenee instantly changed the subject.

"So, I heard that you were re-married."

"Yes; I have a wife and four great children. I can't complain one bit."

"A family, huh," Rhenee chanted. That's the part she hadn't read about in the newspaper. Suddenly, her thoughts left the parking lot. Knowing Sullivan, it was all true. He probably was happy with his wife and family. After all, he was a good, dedicated man with a genuine heart. It was she who had ruined their marriage. All Sullivan wanted to do was work and take care of home. He'd expressed wanting to start a family with Rhenee soon after their marriage, but Rhenee wasn't ready for that. It wasn't that Sullivan didn't want her to work, he simply didn't want her to work so much. Her heart was never into the marriage in the first place. She'd only married Sullivan to make herself feel like she was worthy of a man's full time love. She'd met Sullivan after she was assigned to be a part of the defense team of lawyers, defending the juvenile facility where he worked on a child abuse case. Soon after, they casually dated. Rhenee knew that Sullivan was a good man and at the time, that's what she was looking for. Soon after the marriage, Rhenee realized that being in a committed relationship took more time and work than she was prepared to give. She soon fell out of love with wanting to be that dedicated wife, and continued living as she had when she was single, including spending twelve to fourteen hours at the job.

The affair with Ray was before her marriage to Sullivan. In a way, marrying Sullivan was a revenge tactic. Ray had kept promising to leave his wife for her, but never took the initiative to do so. In retaliation, Rhenee got mad and married Sullivan to show Ray that she wasn't to be tested. Since he didn't want to commit to her, she found a man who did. Unfortunately, Rhenee discovered marriage wasn't what she really wanted. Only months after her marriage to Sullivan, Rhenee found herself back in the arms of the man she truly loved. Her scheming and conniving all ended only one year later when Sullivan came home from work and found her and Ray in the middle of a rendezvous.

Rhenee was snapped back into reality with Sullivan repeatedly calling out her name.

"Rhenee," he called, while looking strangely at her.

Rhenee laughed, looked back toward her car, and then at her watch. "Well, that's wonderful, Sullivan," she finally answered. "I just stopped by to see how you were doing. I was thinking about you while on my way to work and decided to stop by and say hi. I guess I should be going now."

Sullivan stood in silence and confusion. A couple of seconds later, Rhenee turned to leave. She quickly pranced back to her car without saying another word.

"It was nice seeing you again," Sullivan called out.

She turned to Sullivan after reaching her car. She didn't mumble a word, rather she stood with a somber look on her face.

"Is everything okay, Rhenee?" His concern resulted from the whole irony of the situation. First, Rhenee shows up at his job without warning, and then she abruptly leaves having said little more than hello. There had to be something else that she'd wanted to say. *Could she have lost her courage to say what she'd come to say*, Sullivan wondered. *Naw,* he thoughtfully answered himself. *Rhenee had the courage of a lion.*

"I'm fine," she finally replied. "I'll talk to you later." Afterwards, she swiftly climbed into her vehicle and sped away.

What was up with that? Sullivan wondered as he shook his head in confusion and walked inside the building.

Rhenee drove out of the parking lot at a heightened speed. She was so upset that she could feel a headache coming on. Hitting the steering wheel of her Porsche, she yelled, "Damn, why didn't I say what I went there to say?"

When Sullivan informed her of his family situation, Rhenee lost focus. All kinds of thoughts were running through her head at once. She contemplated turning around and going back to scream her regrets and repressed feelings to her ex-husband. Should she go back and tell Sullivan how she'd been tossed to the side by Ray? He left her when his wife got back into town after nearly a year of living in Philadelphia to take care of her mother who'd had a stroke. Rhenee had taken Celeste's place the entire time she was away. Although she always worked long hours, she still found the time to romance Ray. Whether it was at his home, the office, or every now and then, a hotel, Rhenee always made herself available whenever he called. Now that his wife was back in town, Ray suddenly didn't want to be bothered. Since Ray wanted to have nothing to do with her, Renee decided to pay Sullivan a visit. She wanted to go to him, throw herself into his arms, and hope he'd find it in his heart to forgive her and make amends.

"Why, so I can look like a damn fool? Rhenee, what is wrong with you?" she shouted, while nudging her forehead with the palm of her hand. "Get a hold of yourself, why don't you. You're already being played for a fool by one man, so why would you want to go and ridicule yourself in front of another?" For some reason Rhenee always believed that even after the divorce, Sullivan, a saved, and devoted Christian, would eventually forgive her, and would want to reconcile.

Rhenee was so distraught, she cried. At the red light, she reached into her briefcase and pulled out her flask that was half full of the best Scotch money could buy. She took a long gulp and proceeded down the street. Her speed reached about seventy miles per hour in a thirty mile per hour zone. Her mind was not focused on driving; instead, her thoughts kept going back to Ray. *How could Ray do this to me*? she thought. What was she going to do now? She was still in the process of purchasing a new condo, but hadn't found the place that suited her yet. Since most of her nights were spent with Ray, at his home, she hadn't even bothered to go out looking. Now that his woman had returned, Rhenee really had to get back on the ball with finding her own home. She could not believe that Ray had kicked her to the curb, like old furniture, when he was the reason that her marriage was non-existent. And, as soon as she was ready to go back to Sullivan and beg for his forgiveness, he acknowledges being happily married with a new wife and ready-made family.

Rhenee grabbed her flask and tossed her head back to take another drink of the Scotch. The minute she took the flask away from her mouth, she suddenly shifted her foot from the gas pedal to the brake, but it was too late. Before she could even turn to avoid the pedestrians, her car had already collided with them, head on.

"AHH!" she yelled as she heard a couple of loud thumps hit the front of her car. One body slammed across her windshield and a stream of blood trickled down her cracked window. The next thing she knew, the front end of her Porsche was slamming into the carved brownstone sitting out in front of the public library. The car came to a screeching halt as Rhenee's neck jerked and her chest slammed into the steering wheel.

She gasped for breath as she looked around her. Her eyes scanned the area where the people were lying lifelessly on the ground. She wiped her forehead with the back of her hand, and looked in all directions. There weren't any bystanders in sight that could possibly help her or the people she'd barreled her car into. Rhenee had been so preoccupied with taking a drink that she failed to stop at the traffic light. The pedestrians she hit had been crossing at the intersection and she hadn't even seen them until it was too late.

"OH, NO," Rhenee cried. She was lightheaded and overcome with shock, not believing what had occurred. She'd critically injured two people while failing to stop at a red light. She could be disbarred from practicing law if it was discovered that she'd been drinking and hit someone. Her life and career would be ruined if anyone found out.

Glancing around at her surroundings again, she still didn't notice anyone coming to their rescue. Rhenee turned the key in the ignition, and tried to restart the car. It cranked immediately, and she placed her foot on the clutch and shifted the gear in to reverse. Her entire front end was smashed right into the wall. When she placed her foot on the gas and tried to back away, the car hesitated. She moved the gear into first and then quickly back into reverse. On the second try, the car rolled back and away from the brick wall. *What am I doing?* she thought as she took one final look around before shifting the gear into drive and quickly speeding away.

As she drove down the street in tears, Rhenee prayed that the people she'd hit would be okay. Her heart went out to their family members, but there was no way she could risk sticking around. She'd been illegally drinking and had committed a crime, but she wasn't going to sacrifice losing her job, her law license, or risk going to jail for fifteen years. "Dear, God, please let those people be okay," she prayed as her car raced down the street.

CHAPTER 6

Tim sat in his nine o'clock Science class, three rows from the door, and two seats away from where the Professor was standing at the chalkboard, jotting down notes. Tim was unable to focus on the lecture because his mind kept wandering to unrelated issues. He couldn't stop thinking about Andrea showing up at his house. It had been a long time since he'd seen her, but his heart still felt as it always had. He still loved her. In fact, he'd never stopped loving or thinking about her the entire time they'd been apart. He could remember their last day together at the mall, as if it had happened the previous day. That was when both of them were homeless druggies. To support a nearly $300 a day cocaine habit, they shoplifted on a daily basis as if stealing was their employment.

Andrea had gotten her things and made it to the car, but he did not. Before he knew it, two undercover officers approached, asking him to follow them to the back of the store. As a result, Tim ended up serving seven months in the county jail. That's when he lost all ties with Andrea. It had to be fate that brought her to his parents' door.

"All that was in the past," the voice in Tim's head whispered to him, disturbing his thoughts. Now, Tim was working on completing a degree in Education. His goal was to be a middle school teacher. Since obtaining his GED, Tim had been attending the downtown community college. As a part of his recovery, he tried to keep busy, to avoid turning back to the life that had caused him to lose so much. He hoped he and Andrea could get back together and mend the relationship they once had. If Andrea would still have him, he'd love to be her man.

Tim glanced at his wristwatch, and back at the black clock hanging over the chalkboard. In exactly fifty-one minutes, he would be finished with class and meeting up with Andrea. She had told him that they had some important things to talk about, and he hoped it was about them starting over. He was definitely looking forward to their meeting.

≈ ≈ ≈

Caroline drove her own car to work, because she didn't plan on going straight home afterwards. Instead, she needed to get to the mall to pick up some things. Now that she had most of the planning for the party underway, she could focus on the guest of honor, her daughter. She had to find something nice and appropriate for Andrea to wear to the party. Since Caroline had invited a few of her closest friends, she had to make sure that her daughter, along with her mother and sister, would be looking fabulous from head to toe. With that in mind, Caroline decided to make her first stop at Sak's. She wanted Andrea's party to be talked about for months to come. Sunday they would be celebrating the start of a new life for her daughter. Now that Andrea was home, it was her time to prove that she could overcome any obstacle.

After work, Sullivan rushed home to change out of his suit, and into a pair of jeans and a t-shirt. After doing so, he headed to the kitchen to fix a sandwich. In another forty-five minutes, it would be time to take Dwayne to basketball practice. With sandwich in hand, he walked into the living room and grabbed the remote to the television when the flashing message indicator on the answering machine caught his attention. He walked over to the unit, and pressed play to see who'd called. The message was from his wife, calling to inform him that she would be on her way home after she dropped Andrea and the Timya off at home. After listening to the entire message, Sullivan deleted it and headed back into the kitchen. Ten minutes later, he was grabbing his keys from the table and walking out of the house.

"""

As soon as Rhenee sped away from the crime scene, she rushed to her hotel room. Immediately, she closed all of the blinds and windows, and then dove onto the bed and hid her head beneath the fluffy pillows. Her mind was racing a thousand miles a minute and she felt the onset of a pounding headache. Her body was experiencing nervous tremors and she still could not believe what had happened, or what she had done. As her face sank deeper into the pillow, the smell of scotch reeked from her mouth. She didn't know what to do. She was so scared that she took two Valium tablets from a small bottle inside her purse, and tossed them down her throat along with two sips of Scotch. She rested in the bed while waiting for the pills and liquor to calm her nerves. Rhenee wanted to call Ray, but dismissed the thought. She knew calling him would seem suspicious and she didn't want to call any attention to herself.

When she heard the sudden sounds of sirens approaching, Rhenee jumped up and peeked out the window to see where they were headed. She was hoping it wasn't the police coming to take her to jail. With paranoia taking over, she closed the blinds and ran back to the bed where she reached for her flask of Scotch, titled her head back, and sipped until the container was empty. The liquor burned its way down her throat, and into her empty stomach. Frantically, she grabbed the remote control and hit the power button turning on the television. She flicked through the channels, searching for the local news station. If there was a news crew at the accident scene, she wanted to know how much information they had about the fled suspect.

Right now, she needed her mom. Rhenee knew that if she could trust anyone with such a secret, it would be her mother. Although her parents lived in Ohio, she felt the need to call and have a heart to heart conversation with her mother. She needed to tell her how she had been a bad girl and hit two pedestrians while drinking and driving. Of all people, Rhenee knew better than to drink and drive, not to mention leave the scene of the accident.

Rhenee got up from the bed to walk to the place where her telephone sat. All of a sudden, her head was spinning. The liquor and Valium had taken affect at a moment when she was unprepared. Instantly feeling bubbly and relaxed, like she was floating on a cloud, Rhenee felt herself slowly losing control as the illicit concoction took over. Instead of going to retrieve the telephone, Rhenee fell back onto the bed. Her eyes slammed shut as her mind drifted off into a relaxing euphoria.

∾ ∾ ∾

When Sullivan and Dwayne made it back home from practice, they noticed Delvin's car sitting in the driveway. Before Sullivan could put his vehicle in park, Dwayne was halfway out of the car. He ran straight into the house, searching for his father. Sullivan smiled as he continued parking. Although, he had a genuine love for all the children, he'd never seen their eyes light up more than when their father came around.

Delvin stood in the kitchen listening to Dwayne explain the details of his basketball practice. Sullivan walked into the house on the tail end of the conversation and as soon as Delvin noticed him, he quickly turned to greet him. The two men shook hands and continued listening to Dwayne, who was giving the play-by-play of how he'd slam dunked on a team member.

Sullivan interrupted by saying, "He's one of the tallest boys on the team. I think he makes a great guard. His opponent could barely get any balls past him. I think he's going to do well at the real game next week."

"They ain't gon' be able to take me," Dwayne bragged as his dad and Sullivan laughed in unison.

Keisha walked into the living room, where the guys were, and announced that she and Tonya were ready to go.

"I'm about to go and get my stuff too, Dad," Dwayne said before quickly disappearing.

Since Delvin had stopped using drugs, he'd become more firm with the promises he made to his children. He no longer lied to them about coming to get them, and he also kept up on his child support payments. Dorothy no longer had to stay on his case, the way she used to. He'd been working the same job and maintaining his own place for over two years.

When Tonya walked into the living room, Sullivan excused himself to go and call Dorothy. He knew that if she got caught up in those stores, she'd be there for hours. He got no answer from his wife, so Sullivan hung up and walked out with Delvin and the children. "I will see you all on Sunday," Sullivan waved, as he stood in the front doorway until Delvin and the children drove away. As soon as he closed the front door, the telephone rang. Sullivan rushed to answer it. He was suspecting it was Dorothy.

"Hello," Sullivan spoke into the receiver.

"Hi, may I speak with a Mr. Sullivan Edwards," said the voice on the other end.

"This is he."

"Mr. Edwards, this is Nurse Fletcher at Spectrum Health Hospital. I was calling to inform you that your wife was brought in by the ambulance this afternoon."

Sullivan became worried. He nervously placed his hand over his chest, barely believing what he was hearing. He looked around the room blankly. His wife, the love of his life! What could possibly be wrong with his Dorothy? He didn't recall the rest of the conversation with the nurse, because anything that she said after the words, "your wife has been brought in by the ambulance," were cut off when he dropped the telephone and dashed off in search of his car keys. Snatching his keys from the counter, Sullivan rushed out the door toward his car. He had no knowledge of what happened to his wife, nor did he know her status. All Sullivan could think of was getting to the hospital as fast as he could.

Sullivan's car glided down the street like a Boeing jet. His thoughts were racing out of control and he needed to get to Dorothy's rescue as soon as possible. He prayed to God that his wife would be okay. He'd been warning Dorothy about watching her cholesterol. He had been telling her that she needed to cut back on eating the fried food that she loved to enjoy in the wee hours of the night. As he coasted down the residential neighborhood, driving at a speed of about seventy miles per hour, Sullivan continued praying, and asking God to look over his wife.

"I don't know what I'd do without her, Lord," he prayed. Sullivan stopped briefly at a red light, looked in both directions, and, when all was clear, he took off. He had to get to his wife. The hospital was about fifteen minutes away from his house, but with the way he was driving, he was hoping to be there in about five.

His car screeched, then came to a complete halt, in an available parking space in the parking lot. Sullivan quickly jumped from his vehicle and dashed through the lot toward the doors of the Emergency Room. He rushed up to the woman sitting at the desk and gave her his wife's name, explaining how he'd gotten a call from a Nurse Fletcher saying that his wife was brought in by the ambulance. The woman typed Dorothy's name into the computer and waited for some information on her to download. She later explained that Nurse Fletcher was assisting with a surgery in Operating Room 109. The receptionist directed Sullivan toward the nurses station through the double doors. There he would be able to speak with another nurse, who'd have more information. Sullivan thanked her and then rushed through the double doors.

So far, he had no information on the status of his wife and not knowing was causing panic to set in. Sullivan stopped the first doctor that he saw walking down the hall and asked if he knew anything about his wife. The doctor knew nothing, and kindly told him so.

"You are welcome to have a seat in the family waiting room down the hall. It's the third door on the left. As soon as the nurse comes out, you can ask about your wife's status. I am sorry that I couldn't be more help, but good luck to you and your spouse, sir." The doctor then excused himself and walked away.

Sullivan sat in the waiting room with his head stuck between his legs, praying that Nurse Fletcher would soon make an appearance. The room was calm and still, with only two other people waiting inside. Sullivan wanted to know what was going on with his wife. He wondered what had happened to cause her to go from a shopping trip, to the emergency room. With tears in his eyes, he raised his head and looked around the somber room.

For what seemed like hours, Sullivan continued to wait. He didn't want to call Caroline until he knew exactly what was going on. He knew how upset she would become, so he continued to wait alone.

The sounds of approaching footsteps brought Sullivan to his feet. He hoped it was Nurse Fletcher, but to his surprise, it was his sister-in-law, Caroline, and her husband, Thomas. Thomas looked more worried than Caroline.

"I'm sorry I didn't call you guys but I didn't want you all to get all worked up until after I spoke to the doctor." Sullivan exchanged hugs with the couple and then said, "I guess you all heard about Dorothy, huh?"

Caroline burst into a well of tears. "My baby, Sullivan! My baby, Timya, is gone!"

Sullivan was startled and confused. He didn't understand what Caroline was talking about. He grabbed Caroline and embraced her. Thomas stood off to the side crying silent tears.

"What's going on?" Sullivan asked Thomas. "What happened to Timya?"

"She was killed in a car accident, Sullivan," Thomas cried. "They were all hit, and whoever hit them pulled off. Timya died before she made it to the hospital."

Sullivan suddenly felt weak. He looked at Caroline, and back at Thomas. He could not believe what they were saying, but now, it was all making sense. They must have been notified, as he was. Sullivan hadn't taken the time to get the entire story from the nurse. "Oh my Lord," Sullivan shouted. "What kind of a person would do something like this?" His hands grazed through his hair. "How is my wife?" he shouted out. "Does anyone know the status of my wife?"

"We were told that Dorothy has a collapsed lung and is in surgery," Thomas explained. "Andrea has a broken arm and leg, and is having a cast put on. They said she will be fine. We just left from visiting with Andrea, and she is in total shock. They said they needed to keep her for observation. We must pray that Dorothy will be okay. The nurse said that she has a very good chance of recovering."

Sullivan left the room without saying anything further to his in-laws. He rushed down the hallway toward the elevator, heading for the downstairs chapel. He needed to talk to God in private, because he had some personal favors to ask of Him.

CHAPTER 7

Tim sat in traffic for a long time before he was redirected onto a different street. He was sure that Andrea had left, but since he didn't have a telephone number to reach her, he couldn't call and tell her about his traffic dilemma. Anxious to see Andrea all morning and now that the time had come for him to meet with her, Tim was nearly an hour late. All he could do was hope that she hadn't left McDonald's by the time he got there. The two of them had a lot of catching up to do.

Monet hung up the telephone in a panic. Her Aunt Caroline had informed her that her mother was in a car accident and that she needed to get to the hospital. Monet's hands were trembling, and suddenly, she couldn't focus. Because Caroline didn't give her any specifics, Monet was left to wonder about the severity of her mother's condition. Monet knew that she had to get to the hospital as soon as possible.

When Monet dialed her mother's house to see if anyone was there, she got no answer. "Dang," she sighed when she hung up the telephone. Monet didn't know what to do with her son. She didn't want to take Deshawn to the hospital with her because she didn't know how long she would be there. A hospital was no place for him to hang around because after a while, the child would get agitated. Unable to come up with an idea for a reliable sitter, Monet got frustrated. The only person she could think to call was Derrick, and although he was her absolute last resource, limited time and options left her with no other choice.

Derrick answered on the second ring. "Derrick, I need you to watch Deshawn for me while I go to the hospital. My mother was in a car accident, and I need to go and see about her. Can you keep him for me? And I mean *you* keep him, I don't want my son being left with one of your lil' stankin' tricks. "

"What?" he huffed, sounding preoccupied. Wherever Derrick was, Monet could hear lots of people in the background.

"My mother is in the hospital, Derrick. I need you to keep your son while I go up there and see how she's doing."

"Is she okay?"

"Damn, Derrick, what did I just say? Can I drop Deshawn off to you for an hour or two or what?"

"For a lil' while, man. I got something to do later. You can go 'head and shoot him over here," Derrick finally agreed.

"Where are you?"

"I'm at Mom's crib."

"I'm on my way," Monet said, then slammed down the telephone.

Before leaving her son with Derrick, Monet told him, "Please do not leave my son with anyone. If I'm not back by the time you have to do what you have to do, call me."

"Man, I got him," Derrick huffed as he grabbed his son from Monet's hip.

Kissing her son's forehead, Monet returned to her car, and after a moment of hesitation, she drove away.

CHAPTER 8

"A family emergency; damn," Sheila cursed as she hung up the telephone, after speaking with Thomas. It was his week to keep Thomas Jr., and due to some family emergency, she now had to cancel her plans and make other arrangements for her son. Sheila had called Thomas' cell phone when he didn't come to pick up Thomas Jr. Only then did he inform her of his family crisis, which resulted in him not being able to keep Thomas Jr. for the weekend.

Her date, Cameron Wilkes, was a lawyer who worked for Walker, Belingsly, and Burke, another law firm whose office was in the same building that Sheila worked in. Cameron had wanted to take her out for months, but Sheila hadn't taken him up on any of his offers. Although she'd been attracted to him, she never led him to believe so. Cameron was very persistent. Sheila could tell that he was the type of man who got what he wanted, and at first, she didn't want to chance being another conquer. But Sheila had just cause to change her mind. She hadn't had sex in so long that if Cameron blew on her, she believed she would have an orgasm. Being without the intimate company of a man for over nine months had been a difficult existence.

Sheila pondered for a minute before she came up with a possible idea for a babysitter. She could call Cheronda, her ex-best friend, Elaine's, daughter. Cheronda used to baby sit for Sheila when she and Elaine were on good terms, and used to party a lot. They had been best friends for over ten years until the year prior to their complete disassociation. She and Elaine stopped being inseparable after Shelia helped Elaine escape from her whoreish and abusive husband, Dennis, after catching him cheating with another woman. Sheila and her friend worked expeditiously to get all of Dennis's things out of the house before he could come home and change Elaine's mind about putting him out. While they moved out his things, Elaine had a locksmith come and change all the locks on the doors of her house. Dennis was out for only twenty-four hours before Elaine allowed him to come back home. Sheila was upset because she'd missed a day of work to help Elaine get all of Dennis's belongings out of the house. Once she found out that Elaine let him right back in, Sheila vowed not to deal with Elaine anymore. She was tired of being caught in the middle of Elaine's and her husband's mess, only for Elaine to be right back with him.

It saddened Sheila to see her friend invest so much into her husband, until she had nothing left. Elaine had no self-esteem to feel that she deserved better, and no courage to believe that she could live without Dennis. Although they had been married for nearly fifteen years, the marriage was over after the first year. For some reason, Elaine couldn't walk away. When Sheila got tired of the drama, she backed off and found other ways to occupy her time. There was no animosity with her and Elaine, they simply didn't spend time together like they used to.

Even though Sheila hadn't spoken to Elaine in quite some time, she was going to call Cheronda anyway. She needed a babysitter and Cheronda was the only person, besides Thomas, that Sheila left her son with. Without further thought, she crossed her fingers, dialed Elaine's telephone number, and waited for someone to answer.

Elaine picked up. "Hello."

"What's up stranger," Sheila muffled into the phone.

"Nothing much," Elaine happily commented. She sounded very happy to hear Sheila's voice. "How's life been treating you?"

"Let's just say, I'm here," Sheila huffed. "That job's been keeping me plenty busy. I hadn't had a weekend off in over a month, and when they finally give a sister a weekend off, I can't find a babysitter, and I even have a date. Thomas was supposed to keep Thomas Jr. for the weekend, but he suddenly had a family emergency. So, I'm calling to see if Cheronda wants to make some extra money by babysitting for me."

"Oh, you're still on the market? What happened to Delvin? I thought y'all was madly in love," Elaine quizzed.

"Oh, girl, that's been over. I let that go a long time ago. Now, I'm working on Cameron."

Elaine's laughter radiated into the phone.

"Of course, I want to get your permission for Cheronda to baby sit."

"It's okay with me, if she wants to. I mean, I'll be here the whole time, but hold on a minute. Let me get Cheronda."

Sheila heard Elaine call for her daughter and after a couple minutes, Cheronda came to the telephone.

"Hello," Cheronda answered.

"Hey niece," Sheila sang. "What's up wit cha?"

"Nothing, just trying to focus on school and the Pom Pom team."

"Oh? How is everything coming?"

"Real good."

"Well look I need you to do me a favor if you're not busy this weekend."

"You want me to baby sit, don't you?" Cheronda blurted.

"Yes, I have a date, and I wanted to know if you could watch my son for the weekend. I will pay you $100, and I'll drop him off tonight and pick him up Sunday afternoon."

"All right," Cheronda happily replied. "What time are you going to bring him over?"

"I'll be there in about an hour."

"I'll be waiting."

"Alright, I'll see you then," After hanging up, Sheila yelled, "Yes!" then ran into her son's bedroom and grabbed his overnight bag that was already packed.

When she told Thomas Jr. to get ready to go over to Auntie Elaine's, he jumped up with excitement, because he loved spending time at Elaine's. Even though he hadn't been there in a long time, he was still excited with the mention of Elaine's name. After taking her son to spend a few days with Cheronda and her mother, Sheila returned home to get ready for her long awaited, romantic weekend.

Carefully packing her belongings into a small rolling suitcase, Sheila selectively picked out an outfit to wear for each day that she would be gone, and one to put on for the evening. Next, she took a relaxing and rejuvenating shower, and within an hour, she was dressed and waiting on Cameron.

Not a minute past their planned meeting time, he showed up at her front door with a dozen white roses in hand, and stepped into her apartment with a smile on his face. Nosily, he glanced around her apartment. "So you live here alone, huh?" he quizzed.

"Just my son, and me," she answered while accepting her flowers with gratefulness.

Apparently unconvinced, Cameron continued peeking back and forth, from the kitchen to the living room. "I'm looking because I don't want no brothers jumping out of any closets, trying to bust my head over you."

Sheila rolled her eyes and bit her tongue to prevent herself from responding to Cameron's snide remark. He hadn't been there five minutes and already, she was starting to think that going out with Cameron was a bad idea. Now, she knew why it had taken her so long to say yes.

"This is a really nice place," he said, smacking his lips. "I guess you must get paid pretty good to sit behind that desk all day long."

Sheila didn't know if he was being sarcastic or offering her a compliment, but one thing was for sure, she wasn't feeling good about it. To Sheila, Cameron's tone sounded belittling, and for a minute, she contemplated asking him to leave. She didn't feel like dealing with an arrogant pompous, merely for the sake of having her sexual needs met, and if Cameron kept saying the wrong things, she was going to forget the whole evening and put him out of her house. He was sadly mistaken if he thought she needed him, because if necessary, she knew how to please herself. She had a little black box that contained her hand-held pleaser. It could go long and strong all night, giving her all pleasure, minus the bullshit.

Sheila was trying hard not to get mad before she used him for the purpose of her gratification, so she changed the subject before her thoughts became verbal. "So, where did you say you were taking me for the weekend? All that sitting behind the desk has kept me so confined, I can't wait to get loose," she laughed, as she stood in the doorway, waiting for Cameron to say something about what she was wearing. She had taken over two hours to pick out the perfect outfit, and Cameron had been in her apartment for nearly ten minutes, and hadn't complimented her once. She gritted her teeth and thought, *damn; he's got two strikes against him already. Pretty soon, this punk was going to be out of getting some pussy that I was more than willing to give up.*

Cameron pulled an envelope from his suit jacket. Inside, were two first class airplane tickets to Atlanta, Georgia. Sheila's face lit up with excitement.

"I am taking you to dinner in Atlanta. Afterwards, we'll ride down Peachtree Street so that you can see the city, and we can discuss how we'll spend our future together. I like to spoil my woman, and as long as you can conform and be faithful to your man, I'll treat you like the queen that you are," he whispered seductively to her.

Sheila's eyebrows rose awkwardly. She was thinking that Cameron was definitely getting ahead of himself. They hadn't even gone out on their first date, yet, and here he was, claiming her future. Although flying to Atlanta for a dinner date was a first for her, and she was looking forward to it, Sheila already knew that she would have to keep her guard up with Cameron. Even though it was early on in their dating relationship, he was already showing signs of having a control issue.

He grabbed her hand and led her into a spin. "This sexy evening gown that you are wearing just happens to be the perfect outfit for the occasion." Cameron marveled at the sight of her. He was delighted with how good Sheila looked from all angles.

She smacked her lips and softly replied, "Oh, now he notices."

"What was that?" Cameron thought he'd heard Sheila say something.

"Oh, nothing."

Sheila went to get her purse, and Cameron grabbed her luggage. Lastly, she picked up her keys from the kitchen counter and then left with her date.

Sheila and Cameron arrived at the airport sometime after five that evening. They checked in and rushed toward the Delta Airlines departure gates. Their flight was scheduled to depart out from Kent County Airport at six o'clock. It was due to arrive in Atlanta, around seven-thirty. Once the couple boarded the plane, they immediately engaged in conversation. Sheila tried to get to know as much as she could about Cameron before they arrived in Atlanta. Although, Sheila had known of him for over two years, his personal life wasn't something they'd discussed in detail. In fact, all that she really knew about Cameron was that he was a middle-aged, attractive, highly recommended defense attorney, who didn't sport a wedding band. When she asked Cameron to tell her more about himself, he didn't hesitate to inform her.

He expressed that he'd hurdled many obstacles in his past in order to relish in his present success. He claimed that he was single by choice, and only spent time with a select few women, due to his reputation. His name was well known and Cameron said that he'd learned to stay away from women with ulterior motives. He knew most of them only wanted to be with him because of who he was.

Riding in first class, for the first time in her life, made Sheila feel like a celebrity. As soon as the plane pulled away from the gate, she cuddled close to Cameron, while listening to the flight attendant explain the emergency evacuation procedures. Even though the travel time was short, Sheila and her date ordered lite dinner entrees to hold them until they arrived in Georgia. Sheila only nibbled on her meal, not wanting to eat so much that, when she stood, her belly would poke out of her closely fitted dress. While sipping on a glass of wine, Cameron continued to talk about himself.

He was thirty-eight years old, and had been practicing law for twelve years. He had been divorced twice, and had a six-year-old daughter from his second marriage. Cameron owned his own home in Michigan, and also had a vacation condo in Florida. Learning more about him led Sheila to believe that they didn't have much in common. Basically, he was a bull-headed workaholic, and Sheila was an easy going, single female, who loved partying more than working.

After arriving in Atlanta, Sheila and Cameron walked to the rental car counter to pick up the reserved Benz, then headed straight to upscale Buckhead's, Cheesecake Factory, where Cameron had pre-arranged dinner reservations.

The attending hostess escorted Cameron and Sheila upstairs. The place was packed, from wall to wall, and Sheila felt like a VIP when she and Cameron weren't passed a coaster that would light up when an available table was ready for them. The hostess escorted them straight through the crowded room of people, to a private section of the restaurant. Sheila couldn't help but to feel important.

As she followed the hostess, she marveled at the décor of the place. The lighting was dim, and the section they sat in was secluded. Even though they were in a private sector of the restaurant, chatter and noise still managed to move about the room. Sheila had to speak in elevated voice to ensure that her date could hear her from across the table. Cameron was such a gentleman, and despite the fact that he didn't talk much while waiting on his dinner to arrive, he was a very attentive listener. He held onto her every word, with an expressionless face, as she spoke of all the stress she endured at the law firm where she worked. Sheila went on explaining to Cameron that she was starting to get burned out, working as a paralegal, and now wished she would have gone on to become a lawyer. "At least then, I would actually be paid well for my hard work," she commented.

Their waitress approached, and Sheila's words froze. After Sara sat the serving tray down on a tray caddy, she carefully distributed the hot entrées. Once she finished, and before leaving the table, Sara asked if they needed anything else. As soon as she left, the couple dug into their meals. Everything was delicious, despite the fact that they'd waited almost an hour to be served. They finished their dinners, and then Sheila ordered a slice of the signature turtle cheesecake. There was no way that she could leave Georgia without a piece. For his dessert, Cameron chose the apple pie, with French vanilla ice cream. After spending a couple of hours at the restaurant, it was time to go out and see the city, while the night was still young.

The Benz cruised down Peachtree, headed toward highway 85N. The art gallery they were on their way to was supposed to be right off of the exit. Sheila was both nervous and excited about attending the party at the art gallery. Cameron wanted Sheila to see a painting that he was planning to purchase, and the artist was actually going to be at the party in Buckhead. Cameron told Sheila that the piece he was interested in cost nearly $15,000, and he was seriously considering it.

Her eyes lit up immediately, but she didn't comment. She simply didn't know what to say. She knew absolutely nothing about art. All the pictures hanging on her wall at home had been purchased for less than $50, most under $20, and here he was, about to spend thousands. But, Sheila could appreciate the fact that Cameron was exposing her to something new. Not only had he awed her by flying her out of town for a weekend date, but now he was exposing her to a whole new world. Sheila found herself being aroused by Cameron's knowledge.

The gallery wasn't far from downtown Atlanta. The building was well lit, and had high ceilings, like that of a cathedral. The large walls were draped with each artist's painting, separated by three feet of spacing. People stood around in small groups, admiring their favorite artwork, while sipping wine and mingling amongst each other. Several uniformed servers paced the gallery's floors, serving hors d'oeuvres and drinks to the guests. The gallery was definitely nothing like Sheila envisioned it being. As she nervously held on to Cameron, he explained what he thought each of the paintings represented. He definitely made each one seem more interesting than it actually looked. She had never been so turned on by looking at a piece of art. Now, Sheila viewed each piece differently than when she had looked before. She still had no idea why the paintings cost so much, but she was still learning.

Back at the hotel, Cameron hooked his arm around Sheila's waist as he escorted her toward their suite. Before unlocking the door, Cameron did something he'd wanted to do all night. He planted a deep kiss on Sheila's lips. His actions totally caught her off guard, but she responded. Their lips stayed locked even after Cameron opened the door. He scooped Sheila off her feet and carried her into the room. It was dark, but he made his way to the couch, where he laid her down and continued kissing her. He stopped briefly, and stared into her eyes. "I can't wait to make love to you," he mumbled. "These two years, I've waited to get to know you better have been pure torture. I've wanted you ever since the first time I saw you waltz into the office with that white suit on. It killed me to have this yearning for you for so long."

"You know exactly what to say, don't you?"

"I'll feel that my words have accomplished something once I see what you're hiding under this black dress."

After their embrace, Cameron stood to his feet and took off his suit jacket. Sheila sat up on the sofa and waited for his next move. "Let's take it to the bedroom," Cameron said as he lifted her from the couch.

Once they made it to his bedroom, Cameron sat her on the bed, walked over to the fireplace and lit it. The fireplace added a nice ambience to the room, which was already decorated in a romantic decor. He took a few steps toward the nightstand and tuned the radio in to 104.1 FM. It was the station that played all the good R&B slow jams.

As he walked toward the bed, Cameron unbuttoned his shirt, while Sheila knelt on the bed, with her arms stretched wide open, waiting for his embrace. She was so anxious, that she immediately planted soft kisses all over his hairy chest. Cameron released a few soft moans of satisfaction, as he stood, enjoying the trail of kisses left by her teasing lips. Sheila then unbuckled his belt, unsnapped his trousers and allowed them to fall down onto the plush white carpet. As she lay back on the bed, Cameron quickly stepped out of his shoes, kicked them across the room and softly kissed her succulent skin. Wrapping her arms around his muscular frame, Sheila was enjoying every minute of Cameron kissing and caressing her body as he pulled the straps of her dress over her shoulders and down her arms..

"Take this off, baby," he whispered in her ear.

As Sheila gazed into his eyes, she eased out of her dress. Cameron peered at her breast, amazed at how supple and beautiful they were. Gently he cupped her heaving bosom and softly squeezed, his thumbs stroking her nipples as if they were delicate rose petals. Her body was on fire. She wanted him so bad, the throb between her legs was unbearable. *Take me* now, she thought.

Moving down her torso, his fingertips found their way over her abdomen toward the warmth of her mound. His fingers entered her with ease, as their tongues danced. Releasing sensual cries, Sheila's hips slowly gyrated as his fingers skillfully drilled in and out of her, with precision. Cameron whispered in her ear. "Are you ready for me to make love to you?"

"Yes," she cooed, anticipating that the best was yet to come.

"Roll over," he ordered.

Sheila did as she was told and rolled over onto her stomach. On her knees, as Cameron raised her hips, Sheila arched her back, before his tongue entered her already moist center from behind. It was electrifying. She was so ready! As Cameron licked and sucked on the swelling between her thighs, she remained in position waiting for the great moment when she would feel that stiff, hard mass of thickness enter her anticipating womb.

Cameron took one final lick before walking away. "Come on over here," he instructed, pointing to the velvet sofa in the bedroom. With one hand, he stroked himself and with the other, he escorted her over to the small sofa that was about six feet away from the bed. He stood behind her and said, "Bend over. I don't want you to see me coming."

Sheila smiled, and quickly reached in her purse and retrieved a condom. After passing it to Cameron, he rolled the latex over his hardened shaft, as Sheila positioned herself over the sofa.

Placing his hands on her hips, Cameron aimed his erectness toward her opening and slid, with ease, into her abyss. Sheila moaned with satisfaction, as he stirred his straw deep inside her juice, his hips grinding rhythmically. Sheila worked with him as they moved together sensually, as the mellow, sultry voice of Anita Baker clouded the room.

Right in the midst of Sheila experiencing pure enjoyment, her euphoria was suddenly interrupted by a loud howl. The noise not only startled her, but it broke her concentration. It was Cameron expressing his satisfaction to what she was giving.

"Oh shit!" Faster, and faster, Cameron pumped as he cried out, "Um, um, oooh," and then there was silence. His body stiffened, and then he released the hold he had on her. Sheila could not believe what had happened. Not even five minutes into their sex session and here he was, ending it.

Her face frowned as she turned toward him. "What was that about?"

"Aw, man," Cameron huffed as he pulled away from her, and sighed. "Whew. Either I was a little anxious, or you have some bomb ass stuff. That was great."

"T'ss," she hissed, as she stood straight up. "Come on now, Cameron. I know you can do better than that."

"Damn, baby, I'm sorry. I just told you that I was a little too excited."

Sheila watched the silhouette of his bronze frame as he stood in front of the crackling fireplace huffing and sweating as if he'd completed a strenuous workout. Afterwards, Cameron walked into the bathroom. She heard the toilet flush, then Cameron re-entered the room. He walked over to the bed, where he fell straight down onto his stomach.

Sheila was appalled. She sat on the sofa with her mouth gaped wide open. Within minutes, Cameron was sound asleep, and snoring.

CHAPTER 9

As soon as Monet arrived at the hospital, she received the awful news that her mother and two cousins had been in a car accident. Dorothy was still undergoing surgery, and Andrea was waiting for the nurse to come in and start closing her womb with stitches. Poor little Timya had died. When Monet heard this, she cried. That baby was definitely a warrior, although her cavalier spirit had taken its final rest. Monet couldn't begin to imagine what her cousin, Andrea, was going through. Her child had been taken from her soon after she was born, and no sooner than Andrea was given a second chance to be a good mother to Timya, she was gone. Right when Andrea was starting to get her life on track, her whole world was suddenly snatched away from her.

The nurse walked into the family waiting room, and informed everyone that Dorothy was on her way to the recovery room, and that she was going to be okay. "Once Mrs. Edwards is settled into her room, the family can go in to see her. She's still going to be heavily sedated, more than likely sleep, but you all are welcomed to go in for a few minutes of visitation."

"Thanks," Monet said to the nurse as she prepared to leave.

Thomas walked into the waiting room. He'd been in the hallway talking to police who were assigned to investigate the accident. The officer stated to Thomas that they didn't have too many leads to catching the assailant, but for them to remain hopeful. Subsequent to his informing everyone of what he'd learned, Thomas took a seat, next to his wife.

Caroline remained seated with her head down. Her body was still, her eyes were dazed, and she seemed to have incoherently drifted off into her own little world. She'd been that way for at least a half hour. She was sad, hurt, and confused. It seemed that the events in her life always went from one extreme to the other. What was she doing wrong? What was she going to do without her Timya, who'd become a permanent fixture in her life? She loved Timya like she was her own daughter. Nervous and afraid, Caroline felt like giving up. There was only so much she could take. To think, her family was supposed to be celebrating Andrea's homecoming, but instead, they had to prepare for a home going for her dear sweet granddaughter, Timya.

"Why," she screamed out, alarming the entire room of people. Monet, Thomas, and Sullivan all turned toward Caroline. Thomas jumped up to comfort his wife by hugging her and telling her that everything was going to be okay. Caroline's outbursts grew louder, and her body trembled. Thomas held on to his wife and tried to rock her into comfort.

"It's okay, sweetie. This is God's plan. Timya is gone to a better place," he spoke, trying to console her. Thomas really needed to get his wife home and into bed so she could rest. He wasn't sure how much more Caroline could bear. Besides, it was going on six o'clock, and Taylor had to be picked up from the after school program.

He was heartbroken, sad, tired, and hungry. It was hard for him to believe how much life had changed since morning. Timya was such a happy baby. Her bright smile would no longer be there to brighten his day. Contrary to professional opinion, Timya had grown to be a healthy, cheerful, baby, and she would be dearly missed.

Thomas felt so sorry for his daughter, Andrea. He wasn't sure if she knew about the baby's death or not, but he knew it would be hard for her to cope with the news. Sadly, Andrea never had the opportunity to be a mother to her child. Thomas tried to hold back the tears, but the emotional loss he was experiencing wouldn't allow him to hold on to them in any longer. Instead of trying to be strong, he needed to allow himself some grieving time as everyone else did.

Sullivan fidgeted in his chair as he sat waiting for the doctor to come out and say it was okay for him to go in to see his wife. He was so worried, that he didn't know what to do. Monet was sitting in the chair next to him, and every five minutes or so, she would announce that she was cold, and then she would change positions in the chair, hoping to settle in a more comfortable one. Sullivan knew that Monet was creating excuses so they wouldn't see how nervous she was about not knowing the status of her mom. Neither of them could wait to hear the word.

Finally, a white-haired doctor walked into the waiting room with a clipboard in his hand. "Who are the family members here on behalf of Mrs. Edwards?"

Sullivan jumped up from his chair before the doctor could finish speaking. "I am, sir. I am Mr. Sullivan Edwards. My family and I are here on behalf of my wife. How is she?"

The doctor scratched his head and slowly offered details of Dorothy's condition. Dr. Harvey explained that Dorothy's left lung had been punctured. The handle from the baby's stroller had stabbed her in the side, causing the injury. The resulting surgery had been a difficult one, because they had to remove most of the left lung, due to extensive damage. Although the doctor told them that Dorothy would have to remain in the hospital for two weeks of treatment and observation, he ended with the good news that she was expected to make a full recovery.

Sullivan quickly shook the doctor's hand, while thanking him for saving his wife's life. Monet was so relieved; she cried. Her aunt and uncle walked up and hugged her.

"Can I go in to see my wife now?" Sullivan finally asked the question that was most pressing in his heart.

"You may go in to see her, although she's still heavily sedated. I'd like for you to keep the visit short, because Mrs. Edwards will need as much rest as possible. When you come back tomorrow, she should be coherent." The doctor then looked at his clipboard and said, "She is on the forth floor, in Room 441." He then turned to Andrea's parents and told them that their daughter was okay. "She and Mrs. Edwards are assigned to rooms on the same floor. Andrea is in Room 412. I left her a few moments ago and she's doing fine. She has asked about her daughter though."

"Don't worry, we'll take care of that," Thomas said.

Dr. Harvey then stated his condolences and left the room. The family all gathered their things and headed up to the forth floor.

Monet was the first to enter Dorothy's room. There were several machines lit up with tubes running from them and connecting to her mother. Dorothy had one thick tube hanging out of her mouth and a thin one was connected to her nose. She had an I.V. and another tube that was draped under the sheets, on the side of her. At the first sight of her mother, Monet burst into tears. She could not stand seeing her this way. Dorothy didn't appear to be okay, nor did she look like herself. Monet ran into the arms of her stepfather, who was silently crying himself.

"Oh, Sullivan," she cried. "Look at her."

"I know, sweetie," he whispered. "I know how bad things look, but she's really going to be okay. Let's pray for her," he stated. He and Monet joined hands, and bowed their heads, as Sullivan prayed.

Monet was wearing a cellular telephone on her hip. It vibrated during the prayer, but she ignored it. Now was not the time. She didn't feel like talking to anyone. After the prayer ended, Monet and her stepfather approached Dorothy's bedside. Sullivan immediately bent over and kissed his wife on the forehead.

Monet held her mother's hand and felt the coldness of her flesh. She cried, "Mama, I'm here. This is Monet, your daughter. Can you hear me?"

Dorothy didn't budge. Sullivan stood peacefully, staring at his wife. He knew that she was going to be okay, so he was no longer worried. He did want to talk to her though. He wished she would open her eyes.

Monet and Sullivan sat with Dorothy for over an hour, but her eyes still didn't open. It was getting late, so Monet told her stepfather that she had to leave to go and pick up Deshawn. She rose from the chair and said, "I'll have to come back tomorrow."

"Where is Deshawn?"

Monet rolled her eyes upward. "He's with his father. I told Derrick that I would only be gone for a couple hours, so I better hurry up and go and get my son because Derrick will use any excuse to not have to keep his own child. He is so pitiful."

"Well, you and I can walk out together, because I want to stop by and see how Andrea's doing before we leave."

Monet nodded, then she and Sullivan said their goodbyes to Dorothy, and left. Sullivan was going home to get some much-needed rest, and something to eat, and since the children were gone with Delvin for the weekend, he planned to return to the hospital and stay all night, with his wife.

Sullivan opened the door to Andrea's room, after softly knocking. As he was about to enter, Caroline and Thomas exited. "Are you all about to leave?"

"Yes," Thomas answered. "Andrea didn't take the news about the baby too well, so the nurse came in and gave her a shot to sedate her. Right now, she's sleeping, so we're going to head home. Our next door neighbor has Taylor and we don't want to inconvenience them for too long."

Caroline didn't say a word. She continued walking toward the elevator with the rest of her family.

"I'll check back in with her later," Sullivan stated. "I'm coming back to spend the night with Dorothy. If Andrea is not sleeping, I'll visit with her before I go in to see my wife."

"That'll be great," Thomas said. "We'd appreciate that very much."

The elevator door opened, and they all entered it and rode down to the parking lot together. It had been a long, sad day for them all.

Monet merely wanted to pick up her son, go home and climb into her bed. She would have to skip class and somehow make up the test she would miss in her absence. There was no way she could sit and focus on an exam when her mother was fighting for her life. Right now, Monet felt compelled to hold on to her son and appreciate him like she never had before.

Her stepfather saw to it that Monet got into her car safely. After he waved to her and headed toward his car, Monet sat alone in her vehicle for a brief, peaceful moment. She needed to clear her mind so she could focus on being strong for her mother. She knew that Dorothy would be okay, because she'd put it in God's hands. While her car warmed, Monet decided to check her phone to see who'd been trying to contact her. As she scrolled down the list of missed calls, she noticed that one was from Malcolm, her fiancé, who was away in dental school. The other three calls were from Derrick. She sucked her teeth and sighed. "It doesn't make sense for him to call me this many times. He acts as if it would kill him to keep his own child for a few hours." Disgusted, Monet pulled the shift into reverse and backed out of the space. As she pulled out of the parking lot, she huffed, "I am not even about to call him back. He can wait until I get there."

Monet pulled up in front of Derrick's place about twenty minutes after leaving the hospital. She glanced toward the house and the darkness of it made her assume that Derrick's mother was still out at her friend's card game. If she were home, everything would be lit up. She wondered if Derrick had gone to bed. Certainly, she hoped he had not left. Monet shut off her car and checked out her surroundings, before she climbed out. Quickly, she jetted to the front door. From the porch, she glanced through a window and saw light coming from a television set. Monet turned the knob while knocking on the door. As usual, the door was unlocked. While slowly walking inside, she simultaneously called out Derrick's name. The living room was empty and Monet called for him again as she proceeded through the house. Still, he didn't answer.

As she stepped toward Derrick's bedroom, Monet noticed that the door was slightly open. She knocked a few times, but got no response. Suddenly, an eerie feeling came over her.

"Oh, Lord, please let my baby be okay," Monet chanted softly.

With Derrick still living the street life, there was no telling what had happened. It was not even an hour ago that he'd called her telephone. Hysterical, and with her heart beating in quick rhythm, she continued into the room. As she stepped inside, she heard moaning and crying sounds. Right away, her eyes were not pleased with what they observed. Deshawn, was lying at the foot of Derrick's bed, and Derrick and some female were lying at the head, completely nude and sound asleep. The room reeked of the pheromones of sex. An adult movie, with a couple, heavily involved in a very explicit sexual act, was displayed on the television. Monet was totally outdone. She could only imagine what had taken place in the presence of her son.

Deshawn's cries grew louder when he saw his mother. Monet screamed out Derrick's name so loud, that his eyes, and the eyes of the woman in the bed with him, popped wide open. Monet grabbed her son from the bed, and immediately scolded her baby's father.

"Just when I thought you couldn't stoop any lower," she fussed. "You know, you are one trifling dog, Derrick. You don't never have to worry about keeping my son anymore. You'll be lucky if you see him," Monet yelled.

Derrick didn't even attempt to get up out of the bed, nor did he cover himself. The female grabbed the covers and pulled them over both their naked bodies, then turned over onto her stomach. She didn't seem to be bothered by Monet's presence, or the argument between her and Derrick.

"Man, stop yelling, Monet, Can't you see that people are trying to sleep? I called you three or four times. You didn't answer your phone, and I know you knew that I called. I had something to do; you didn't say yo' ass was going to be gone that long."

Tears crowded Monet's eyes. She couldn't believe how inconsiderate Derrick was. He knew perfectly well that she was at the hospital seeing about her mother, and for him to even consider saying what he had said, disgusted her. Without saying another word, Monet turned and walked out of the room before she risked imprisonment for busting Derrick's head wide open with something. As mad as she was, she even wanted to put her fist through the mouth of the strange woman he was lying with.

What kind of female would be in the bed screwing, with the high probability of someone's child watching? Monet's thoughts raced as the thought of it all made her angrier.

She had absolutely no more words for Derrick. At this point, she didn't care if she or her son never saw him again. As far as Monet was concerned, Derrick was a pathetic excuse for a father.

CHAPTER 10

Monday morning, three days after the accident, was Rhenee's first day back in the office. Ever since the accident, she'd been a nervous wreck, and drinking heavily. Over the weekend, she diligently watched the news morning, noon, and night. Rhenee had to make sure there were no updates of the accident being aired without her being aware of it. She couldn't be caught off guard. If there were any new leads linked to the accident, she needed to know. The odds were still in her favor since there was no witness who could identify her or her car.

To place herself in a functional working mode, Rhenee tried to sit at her desk and meditate, but she couldn't. Flashbacks of the accident kept clouding her mind. Her ears could still hear the screams of the pedestrians she'd hit as her car collided with their bodies. Even though she'd had a few shots of Scotch on the morning of the accident, Rhenee didn't feel that she was intoxicated. She simply hadn't seen the people as they stepped out into the street. She could clearly remember staring into the woman's eyes when her face smashed into the windshield of her Porsche. The memories had been haunting her so much, that she couldn't sleep. In order to maintain her sanity, Rhenee needed to talk to someone. Hiding away from the world, and trying to hold on to such a secret would not help the situation. To free herself of the guilt associated with the car accident, Rhenee needed to continue on with her normal life, and pray that God would relieve her of the sleepless nights that were a reflection of the awful tragedy of which she was an accomplice.

She'd told herself that she was going to call her mother, but Rhenee simply had not gotten around to following through. Frustrated, she shook away her thoughts and tried to focus on the three files lying on her desk. She hadn't opened either one of them in over a week, and she was due to be in court in only three days, for the preliminary hearing on one of the cases.

"Cheryl," she mumbled aloud when she realized that she was about to be late for her lunch appointment with her friend. Taking her eyes away from the clock on her desk, Rhenee jumped from her seat, grabbed her purse from her closet, and dashed out of the office.

Any minute now, she was expecting Cheryl to call and remind her of their lunch plans. Cheryl was habitually punctual and had probably been at the restaurant for thirty minutes already. Rhenee had planned the meeting with her co-worker Cheryl Adams after deciding that she was the chosen one for Rhenee to unveil her secret to. Rhenee could no longer harbor what she had done, without going crazy, and if she could trust anyone, it would be Cheryl. They had been co-workers for eight years. She was also the one who Rhenee confided in about her and Ray's love affair.

After lunch with Cheryl, Rhenee felt somewhat relieved, although, she didn't get around to telling her about the accident. It wasn't that she didn't feel compelled to share the ordeal with her, but, once meeting with Cheryl, Rhenee couldn't gather the nerve to break her silence just yet. While Cheryl went on and on, about how much her boss worked her nerves, how money hungry he was, how he'd do anything for wealth and status, Rhenee decided against telling her. Her friend had problems of her own. Besides, Rhenee had too much to lose if the truth was exposed. She didn't want Cheryl to think that she was a heartless, evil person, when she wasn't.

Another reason why Rhenee decided not to expose herself was because she didn't want anyone trying to convince her to turn herself in. She simply wasn't prepared to do that yet. Having not spoken to anyone in days, only talking with Cheryl served as a much-needed source of relief. Rhenee had let her voicemail catch all her calls, the entire weekend, while she sat in her apartment trying to figure out what she was going to do.

Returning to work, Rhenee felt a great deal better than she did before her casual meeting, and she was even able to focus on the files on her desk. She had gone over the three cases that most urgently needed her attention, and she was also able to speak with the judge presiding over one of the cases, successfully obtaining a continuance. For that particular case, she needed to be at her best, and if she was going to do her best, she needed ample time to prepare for it.

Her day ended early. Even though Rhenee had more work that she could have stayed over time to complete, she had plans to go condo shopping. She seriously needed to find a home, and be closing on it by the end of the month. She left work at three o'clock to meet with a realtor, who'd be showing her a condo. The place that Rhenee was checking out would be quite convenient because it was located downtown, only about a five-minute drive from her job.

The agent, Shelly, said she'd meet Rhenee there. Shelly told Rhenee that she'd be waiting in the parking lot, in a dark blue Mercedes. Since Rhenee's car sustained extensive damage, and she hadn't yet taken it to the shop for the needed repairs, she parked her car around the corner from where she had to meet Shelly, and walked the rest of the way. She didn't want to risk Shelly asking any questions about the obvious dents in her vehicle. Rhenee wasn't planning on reporting the accident to her insurance company, and she hadn't gotten around to getting a rental car or finding a bootleg mechanic to repair her own battered automobile.

Rhenee noticed Shelly's car as soon as she walked around to the front of the condo complex. Since Shelly hadn't gotten out of her car, Rhenee pranced toward it, while trying to get Shelly's attention. Shelly smiled when she noticed Rhenee waving her arms.

Shelly rolled down her window. "Ms. Edwards?" Her voice sounded unsure.

Rhenee smiled and nodded her head and, with the verification she needed, Shelly climbed out of her vehicle. She grabbed her briefcase from the backseat, closed the door and rushed to shake hands with her potential new client.

"Hi," Rhenee said as she shook Shelly's hand.

"Nice to meet you," Shelly responded. She sported a very welcoming smile. Shelly was a tall, white woman with wide hips. Her hair was long, brown and curly. She was wearing an attractive, tan pantsuit and the colors in it called attention to her green eyes. As she and Rhenee walked toward the building, Shelly went to work.

"Once we step inside the lobby, I'll show you the seven different floor plans we have available; that way, we'll avoid showing you those that are not accommodating to your needs."

"Sounds great."

As they headed toward the door of the lobby, Rhenee took a moment to check out the architectural layout of the building. It looked to be about nine stories high. Rhenee wanted to be right on the middle floor. She'd love to look at a place on the fifth or sixth floor. As soon as they entered the building, Shelly went to work, selling the place. She first mentioned how quiet the community was, and referred to the majority of the residents as yuppies. She also mentioned that there were only four families with children who lived in the entire building. Shelly made it a point to stress this perk because Rhenee had questioned the ratio of children when she inquired about the condo. Rhenee mentioned not wanting to purchase a place in a community where many children lived. Not that she had anything against children; but after putting in thirteen- or fourteen-hour workdays, she definitely didn't want to come home to a building full of noise.

Rhenee took her time to look over all the floor plans for the remaining available condos in the building. Of the nine, Rhenee chose to tour four of them. The first two didn't meet her expectations, but Rhenee kept her hopes up. She still had two more to see. One was a 1,700-square-foot, one-bedroom condo, and the other was a 2,450-square-foot, two-bedroom. Since Rhenee liked having extra space, she opted to see the two-bedroom unit first.

Upon entrance, Rhenee fell in love with the condo. The foyer had high ceilings with sun windows. The floors were hardwood and had a sparkling shine that showed her reflection as she walked across it. Rhenee happily followed Shelly during the tour through the rest of the place. The living room was huge and also had hardwood floors, and high ceilings. There was a massive brick fireplace with a stone mantel. To the right of the mantel, was a walkout balcony with a great view of downtown Grand Rapids.

Next, Shelly showed Rhenee the kitchen and the dining room, both of which had black and grey stone, marble floors. Separating the two rooms was a built-in bar, with a counter long enough for at least four people to occupy. The master bedroom was so roomy that it seemed to be about half the size of the entire condo. Inside that bedroom was a living room suite, a humongous walk-in closet, and a king-sized garden whirlpool bathtub. The step down tub was in the middle of the floor, and a built-in vanity area sat on the side of it. Rhenee's love for the condo could be seen all over her face. As she stood in the middle of the bedroom, she looked up to the sky, closed her eyes, and took a deep breath. Once she opened her eyes, she smiled, because this place truly felt like home.

"You know, Shelly, I think I've made my selection. I want this place. With a few minor adjustments, I think I can make this into my castle in the sky."

Shelly smiled, then asked Rhenee into the kitchen where she could use the counter to jot down a few notes. Afterwards, Rhenee asked for a couple days to look over the paperwork, and told Shelly that she would get back with her.

"Sounds real good," Shelly said as she and her new client exited the condo and headed toward the elevator. "The sooner you call me, the sooner I can get started on submitting your paperwork for the loan."

"Be expecting to hear from me soon," Rhenee retorted as they exited the building, each going their separate ways.

CHAPTER 11

Wednesday morning was a sad and dreadful day for Andrea. It was the day she was released from the hospital. It felt like the worst day of her life. She had lost her child, her baby, the love of her life, and all that she sustained was a broken leg and arm. *How could it be*, she wondered as the nurse pushed her in the wheelchair, through the hospital. Tears poured from her eyes. She could not believe how, with a quick turns of events, she could again be without the precious love of her life. And this time, it was forever. Andrea wanted to know why God had taken her child. Timya deserved life.

As her father and the hospital staff helped her into the car, Andrea continued to cry. In less than a week, she would have to say her final goodbye to her daughter. This would be an entirely different experience than when she went away to jail because she knew that one day, she'd be back with her daughter. Now, there was no coming back. After the funeral, Andrea would see her daughter no more. She felt so sad that she simply wanted to lie down and never get up to face another day. Even though she hadn't been there to raise her daughter, Timya was her other half. Ever since the day she entered into Andrea's life, all Andrea wanted to do from that point on was get better; and now it felt as though she didn't care about anything anymore, which was exactly the attitude she had before going to jail. Andrea felt so cheated. Everything that she'd planned to do was for the sake of her daughter and without Timya, what was she to do? As she depreciated further into her somber sadness, Andrea leaned back in the seat of her father's car and wept heavily.

Her Aunt Dorothy was going to be in the hospital for at least another week. She would miss Timya's funeral, because her doctor wanted to keep a close eye on her progression. And once Dorothy woke up and heard the news of Timya's death, emotionally, she would be in no condition to attend the funeral anyway. She would have no strength to mourn.

When they arrived home, Thomas helped Andrea get settled into her bedroom before he went in to check on his wife. Since the accident, Caroline had remained locked away in the bedroom, lying in bed. She hadn't eaten a decent meal for days, and hadn't gone to the hospital to see her sister, nor was she there for Taylor. Pastor Gaines, the pastor of her church, came over to pray with her, but even that didn't break her from her depression.

Caroline preferred to remain in bed, and avoid everyone and everything. She refused to go to work, and refused all phone calls. It wasn't that she didn't want to be there for her family and friends; the truth was, she wasn't strong enough to face anyone. Timya was her baby, and losing her felt like a piece of Caroline's soul had been ripped away. Caroline could not believe that such a terrible thing could happen to such an innocent child.

Taylor and her father sat alone at the kitchen table, eating dinner. Not particularly skilled in the kitchen, Thomas prepared chilidogs and fries for the two of them, since the women of the house, who normally did the cooking, were in no condition to do so. For the mourning women, Thomas made chicken noodle soup and grilled cheese sandwiches, but neither of them touched their food. He left the food trays in their rooms in case either of them wanted to eat it later.

"When is Mommy going to come out of her room? Doesn't she have to go to work?"

"I don't know, honey. I guess she'll come out when she feels better. After she's better, she can get back to spending time with you and she can get back to work. I think we should be considerate and give her and Andrea all the time they need to heal."

Taylor took a bite of her hot dog, and after swallowing, said, "I'm sad too, Daddy."

Thomas wiped his hands on the paper towel, and reached over to give his daughter a hug and a kiss on the cheek. "It's okay, baby. We all have a right to be sad. We have suffered a great loss. I've been a little down myself, but sooner or later, all the pain will start to ease and our lives will start to feel normal again. Although we're all suffering from losing Timya, we have to be thankful, and keep praying that Auntie Dorothy is going to be okay."

Taylor was silent and a puzzled expression overtook her face. Thomas saw the confusion and reached over the table to give his baby girl another hug. She smiled and told her father that she loved him, and hoped that nothing never happened to him.

"I don't know what I would do if I didn't have you, Daddy."

Thomas smiled. After the two of them finished dinner, they headed into the den. Together, they picked out a movie to watch. Once they agreed on one, Taylor and her father sat in front of the television and watched it together.

The next day, Thomas and Taylor went to the mall to pick out an outfit for the funeral home to dress Timya in. Since Andrea and Caroline were both out of commission, it was up to Thomas to carry on with the burial arrangements. So far, he'd already reserved the church and had an okay from the pastor, who agreed to deliver the eulogy. Thomas had also made phone calls to their close friends and family members, informing them of the home going ceremony for Timya.

He and Taylor picked out a beautiful, white, lace gown that resembled a christening outfit. The clerk assisting Thomas bagged the dress and accessories neatly, and then she recited the total of his purchase. Thomas whipped out his credit card, and handed it to her. Once it dawned on him what the purchase was for, he suddenly became emotionally panicked. His heart was beating expeditiously, and his eyes became watery and red. He could not believe he was purchasing the very last dress he'd see Timya in.

The clerk handed the card back to Thomas. He placed it back in his wallet as they both waited in silence, while the transaction was being approved. Finally, the receipt popped up. The sales clerk ripped it from the cash register, and handed it to Thomas, along with an ink pen. The woman looked at him with concern. Thomas' face was covered with worry lines. He looked as if he were about to cry.

"I need you to sign at the bottom, sir."

Thomas stood blankly in front of her station with the pen in hand. He looked as if he had no clue as to why she handed it to him in the first place.

Coming to himself, Thomas quickly jotted his signature onto the receipt, and then waited for the woman to hand him the bag containing his purchases. He and his daughter then turned and walked out of the store. Although he desperately wanted to shed a few tears for the tragic loss of his granddaughter, Thomas had to be strong for the others.

When he and Taylor arrived back at the house, they were surprised to see that Andrea and Caroline were out of bed and sitting at the kitchen table together. They each had sandwiches sitting on a saucer in front of them. Taylor ran straight into her mother's arms as soon as she stepped into the house.

"I'm so happy to see you up and feeling better, Mom. I thought you and Andrea would never get out of bed. Dad and I just came from the mall."

Caroline eased out a slight smile. "I'm sorry I couldn't come with you, baby. I've just had a lot of things on my mind that's kept me from being in a shopping mood."

"I understand, Mom. I know that you have been going through a lot." She looked at her sister. "You and Andrea are going to be okay. God is going to heal you guys' hurt in due time. If either of you need me to do anything for you, let me know. Daddy and I are going to help you all out as much as possible."

Caroline smiled as she reached out to hug her daughter. Taylor sounded and looked so sincere. Her daughter's words had made her day. She knew that if she didn't get up and get herself together for herself, then at least she could do it for her family.

ぬ ぬ ぬ ぬ ぬ

The morning of the funeral was rainy and dreary. Everyone in Caroline's house was dressed and ready for the limousine to pick them up. It was due to arrive at eleven o'clock so that they could all be situated inside the church in time for the noonday service.

Caroline was trying her best to be as strong as she could. Her daughter needed her today as never before. Andrea was emotionless. Her face showed no sign of happiness or sorrow; she said nothing.

Thomas hoped that she didn't break down at the funeral. He knew that although Andrea appeared to be okay, she was hurting tremendously inside.

The limo finally arrived and as soon as the rest of the family gathered, the funeral home staff attached miniature flags onto the hoods of all of the cars. Andrea and her dad sat beside each other in one of the vehicles, and Caroline and Taylor sat across from them. In silence, they all sat somberly, waiting for the chauffeur to get back into the limousine and lead the procession of cars to the church. About fifteen cars, loaded with family and friends ushered the mourning family to the church.

Once there, Caroline and her family were led inside the sanctuary where they were escorted down the aisle to the front of the church. As soon as the immediate family was seated, the rest of the relatives and supporters were permitted inside the church. The benches filled rather quickly. While she sat, trying to hold back her tears, Caroline glanced around the church and admired the way the flowers had been placed all throughout the sanctuary. Pink roses on pine green vines, lined all the pews and surrounded the casket. Two large photos of Timya stood on each side of the casket. Thomas had purchased so many flowers to be placed around the casket that the church looked like a floral shop. As people continued to gather inside the church, the now assembled choir commenced humming the spiritual, *I'm Going Home,* as the requested red carpet was laid. Thomas chose to add the laying of the red carpet to the ceremony, because in his eye, his Star was going home, and she needed to be represented as such.

Caroline's eyes watered when she took a long look at the pearl white casket that housed her precious little granddaughter. The thought of Timya being in the casket, her final resting place, caused the tears that Caroline had been holding back all morning, to burst free. "Granny is going to miss you, Timya," she cried softly.

Thomas wrapped one arm around his wife, and with the other, he used a napkin to wipe away her tears. Up until that moment, the entire family had held up pretty well, but as soon as Caroline broke down, Thomas, Andrea, and Taylor did the same. The volume of the music increased as the Pastor entered the sanctuary and stepped up to the pulpit. The choir continued humming as Caroline looked back at the row behind her, to see if Dorothy's family had arrived. Caroline had reserved seats for Sullivan, Monet, and the kids, but they still hadn't made an appearance. It looked as if they'd miss the beginning of the ceremony, because Pastor Gaines was ready to begin.

Fifteen minutes into the sermon, Thomas felt a tap on his shoulder and turned to see that the bench behind him being occupied. It was Sullivan who had tapped him on the shoulders to let him know that he and the kids had arrived. Monet took her and Deshawn's coats and neatly laid them on the floor in front of her. When she finished, she sat her son on the pew, and instructed him to remain there while she went to hug her cousin, Andrea. Embracing, the two women cried together as Monet used comforting words to assure Andrea that everything was going to be okay.

"God knows best," she told Andrea as they stared into each other's teary eyes.

Shortly after Monet took her seat, a tall brown-skinned woman, wearing a navy blue skirt suit, approached Caroline. When Caroline rose to exchange hugs with the woman, the woman wept heavily. She appeared to be as shaken up as Carolyn. The mascara that lined her eyes ran, leaving a dark trail of tears, and different shades of lipstick impressions were covering her face. Monet didn't know the woman personally, but she recognized her as being one of their distant cousins. Monet remembered seeing the woman at one of their family reunions, about two summer's ago. Everyone in the family referred to her as Kat, but Monet assumed that was her nickname. Now, Kat looked about ten years older than she had when Monet had seen her last. Her mid-back length hair weave was tangled into a lump that piled up on Kat's right shoulder and remained there. No matter how much she moved her head, the hair didn't budge. Although the suit Kat wore was eye-catching and looked very expensive, her weave looked liked a tangled web ball extending from the nape of her neck.

Dorothy's best friend, Punkin, finally showed up. She slid onto the end of the bench where Monet and the others were sitting. All eyes were on her, especially those belonging to the men. Monet was surprised to see Punkin in a dress that hung barely past her knees. What didn't surprise Monet was that Punkin's dress was skin tight, and made of a leather material that had to be at least eighty percent spandex. Punkin was breathing heavily, as if she'd run a marathon. Onlookers found it entertaining as they watched her try to maneuver herself into the seat comfortably, while the black dress she wore stuck to her body. Monet could not wait to tell her mother about that dress. Dorothy was bound to have a good laugh after Monet told her how her friend sat on the end of the church bench, as stiff as a board, while trying to hold on to her flirtatious Kodak smile.

Once the pastor finished his sermon, he then announced that it was time for everyone to line up for the final viewing of the body. Instead of Caroline and her family leading the way, she requested that everyone else go first, and they would follow. Monet got up and slowly walked toward the casket with Punkin, Tonya, and Keisha, who was carrying Deshawn. Dwayne remained in his seat, waiting with Sullivan, who'd decided to accompany Caroline and Andrea. He wasn't sure if either of them were strong enough to go up alone.

Slowly, the line moved and Monet's turn to approach the casket was nearing. When Punkin walked up to the casket, she briefly closed her eyes, and when she opened them, they were watery and red. She placed her napkin under her nose, bowed her head, and then stepped away.

By that time, Monet was already in tears. She took the final step and froze as she looked down into the casket. She was crying for several reasons, but mostly because she'd miss Timya. Some of her tears were for her cousin, Andrea, and what she was going through. Monet could not imagine what she would do if such a tragedy was brought upon her. Deshawn was her whole world, and ever since the day she first set eyes on him, she couldn't imagine her life without him. After saying a short prayer, Monet whispered, "Bye, Timya," then she stepped to the side and waited for her sisters.

Once they all finished bidding Timya farewell, they waited for the next usher who would escort them back to their seats. The gentleman walked up quickly and smiled at Punkin. Instead of simply leading her, he slid his arm around hers, and walked beside her. Punkin smiled when she turned to Monet who was walking behind them. Monet shook her head and continued walking.

The male usher was a new member of the church. Monet remembered seeing him join a couple of weeks prior. She wasn't good at remembering names, but Monet did recall the man telling the church that he was an electrician. He indicated that he'd bought a small piece of property on the corner of Eastern and Oakdale, and was planning on turning it into an office space to house his business, and that he would build his business' reputation by offering great, friendly, reasonable service. Monet imaged that all the women in the church were impressed because not only was the newcomer attractive, but he had mentioned nothing about having a wife or family.

It was Caroline's turn to view the remains and when she saw her granddaughter lying there peacefully, Caroline had to be caught from falling to the floor. Her husband was forced to carry her back to her seat.

"No! No, Lord, don't take my baby!" she screamed repeatedly.

Thomas continued to hold on to her as they wept together.

Andrea asked Monet if she could walk with her up to the front. Andrea was still very calm, although her face was full of tears. As soon as she made her way to the resting place of her daughter, Andrea laid her head into the bed of the casket, and closed her eyes. Sullivan and Monet stood on both sides of her.

"I love you Timya," Andrea whispered. "No matter what, you will always remain in my heart. You are what gave my life purpose." As the tears streamed continuously down her face, Andrea raised her head and placed a gentle kiss on her daughter's lips. "I love you, baby," she repeated before standing upright and walking away with Monet at her side.

A few latecomers scurried up to view the body before the funeral attendants prepared to close the casket indefinitely. For some odd reason, Kat had to get one last glimpse as well. As she viewed the body one last time, the roar of her voice echoed throughout the church, as she cried out Timya's name and fell to her knees.

"Oh, Lord, why!" she cried out. Two ushers immediately rushed to help Kat back to her feet. She could have received an Oscar for her performance. "NO, LAWD, NO! NOT TIMYA, LAWD. She was only a baby. Please, God, please don't take the baby." Big crocodile tears fell from her eyes as the two gentlemen continued trying to keep Kat on her feet. It seemed that every time they tried to lift her, she'd suddenly fall back down. Her legs were wobbling like Jello, and her head was jerking back and forth. But even with all of her theatrics, her hair still did not move. To the average outsider, Kat was mourning the loss of a child that she really had some emotional attachment to.

Thomas looked toward the ground and shook his head with embarrassment. Kat was making quite the scene and everyone in the church was staring at her. He couldn't believe the way she was making such a fool of herself. It was all a ploy for attention because the only time Kat had ever seen Timya was on the one occasion when she came to their house. Timya was a year old at the time and Caroline thought the visit was suspicious and later found out the exact reason for Kat's impromptu visit. Kat had only come over to see Timya because she'd heard that Andrea had given birth to a crack baby, and she wanted to come and see if there was any truth to the gossip. She stayed for about thirty minutes and left. Now that Timya's life was no more, Kat was acting like she couldn't live her life without the baby. As Thomas observed the two ushers wiping Kat's face and carrying her down the aisle, he continued trying to hide his face, while shaking his head in disgust.

Monet was too disgusted. Kat's performance was another thing she couldn't wait to tell her mother about. If it weren't for their bloodline, Kat would be a stranger to the family, because there was little anyone knew of her.

Andrea looked up when she noticed that Tim was the very last one to view his daughter's body. After he walked away, the casket closed. Andrea watched carefully as the attendants locked the casket and rolled it down the isle. She tried to make it. She tried to remain strong until they got to the gravesite, but she could hold out no longer. Realizing that she'd seen her daughter's face, for the very last time, Andrea passed out in the chair.

CHAPTER 12

A week and two days after the funeral, Dorothy was released from the hospital. Sullivan arrived precisely at eight o'clock in the morning to pick her up. He missed having his wife around the house, and their bed didn't sleep the same without her. He couldn't wait until his wife was back at home with him. Dorothy had been away from home for nearly three weeks. The doctor wanted her to take it easy, although he recommended that she do as much walking as possible. He advised that walking would be good exercise to help her regain the strength in her lung. The hospital prescribed an oxygen machine for Dorothy to take home with her, and Dr. Harvey assured her that it would not be permanent. He suggested that Dorothy use the machine only as needed.

"The sooner your lungs build up their strength, the sooner you can do away with the oxygen machine," he said. "During the first couple of weeks, any time you walk long distances or perform any strenuous activities, you'll need the oxygen."

After passing along the instructions, Dr. Harvey pulled Sullivan aside so that they could speak in private. As they stood outside of Dorothy's room, the doctor explained to Sullivan, that Dorothy would seem somewhat depressed from time to time, so as a precautionary measure, in addition to pain relievers, he was also prescribing anti-depressants, and wanted Dorothy took take them as needed.

"She will definitely need these painkillers after the morphine wears off, so get this prescription filled as soon as possible," Dr. Harvey stated. "She'll be experiencing some level of pain, for the first couple of months." He advised that Dorothy take the painkillers every four hours, instead of waiting to take them when she was in pain. In conclusion, he told Sullivan, "I've explained everything to your wife as I am telling you now. I just needed you to know so that you can make sure she stays on track with all of my orders and recommendations."

"Thanks a lot," Sullivan replied. "I will make sure that she gets all the proper care that she needs."

After watching the doctor walk away, Sullivan turned and walked back into his wife's room, where the nurse was assisting her into the wheelchair.

∝ ∝ ∝ ∝ ∝

Dorothy felt relieved when she finally walked through the door of her own home. Once inside, she took a deep breath, inhaling the fumes of fresh laundry. The smell lingered throughout the air. "Yes," she remarked. "It truly is good to be home."

Sullivan smiled and kissed his wife on her head. "It's good to have you back, honey."

Dorothy slowly strolled throughout the house. She took her time, although by the time she reached the kitchen, she was already breathing heavier than normal.

Sullivan observed her every move. "Are you sure you don't want to go and lie down in the bed, baby?"

"No," she answered quickly. "I am tired of lying down. I've been lying down for the last couple of weeks. I want to walk. I need the strength back in my legs."

Sullivan shook his head and continued into the bedroom carrying his wife's things. The house was well kept and Dorothy felt relieved to come home to such a clean place. She was happy that she didn't have to come home fussing about housework not being done.

"Monet said that she'd be over some time this morning. She doesn't have class today," Sullivan informed his wife.

"Oh, yeah," Dorothy answered. "I can't wait. I haven't seen my grandbaby in weeks." She paused, and breathed heavily, struggling to catch her breath.

Sullivan stood in silence while carefully observing his wife. He didn't want to say anything, but he did need to be assured that she was okay. After a few short seconds, Dorothy lifted her head, and replied, "I'm okay."

With her reassurance, Sullivan continued talking. "Caroline, Thomas, and the girls said they'd be over later on this evening. Your best buddy, Punkin, called last night and said that she would come some time today as well. I don't know if you feel like a whole bunch of company, but I invited Pastor Gaines to drop in for a visit later on. We should be expecting him this evening around eight o'clock. I wanted to him come after everyone else has left so that we can have a family prayer."

"That's all fine," Dorothy smiled. "I have plenty of energy," she huffed as she continued pacing back and forth down the hallway. Sullivan stood at the end of the hall watching her. Suddenly, Dorothy bent over and rubbed her chest. She was breathing hard, again.

"Are you sure you're okay, honey?"

"I'm fine," Dorothy snapped. "I'm just trying to exercise my lung. I want to get back to normal as soon as possible. The sooner I'm breathing well on my own, the sooner the hospital can have that machine back. I definitely do not plan on using that for too long, God willing. I'll only be using it for a little while."

Sullivan walked away, shaking his head. He took a seat on the sofa, and opened up the newspaper. Before long, Dorothy entered the room looking as if she'd finished running a marathon. Sweat beads had gathered on her forehead, and her breathing pattern was still erratic. Sullivan looked up at her and suddenly back at his paper. It wasn't until his wife finally took a seat beside him that he was able to relax his nerves.

"I think you should try and take it easy," he advised. "You're going to be having visitors later, and you don't want to wear yourself out, so that you have no strength to entertain once they get here."

"I'll be fine, sweetheart, and if it'll make you feel any better, I'll remain seated so you won't continue to worry. It's written all over your face," she smiled. Sullivan returned her smile and resumed reading the paper.

Spotting a fresh glass of ice water resting on a coaster on the end table, Dorothy hurried to pick it up. As soon as the chilled fluid hit her throat, she let out a refreshing, "Ahhh." Within minutes, Dorothy found herself becoming more comfortable on the couch. Sullivan got up once she turned and kicked her feet up. The two Vicodin tablets she'd taken before leaving the hospital were beginning to take effect, and slowly she was starting to drift off. Dorothy felt so relaxed, that she rested her head on the pillow of the couch, and closed her eyes. She fought the sleep that was coming over her for as long as she could, but before long, her vision became blurry, and her head heavy. Ten minutes later, Dorothy's eyelids became so heavy, that she could no longer fight off the sleep. Her eyes closed in slow motion, as if they had a mind of their own.

The room was still and quiet when Sullivan re-appeared. Dorothy could see her husband through a blur, as he called her name, awakening her from her catnap. "Honey, I think that you'd be much more comfortable in the bed. I just changed the sheets this morning. I know you miss sleeping in your own bed, and that couch will have you with a crook in your neck."

Dorothy got up from the sofa and ran her hands through her hair. "Where were you?"

"I was in the kitchen putting your flowers in water. I set the vase of roses, and the balloons in the bedroom."

"Thanks, baby. I'm sorry that I dosed off on you. That medicine kicked in before I was expecting it to. I'm feeling like I'm on cloud nine. I think it's a good idea that I go and get in the bed. I can barely hold my head up."

Sullivan led Dorothy to the bedroom and helped her get out of the clothes she was wearing, and into a comfortable nightgown. He then assisted his wife into the bed, and pulled the covers over her. As soon as her head hit the pillow, Dorothy was sleep.

As Dorothy pushed Timya in the buggy, down the street, she and her niece, Andrea, conversed. Andrea wanted her aunt's help in figuring out the best way to break the news to Tim about him being Timya's father.

"Well, Andrea. I think that the best thing for you to do is to be straight up, and straight to the point with Tim. I mean, I've never met the boy, but as high yellow as this here little girl is, she has to be his. It's quite apparent that my Mya-Mya got some white in her," Dorothy laughed. "If he has any doubts, tell him to get a paternity test. DNA don't lie, baby," were the last words Dorothy uttered before she turned to see the car veering into their direction.

Ear piercing was the sound of the brakes on the car that screeched off the road, and collided into them. The impact swept them off their feet and hurling them into a brick wall. Dorothy and Andrea screamed, and threw up their hands, but it was already too late. There was no time to get out of the way, no time to run.

"*AWWH,*" Dorothy screamed as she was awakened from her sleep.

In a state of panic, Sullivan rushed into the bedroom "What's wrong, sweetheart? Are you in pain? Do you need me to call the doctor?"

Dorothy looked toward her husband. Her forehead was covered with sweat and tears were streaming down her face. "I tried to get out of the way, but it was too late," she screamed. "It was too late for me to do anything, Sullivan. I wanted to save Timya, but it was too late," she cried as she fell back onto the pillow.

Sullivan walked over to the bed and sat on the edge. He reached over and wrapped his arms around his wife. "Don't worry about it, Dorothy. It's all over now. You were just having a bad dream. What happened to you guys wasn't your fault. It was no one's fault." Sullivan lifted his wife into his arms and rocked with her. "It's okay, baby. Would you like for me to get you something cold to drink? You are burning up."

Dorothy nodded yes. She then sat still while her husband wiped her eyes dry. Afterwards, he left the room and returned with a cold glass of lemonade. Dorothy quickly grabbed the glass and sipped the cold liquid.

At the sound of the doorbell, Sullivan told his wife, "That's either Monet or Punkin. Let me go and get the door, and then I'll be right back." He left the room, and headed toward the front door, leaving Dorothy to herself to try to clear her thoughts.

When Sullivan opened the front door, his grandson, Deshawn, as full of energy as always, burst forward into his Pa Pa's legs. It was obvious that he was happy to see Sullivan. Sullivan quickly grabbed Deshawn and threw him into the air, causing the little boy to burst into laughter.

Monet stepped past the two of them "Where's Mother?"

"She's in the bedroom, but I think she'll probably be in here in a minute," Sullivan answered while still playing with Deshawn. Monet shook her head, took a seat on the couch and admired the way her mother had the living room decorated. Dorothy's favorite color was purple, and it was accented throughout the entire room. Monet found the room to be very relaxing.

After placing Deshawn back on the floor, Sullivan looked at Monet and said, "Let me go and check on your mother. She just woke up from a really bad dream, and I want to make sure she is okay. I will see if she wants to visit with you out here, or if she wants you to come to her room."

Monet was now wearing a worried look on her face. "Is she going to be okay?"

"I hope so," Sullivan said as he exited.

Shortly after Monet and Deshawn arrived, the doorbell rang again. Dorothy still hadn't made it to the living room yet, so as Sullivan returned to answer the door, Monet tipped into her mother's bedroom to see what she was up to.

"That's probably Punkin," Sullivan said, en route to the front door. Deshawn was right behind him. Once Sullivan looked through the peephole and saw that his guess was correct, he hurried to open the door. Punkin was full of smiles, but her eyes were hidden by a large pair of dark sunglasses.

"What's up?" Punkin greeted as she stepped into the house while smacking on chewing gum.

From the strong smell of cinnamon that Sullivan got a whiff of as she stepped past him and into the house, he figured it was Big Red. As usual, she was wearing skintight jeans, and a shirt that revealed far too much cleavage.

"Hey, Punkin," Sullivan finally greeted as he took a very quick look at her. "My wife was supposed to be coming in here ten minutes ago, and she hasn't made it yet. I'll go and check to see what she is doing, and let her know that you are here," he added before leaving the room to find out what was delaying Dorothy.

Punkin didn't wait for him to go and check on her friend as Sullivan thought she would. Instead, she followed him into the bedroom where Dorothy and Monet were sitting together.

"Hey, Dorothy," she yelled as soon as she stepped into the room. Dorothy was sitting up in the bed, and Monet was sitting on the end of it. Dorothy smiled when she saw her friend for the first time in a long while. Punkin approached the bed and gave Dorothy a massive hug.

"Be, careful," Dorothy moaned. I know you love me, but you don't have to squeeze so hard. You know I just had a surgery."

"I'm so sorry," Punkin said while releasing her. "You ain't never too sick to get some love from your girl."

Dorothy smiled, and, with caution, climbed out of the bed. "Let's go into the living room. I am tired of lying down."

Monet and Punkin walked ahead, as Dorothy followed slowly behind them into the living room. Sullivan was already in there and he propped a pillow on the couch for his wife.

"Thanks, baby, but I'll stand up for a minute. I'll sit down if I get tired."

Monet and her stepfather exchanged familiar expressions as they looked at each other and then back at Dorothy. Neither of them dared to say anything.

Punkin wasted no time jumping right into a conversation with her friend. She missed Dorothy and had a lot of gossip to catch her up on. So much had happened since she'd last seen Dorothy, but she made sure to fill her in on every dramatic detail of her life. Before long, Punkin was discussing details of Timya's funeral. Dorothy was not interested in hearing about it, and the expression on her face confirmed it, but Punkin wasn't even paying attention. As Punkin continued talking, Dorothy listened without interrupting, since Punkin didn't mention anything about Timya. She was busy trying to tell her friend about the performance put on by Dorothy's cousin, Kat. She theatrically described how Kat got to the front of the church and screamed how much she would miss Timya, while collapsing onto the floor. While telling the story, Punkin made funny gestures, mocking Kat's performance. Dorothy tried hard not to laugh, because she was trying to prevent busting her stitches, but Punkin's dramatics were hilarious. This was Dorothy's first time hearing the story, and she knew no one could tell it and make it sound as humorous, as Punkin did. By the time Punkin finished telling the story, even Monet and Sullivan were laughing.

After hearing Kat's story, Dorothy's spirits were lifted and Punkin sat with Dorothy and Monet for about an hour before she prepared to leave. She was on schedule to work the night shift, but had been thoughtful enough to stop by and see her friend before clocking in.

Right before she left, Sullivan said, "You have a secret admirer at the church, you know."

Punkin laughed. "A secret admirer?"

"Yes, the guy is new in town and just recently became a member of the church."

Punkin blushed. "So does this secret admirer have a name? And how much do you know about him?"

"His name is Brother Mark Woods. He's an electrician, and he just opened his own business right down on Oakdale Street. He's in the same building where the old hardware store used to be."

"Oh, yeah," Punkin answered. "I think I may have to pay a visit to the church. I just happen to be off next Sunday." After marveling at the idea, Punkin got up to leave, saying her goodbyes to Dorothy and Monet, before she left the room.

Shaking his head back and forth, Sullivan led Punkin to the front door. "Girl, you are a trip," he stated, before saying goodbye and closing the door behind her.

CHAPTER 13

Andrea was anxious to get home from Dorothy's. She was happy that her auntie was doing okay, but Andrea had other plans for the rest of the day. She had gone with her parents and sister to check on Dorothy, but she didn't think they'd be staying as long as they had. Although Dorothy wanted to be good company, she couldn't seem to stay awake long enough to hold a lasting conversation. She was on some heavy medication, and kept apologizing for dozing off. Eventually, Caroline realized that she wasn't going to get much conversation out of her sister, so she kissed Dorothy on the cheek and told her that she would call her later. Andrea had been waiting to hear those words for what seemed like forever. She couldn't wait to get back home, because she had a dinner date with Tim. Tonight, Andrea was going to tell him all the details of her life that transpired after the two of them separated. It was unfortunate that Tim had never gotten the chance to meet their daughter.

As soon as she entered the house, the telephone rang. Caroline was puzzled by the way that Andrea rushed to answer it. Andrea knew it was Tim, and didn't want her mother to answer. The way Caroline stared as she rushed to the phone caused Andrea to ponder. She knew she needed to get her own phone line before she and her mother would have problems. She could tell by the look in Caroline's eye that her mother couldn't wait to get in her business.

Andrea's conversation with Tim was short. He was calling to let her know that he was on his way. He informed her that they had dinner reservations for seven o'clock and didn't want to be late. Andrea excitedly hung up the telephone and rushed upstairs to her bedroom to freshen up before Tim arrived.

Taking a quick look in the mirror, she patted down a few loose strands of hair, and re-applied her black eyeliner. Afterwards, she misted herself with a few squirts of her favorite perfume, True Star. Within minutes, she was rushing out of the bathroom, and back downstairs to wait for her ride. Andrea window-watched for Tim's arrival and once she saw his car pull into her driveway, she hurried out the front door. Jumping into the passenger seat, she smiled as the car pulled away from her house and cruised down the street. Besides the music playing, the car was silent. Tim and Andrea were both nervous about seeing each other, but Andrea was the first to break the calm.

"This is a change for you, but it's a nice ride"

Tim smiled. "My parents helped me get this car after I got out. I'm trying to live the more conservative life."

"So am I." Again, there was silence. Andrea's smile diminished when a flashback emerged in her thoughts. "I'm trying to stay as far away from that old life as I can. Our daughter saved me." Andrea's hoarse voice silenced, as the tears formed in her eyes, trying not to make an appearance.

Tim could tell that talking about Timya was still a little hard for Andrea, but it was a good form of mental rehabilitation for her to express her true feelings. Besides, he wanted to know more about the baby he never got the chance to know. "When was she born?"

"On August fifth, she turned two."

"So did you go back home to live when you found out you were pregnant?"

Andrea shook her head no. "Tim, I found out that I was pregnant with our daughter when I was going into labor with her, she arrived nearly four months early. Up until then, I was still living on the streets and getting high. It was horrible; I had no idea that I was pregnant. After you went to jail, I was so sad. That same day, I met these two females at the house where we used to go and get blow from. They let me move in with them, and for the next couple of months, we partied and got high every single day of the week. I was so alone and lost without you, Tim." Andrea's words were accompanied by tears as Tim navigated the car into the parking lot of Ruby Tuesday's and shut off the engine. He reached over and pulled Andrea into his arms.

"I never got the chance to tell her how sorry I was for what I did to her," Andrea whispered into his ear. Tim held her in his arms until she was ready to get out and go inside the restaurant.

Tim wiped Andrea's face with a Kleenex, and the two of them climbed out of the gold Camry and walked in each other's arms into the restaurant. Tim held the door for Andrea as she stepped into the dimly lit restaurant. They walked down two stairs and stood at the hostess stand behind the sign that read: WAIT TO BE SEATED.

Soon, the hostess approached. "Two for smoking, or non-smoking?"

"Non-smoking," Tim answered, "and we have reservations."

The woman smiled as Tim gave her his name and waited for the hostess to respond. After locating Tim's name on the ledger, the hostess grabbed two menus from behind the podium. "Follow me, please."

Tim walked behind Andrea as they followed the lady to their seats. The woman escorted them to a booth in the back corner of the non-smoking section. The section was cozy and the atmosphere was quiet. There were only four other occupied tables in the section.

The interior of the brick structure was painted a soft yellow color and artwork of various painters decorated the otherwise barren walls. The waitress, who introduced herself as Aleece, came to the table right away to take their drink orders. Tim ordered a coke, and Andrea chose lemonade. As soon as Aleece walked away from the table, Tim continued with his questions. There was so much about Andrea and the baby that he wanted to know, and now was as perfect time, as any, to find out. This was the first time that they'd been able to talk since Andrea had come to his parents' home to see if he was out of jail.

"So, how long have you been out?"

"Almost a month, I was locked up for sixteen months. As soon as I got out of the hospital, after having the baby, I got locked up. I went to see my probation officer that Monday, and he had me arrested on a prior shoplifting case where I was sentenced to do community service work and never showed up. My probation officer sited that was a violation and they waited good until I turned eighteen years old so that they could charge me as an adult. In addition to that, I was charged with child cruelty, and child abuse. That's what they do when you have a baby that is born addicted." Andrea shook her head. "It was an absolute disgrace that I could be so dedicated to getting high, that I didn't even know that I was pregnant. It took me a long time to forgive myself for what I did to our baby." Tears filled her eyes.

Tim got up and walked to her side of the booth. He took a seat beside her and held Andrea in her arms, reminding her that everything was okay.

"Just when I was prepared to start all over being a mother to my daughter, she was taken from me for good, just like that," Andrea cried. Now her entire face was covered with tears. Tim held Andrea in his arms until the waitress came back to the table.

"Can we please have some napkins," Tim asked the girl. She reached into her apron and handed him a few.

The waitress looked at Andrea. "Is she okay?"

Tim took the napkins, wiped Andrea's face and smiled. "She'll be fine. Just give us a few minutes. We haven't had time to look over the menus yet."

The waitress quickly walked away from the table with a concerned look on her face.

"I'm sorry."

"No, I'm sorry. I promise not to mention anything about the baby. When you feel more comfortable discussing it, you just let me know."

"No, it's okay," Andrea sniffed. "I'll be alright." After she finished composing herself, Andrea reached into her purse and pulled out a photo. She handed it to Tim. It was a four-by-six picture of Timya sitting on a scooter that was taken a month prior to her death. Tim looked at the picture and smiled. It was amazing how much the baby looked like him. Her eyes were green, and her golden brown hair was full of ringlet curls. There was absolutely no doubt in his mind that Timya was his daughter.

"She does look like me, doesn't she?"

"Yes." Andrea handed Tim an envelope. "Although you never had the chance to meet her, I wanted you to have something to remember her by."

Tim immediately opened the envelope to reveal the contents. There were two documents, folded in half. Once he unfolded the documents, he read the header of each. One was a copy of Timya's birth certificate, and the other was a copy of her death certificate.

For a couple of moments, he stared blankly at the documents. "Thanks Andrea, I really appreciate this."

As Andrea was about to speak, the waitress approached the table again, and asked if they were ready to order. Nodding in unison, the couple ordered their meals and then continued their conversation while waiting for their dinners. Even after their meals were delivered, they continued talking, sharing all of the things that they both had been forced to withhold for months. After eating, the couple, both stuffed, got up to leave the restaurant.

Tim drove down the street, heading nowhere in particular "Do you have to go straight home, or would you like to ride and talk for awhile? I'm not ready to start missing you again."

Andrea blushed, because she felt the same way. She loved and missed Tim more than she'd realized. "Let's go to Lookout Mountain," she suggested. "We can sit in the car, on top of the mountain, and just talk. I'm not ready to go home. At home, I feel like I'm living with the enemy. I need to hurry up and find me a job so that I can get my own place. So far, we've all been one happy family, but I know that it's only a matter of time before my mother starts to reveal her true colors. I'm surprised that she and I have been getting along thus far."

Tim chuckled. "Yeah, I know what you mean. You just don't have the privacy you want when you live with your parents, do ya? I'd love to have a place to invite you to. I guess I need to get myself together, if we're going to maintain a relationship."

"Well, I know that you're working toward your degree and all you have to offer me right now is your love, and some of your time; but that's fine with me."

Tim smiled as he turned onto Michigan Street. Lookout Mountain was an area near downtown, where sightseers often went to get a great view of the city. It was also a secluded cul-de-sac area frequented by young lovers. Andrea and Tim often spent time at the landmark before they went to jail. When they were addicts, they'd sometimes park and sleep there.

Tim parked the car in a nice secluded area of the mountain. There weren't many cars there, but it was still early. Couples usually showed up later in the evening. The sun had not long ago gone down, and dusk was slowly turning into night. After turning off the engine, Tim turned to Andrea and quickly kissed her, thrusting his tongue into her mouth. Andrea's head fell back onto the headrest of the seat as Tim's hands eased their way down her waist. He immediately unfastened her pants.

Andrea thought, *Oh, no!* Her body was starting to do things that her mind objected too. *Not in the car*, she thought, while her body said, *yes, here, in the car*.

Passionate moans roared from her lips, Andrea raised her hips as Tim swiftly pulled her pants down over her ankles. With her legs slightly apart, Tim rubbed his hand between her thighs, and Andrea wailed. Her hips slowly gyrating, grinding in motion with the rhythm of his stroking finger against the swelling between her thighs. She hadn't been touched in so long, that his initial contact immediately ignited her passions.

Tim didn't let up. He kept kissing her, and fingering her middle. He hadn't been with anyone in nearly three years, and could no longer hold back. He was anxious to try some things out on Andrea that he'd heard inmates discuss while he was in jail. After sitting around and listening to some of the more experienced prisoners, Tim learned that his bedroom tactics weren't as sharp as he thought. So, he'd hear the brothers brag on how good they had it with the ladies, and what it took to keep them satisfied. By the time he was released from jail, his ears were ringing with knowledge on how to satisfy a woman in the bedroom. Tim felt like he was the youngest, pussyologist that ever walked out of the county jail. He'd been taught by some men who had four and five different ladies coming to see them, and keeping money on their books. Tim couldn't wait to try out his skills. Although he'd never licked a clit before, he was dying to test some moves out on Andrea.

Tim pushed the passenger seat as far back as it would go, and told Andrea to let the back down, then he pulled down his pants. After reclining his seat, Tim kissed her again. He stopped suddenly and told Andrea that he had something for her. He asked her to turn and lean her back against her window. She propped one leg on the dashboard of the car, and one on the back of the driver's seat. Tim smiled, as his head disappeared. Andrea suddenly felt his tongue slide swiftly across her clitoris. In no time at all, she was pre-ejaculating. Her stomach muscles clenched. Her legs spread wider, as Tim's tongue moved back and forth along her clit. It was moving so fast, it felt as if it were battery operated. Andrea could feel her pressed hair reverting back to its naturally curly state. She'd never been so pleased in her life. She became so wet, with lust juice, that she begged for Tim to grace her walls of ecstasy. He slid between her legs, and entered her womb. From deep within, Andrea cried a shrill of ecstasy. She felt angelic, like a virgin who was experiencing pleasure for the first time in life. Her mind, body, and soul, succumbed. Andrea was relieved and rejuvenated.

After they finished, the both of them dressed and found themselves locked in another kiss. When their lips finally parted, Tim said, "I don't want to leave you, Andrea."

"What are we going to do?"

Tim looked her straight in the eyes and said, "Marry me," totally catching Andrea off guard. Her eyes grew wide as she looked into Tim's eyes.

"Are you serious?"

"As a heart attack."

Andrea smiled as she reached over to give Tim a hug.

"Yes, I'll marry you. Tim, I love you so much, of course I'll marry you," she sighed. "When shall we do it? Do we do it right away, or do we have a long engagement?" Anxiety had taken over and she was ready to live the rest of her life with the man she'd loved since high school.

"Well, we'll have to wait until after I graduate."

"Sounds good to me," Andrea chided. "I would love to be Mrs. Tim Doberson."

CHAPTER 14

Sunday morning, Punkin showed up at Dorothy's house at nine o'clock sharp. She'd been telling Dorothy all week, that she was going to church with her, but Dorothy didn't believe her until she showed up at her front door. When Dorothy opened up her front door, to her surprise there was her best friend, Punkin, standing in a navy blue mini-skirt suit. The skirt was way above knee length, and underneath the jacket, she wore a solid white, cotton blouse, and a set of faux pearls draped around her neck. She was also wearing a pair of pearl earrings and matching bracelet. When Dorothy looked down at Punkin's feet, she shook her head. Punkin's navy blue, leather pumps lifted her about five inches into the air.

Dorothy smiled, turned on her heels and headed toward the kitchen, with Punkin in tow. "Girl, where are you going with that outfit and those shoes? Is that what you're wearing to church?"

"Of course," Punkin answered as she did a spin in the middle of the floor. "You know you never should have told me about having a secret admirer at your church. How do I look?"

"Are you sure you want me to answer that," Dorothy huffed.

Punkin waved her hand in the air. "Girl, I ain't thinking about you. I just hope this man is fine."

Dorothy laughed aloud as she continued loading the dishwasher with the soiled breakfast dishes.

"I'm trying to do things right this year, Dorothy. I am looking for me a God-fearing man, like Sullivan. I hope this Brother Woods has himself together. I need a mad I can keep, not one with a whole lot of issues."

Dorothy tried to sustain her laughter because she knew that Punkin was as serious as a heart attack. Instead of bursting into tears, Dorothy called for her husband to come into the kitchen. Once Sullivan entered the kitchen, Dorothy asked him if he could finish loading the dishwasher so that she could get Punkin to comb her hair out. Tonya had rolled Dorothy's hair the night before, and Dorothy wanted to get Punkin to comb the style in. It still astounded her when she lifted her arms for too long.

Sullivan looked Punkin up and down as she stood in the middle of the floor. Punkin noticed him staring at her.

"How do I look, Sullivan?" Sullivan looked at his wife and back at Punkin without speaking. He didn't know what to say. "What's wrong, cat got ya tongue, Sullivan?" Sullivan smiled.

"What he is failing to say is that you look like a stripper who's getting ready to perform her naughty school girl routine."

Sullivan and Dorothy fell out with laughter.

"Whatever, Dorothy. Don't be a hater! You know I've got to be sexy no matter where it is I go."

"The Lord says come as you are, Punkin, so you'll be okay," Sullivan stated, trying to sound positive.

Dorothy pursed her lips and said, "Girl, come on in here, and fix my hair, before you make me bust a stitch laughing at your crazy behind." She and Punkin then left the kitchen and walked into Dorothy's bedroom.

They arrived at church too late to get a parking space in close walking distance, so Sullivan pulled his car up to the front door and let everyone out. He didn't want Dorothy to have to walk too far, so he parked the car three blocks down the street and walked back toward the church alone.

As soon as Dorothy and her family stepped inside the church, she was greeted by a great number of her church members. Everyone greeted her with open arms, saying how much they had missed her, and had prayed for her speedy recovery. Punkin stood off to the side with the children, while waiting for Sullivan to come inside, so they could all be seated together. While the children conversed with people they knew, Punkin looked around trying to see if she recognized any familiar faces from the funeral a few weeks prior.

Pastor Gaines preached a good sermon, as usual, and before calling for new members, he asked if there was anyone who needed special prayer. An evangelist team walked from the back of the church, and met at the altar. As the choir hummed a hymn, Punkin tapped Dorothy on the arm and asked if she would walk up with her for special prayer. She was thankful to be alive and well. Dorothy wiped her tears away, and smiled at her friend, as she rose from her seat. Sullivan stood with them, but Dorothy told him that she would be okay, so he sat back down. *He was so considerate*, Dorothy thought to herself.

Punkin got up and followed her friend to the front of the church. She was so nervous. Besides attending Timya's funeral, she hadn't been inside a church in years. Sensing Punkin's frenzy, Dorothy grabbed her friend's hand as they continued down the aisle. The church applauded as a few more attendee's headed toward the altar for prayer. Dorothy and Punkin continued to hold hands until a member of the prayer team was free, and asked them to step forward. Dorothy told Punkin, "Let's go up together."

The two of them walked up to Sister Johnson. "God Bless you," Sister Johnson mouthed as she hugged each of the women and took their hands. Dorothy whispered something into the woman's ear. Afterwards, the three women bowed their heads, and closed their eyes, as Sister Johnson prayed. A few seconds into the prayer, Dorothy's legs suddenly felt weak and wobbly, like Jello. Her lips trembled and her body shook. Before she knew it, her flesh had been taken over by a force she couldn't control. Another member of the prayer team walked up behind Dorothy as she spoke in tongue. Punkin released Dorothy's hand and let her shout and dance freely. Sullivan rose in his seat, but did not move. He closed his eyes, bowed his head, and threw his arms into the air. He prayed with her because they had a lot to be thankful for.

Once Dorothy was calm, the Pastor handed her the microphone. She turned to face the congregation, and explained to everyone what she'd been through in the past month, and how thankful she was to be alive and in church.

When morning service ended, the members inside the sanctuary moved toward the vestibule. It took over twenty minutes for Dorothy and her family to gather in a group near the front door. There were so many people stopping and praising each other that you just had to smile, and have patients to wait until someone moved on. Just when Dorothy thought she had a free chance to get to the door, Sister Nelson called out her name.

"Sister Edwards, it's so nice to see you back in church. I thought it was awful brave of you to go up and speak your testimony. I'm glad to see you give God the glory, because it is he, who has brought you through. Sister Edwards, you're living proof of his work. God is an awesome God. He will help you make it through the most trying times, won't he?"

"Yes he will," Dorothy testified.

"Well, God bless you, and your family," Sister Nelson finally said, before walking away.

Punkin looked at Dorothy, and then at the woman. She rolled her eyes. She was so tired of all the fake people walking up in Dorothy's face. Punkin needed for all them to clear the path so that her secret admirer could make his way up to Sister Edwards, and notice that she was standing there beside her. Brother Woods needed to show his face soon, because Punkin was becoming impatient.

After one parishioner walked off, soon approached a smiling, six-foot, brown-skinned brother with a short cut fade. He first shook Sullivan's hand, and then he spoke to the others, as he gave each of them hugs. When he turned to Punkin, he smiled flirtatiously and said, "Hello, sister, I don't believe that we've met."

Punkin's face lit up, as she extended her hand to shake the hand of the man she hoped was one who had been admiring her from afar. If this was Brother Woods, she was impressed already. Sullivan failed to mention to her, how fine her admirer was.

"I'm Brother Wilson. Brother Sam Wilson." He offered his hand, which carried a shiny wedding band.

Punkin's smile dropped instantly. "I'm Charlotte," she mouthed quietly.

"Well Charlotte, I hope to see you around here more often." After speaking to everyone, Brother Wilson said goodbye, and then walked off.

"Brother Edwards, my man," yelled a deep voice from behind. Sullivan turned around, to see whom the voice belonged to. Approaching was another church member. He walked up and cheerfully greeted everyone. Punkin's head turned immediately in the direction of the voice. The face that matched the voice wasn't as appealing to Punkin, as the first guy who'd recently walked off, but the cologne he wore, was intoxicating. Punkin could smell him even before she turned to see who he was. She smiled and waited to be introduced. Dorothy served as the moderator.

"Brother Woods, I'd like for you to meet one of my long time, and dear friend, Charlotte. I've known her so long, she's like family."

"Everyone calls me Punkin," Charlotte interrupted.

"Well, *Punkin*," Brother Woods, repeated, with emphasis, "it's a pleasure to finally meet you." He extended his hand to shake hers. "And you can call me Mark." He looked Punkin up and down and then looked over toward Sullivan. "Ain't God good?"

Sullivan smiled. "Yes, he is."

"So what do you guys have planned for the rest of this beautiful Sunday afternoon?" Mark asked with his eyes seductively planted on Punkin, admiring every curve she offered.

"Well, we've been invited over to Deacon Brown's for dinner. We are heading over there right after we drop Punkin at her car. She parked it at our house," Sullivan stated.

Brother Woods nodded. "That sounds real good. I guess I'll just stop by Popeye's chicken, to get me a three piece to go, on my way home."

"Now, Popeye's is right up my alley," Punkin chuckled. "They put there foot in that dirty rice and those buttermilk biscuits."

"Mom, can we go to the car?" Tonya interrupted.

Dorothy looked over at her husband, who was already handing the car keys to their daughter.

"The car is straight down the street. We'll be out in a minute," Sullivan said.

Tonya huffed and walked off with the keys. Her other siblings followed closely behind her. They knew that their parents would be in the church talking all day. At least in the car they could listen to the radio.

Brother Woods immediately continued on with the conversation. "Well, Sister Charlotte, you care to join me at Popeye's, to munch down on some chicken and biscuits? We won't call it a date, but it'll be my treat."

"Sure I will," Punkin smiled with excitement, before turning to her best friend. "That's if you don't mind, Dorothy."

"Oh, no, I don't mind at all, Punkin. It's no big deal."

"I will be happy to take you to your car afterwards," Mark quickly added.

"All right then, let's roll," Punkin said. "I guess I will see you later, Dorothy. If you all are not home when I go to pick up my car, then I'll just call you tomorrow."

After shaking hands with Sullivan, Brother Woods and Punkin walked off. Sullivan and Dorothy exited the church with the Watsons. Once outside, the four of them walked down the street, parting ways as they approached their cars.

As Punkin and Mark walked away together, Punkin noticed a few stares from other members of the church. It didn't bother her though, Punkin just made it her business to walk a little closer to Brother Woods. They entered the parking lot and stopped abruptly as Mark patted his pocket for his keys. Punkin stood patiently. She wasn't sure which car they were about to get into because Mark was sort of standing in between a shiny, new looking, Nissan 350Z, and a late model four door, brown Oldsmobile. Punkin hoped that they were about to get into the Nissan because it resembled a Porsche and she couldn't wait to hop in. Finally, Mark unzipped his leather bible cover and found his car keys inside. He smiled at Punkin and pressed the disarm button on his keychain. The lights on the Nissan lit up and so did Punkin's eyes. It was nice to see that Brother Woods at least had a decent car.

Mark walked over to the passenger side of the car and opened the door for her. Punkin hurried and climbed down into the low rider, and waited for Mark to get in. He soon climbed inside and turned on the engine. Within seconds, the sports car was screeching out of the parking lot. Immediately, Mark sparked up a conversation.

"So, I guess you got the message about me wanting to meet you."

"Yeah, I guess you can say that. I have heard a few things about you, but that's all hearsay. I want to see how much I can find out for myself."

Mark flashed a smile that revealed his pearly white teeth. As they furthered down the street, Mark looked to Punkin. "So, where can we go to sit and talk, while having a nice meal?"

"I thought we were on our way to Popeye's," Punkin inquired with a confused expression on her face.

"Well, Popeye's is cool with me, but I don't want you going back to your friends talking about," he pierced his lips and rolled his neck, "Mark knows he is cheap. On our first date he gon' have the nerve to take me to some ole greasy Popeye's chicken instead of taking me to a classy restaurant." He spoke in a high-pitched voice, trying to sound like a woman, as he gestured. "You know how you women are."

Punkin was rolled over with laughter. Mark did a pretty good impression of an ugly woman. "No, you didn't," she laughed. "I promise you that Popeye's is okay. If I still like you after that, then I'll let you take me out to a classy restaurant, the next time. Since Popeye's was the original plan, that's the one we'll stick to. Besides, my mouth is watering for some of that dirty rice."

They pulled up into Popeye's, and surprisingly the restaurant wasn't very busy. They ordered, got their food, and sat down at a table in the back. Punkin and Mark got personal with each other during dinner. Punkin found out that Mark was single, had no children, owned his own business, and had only been living in town for about eight months. He was from Mississippi, and, after a friend, who he served time with in the Army, invited him to Michigan. He found himself liking the city, and the change of place. Shortly after, he found an apartment and a building to start his business.

Mark found out that Punkin had a fourteen-year-old son, who lived with his father. She worked as a certified nurse's assistant, and lived alone. Although Punkin wouldn't reveal her age, Mark guessed that she had to be in her late thirties or early forties, but he dare not reveal his guess to her. He did tell her that he was thirty-seven, and that he was ready to settle down with a good woman and start his own family.

"I am trying to do the right things these days. I am getting too old to play games, and that's part of the reason why I joined the church. At this point in my life, I don't want to be in a relationship with anyone who is not ready for commitment."

Punkin was surprised by his up-front attitude, but she understood what he was looking for. She was looking for someone who was ready to settle down and be serious as well. She was tired of dealing with deceitful brothers who claimed they wanted to be committed, but really didn't mean it. She was happy to have finally met a brother who had a plan, and had something going for himself.

After stuffing themselves with chicken, biscuits and dirty rice, they left the restaurant and headed to Dorothy's so that Punkin could pick up her car. Once they arrived, they noticed that Dorothy and her family had not made it home yet. Before climbing out of Mark's vehicle, Punkin thanked him again for the dinner.

Mark took her by the hand. "So when will I see you again, Punkin?"

"I don't know," she answered while staring into his eyes. She was trying to see if she could tell what he was thinking. "When would you like to see me again?

"To be truthful, I want to spend every single day with you, for the rest of my life," he whispered charmingly. He spoke in a sensual tone that sent chills through her.

Punkin was taken aback. "Isn't it a little too soon to be talking like that?" Punkin blushed. "I mean I know that I can be quite overwhelming, but we just met today."

Brother Woods was a very charming man, but his words definitely caught her off guard. She didn't know if he was crazy, or if God had finally sent her what she'd been looking for all her life, a good man. Was this fate or what, she gawked.

Without an answer, Mark lifted her hand to his mouth, and planted the softest kiss. When his soft, juicy, lips touched her flesh, Punkin became moist between her legs. Now silently quivering, Punkin closed her eyes, and reached for the door handle. Although she did want to be the first woman to break him in with some good ole up north coochie, it was just too soon. She didn't want to mess up what could potentially be a good thing. So, she climbed out of the car, and told Mark to call her. Punkin jumped straight into her car and pulled off. She needed to get home and in a cold shower as soon as possible.

CHAPTER 15

The week that Rhenee moved into her new condo, was a very hectic one. She had been working fourteen-hour days and had not yet been able to unpack any of her things. It was a good thing she purchased new furniture and a bedroom set, which had been delivered, and set up where she wanted them to go. At least, that was one thing she didn't have to worry about. As she rushed down the hall to her bedroom, Rhenee kept repeating to herself that she needed to calm down. She was supposed to have been at the office an hour ago but as usual, she was running a little late. She was so disgusted with the disarray of her condo; she needed to take a day off to get it together. Every outfit that she'd worn for the last two weeks, was scattered about, either on the floor, or draped on the snow white, three piece, leather living room sectional.

As she stepped into the bathroom, adjacent to her bedroom suite, Rhenee placed her half-eaten bagel on a napkin, and then she sat her cup of coffee down on the counter. She took a deep breath, and then a long look at herself in the mirror. As she applied her make-up, Rhenee thought about the day ahead of her. She was scheduled to meet with a client, to prepare him for his preliminary hearing, but she wasn't fully focused, due to her own personal issues. Although she had not incurred any nightmares since she'd moved into her new place, she still wasn't able to sleep peacefully.

Last night, she had gotten down on her knees, and asked God for forgiveness. She prayed for the family members of the victims. She asked God to help them to, quickly, recover from the mourning and loss of their loved ones. She also asked Him to deliver her a clear conscience, and to rejuvenate her body so that she could be mentally focused and strong because she needed to win her case. Rhenee read in the Bible about repentance, and understood that if she asked God to forgive her, then He would cleanse her of her sins, and her slate would be wiped clean, so that's what Rhenee did. She prayed for a clean slate. After all, she was going up against a very experienced attorney, with an extensive track record, and she needed to be prepared to battle him to the end, for the win. She'd spent over twenty minutes on her knees praying, so today was going to be the day of her new beginning. If she won this case, it could mean great things for her career. Rhenee would be able to take some time off to start planning for the opening of her own law firm. From now on, she was putting the past behind her, and dealing with what each day brought about.

After applying her make-up, Rhenee washed her hands, grabbed her bagel and coffee, and headed toward the front door. Her nylon-covered feet slipped into her black pumps, and left the condo.

On her way to the office, Rhenee couldn't stop thinking about how incomplete her life was. According to her ten-year plan, she was supposed to have been married, and preparing to start her family. The major problem was that she still didn't have the man. She thought that she could rekindle things with her ex-husband, Sullivan, but found him to be in love with someone else. Now Rhenee would have to shift her focus back to Ray, because that's truly where her heart was. Last week, she had seen Ray at work twice, but he was trying to play hard to get. He told Rhenee that he was trying to do right by being faithful to his wife, which meant that he and Rhenee had to cut off their secret relationship that had been going on for too long. Ray was the reason for the demise of her marriage to Sullivan. However, now that his wife, had returned home, Ray was acting like a married man again, trying to dismiss his feelings for her. But, Rhenee knew that it was only a matter of time before he came to his senses. They'd been through the same thing before, and all Rhenee had to do was be patient. She'd give him two weeks before Ray would be running back to sniff between her legs. What the two of them had was real love, and love didn't fade overnight.

Rhenee stormed into her office, and dropped her briefcase on her desk. After starting a fresh pot of coffee, she sat down, and retrieved a folder from her briefcase. She was meeting with her client, Alan Shapen, in thirty minutes, and she only had a few minutes to prepare her talking points. She also needed to collect the balance on the retainer fee, that she was charging Alan to defend him. Earlier in the week, a woman barged into Rhenee's office and pulled out several wads of cash from her designer handbag. As she stared down at Rhenee, she placed a $25,000 down payment on Rhenee's desk. She appeared to be more upset with Rhenee, than she was worried about her man getting out of jail. Rhenee couldn't believe that the woman didn't have enough sense to, at least, have the cash transferred into money orders or a cashier's check. Without prejudice,

Rhenee buzzed her secretary to collect the money, and to return with Ms. Vincent's receipt.

After receiving the retainer from Alan's girlfriend, Rhenee drove out to the county jail for her first meeting with Alan. He was accused of being an accessory to a murder. The prosecution was trying to convict Allen for riding in the car with the gunmen, while a drive-by shooting took place. Alan's defense was that he was a victim of accepting a ride. He claimed to have had no knowledge of the murder, until it took place. He was entering a plea of not guilty. Since Alan was a known drug dealer, with a few prior charges on his record, his bond was set at $500,000. He was released from jail, three days after the preliminary hearing. His girlfriend had contacted a bails bondsman who got Alan back out on the streets until the date of the trial.

Her intercom buzzed. It was her secretary. "Mr. Shapen has arrived."

"Send him in," Rhenee told her. She rose from her chair, and walked toward the door.

Alan walked into Rhenee's office sporting a brown and beige , Rocca wear outfit . In his right hand, he carried a Nextel cellular phone. He had been talking to someone while walking in, but dismissed the caller after Rhenee greeted him. She closed the office door, and offered him a seat. She pointed her finger in the direction of the empty chair in front of her desk. As Rhenee walked around her desk, to take her seat, her eyes scanned Alan. He was an attractive, brown skin man, with short, curly hair, smooth skin, and dark, dreary eyes. He had a baby face, with really thick eyebrows, and a thin mustache. He reminded Rhenee of the singer Johnny Gill, in a roughneck kind of way. Rhenee could see how a girl could easily find herself turned on by him.

As Rhenee took her seat, Alan held a dead stare on her, staring directly into her eyes, with a gigantic smile on his face. You could tell by his demeanor, that he wasn't taking the visit with his lawyer too serious.

"So," Rhenee proceeded, while opening up Alan's folder. Her eyes scanned the forms, and then she looked up at her client. "Do you have anyone we can call, who will testify that it was Sean Blakely, and not you, in the front seat of the car in question?"

Alan looked at Rhenee and then at her voluptuous breasts. He licked his lips. "I'm working on it."

Rhenee's facial expression revealed the disgust she felt.

Alan continued. "See, the thing is that, everyone at my crib, that day, can tell you that I was preparing for my cookout. My boy James pulled up, and asked if he could help out with the preparations, so I asked him to shoot me to the store real quick to get the charcoal. My ride was gettin' washed so I couldn't drive myself. I jumped in the car with him and Sean, not knowing that they was about to go and spray nobody."

For the next hour, Rhenee and Alan went over the details of his case with a fine toothed comb. By the end of the meeting, Rhenee had an idea of how she wanted to prepare her statement for the hearing that was scheduled for the following week. At the conclusion of their meeting, Alan stood from his seat, and extended his hand to Rhenee. Since he held on to her hand longer than necessary, Rhenee cleared her throat, and stared into his eyes in an aggravating manner. Alan smiled, and said that he was gladly looking forward to seeing her again. He failed to realize, that his flirting was not gaining him any brownie points. It was his money that she needed, not his charm. After Alan left her office, Rhenee cleared her desk. Since Alan had been her only client for the day, she was taking the rest of the afternoon off. Rhenee planned to take advantage of the free time to go home and get some much-needed rest.

Rhenee arrived at her condo around three o'clock. Once she stepped through the door, off came her shoes and her suit jacket. She placed her briefcase, keys and purse on the table, and stood with her brand new floor planted beneath her feet. She ran her fingers through her hair took a long, deep, breath and exhaled. As her ears soaked in the ambience of her condo, Rhenee felt relieved to be home. She walked over toward the window, and picked up the pitcher of water to feed her two Ficus plants. A few leaves had turned brown since the last time she watered them, so she gently pulled off the dead ones, and discarded them. She stepped over the previous days' outfits scattered about, as she entered the bedroom, letting her navy blue skirt drop to the floor. Once she removed her blouse, Rhenee tossed it onto the bed, along with the other clothes, two of her law books, and the towel she used after showering that morning. As she looked around the room, she thought, *I need a housekeeper.* She never was able to keep a clean house, and her bedroom was always the worst kept room in any place that she lived. When she was married to Sullivan, he did all the cooking and cleaning, so she never really noticed how much of a slob she really was. Since she didn't have a man to invite over, she really didn't care if her house was cleaned on a regular basis or not. Whenever Ray called to say that he was coming over, she'd rush to get the place as tidy as she could before he got there.

Since Rhenee didn't feel like cooking, she looked into the freezer and pulled out a Marie Callender's turkey and dressing frozen dinner. After popping it into the oven, she set the timer, and went back into the living room, where she decided to straighten up a little bit. First, she picked up the dirty clothes that were strewn all over the place. She carried them to the laundry room where she sorted the articles she was going to take to the cleaners, from the ones she needed to put into the washing machine. Rhenee then walked into her bedroom to change the sheets on her bed, before starting the first load of laundry. As her stomach growled, the oven's timer buzzed. Her dinner was ready. She dashed into the kitchen to cut off the timer, and then Rhenee removed her meal from the oven and placed it on the stovetop to cool.

Once she poured a cup of Tide into the washing machine, she set the temperature to hot. When she finished putting all the clothes into the washer, Rhenee closed the top and headed into the kitchen to eat. She peeled back the cellophane, and inhaled the aroma of the hot food. Transferring the dinner onto a plate, the smell of roasted garlic enticed her empty stomach. Within minutes, she was in her living room, comfortably nestled on the couch. Reaching for the television's remote control, she surfed through the channels, searching for a good program to watch. Unexpectedly, the telephone rang. She released an aggravating moan because she simply did not feel like being bothered. On the very day that she was trying to kick back and relax, someone had to call and disturb her.

She looked over at the illuminated screen, on the caller ID, to see who was calling. It read Private Caller, so Rhenee decided not to answer. She'd let the answering machine pick it up.

After hearing her pre-recorded message greet the caller, followed by the beep, the caller spoke. "Aye, yo, Rhenee, this is Crip Lee. I wanted to know if you were still coming down to the shop tomorrow to get the front end of your whip fixed. Yo, when you get thi–"

Rhenee quickly picked up. "Hey, Crip Lee, I'm here."

"Yo, you still coming by tomorrow?"

"What time did you want me to come?"

"Come over early in the morning, around nine, if you want it to be out the following day."

Rhenee hesitated before answering. She was still a little leery about dealing with Crip Lee, aka Charles Lee, a previous client from a few years back, whom she'd worked her ass off to keep out of prison. Charles was accused of running an illegal chop shop. Since the police had illegally raided his business, Rhenee was able to get the charges thrown out after a two-week jury trial. Since Rhenee had gotten him off, Charles told her that if she needed him for anything, just to let him know. Last week she decided to call him, when she remembered that he had his own body shop. She was so tired of riding around on edge, but was too paranoid to file a claim with her insurance company, because she didn't want to leave a paper trail. Now, Rhenee was elated that Charles owed her a favor. She knew that if he fixed her car, they could skip all the paperwork and settle everything in cash. Unbeknownst to Charles, he was the answer to her prayers.

"That's cool. I'll be there!" Rhenee exclaimed, hanging up the telephone.

Charles truly was a savior. It had been two months since the accident and Rhenee was still driving around, scared to death about being pulled over, and questioned about her bumper being so badly damaged.

Rhenee inhaled her meal, and decided to go into her bedroom to lie down and watch television. She carried her plate into the kitchen and sat it on the counter. She threw the empty aluminum tray into the trash, and crept off to her most favorite spot in the condo. Still, she couldn't believe that she had some time to herself, after all the hard work, and long hours she'd been putting in. As soon as she stepped into the room, she rushed to the freshly made bed, pulling back the covers, and climbed in.

Perhaps she could catch a re-run of Law and Order, her favorite show. Since nothing else was on, Rhenee decided to see what good drama was playing on Lifetime. As she surfed through a few more channels, Rhenee suddenly released the button when she thought she recognized a man, who resembled her ex-husband Sullivan. She quickly flipped back a few channels. Her jaw dropped. It *was* Sullivan, and standing behind him was about twenty reporters with microphones of all shapes and sizes. Apparently,

Sullivan was a hot topic. When Rhenee noticed tears in his eyes, she turned up the volume to hear what was going on. It was imperative that she knew all the details of what was going on just in case Sullivan would need her to represent him. No matter what happened with them in the past, she would defend him regardless.

"I am asking that the person responsible for injuring my wife, and killing my young niece, would stop being a coward and come forward with a confession. Our family has suffered a great loss and we want answers. We are asking that if anyone knows anything about the accident, we'd appreciate it if they'd inform the police with that information. We want justice," he strongly stated. "So, if anyone saw anything, or knows anything, about the car accident, that took place on August 16th, at the corner of Madison and Hall Street, please come forward. Please, people, if you know anything, call the hotline," he preached.

As the words from his mouth, to her ears, played over and over in her mind, she continued watching, with her eyes glued on Sullivan , who was now holding up a flyer with a baby girl's picture on it. He continued to talk as the camera zoomed in on the picture of a little girl. Rhenee felt a migraine coming on. Her heart was pounding as she perspired profusely. In a panicked frenzy, Rhenee shook her head back and forth, screaming, "No!" She jumped up from the bed and paced the floor. "No," she continuously repeated.

All of this was too much for Rhenee. Feeling nauseas, she sat on the edge of the bed and leaned over, resting her elbows on her knees. An overwhelming chill shot through her and, as much as she tried to suppress it, the inevitable occurred; remnants of dinner left her stomach, worked its way up to her throat and poured out onto her brand new carpeting. Food decorated the floor and down her leg. When she entered the bathroom, the first thing she noticed was her reflection in the mirror. It revealed to her what she'd been trying to deny for the past few months. The devil in the flesh.

"Oh, God, Oh, God," she screamed repeatedly.

CHAPTER 16

Before leaving to take Dorothy to her doctor's appointment, Sullivan dialed his friend Erwin's number. He wanted to thank Erwin for getting him the hook up on the news spot the day before. Erwin was friends with one of the Channel 8 news anchors, who, as a favor, allowed Sullivan on the air for sixty seconds, to inform the public on his quest to find the person responsible for the accident. Erwin didn't answer the telephone, so Sullivan left him a thank you message. Afterwards, he and Dorothy left out the front door. It had been eight weeks since the accident and Dr. Muhammad wanted to examine Dorothy to see how well her lung was healing.

Sullivan opened the door to the clinic, and stood off to the side as Dorothy walked inside. Dorothy walked up to the counter, while Sullivan took a seat in the partially filled waiting room. Besides he and Dorothy, there were only six others seated in the waiting area. Sullivan looked around the room, admiring the décor. It seemed that the earthy colors, and the dim lights, made the room seem more soothing. Except for the soft jazz music playing overhead, the waiting area was otherwise quiet. Sullivan took a seat on the plush sofa and waited for Dorothy to join him.

After signing in, Dorothy was handed a clipboard, with a couple of forms attached. The receptionist handed her an ink pen and instructed her to return the forms to the desk, after she had finished filling them out. Dorothy smiled and carried the clipboard away with her. She took a seat beside Sullivan and immediately scanned through the questions on the first form. By the time she made it to the last form, Dorothy was about fed up with answering the same questions that had been reworded. Dorothy returned the paperwork to the receptionist, and walked back to her seat.

Before long, one of the doctor's assistants came from behind the door leading to the examining rooms, and called her name. Dorothy happily jumped up from her seat and turned to her Sullivan, who was reading an issue of *Black Enterprise* magazine. "Are you coming or staying, honey?

"I think I'll just sit here until you come back."

"Okay," Dorothy said, before walking away with the assistant.

Kelly, the assistant, escorted Dorothy into Examining Room 8. Once they were behind closed doors, Kelly asked Dorothy to remove her blouse only cover up with the thin paper top lying on the examining table. "After you finish, just take a seat, and the nurse will be in shortly."

After sliding into the gown, Dorothy climbed onto the examining table and waited for the nurse to come. There was a knock at the door, and a few seconds later, the nurse entered, smiling. Nurse Walker immediately greeted Dorothy. "How are you feeling?"

"I am feeling wonderful, thank God."

"Okay, then," the nurse said as she glanced over a form that was attached to the clipboard.

"Let me take a listen to your lungs, I'd like to hear how strong they've gotten."

"No problem." Dorothy reclined back and took a deep breath. The nurse rested her cold stethoscope, on Dorothy's bare chest. Dorothy jumped when the instrument touched her skin.

"I'm sorry. I should have warmed it on my overcoat first." Nurse Walker listened intently to the steady, rhythmic beat of Dorothy's heart. "It sounds real good." She then proceeded to check Dorothy's blood pressure, temperature, and weight. After documenting everything, Nurse Walker patted Dorothy on her shoulder. "I will need to get a urine sample as well." She then walked over to the cabinet and took out a plastic cup. She took out her pen and wrote Dorothy's full name on it. "You can go to the bathroom right outside the room, to the left. When you're finished, you can place the cup in the window next to the toilet."

"Okay." Dorothy climbed down from the table.

"You can come back in here once you're finished, and Dr. Muhammad will be in shortly."

"I'll be right here," Dorothy cheerfully responded, as she walked out of the room ahead of the nurse.

The door finally sprung open, and the doctor's friendly smile greeted her right away. "How have you been doing, Mrs. Edwards?" Dr. Muhammad was a dark-skinned, middle-aged man who spoke with an accent. He was about five-foot-six, with large oval-shaped, black eyes, and dark black, wavy hair. His smile was warm and friendly. His cheerful entrance perked her up.

"I feel fine, doctor. The first week at home was a little rough, but in my mind, I've been getting along as if I've never had the surgery, and Dr. Harvey told me that I would. My husband is constantly reminding me of how I need to take it easy, but I just can't sit around all day and do nothing. I get tired, and may feel out of breath from time to time, but when that occurs, I just get my behind someplace and sit it down. I think I know my limits."

As she spoke, the doctor took notes, all the while still holding on to his smile. "It's not unusual for you to feel tired. You had major surgery. And, in some cases, it may take a patient any where from a couple months, up to a couple of years before they start to regain all their strength." Dorothy nodded, as the doctor placed his clipboard behind Dorothy, on the examining table, and stepped closer to her. "Let me just check to see how your lung sounds." Removing the stethoscope from around his neck, he slid his hand under the thin paper top and pressed it against her chest. Dr. Muhammad said. "Now, breathe in for me, and hold it."

Dorothy did as she was told.

"Now, exhale."

Dorothy exhaled.

"Again."

Dorothy inhaled and then exhaled.

Dr. Muhammad took a seat and continued asking Dorothy questions. "Did the nurse get any blood from you today?"

"No," Dorothy answered with a nervous look on her face.

"We'll I'm going to need a few blood samples." He rose from the chair. "You can go ahead and get dressed, and I'll send the nurse in to get some blood from you. After that, you will be finished. I will look over all your tests and let you know how everything turns out. In the meantime, I'm going to go ahead and write you a prescription for an inhaler. I don't think you will be needing the oxygen anymore. You are recovering well, but I'll want to see you again in six weeks. Okay?"

"Sure thing," Dorothy cheerfully answered.

After shaking her hand, Dr. Muhammad left the room. Dorothy was glad to hear the good news. She couldn't wait to call Option Care to tell them to come and pick up that big oxygen machine that wasn't doing anything but taking up space in her bedroom.

Before long, the nurse returned to the examining room and drew three tubes of blood from Dorothy, before leaving. For the next ten or fifteen minutes, Dorothy was getting antsy. *She could've made the inhaler thing by* now, Dorothy thought, wondering what was taking Nurse Walker so long to return with her prescription. Dorothy was quite anxious to tell her husband the good news.

When Nurse Walker returned, forty minutes later—Dorothy had dozed off—she'd taken so long.

"Mrs. Edwards." Dorothy's eyes popped open as her lips parted to smile. "I'm sorry it took so long, but I had to look up the information on the doctor we're referring you to." She took a seat beside Dorothy. As the nurse spoke, she flipped through papers. "Here are the prescriptions for your inhalers, and we will need to see you back in six weeks, although, we're referring you to an OB/Gyn whom you'll need to schedule an appointment with as soon as possible." Handing Dorothy a slip of stationary with a name and telephone number on it, she continued. "He is highly recommended for women with high risk pregnancies, which we have to take into consideration, due to your age."

Dorothy wasn't sure if she was hearing correctly. "OB/Gyn, pregnancy. Nurse Walker, what are you talking about? I am here to have my lung checked out. You must have grabbed someone else's paperwork," Dorothy said with a stern, aggravating look on her face.

"I take it this pregnancy comes as a surprise to you, Mrs. Edwards."

"Pregnancy," Dorothy snapped. "What are you talking about. My tubes were tied fifteen years ago, so I know for a fact that you have your information wrong. Don't make me loose my religion up in here, Nurse Walker," Dorothy warned.

The nurse looked confused. She looked at the paperwork to make sure that the name read Dorothy Edwards, and then she looked back at Dorothy. She was nervous. She had no idea what to say. She'd tested the urine herself, and she was sure that the cup she got the urine from had Edwards, Dorothy written on it. It was also the only sample sitting in the window. The doctor had specifically asked the nurse to test Mrs. Edward's urine sample for a possible pregnancy, because they needed to keep a close monitor on her healing lung, and a pregnancy would definitely affect that.

"Well, Mrs. Edwards, I am sorry to tell you this, but, your urine sample was the only one there, it had your name on it, and when I tested it, the test came back positive. If you'd like, I can re-test you."

Immediately, Dorothy lost it. "Re-test it for what? It ain't no need for all that Nurse Walker, are you listening to me? I just told you that my tubes are tied. I had tubal ligation surgery, fifteen years ago, right after I had my son Dwayne. I am forty-two years old, so how can I possibly be pregnant?" Dorothy fussed. "I don't think you know what you are doing. Can you please get Dr. Muhammad?" Dorothy demanded. The nurse immediately left the room.

No matter how much Dorothy fussed and cursed, she could not change the results of the second pregnancy test, which the doctor tested in front of her. For the second test, results came up positive like the first one. Dorothy was in such shock, she refused to leave the examining room. She requested that the doctor test her blood instead of using the cheap pregnancy test. They had to be no good. Even after the doctor explained to her that the tubal ligation surgery, in which she very well could have had fifteen years ago, was not permanent, nor was it one hundred percent guaranteed, still, Dorothy wanted to hear something to justify that they were all wrong about her being pregnant.

If Sullivan hadn't come back to nearly drag her out of the doctor's office, Dorothy would probably have been still sitting there. She rode home in a ghostly silence. When she finally spoke, she muffled, "Sullivan, the doctor said I'm pregnant."

"Hallelujah," he shouted, like he'd never shouted before. That was the best news he'd heard in his life. "Yes, honey, we're going to have a baby. Isn't that wonderful?" As the car slowed down before coming to a complete stop at the red light, Sullivan reached over and gave Dorothy a big kiss. "A baby," he repeated, as the car proceeded through the green light.

Dorothy continued riding in the car in a state of total disbelief.

CHAPTER 17

Andrea stepped out of the Human Resources office of the General Motors plant, where both of her parents worked. She was hired to work on the assembly line, and she couldn't wait to get home to call Tim. He would be expecting her phone call during his lunch break at school. Every since their engagement, they'd been spending a lot of time with each other. Since Andrea now had a job, they could discuss planning an official wedding date. Last week, Andrea had gotten her driver's license, so her parents bought her a brand new Chevy Malibu. It was bright red, very sporty, and good on gas. Andrea drove the car every chance she got. The Malibu was her first car, and she absolutely loved it. Andrea told her parents that she planned to pay them off, a little at a time, for the car, because she didn't want her mother to have something else to hold over her head. Andrea was happy with the progress of her new start.

As soon as Andrea returned home from her interview, she placed her orientation folder, purse and keys, on the kitchen table, and made herself a turkey sandwich. Since no one was home, Andrea took her sandwich and the orientation materials to her room, to read over the documents. It was only 11:10, and Tim's lunch break wasn't until a quarter to one. Inside her bedroom, Andrea turned on the television and, twenty minutes later, she drifted off to sleep.

In her dream, *she sees her daughter sitting in her stroller, with a smile on her face, as bright as the sun. She looks so pretty with her golden brown hair tied off to the side in two ponytails. From out of nowhere, a black vehicle barrels toward them. Andrea quickly turns to her Aunt Dorothy and attempts to warn her to get out of the way. But, when she opened her mouth to scream, it was too late. Before they could run to safety, the car slammed into the three of them. Timya is the first one to be struck by the vehicle.* Suddenly, Andrea tossed and turned, screaming, "NO! NO!"

Anxiety taking over, Andrea jumped up in the bed, and as beads of sweat drenched her, tears took over and poured from her eyes; strands of hair stuck to her face. Sitting up on the bed, Andrea cried uncontrollably. *If only I could've pushed the stroller to the side a minute sooner, I'd still have my daughter,* she thought through streams of tears. Why hadn't she seen the car coming before it was so close up on them? In the back of her mind, Andrea felt like she let Timya down, by not being there for her as a mother, and for not protecting her from the vehicle that took her life. Even though her family members told her that there was nothing she could have done to change what happened, Andrea still felt responsible. Tears continued streaming down her cheeks as she cried out, "I'm sorry, Timya. Mama is so sorry that I couldn't be there for you when you needed me."

Attempting to rise out of bed, Andrea's body felt like lead, she couldn't move. She tried to stop herself from crying, but it didn't work. All that she'd been through, in the past few years of her life, was flashing before her eyes, and she had so many regrets. Andrea cried for all the mistakes that she'd made, and wished that there were something different she could have done. If she could turn back the hands of time and rewrite her life, she would. She'd been through more in her nearly twenty years of living than someone twice her age, missing out on experience that of a normal teenager. At that time, Andrea was too busy running the streets, stealing and getting high. Whenever she took two steps forward, she would fall three steps backward.

Andrea climbed out of bed, and got down on her knees. Closing her eyes, she prayed to God, asking Him to help her get her life in order. She asked Him for the strength she needed to move forward, and to stop blaming herself for the loss of her child, so that she could go on with her life. And lastly, Andrea thanked God for her family, who'd supported her through it all. She promised God that she wouldn't take them, or anyone else for granted, because now she knew better. She'd learned from her own experience that God giveth and He taketh away.

"Amen," she prayed, before she headed to the bathroom to wash her face. She had to gather her composure before her parents came home. She didn't want them to worrying about her. If her parents had so much as a hunch that she was having bad dreams, they'd haul her off to the doctor's office, no later than the next day. Andrea had refused counseling several times because she was convinced that she was okay. Her mother knew otherwise, but she didn't want to push Andrea into doing something she wasn't comfortable with doing.

Turning on the hot water faucet, Andrea gazed into the mirror, feeling sorry for the woman staring back at her. Closing her eyes and inhaling deeply, she lowered her head and tested and water's temperature with her fingertips. Lowering her face toward the sink, Andrea filled her hands with water and splashed it on her face. She grabbed the white thick towel from the steel rack and patted her face dry. She felt refreshed and inspired. Andrea refused to be bound. No matter what situation she faced, she'd face it with confidence and faith that it was going to get better with time.

The clock on Andrea's dresser read 1:40 PM. "Dang," she shouted in frustration as she looked over toward the telephone. She hadn't even heard it ringing. She noticed the red message waiting light blinking. Andrea rushed over to see if it was left by Tim. Before playing the message, she noticed his number on the caller ID. Tim called at 12:49 PM. "Dang," she hissed. She hated that she'd missed his call, because now she wouldn't be able to talk to him until his second class ended at 3:40. Disappointed, Andrea pressed play the answering machine and waited to hear the message. Tim explained how he was sorry that he missed her, but assured Andrea that he would call her back as soon as class ended. After listening, Andrea, went downstairs to watch television, while she waited for her family to return home.

CHAPTER 18

Since their formal introduction at the church, Punkin and Mark spent most of their spare time together. She felt so comfortable talking with him. Mark was so attentive and considerate. He reminded Punkin of a boy named Kirk Johnson, whom she befriended her junior year of high school. Kirk was one of the few boys in high school who was a genuine friend, not one wanting to talk to her just so she would go out with them. Even back then, she already had a fat backside, and grown woman hips. When she was younger, she was insecure about her looks because she also had big lips and acne all over her face.

Her experience at Henry Park Elementary school was a nightmare, compared to the way she was worshiped by the boys in high school. In elementary school, she was always teased by her classmates, not just for big lips, but also for having bulging eyes, and big ears protruding from the side of her head. She was teased by the girls and the boys. She could remember coming home from school and running to her bedroom to cry, because of the ridicule she'd endured from her classmates. Sometimes she wished she were a groundhog so she could crawl in a hole and stay there until her big eyes, and pokey ears caught up with the rest of her body. Kirk was the only one who made her feel like she was just as pretty as all the other girls. He would say things like, "Your lips and eyes aren't too big, they fit your body perfectly." It was comments like that that helped Punkin build the confidence she now had.

In high school, she was infamous amongst her female classmates, because all the boys seemed to flock her way whenever she came around. By her second year at Creston High School, she was already in size eight jeans, and was wearing a 36C bra. Those were her glory years; she loved the attention that she received from the boys, and rolled her eyes at the girls who hated on her for being loved by them. Back then, she thought that having a grown woman's body was all it took to get a good man. Her way of thinking resulted in a lot of hurt feelings and broken promises, during the years that followed.

Mark spoke with good diction, and a southern drawl that turned her on. It was that distinctiveness about him that made him different from any other man she'd been with. Every time he opened his mouth to say something, she smiled. Since being with her son's father, all Punkin's acquaintances had been part-time lovers. Spending time with Mark allowed her to reflect and evaluate what her past relationships lacked. She couldn't remember having a decent relationship, or a man in her life that wasn't with her because of convenience. Punkin could remember only a few times that she'd had what is defined as a date. Her so called dates usually meant inviting a man over to her place, where they'd talk, and maybe have dinner, and a movie or something. She dreaded of the many mornings that followed most of those dates. Those were the dreadful mornings she'd grown accustomed to knowing. The taboo mornings, which resulted from a long night of exhausting sex, with complete strangers that she never heard from again. It was a sin and a shame, that in her adult life, she was still carrying on with habits she'd adapted in high school. She was a sucker for attention and had paid the price dearly. It was now that she realized the meaning of a mantra her grandmother always used to preach: You stand for nothing you'll fall for anything.

It's been two weeks since she'd met Mark, and they'd already gone out to three different restaurants, and have seen two movies. They really enjoyed each other's company. She felt mesmerized when Mark asked questions about the things going on in her life, as well as her interests and dislikes. As they sat in a restaurant enjoying dinner, Mark learned that Punkin's teenage son lived with his father. Her son, Chalon, who was fourteen years old, had been living with his father for four years.

"I wanted him to be raised by a man," Punkin said to Mark. After she took another bite of her steak, she explained, as Mark listened attentively. "I feel that when a boy reaches a certain age, he needs a man in his life, to help with his transition from a boy into a man. I can't teach him to be a man, so after Chalon turned ten, I let him live with his father. Although he loves his mama, Chalon is a daddy's boy. He and his father have a great relationship, and Ralph and I parted amicably after a very short relationship. Every now and then, I'll beg Chalon to come and spend the weekend with me. He and his dad have a bond that even I can't break. I talk to my son at least twice a week though. It is necessary that he call me at least twice a week to fill me in on every detail of his life. The last time we spoke was brief, because Chalon was on his way to basketball practice. He plays basketball and soccer, so he rarely has free time. He has also been an honor roll student for two straight semesters. I am so proud of him," Punkin bragged.

Mark could tell that Punkin was fond of her son, from the way she spoke so highly of him. He couldn't wait to meet Chalon.

"Ralph and I weren't together very long, but he promised me that he would be there for the baby no matter what. He was very excited about being a father. I've never had any problems with him or his wife. They take really good care of our son. Chalon is an only child. His dad's wife doesn't have any children of her own.

Mark told Punkin that he didn't have any children. He, like her, had never been married. Punkin smiled, she thought of Mark as a rare breed. It wasn't often that she ran across a saved man, who was unmarried, had no children, and also owned his own business. Mark being new in town made him an even higher commodity in Punkin's book. She felt like she'd hit the jackpot when she was introduced to Mark Woods. He was like fresh deli meat.

After two months of dating and enjoying each other, Punkin and Mark officially labeled themselves a couple. Mark did a wonderful job of making Punkin feel special. He even gave her a nickname. When he learned that Punkin didn't like being called Charlotte, and since everyone else referred to her as Punkin, he picked a special name that only he would call her. One day, while at the shop, he glanced into her big brown eyes, smiled, and said, "Sunshine."

"What?" Punkin responded.

"You are my sunshine. When I look into those big, bright eyes of yours, it makes me think about the sun shining bright outside, on a warm summer afternoon. I think Sunshine will be a perfect name for you."

Punkin couldn't help but blush. It was that moment, when Punkin fell in love with Mark. He was so caring and considerate. He knew exactly what to say to make her heart flutter. "Of course you can call me Sunshine," Punkin smiled. She was speechless, which was the way he usually left her.

For the next couple of weeks, Mark wined and dined his Sunshine. He would invite her over to his place, where they would have dinner by candlelight. He'd take her shopping on the weekends, and for walks through the park at night. It was so peaceful walking through the park at night because there weren't many people out. Strolling through the park, attached to his arm, as they walked along the river walk downtown, made her feel so special. It seemed so intimate. She and Mark would talk about church, about his family down south, and both of their childhoods, and past relationships. She wanted to be with him all the time. Even while at work, she thought about him, and couldn't wait to get home to call him, hoping that they'd make some type of plans to be with each other by the end of the night. Going into their third month of dating, Punkin knew that Mark was a keeper.

One Friday morning, around 7:30, Punkin was awakened by the ringing telephone. She looked at the clock and then answered the phone. "Hello," she muffled into the mouthpiece, while clearing her throat. It was the soft, sexy voice of her new man on the line.

"Happy three month anniversary," Mark hummed into the phone.

Punkin wiped her eyes with the back of her hand and smiled. Her eyes needed a minute to adjust to the morning sunlight that was shining through her bedroom window. "Has it been that long?" she asked. "I'm sorry but I hadn't really been keeping track, I've just been enjoying the time we've been spending together, especially last night," she chided.

"Yes, today, starts the third month that I've been blessed to have you in my life. I think there is a cause for celebrating. I have planned an entire day of surprises for you. I am going to work until two o'clock, and then I'm going to close the shop. I want you to be ready to be picked up by six o'clock. You should be expecting surprise number one shortly. I'll know when you've received it, so you don't have to call me back. Just have your beautiful self ready at six." Before she could say anything else, he hung up.

Punkin hung up the telephone and sat up in her bed. She shouted as loud as she could. "Thank you, Jesus!" She was thankful that He'd sent Mark her way. Punkin got up from her bed and looked around the room. She was trying to see if she noticed anything new lying around anywhere. She wondered if Mark had stashed the surprise somewhere around her house without her knowing. She ran from room to room, opening doors and looking in closets hoping to unveil the surprise. She found nothing. After thirty minutes of running around her apartment, looking for the secret surprise, she became hungry. Punkin walked into the kitchen to fix a bowl of cereal. After pouring the sugar and milk over her cornflakes, she pranced back into the living room to catch the morning news.

She needed something to distract her thoughts from thinking about this secret surprise that Mark had called and warned her about. She was so anxious, she was about to jump out of her skin. Punkin took a few bites of her cereal, as her thoughts reflected back to Mark. She'd never met such a gentleman. "Dang," she huffed. "This must be the one."

At 8:40, Punkin was in her bedroom, about to hop into the shower when the doorbell rang. She rushed to the front door assuming that it was Mark. She just knew he would be there with his surprise in hand. "I get it, she spoke out loud. He is the surprise," she sang as she headed down the hall, toward the front door. Punkin tied the belt on her robe and flung open the front door. There was a uniformed white man, standing there. He was wearing a grey and black FED EX uniform.

The man smiled and stated. "I have a package for a Ms. Charlotte Evans."

"I'm Charlotte Evans," she answered quickly, almost cutting his words off.

"I have a package for you that require a signature, upon delivery." As he extended his writing tablet to her, she looked around him and noticed his work truck parked in front of her apartment.

Excited, Punkin scribbled her name on the tablet, and handed it back to the man. She didn't even bother to ask who the package was from. The FED EX worker then handed her two medium-sized packages and walked off. "Have a good day, Ma'am," he said.

Before closing her front door, Punkin looked around outside to see if Mark was somewhere preparing to jump out the bushes or something. She closed the door and ran into the living room to open the packages. It was from Mark, but she had no idea what was inside. The card plainly read: *To My Sunshine.* She blushed, and continued to tear open the box. The packages came from Victoria's Secret. As she pulled back the tissue paper, Punkin noticed that the gift-wrapped box, contained a red garment. She reached inside and pulled out a long, red, evening gown. It was made of satin, had spaghetti straps with a long split up the back. The bodice of the dress was covered with beautiful ruby red beads. In the other box was a pair of red satin shoes. "Mark has good taste," she mumbled. They were a size eight, her correct shoe size. "How did he know?" Punkin whispered. She hopped up and held the dress against her body, and screamed. It was so beautiful. She couldn't wait to get to her bedroom to try it on. The dress was a perfect fit and so were the shoes. As she gazed at herself in the mirror, Punkin felt so good, she wanted to cry. Mark was too good to be true.

At 5:25, Punkin sat dressed in her new outfit, waiting for Mark to come and pick her up. Although she hadn't talked to him since earlier that morning, she automatically assumed that Mark was going to come and pick her up. She just knew they'd be going to some fancy restaurant to enjoy a romantic dinner by candlelight or something. After receiving her gift from the deliveryman, Punkin had spent the rest of the day preparing for the night. As soon as she got out of the shower, she called Dorothy and told her about Mark's surprise. Dorothy was happy for her friend. She couldn't wait until Punkin returned from her date to tell her all the rest of the details of Mark's surprise.

Punkin almost drove herself crazy trying to find something to do for the rest of the day. All she could think about was her evening with Mark. After her call to Dorothy, Punkin took her time and sat in front of her vanity, carefully applying her make-up. She was going for a subtle, but sexy look. She chose to wear ruby red lipstick that made her lips pop. It was her favorite color, and it matched perfectly with her outfit. It took her two hours to style her hair, making sure that each strand was curled to a crisp perfection. She didn't want a hair on her head to be out of place. When she finished applying her make-up, Punkin grabbed a bottle of red nail polish and brushed a fresh coat of polish on her nails, and toes. Once they dried, she dressed and walked into the living room to wait for her date. To keep herself occupied, she turned on the stereo and popped in the latest Faith Evans CD. She needed to do something to calm her nerves. She pressed five on the console and waited for the one song that made her think about how Mark was making her feel, *Mesmerized.*

It was a few minutes to six, before the doorbell rung.. Eagerly, Punkin jumped up to answer it. She mouthed, "Right on time," as she approached the door and peered through the peephole. There stood a man wearing a suit; however the silhouette didn't fit Mark's profile. The person at the door was a few inches shorter than Mark, and much slimmer. She had no idea what was going on. The man on the other side of the door was definitely not who she was expecting.

"Who is it," she yelled through the door.

"Ms. Charlotte Evans," said the man, "I am here to escort you to the vehicle where your date is patiently waiting."

Punkin ran to the front window and looked out into the street. She noticed a shiny, black limousine parked in front of her building. She gasped, as her smile stretched from ear to ear. She had never ridden in a limousine before. She didn't know if she wanted to scream or jump up and down like a child with a new toy.

"Just a minute," Punkin yelled as she unlocked the door. "Who sent you?"

"Ma'am, I have been told not to disclose that information." He then extended his arm out to her.

Punkin twisted up the corner of her smile, and said, "Hold on a minute, let me get my purse."

The chauffeur smiled. "Take your time, Ma'am."

As she returned to the living room to cut off the stereo, and to grab her purse, she reached for the ringing telephone. It was Mark.

"Where are you?"

"I'm getting my purse. Where are you?"

"I'm out here, concerned about why you haven't stepped out here in that beautiful gown that I picked out for you."

"I'm on my way out," she quickly spoke into the telephone, before she hung up and scurried to the door.

Punkin was escorted to the limo where Mark sat waiting. He stepped out of the limousine after the chauffeur opened the door. "You look so beautiful." He marveled at his taste in the dress he picked out for her. "I knew when I saw that dress, that it would look good on you." She blushed as her date reached over and kissed her. They climbed into the vehicle. Cuddled closely under each other, the two embraced in a long, passionate kiss. They parted lips as the limo pulled off down the street. Punkin looked around and marveled at the interior, which was decorated with red roses and petals that were draped all about the black leather seats. There was a well-stocked mini bar, and a bottle of Moët chilling on ice. There was enough room inside the limo to seat eight people, comfortably. The windows were tinted, including the glass partition separating them from the driver. There were three red balloons that each read *Happy Anniversary*.

"Balloons, too," Punkin remarked. "Mark, I can't believe you did all of this for me."

"I surely did," Mark smiled, as he poured her a glass of Moet. Mark held his flute up to hers. "A toast to a night filled of fun and surprises" Together they gently tapped the rim of their flutes and took a sip. Gazing at her, Mark kissed Punkin's red lips again. "I am so in love with you, woman," he whispered, as he brushed his nose against hers.

Feeling a little flustered, and madly in love herself, "Where are we going?" Punkin finally asked, as she and Mark's lips parted for a hot second.

"I am taking you to one of the finest restaurants in the city."

"The finest. Ha!"

"Only the best for you."

For a few moments, there was silence. Punkin thoughts had momentarily drifted away. Mark was the man she never felt worthy enough to deserve. He was a real man. Not only did he tell her over and over how much he appreciated her, but he also showed her. She'd never had a man who seemed so dedicated to pleasing her. In only a few months, she'd been exposed to things she'd never known, the two of them had gone places she'd never visited in the city, and she'd lived in Michigan much longer than he had. The joy that Mark brought into her life was like none she'd experienced. Here she was, nearly forty years old, and for the very first time in her life, she could finally say that she'd been out on an official date. The feeling was so overwhelming it almost brought Punkin to tears.

"So, how do you like the dress that I picked out for you?"

"I love it," Punkin smiled, as she snapped back from her daze. "How do I look in it?"

"Absolutely, beautiful. The minute I saw that dress, I said, this looks like it was made to fit the body of my Sunshine. The woman in the magazine looked good in the dress, but it fits your curves like it was designed exquisitely for you. They should have had you modeling it in the magazine. They would have surely sold a million of them."

Punkin couldn't help but to blush. "I'm melting," she told him.

The car pulled up in front of the restaurant and stopped at the front door. Within seconds, the car door opened and the limo driver extended his arm to help Punkin out of the vehicle. Taking his arm, she climbed out with a smile on her face as big as Africa.

She was so happy, she felt like a celebrity stepping out onto the red carpet. As soon as she stepped out of the car, Punkin noticed a few other couples going inside the restaurant dressed up too. Before entering the restaurant, Mark handed the driver a tip, then grabbed the arm of his date, and escorted her into the restaurant. She'd lived in Michigan for almost twenty years and had no idea that the place existed.

Stepping through the front door of the restaurant, Punkin suddenly became nervous. She clung to Mark's arm as if her dear life depended on it. The place was really upscale. The décor inside was quite exquisite. The color scheme of the dining room was white and gold. There were long white drapes, hanging from each window, and tied with gold tassels tiebacks, to reveal the awesome view of the outside patio and deck. As she glanced into the dinning room, she noticed tall white candles, in the middle of each table, which added additional intimacy for the guests. The mood of the room was perfect for the romantic dinner that she and Mark were about to enjoy together.

Punkin stood quietly at the hostess stand, enjoying the soft jazz music playing overhead, as Mark waited for the hostess to locate his name on her lists of reservations. After scaling the list for his name, she looked up from her chart and said. "Right this way."

Mark allowed Punkin to walk ahead of him. The short Asian woman escorted the couple through the dining room, to their reserved table. She pulled out the chair for Punkin, and then for Mark. After seating the couple, the she placed menus in front of each of them, and said, "Your waitress will be with you shortly." As she walked away from the table, almost immediately a waiter stepped up with a wine bottle in his hand. He filled their glasses, smiled, bowed his head, and walked away.

Punkin was totally in awe. She was so nervous, that she picked up her glass of Merlot and took a big sip before Mark could say anything about toasting. She emptied the glass and placed it back on the table. She looked around the restaurant and then back at her date. "How did he know that we wanted wine?"

"I requested it when I made the reservations."

Punkin smiled and raised her hand, signaling to let Mark know that she was impressed. He really knew how to pamper a woman. Punkin wondered how long this fantasy would last. In her mind, she was thinking that if all it took, for her to find a good man, was for her to go to church, she'd have become a steady member a long time ago.

When Mark's arm reached across the table, Punkin reached out for his hand. For a brief moment, they sat in silence, while staring into each other's eyes. Mark lifted her hand to kiss it and Punkin blushed.

"You know you make me wanna–" he stopped in mid sentence.

"I make you wanna what?" she quickly retorted.

"You make me wish that I could wake up staring into your beautiful eyes, and see that gorgeous smile every morning."

"Is that so," she spoke in a soft voice.

"What I need to make my life seem perfect, is having you to spend it with me, forever." He spoke in a serious tone.

"Your woman for life, ha," Punkin remarked jokingly, as her thoughts wandered. She couldn't help but to feel a little guilty. Mark saw her as the perfect woman for him, but there were so many things about her promiscuous past that he didn't know. It was those thoughts that kept flooding her mind every time he spoke of how perfect she was for him.

Mark didn't answer. Instead, he quickly pulled his hand away from hers and slid his chair away from the table. Mark stood up and seemed to be walking away from the table, but instead he fell down on his knee, right on the side of her chair. He reached into his jacket pocket and pulled out a small jewelry box. He popped it open to reveal a sparkling diamond engagement ring. Punkin's mouth fell wide open. Other patrons of the restaurant looked on, as Mark opened his mouth and asked Punkin the question that would change her life.

"Ms. Charlotte Evans, will you do me the honor of being my wife?"

Punkin covered her mouth, as tears formed in her eyes. She was in total shock. She'd never been proposed to, with a ring. She'd had plenty of so-called engagements, but none of them she took seriously because no one had presented her with a ring before. So overwhelmed with the proposal, and without taking a minute to consider if she was ready to take on the responsibilities of being a wife, Punkin quickly answered, "Yes." Despite her uninhibited past, she'd always dreamed of being a wife. "Yes," she reiterated. "Yes, I will be your wife, Mr. Mark Woods."

Mark slid the ring onto her finger, and got up from the floor with a gigantic smile on his face. He and Punkin embraced in a long kiss. The onlookers began to clap. It was legitimate. Punkin was officially engaged.

CHAPTER 19

Monet sat in her Tuesday afternoon lecture class tapping her fingers on her desk. Professor Cartwright was assigning field assignments to students, by paring them up in groups of two. Monet hoped not to be paired with anyone who was a slacker. Whoever her partner was, she wished they were someone who actually cared about the grade they were to receive. Monet knew that some of the students could care less about the grade they got, even though tuition was nearly $900 per class.

As the students lazily paired with their partners, the classroom chatter grew louder. Eventually, her name was called and Monet was told that she was being paired up with Darrell Brown. The only thing that she liked about Darrell, was his slight resemblance of the rapper Ludacris. Darrell was about three feet taller, though, and was also a few shades darker. Darrell Brown was born and raised in Texas, but moved up north to go to college, for a change of scenery. Monet hoped the disappointment she felt, with being partnered with Darrell, didn't show on her face, but she was ticked off. Even though he was one of the excelling students in their class, Monet didn't want to be teamed up with a big flirt. She'd turned him down so many times, it was pitiful, but he was persistent. She constantly reminded Darrell that she had a man, but that never stopped him from trying to run game.

With a flirtatious grin, Darrell wasted no time making his way over to her desk. His shoulder length hair was neatly French braided in small rows. "What's up, Monet?" He smiled so wide, she could see every cavity.

"Hey, Darrell," Monet hesitantly spoke.

"So, it looks like it's me and you, ha?"

"I guess so," she painfully stated.

Darrell took an empty seat next to Monet, and sat silently, while waiting for further instructions from the professor.

Professor Cartwright silenced the classroom's chatter, and asked that each group take the time to discuss their meeting points, and times. The assignment was for each group to work at least ten hours a week, as a volunteer physical therapy aid. Monet and Darrell agreed that St. Mary's Hospital was convenient for the both of them.

"What shift would best suit you?" Darrell asked.

Monet looked down at the handout the professor had given to each student. It listed the time slots that were still available at St. Mary's. After her eyes scanned the document, she looked up at her partner and said, "It looks like the two to six slot is still open. If it's okay with you, we can take the Monday and Thursday, one to six slots. I have a morning class on Thursday that conflicts with any of the other open time slots, for that hospital."

"That's cool with me," Darrell agreed.

Once they settled on the day and times to work together on their field assignments, Monet and Darrell walked up to the front of the class and confirmed it with Professor Cartwright. Afterwards, they were dismissed to go.

That Thursday afternoon, Monet pulled into the parking lot of the hospital at 12:40. After parking, she pulled out her compact and touched up her face. At 12:50, a burgundy Mustang pulled up in front of the hospital. Monet noticed Darrell being dropped off by a light-skinned female. The car sat only for a hot minute before it quickly pulled away. Darrell stepped away from the vehicle, and threw his book bag over his right shoulder. He dug into his pocket and whipped out a pack of cigarettes. He lit one, and let the dangerous smoke fly away into the wind.

Monet finally stepped out of her car and headed toward the employee entrance of the hospital. She hoped that Darrell would be finished smoking his cigarette by the time she approached because she didn't want any of the poisonous smoke seeping into her lungs or her clothes.

"What's up, partner?" Monet said catching Darrell off guard.

"What's up?"

"It's five minutes to, so I guess we better get going." She fanned the smoke flowing past her.

Darrell took one last drag from his cigarette before smashing it out into the white sand-filled ashtray, affixed to the bench where he stood. He threw his bag over his shoulder and said, "Let's do this."

They walked inside the hospital, approached the receptionist, and asked for directions to the Physical Therapy department.

As they exited the elevator, they turned right, toward the Physical Therapy department. You could see the workout equipment through the glass, outside of the physical therapy room. Monet became excited as she opened the door and walked inside. Dr. Wallace walked right over, with his hand extended to greet them. He introduced himself, and proceeded to showing them around the Physical Therapy department. Afterwards, he gave them each a pair of hospital scrubs to put on.

"If you're going to be working in this department, you have to dress the part," he grinned.

When Monet and Darrell returned, donning their work attire, Dr. Wallace discussed the necessary forms that each of them had to complete, and dismissed them for a thirty-minute break.

Once they were back on the first floor, Darrell headed toward the exit saying that he was going to smoke. Monet told him that she would be in the cafeteria eating. She was so hungry, that the lingering smell of food coming from the cafeteria made her stomach growl more. Monet stood in the line contemplating what she wanted to order. The poster board, on the countertop, advertised a meatloaf dinner that was on sale for $3.99. The meatloaf looked pretty fresh, and her favorite, the mashed potatoes, looked delicious, so she ordered the meal, with a side of corn to complete her dinner. After she received her plate, Monet slid her tray down the line, to the cashier who was waiting to collect her money. Since the special didn't come with a drink, she asked for a cup of iced water.

The cashier pointed toward the self-serve drink station and said, "The cups are over there. The clear ones are for water."

"Thanks," Monet said as she accepted her change, picked up her tray and walked over to the drink station.

As she approached an empty table, Monet looked around to see if Darrell had made it back inside. Since she didn't see him, she took a seat, and said her prayers before digging into her plate.

Darrell eventually walked up to the table smelling like a cigarette. "You don't mind if I sit here with you, do you?"

"It's cool," Monet agreed. So far, he had not been trying to hit on her, and as long as he wasn't, she was cool with kicking it with him.

"Well, let me go up here and get me something to drink. I'll be right back."

Monet watched him as he walked over to the drink station. He picked up a Styrofoam cup and filled it with ice and Coke. After filling his cup, Darrell placed a lid on it, grabbed a straw, and then walked away. Monet could not believe her eyes. He didn't even turn back to see if anyone else saw him.

As soon as he made it back to the table, Monet said, "I know you didn't just go up there and steal that drink."

"I wouldn't exactly call it stealing," Darrell mouthed.

"What would you call it?" Monet snapped, obviously irritated by his response, and by what she'd witnessed.

"I'd call it getting a drink," he added. "I was thirsty, and they have a gigantic sign over there that reads self serve, so I served myself a drink. What's wrong with that?"

Monet rolled her eyes, looked around the room to see if any of the cafeteria staff had seen him before she refocused on her food.

Darrell sat across from Monet, sipping on his stolen drink, while she ate. Before long, he leaned over the table and spoke in almost a whisper. "So, Monet, you got someone you kickin it with?"

"I do," she quickly responded, almost cutting him off.

"Dang," Darrell laughed. "You mean that too, don't you? I can see it all over your face. You're faithful to your man ain't you?"

"Yes, I am," Monet stated proudly.

"Who's your man, anyways? I wonder if I know him. I'm sure he goes to the school. Right?"

"Dang, that's three questions in one," Monet huffed, while rolling her eyes.

"Who's your man?" Darrell asked again.

"His name is Malcolm Maddox, and he graduated from Central two years ago. Right now, he's attending dental college in Augusta."

"Oh, you got an out of town man." Darrell took another sip of his drink, as he waited for Monet to clear her mouth, and answer the question.

"Yep," she finally answered, while smiling with confidence.

"And you believe that your man is faithful when he's been away from you for longer than ninety days?"

"I sure do," she answered defensively.

Darrell sat back in his chair and laughed. "Sweetie, I can guarantee you that your man is down there hitting some of them Georgia peaches. Down south, the females come out of the womb with fat asses. You think your man can focus when he got all that temptation in his face everyday?" Darrell was big-time player hating.

"I ain't worried," Monet snapped. Darrell was starting to wear out his welcome. Why did her man have to be a dog just because Darrell obviously was?

"Personally, I just don't think that long distance relationships last. I mean, you don't know what he's doing, he doesn't know what you're doing, so why not just let it go?"

"Well," Monet continued, this time she was holding up her left hand to flash her half carat, class two, diamond engagement ring. "As long as I'm the one wearing this, I'm not worried about those other chics. I know my place in Malcolm's heart." After setting Darrell straight, Monet got up from her seat, grabbed her tray, and walked away from the table. She wasn't about to sit and listen to the devil who was trying to put things in her head. She knew that Malcolm loved her, and Darrell knew nothing about what she and Malcolm had.

After lunch, Monet had only one more hour to look at, and work with player hating, Darrell. Although he tried to apologize to her, Monet brushed him off by continuing to listen to the doctor as he explained the job in detail. As soon as the doctor dismissed them for the day, Darrell followed Monet down the hall, like a puppy dog, apologizing to her.

"Monet, I said that I am sorry. I didn't mean to come to you like that."

Monet threw her hand into the air, as if to say bye, but she mouthed nothing as she headed to her car. Darrell remained standing in front of the hospital waiting for his ride. Monet left the hospital and headed to her mother's place. Even though Darrell had pissed her off, she was not going to allow him to ruin the rest of her day. She knew Darrell's game plan. He was trying to diminish the wall of trust that she had for her man, so that she could become vulnerable and want to end her relationship, but it wasn't going to happen. From now on, she wouldn't allow him the opportunity to inquire about her personal life. She knew what she had, and she wasn't allowing anyone to make her have doubts about her man.

She sat in her car and waited for the traffic light to turn green. Monet needed to pick up her son from her mother's, then she'd have to hurry home to cook and feed him, and then get him in bed so she'd have time to study for her test.

"I guess I'll just go and rub my mother's belly, and talk with her a moment," Monet spoke to herself while yawning. Every since Monet had found out that her mother was pregnant, she wanted to rub her belly every chance that she got. Since it was so hard to believe, Monet had to monitor her mother's growing stomach regularly, to see if it was really so. Monet chuckled at the idea of being big sister to a sibling younger than her own child.

The stay at her mother's was brief, because Monet was so tired. She didn't feel like doing anything but going home and falling into bed. She'd left her house at eight thirty in the morning and it was 8:10 PM when she pulled into the driveway of her apartment. Thank God her mother had already fed her son. He must have played hard all day, because Monet had to wake him up so she could take him out of the car. She released a sigh of relief as soon as she stepped through her front door. She was so happy to be home. She was so looking forward to summer vacation. After dropping hers and Deshawn's book bags to the floor, she stood in the front door waiting on her three-year-old son, who was fifteen feet behind, walking as slow as molasses.

After helping Deshawn unfasten his pants, so he could go potty, Monet ran to the telephone to check her messages. She pressed the button on the machine to see who had called. The first message was Malcolm. He'd called to say that he missed her and couldn't wait to see her. Summer break was coming up and he would be returning home for the entirety of the break. *"I hate that I missed you, but I thought you would have been there. I guess you're over to your mother's or something. Talk to you later, Sweetie."*

The second message was from the sperm donor who contributed to the conception of her son. He was talking about he wanted to see his son. *"I know you ain't been that busy where you haven't brought my son to see me. What are you trying to do, make him think that his daddy don't love him."*

Monet quickly deleted the message and thought that Derrick had a lot of nerve. He didn't really want to see his son. He must have been bored and decided to call her so he could ruin her day. What Derrick needed to do was get down to the Friend of the Court, to catch up on the child support that he was so behind in paying. He was lucky she hadn't told the police where he hung out. She was still upset with him from what happened the last time when he called himself watching their son. She'd cursed him bad, and told him how she felt about his trifling behind. More than likely, Derrick and the girl had engaged sexually, with Deshawn in the bed. Because of that, if he wanted to see Deshawn, he'd have to come to her house and visit him. He was not responsible enough to be trusted alone with her boy anymore.

Monet called out to her son. "What are you doing, son?"

"I'm boo booing, Mama," he yelled back from the bathroom. She tuned her face up.

"Too much information, son." Monet laughed while shaking her head and mumbling, "um, um, um," as the third message played.

"Monet, I wished you had of accepted my apology today, but instead you gone try to diss me by walking away like I wasn't shit." It was Darrell. *"I can't stand when ho's try to act like they're all that when they ain't shit. You ain't no exception either."* Monet wondered how he got her number. *"I hope yo so called man, in Georgia, is banging all the ho's he can, then I hope he comes back and gives your stuck up ass AIDS, or something to make your pussy fall off. I was trying to be nice to you, but you went there. I want you to know that I ain't gone sweat you 'cause I got mad chics who wanna holla at me."* Tears formed in her eyes, as her body remained in a still state of shock. The message played on. *"I hope some niggas rape yo' stuck up ass and bust yo stank ass pussy wide open."* He giggled. *"Yeah, since you acting like a bitch, I'm gone treat you like a bitch. So the next time I see you, I might just slap the shit out of you, so you better watch your back, trick."*

The beep at the end of the message snapped her out of her state of shock. Without even thinking, she quickly erased the message. Her face was full of tears. She stood in disbelief. Monet could not believe that Darrell would leave her such an unpleasant message because she refused to accept his apology. On the answering machine, he sounded like an aggravated stalker. An eerie feeling suddenly came over. Since he had her telephone number, Monet wondered if Darrell knew where she lived.

"Why are you crying, Mommy?" Deshawn entered the bedroom where Monet was standing. Monet reached for him. She picked him up and held him in her arms. She was so scared.

"Mommy is alright baby. I had something in my eye," she lied. With her son in her arms, she walked to the front door to make sure that it was locked, and then she walked into the living room to look out of the window to see if Darrell was lurking outside her apartment. Nothing outside seemed out of place, so Monet headed back to her bedroom. She thought about calling her mother, but later thought against it. She didn't want to worry her.

Monet turned the television on to the Cartoon Network and sat her son down on her bed. After wiping away her tears, she scrolled through the numbers on her caller ID, to see if the number Darrell had called from was there. She needed some type of proof that he'd called and threatened her since she had already erased the message. It was there. How stupid was he to call with a threatening message, and then not even block his number. The thought of how bold he was, made her mad. She, in turn, decided to call him back, to let him know that she would go to the police if he called her house again. Monet picked up the telephone after tiptoeing off into the other room. She dialed the number and waited to see if Darrell would answer. He answered as if he was expecting her call. "Hey, Monet," he answered, in a nonchalant tone. She immediately went off.

"I'm glad you called and left that message on my answering machine because now I have evidence to get you locked up. I did nothing but try to be cordial to you, and you call my house and leave some psycho message on my answering machine. And how did you get my number?" she yelled.

"I saw it when you wrote it on your registration form today." Darrell chuckled. "Why you try to diss me like that, Monet?" Darrell asked in a soft, seductive voice.

"Darrell, you should lose my number because the very next time that you call my house, I'm calling the police to play the message that you left on my answering machine. What is wrong with you?" she cried.

"I don't have no hard feelings. You just made me mad because you hurt my feelings and I wanted you to be hurt the way that you hurt me."

Monet could not believe how calm Darrell was. The creepiness in his voice brought back her tears. She'd felt totally violated by him. There was no telling how much of her personal information that fool had. "I'm also taking this recorded message to the school on Monday. Hopefully they will kick your crazy butt out," Monet said. She then hung up.

Darrell called right back but she didn't answer. She heard him on the answering machine begging her not to get the school involved. He apologized for calling her house and leaving the awful message. Monet didn't answer that call, or the fifteen or so others that he made. Monet got so aggravated that after awhile, she actually called her stepfather and explained to him what had happened. Sullivan asked if she was okay, or if she needed him to come over, but Monet assured him that she was okay, and needed someone to talk to.

Before hanging up, he told her, "I can't do anything right now, but I promise you that I will handle Darrell Brown."

Afterwards, Monet and her son got into their pajamas and went to sleep.

CHAPTER 20

When Caroline found out about her sister having another baby, jealousy ensued. *Why did Dorothy have to have all the luck*, she wondered. Caroline had always wanted to have a third child, a boy for her husband, but had never been able to. She'd had a full hysterectomy shortly after giving birth to her daughter, Taylor, due to health reasons, which ended her possibility of having anymore children. Since her surgery, nearly fifteen years ago, Caroline seemed discontent. The thought of not being able to conceive made her feel inadequate as a woman. From time to time, thinking about it would send her into a state of depression. Sometimes, she'd get so angry when she would see women with children standing at bus stops, fatherless. She would think, those women, who were obviously not ready to have children, were usually the ones who did not have a problem giving birth to them. Then she'd think about her own situation, which was totally opposite. Why did she have to be the unfortunate one? Even though she'd finally gotten over the fact that her husband had an illegitimate child, she'd blamed herself for not being able to have children, as the reason for Thomas' cheating.

Dorothy's pregnancy brought about many buried emotions that Caroline had bottled up for quite some time. Since Caroline found out, she'd experienced flashbacks, hot flashes, and anxiety attacks on a regular basis. She knew it was wrong for her to be so resentful, and she knew that it would probably be wise for her to talk to someone about how she was feeling, but Caroline wouldn't dare tell anyone of her insecurities. She was too ashamed to tell her husband, of all people, how she felt, let alone a doctor.

It was Monday when Caroline first experienced panic attacks, and Friday was General Motor's 12th Annual, Employee Appreciation Award Ceremony, so she needed to get it together. Her husband had been nominated for employee of the year, and she was to accompany him. She decided to take off the entire week to get prepared for it. Caroline told her boss that she was going through a lot of stress and needed some time off. That Tuesday morning, after her family left for work and school, Caroline called her doctor and told her about the panic attacks. The doctor said that she would call in a prescription for thirty more Xanax pills. Caroline found solace in the pills after Andrea went to prison. Conveniently, she continued taking them to calm the stress of her everyday life.

To compensate for the loss she was enduring, Caroline had only one solution to make her feel better, once she fell in these deep stages of depression. She needed to go shopping. Spending money fulfilled her. It made her feel important. So, for the rest of the afternoon she would drive around and prowl the local boutiques for the most fiercest dress she could find to wear to the awards ceremony.

The first three shops that she visited had very nice dresses, but not the dress Caroline was seeking. She was looking for the dress that would turn all heads, as soon as she stepped into the room. After leaving Jacobson's Boutique, she decided to try her luck at the mall. She'd left her house shortly after ten o'clock in the morning and hadn't realized that she'd been out for over three hours searching for a dress. Caroline had originally wanted to make it home before her husband did, but the way that things were looking, it didn't seem possible. If she didn't make it home before Thomas, she wouldn't be able to sneak her new outfit in the house, without having to give an explanation.

She walked past a store in the mall, where a mannequin in the display case was wearing a dress that Caroline knew would turn heads. She had to go inside to try it on. The white satin, black trimmed, A-Line dress seemed to be calling her name. As soon as she walked through the door, she was greeted by a smiling and cheerful sales clerk. The woman was thin, average height, big breasts, and brown-skinned. She looked like she could be related to the actor, Kim Fields. She greeted Caroline. "What can I help you find today, Ma'am?"

"A beautiful gown," Caroline gladly responded. "I would like to know if you carry that white and black dress, on display, in a size eight."

"The Vera Wang gown; of course we do. Follow me."

Caroline followed the woman past a few racks of evening gowns, to the after-five dress section.

"It's such a lovely dress," the woman said. "We only stocked ten of this design, and we only have three left, but I'm almost positive that I saw an eight, earlier." Coincidentally, the first one she picked up was an eight. Tracy, the sales clerk, took the dress down off the rack, and held it up so Caroline could get a good look at it.

Caroline marveled at the dress for a couple of minutes. "It looks like it could be the one. I'd like to try it on."

"Follow, me," Tracy said as she escorted Caroline toward the dressing room, in the back of the store. Tracy was very courteous. She took the dress and hung it on a hook inside dressing room #4. She even unzipped the zipper on the dress. "Do you need any undergarments?" Since the dress was sleeveless, Tracy offered a strapless bra to Caroline.

Sure. I want to get the full effect of the way the dress looks on me, before I purchase it."

Tracy smiled. "What are you, about a 36D cup?"

"Exactly," Caroline answered with an, *how did you know my size*, expression on her face.

"I'll be right back with a few selections."

Caroline looked into the full-length mirror as she slipped into the dress. Perhaps purchasing the dress would take away her blues. While she waited for Tracey to return with the bra, she took the dress and held it up against her, and focused on her stomach area. She peered again into the mirror and closed her eyes. She imagined what if one day she went to the doctor, and he told her she was pregnant.

Tracey's knock on the door snapped her back to reality. "Yes," Caroline answered.

"I'll pass the bras over the door. If you need my assistance in zipping the dress, just yell, I'll be standing right here. I can also pick out a handbag and a pair of shoes, that'll look great with the dress. I guess you are about a size eight in a shoe."

"A seven and a half," Caroline responded.

"I'll be right back."

"Thanks."

She was mesmerized at how she looked in the dress. It hid all of her flaws and accentuated all of her curves. There was no way she could leave the store without it, although it needed a few alterations. Once she tried on the shoes and accessories, Caroline was set.

Tracey took her measurements, and then escorted her client to the register to pay. Caroline ended up charging almost $3,000 on the Preferred Platinum Visa, and she still had to have her manicure, pedicure, facial, and hair done. For the works, at the spa she often frequented, it cost her around $450, but since it was a special occasion, she would go all out and get the house special for $750, which included a one-hour deep tissue body massage, esthetician services and free samples of different lotions and massage oils to take home. Once she finished pampering herself, she was sure to feel like a million bucks.

The party was scheduled for six that evening. By the time she made it home, it was 5:10, and she still had to get dressed, and put on her make-up.

Thomas was so upset, he yelled at Caroline saying that he should go on without her. She insisted that she could be ready in forty-five minutes. He knew that was a lie, but he sat in the living room, upset until his wife was ready to go. Caroline stepped into the living room looking stunningly beautiful. The sight of her stole Thomas' breath. She had bangs that were swooped into an updo, and small spiral curls draped down in the front, partially covering her right eye. Her make-up was flawless, and the gown fit her like a glove. He gladly jumped up from the couch and complimented her on the way she looked. He kissed her lips and held out his arm for his wife to grab a hold of it. Although it was 6:45, he was glad to escort his beautiful wife to the awards ceremony. He knew that as soon as she stepped through the door, all eyes would be on her.

When Caroline and Thomas arrived, they noticed a few others arriving late as well. Thomas seemed to know most of the people staggering in, but Caroline didn't. The awards ceremony was a celebrated event for the cooperate employees of General Motors, and since Caroline worked in the plant, she didn't know anyone at the event. Once inside, Thomas and Caroline were quickly escorted to their designated table. Immediately after being seated, the waitress approached to take there food and drink orders. Caroline was all smiles. Her husband immediately introduced her to the couple they were sharing a table with—Al Winesberg and his wife, Uniss—once they returned from the dance floor. Al told Thomas that the band played so well, he had to get a dance in while the night was still young. Winesberg was Thomas' supervising manager. Thomas had been working under his supervision for over ten years. Al was one of the few Caucasian co-workers who worked with Thomas, who didn't feel intimidated by working with a black man, who was in a high paying corporate position. Al was the one who nominated Thomas for the Employee of the Year Award.

After kissing her hand, Al commented Thomas on how beautiful his wife was.

Uniss yelled to Caroline over the music. "I just love the way they've decorated the place. It brings back memories of my high school prom. Teal and Beige were our same theme colors and everything."

"I know I just love these flower arrangements." Caroline referred to the vases decorated in the center of each table. "Water lilies are my favorite flower."

The room was huge. On one side, was the bar area, and the bartenders were serving the guest as they exited the dance floor. Since it was open bar, the line was long, which was surprising, since the wait staff would happily deliver a drink of your choice, right to your table. Beside the bar, was a long table holding the plaques that were going to be given out to the award recipients.

For an evening spent with a bunch of stiff dancing white people, the ceremony turned out to be very enjoyable. After a few glasses of chardonnay, some of them actually seemed to catch up with the rhythm of the music. Besides Caroline and Thomas, there was only one other black man at the ceremony. Every now and again, Caroline would see a couple or two turn their noses up to her, but she continued getting her groove on, dismissing their nose tooting to them being jealous of her and her rhythm.

The marinated Mahi-Mahi entrée, that Caroline chose, was surprisingly delicious, and so was the Teriyaki Chicken Thomas ordered. Caroline received so many compliments on her dress that her happy face remained throughout the entire night. Wearing the dress made her feel so good, she felt like she'd stepped outside herself and had taken on a new role. Gone was the troubled, insecure woman with the infidelity issues. Now, she felt powerful, like she could conquer anything.

After dinner, the award winners were announced. Although Thomas didn't receive the award for Employee of the Year, he had fun, and was delighted about receiving the nomination. When the ceremony ended, they tried to beat the crowd by heading to the car early. Caroline followed closely behind Thomas as they trucked through the parking lot toward their car. The night air was a bit brisk, so Caroline rushed to the car since she wasn't wearing a coat.

As the car pulled out of the parking lot, she said, "I really enjoyed myself tonight, even though most of your co-workers are a little lame. The band was rocking out though, which made up for all of the shortcomings."

"As long as you enjoyed yourself, I'm satisfied"

"Not only did I enjoy myself, I looked good doing it!" she exclaimed. "You know I was the best looking female in there."

"Now that I agree with," Thomas laughed, "although I would have been just as satisfied, seeing you in that red one that I bought you when we went to the play last month."

"That old thing," Caroline commented, while smacking her lips. "You know that I cannot go out to a function, as important as the award ceremony, in a dress that I wore a month ago."

"Of course you could have." Thomas loosened his tie. "I was the one nominated for the award and I wore an old suit. You, my dear, were just an attendee, and you spent a lot of money, unnecessarily. There were things that I needed to do this month, but once I looked at the credit card statement and saw how much you'd spent, I wasn't able to do what I had planned."

Now she was pissed. She spoke in an elevated voice. "There is plenty of money in our bank account, why didn't you get money from there?"

"The point is that we are on a monthly budget, and like always, you are spending over your allowed spending limit, which causes problems for me being able to purchase the things that I want to purchase."

"Well, Thomas, just do what you have to do, and I'll deposit my next paycheck to make up for whatever you spend."

"Again, sweetie, that's not the issue. The issue is your excessive spending," he remarked, in a passive aggressive manner.

"Look, Thomas, why are you making a big deal of something that isn't even an issue. The credit card bill will get paid, as it always does," she snapped.

"I just want you to be careful with your spending. So please don't turn this into an argument."

"Look, I was trying to make sure that I was looking good. You can't look this good in anything cheap. Shit, I work everyday, and feel that I should be able to buy what I want without being questioned about it."

"Caroline, you spent nearly $5,000 on a one-night affair. That could have been nearly a whole semester of college tuition for Taylor."

"Okay, Thomas, I hear you, now can we talk about something else."

Thomas didn't delay ending the conversation. He turned the music up and redirected his focus on guiding the car down the highway. He'd also had a great evening, and did not want to ruin the rest of the night by arguing with his wife. He had other plans for her after they got home.

That following Sunday, Thomas left to go over to his friend Vernon's house to watch the football game. Andrea was gone with Tim, as usual, so Caroline stayed home to help Taylor with a school project. Tim and Andrea's relationship seemed to have picked up where it left off, before they both went to jail. Knowing that Andrea was on probation and had to take random drug tests, Caroline didn't worry about the amount of time that she spent with Tim.

Caroline and Taylor sat at the kitchen table working on Taylor's science project when they were alarmed by a sudden ringing noise. By the time she traced the noise to the living room, Caroline realized that her husband had run off and left his cellular phone on the sofa. By the time she reached it, the telephone had stopped ringing. She picked it up, and glanced at the tiny display screen on the Nextel. It read, *1 Missed Call*. Out of curiosity, she pressed the button that allowed her to retrieve the last incoming number. Her head fell back in disbelief. It was Sheila. Caroline recognized the number right away. *Now why would Sheila be calling, on the day that Thomas just happened to be going over to Vernon's to watch a game*, she thought. Something was definitely suspicious about the whole situation. She hissed, as the telephone rang. By the third ring, Caroline was still debating if she should answer it or not. On the fourth ring, the decision had been made.

"Hello."

"Hello," the voice on the other end stuttered.

"Yes." Caroline spoke sternly and with an attitude..

The caller hesitated. "Uh… is Thomas around?"

"No, he is not," Caroline snapped.

"Well, can you please tell him that I am trying to get in touch with him?" Sheila asked.

"You are, huh," Caroline inquired suspiciously.

"Look, Caroline, I don't have time for this. Tell Thomas that I need to speak to him about his son's daycare fees, which are due by tomorrow," Sheila snapped.

"Daycare fees? Isn't that something you can pay with the child support check he sends you?"

"Look, my son's father agreed to pay for his childcare expenses, and since he's been doing it ever since our son has been going to childcare, I don't see why he would have a problem with paying this time."

Caroline hung up on Sheila. She didn't know what else to say. She was stunned by the information she'd received, and could not believe that Thomas didn't inform her that he was paying extra money to Sheila. The way Sheila emphasized, *my son's father*, made Caroline want to jump through the phone, and rip Sheila's tongue out, so she could never mouth those words again.

The cellular phone rang again, but Caroline didn't answer. She knew it was Sheila calling back. Caroline was so mad, that she felt like climbing into her car, and going over to Sheila's, to whip her ass, but Caroline simply refused to stoop to Sheila's level. She was too old for that. She could deal with her later. In the meantime, Caroline needed to get with her husband, to get him in check.

"Mom," Taylor yelled from the other room, "I need you," she whined.

"Here I come," Caroline shouted back. She then tossed the ringing telephone on the couch and headed back into the kitchen to join her daughter. She was on fire, and couldn't wait until her husband returned home.

Thomas arrived home around eight-thirty that night. Andrea was in her bedroom, and Taylor was in the bathtub. As soon as Thomas stepped into their bedroom, Caroline badgered him with questions. Thomas unapologetically explained to her that he was, paying for Thomas Juniors' daycare fees, and that he would continue to do so until the boy was old enough to attend school.

"If you don't question the amount of money that we put out on the girls, then don't question the amount of money that I spend on our son." Thomas stormed toward the bathroom. He'd already been disgusted, and disappointed because his team had lost the game, by over fifteen points, and as soon as he stepped in the front door, there was his wife, all in his face bitching about something that didn't call for any discussion. He stepped into the bathroom, closed the door behind him, and exhaled. After turning on the shower, he slowly undressed. *Can't a man just come home to a peaceful, loving wife, without an attitude*, Thomas thought.

Caroline was so upset that she went to bed without saying anything else to her husband. She didn't even ask if he was hungry. She couldn't believe that he had the audacity to say something to her about the money she was spending, without his knowledge, when he was spending extra money behind her back as well. As the thought crossed her mind again, Caroline rolled her eyes, and pulled the bedspread over her head.

The next morning, Caroline woke up with the same bad attitude. She and Thomas passed each other as she exited the bathroom. "I'll be driving myself to work today."

Thomas shrugged his shoulders and went on about his business. If that's what she needed to do, to get her mind right, then he was delighted to give her all the alone time she felt it would take, to do so.

When lunchtime rolled around, Caroline refused to make her routine trip to her husband's office. As she sat alone, eating her lunch, Caroline thought about the situation. She tried putting herself in Thomas' shoes. Maybe she did overreact, a little, the night before. Maybe she should have approached him differently. Now, as she thought about it, she wanted to go back and right her wrong. She wanted to do something good, to let her husband know that she was sorry. Thomas was right. She had no right to interfere on what his agreement was with Sheila, regarding Thomas Jr. She knew that he would make sure his son didn't go without anything, like he wouldn't let their daughters go without. And, even with Thomas paying daycare fees for the boy, it wasn't taking a dime away from her household. After moments of contemplation, she thought that since Thomas was the one who always gave in after they had an argument; she wanted to be the bigger person this time. After work, she planned to cook a nice dinner for her family, and, after apologizing to her husband, she was going to have a romantic make-up session with him.

In her car, heading home from work, Caroline decided to call and see if her husband had made it home, since she noticed his car was gone from its usual parking space. She sincerely wanted to apologize to him, and she wanted to remind him how much she appreciated and loved him. She dialed his cellular, but got no answer, so Caroline decided to go on to the grocery store, to pick up a few items. Even though Meijer's Supermarket was ten minutes out of her way, she chose to shop there; it was well worth it because they had a fresh meat delicatessen, which was her preference.

Amazingly, she was in and out of the store in forty minutes. After loading her groceries into her car, Caroline jumped in and headed home. Because of the high volume of traffic, she opted not to get on the expressway, and decided to take the street route home. Caroline huffed when she was stopped by yet another red light. Instead of loosing her cool, she exhaled, and tried to remain patient, until it was her turn to move again. Traffic was moving so slow. She dreaded nothing more than to be caught driving in afternoon rush hour traffic. Finally, her car was able to proceed thru the intersection. Her head did a double take when she noticed a Lexus, the same color as her husbands, driving in the oncoming traffic lane. As she passed the car, Caroline made sure to get a good look at the driver. Coincidentally, it was her husband. She blew her horn to get his attention, when she noticed a female riding in his passenger seat.

"What the hell?" she cursed, as she floored the gas pedal, and quickly made a U-turn in front of an oncoming car. The car she'd cut off honked its horn at her. Although she had nearly caused an accident, Caroline still paid him no mind. Instead, she Bo guarded her way into the lane, in front of Mr. Upset, who continued honking his horn. Now, she was headed in the same direction as her husband. Only three cars behind him, she immediately dug through her purse for her cellular phone. She speed-dialed her husband's number. After the second ring, Caroline lost her patience and hung up. She would do much better if she could catch up with him.

From out of nowhere, a white Honda Accord dashed out of a parallel parking space, in front of the convenience store. Caroline honked her horn, and slammed on her brakes to prevent from hitting the car. Karma was something. She became so irritated that she cursed her husband, as if he were in the car with her. After ducking and dodging traffic, Caroline finally caught up to her husbands' car and got him to pull over. She wondered how he would explain this one.

Thomas slowly pulled his vehicle over into an Amoco gas station, and waited for his wife to pull in after him. He asked Sheila to remain in the car. Caroline pulled up, shifted her car into park and jumped out. She ran toward the passenger side of Thomas' vehicle to see who the woman was. Thomas quickly jumped out of the car to stop his wife before she got to Sheila. He hoped to explain everything to his wife without their being any confrontations.

"What are you doing with Sheila, Thomas?" Caroline swung open the passenger side door.

Sheila jumped out swinging, arms flailing like a wild woman. For a moment, Thomas stood in shock, but after his mind registered what was going on, he tried to pull the two women apart. Through swinging fists, slaps and verbal insults, Thomas continued to try to get in between the fighting women, but it proved to be a more of a difficult task than expected. Caroline had a grip on Sheila's hair and Sheila was busy swinging wild, closed fists at Caroline's face.

"Caroline," Thomas yelled, "please let me explain. it's not what you think."

"I am going to kill this ho," Caroline threatened while landing a good right to the side of Sheila's jaw. The two women continued tussling, as Thomas busied himself trying to rid Caroline's left hand from Sheila's hair.

"Do...what...you...gon' do, Bitch," Sheila huffed, as she continued swinging. After punching Caroline, she drew her hand back. There was blood on it.

When Thomas saw the blood, he panicked and pulled Sheila away from Caroline. Caroline released her hair. Sheila felt herself being separated from her component, so she kicked her foot, with all her might. It landed in her opponent's mid section. Caroline screamed out, as onlookers gathered.

Once the women were separated, Thomas lost his temper and exploded. "Caroline, get your ass back in the car, right now. And Sheila, if you don't get back in the car, I'll pull off without you." He was fed up with the two of them acting foolish, especially his wife. Cursing at her husband, Caroline ranted about how he was going to be put out, once she got home. Her lip was bleeding, and she could feel that it was starting to swell. Her clothing was falling off her body. Her hair was flying all over the place, and here her husband was about to pull off, with his baby's mother in the car with him. Disappointed, and disgusted, Caroline gathered her things, and watched as her husband escorted the battered and bloody-nosed Sheila to his car.

"How dare you, Thomas. How dare you turn on me, for that dirty bitch," Caroline yelled, as she walked toward her vehicle. She threw her arms in the air and yelled as loud as she could, "I want you out of my house, and out of my life."

"Get in your car, and go home Caroline," Thomas warned with his finger pointing at her as if it were a deadly nine millimeter shot gun.

Without further ado, Caroline climbed into her car, started the engine and revved it. Thomas was still standing outside of his car, so she placed her foot on the gas pedal and sped over to his car. She contemplated running him over, but changed her mind, as the SUV screeched to a halt, about two feet away from him. She sat in her vehicle, gazing out at her husband. Thomas stared into his wife's face with hate in his eyes. He shook his head, in disgust, while gazing toward the back seat of his car.

"They broke down on the way to a doctor's appointment, Caroline."

For the first time, Caroline looked toward the back of her husband's car and noticed little Thomas sitting in tears, in the back seat. His face was stuck to the glass of the window and his eyes were focused on the mad woman who had attacked his mother.

"She called me to take her to an appointment, because her car broke down, and she and my son were stranded on the side of the road. I absolutely, cannot believe that you are out here acting a fool in front of my son," Thomas reiterated. Disgustingly, he shook his head again, and climbed into his vehicle. "All you needed to do was give me a chance to explain, and all of this could have been avoided."

Caroline felt ashamed, embarrassed, and apologetic. She knew that she had overreacted, yet again, and this time, she was afraid that she might have taken it a little too far. To save herself from further embarrassment, she burned rubber out of the parking lot.

CHAPTER 21

From the moment Mark placed the diamond engagement ring on her finger, Punkin couldn't help but to keep marveling at it every chance she got. She could not believe that she was finally getting married. It took her thirty-five years to find someone who she seriously wanted to spend the rest of her life with. She couldn't wait to get off work, so she could go over to Dorothy's, and tell her about her upcoming nuptials. The night that the ring was presented to her, Punkin called her family to let them know, although no one got excited. Punkin had three brothers, two sisters, and a mother back in Chicago, and neither of them had been, or had any plans about getting married, so her news didn't seem to spark any happy fuses with anyone. It didn't bother Punkin much, because as long as she had Dorothy around, big belly or not, she was going to be her maid of honor, and everything was going to be fine.

Mark was like a dream come true. He was what Punkin had not been looking for, all of her life. Mark was a good man, with no children. Since day one, he'd treated her like a queen. He was so genuine. Punkin knew Mark was the real thing because they'd been seeing each other for over ninety days, and he still hadn't changed. She couldn't wait until he met her son, Chalon, who didn't spend too much time with her, because he always complained about being bored when he came over to visit. Besides that, Chalon had a girlfriend, so he preferred to stick around his own neighborhood to keep his eye on her.

On her way to Dorothy's, Punkin decided to call her fiancé to say hi. She had been thinking about him all day, and wanted to hear his voice. It was something about Mark that had her losing her mind. It was as if she couldn't get enough of him.

"Hello," Mark answered.

"Hey, baby," she whispered.

"It's so nice to hear such a sweet voice, so early in the morning," he spoke in a deep, masculine voice.

"I was calling so to say hey, and I also wanted to hear your voice. I'm on my way to Dorothy's right now."

"Will I get a chance to see you later on?"

"Of course, I have to find the time to spend with my handsome husband-to-be," Punkin softly spoke. "If I plan to spend the rest of my life with you, I have to get used to spending as much of my time with you as I possibly can. I'll stop over to your place right after I leave Dorothy's."

"What are you ladies planning on getting into?"

"Oh, nothing. I haven't told her about our engagement yet. The only thing I said to her was that I had some good news to share with her, but I wanted to tell her in person. I love getting her all anxious and worked up. She doesn't have a clue as to what the news is, and she keeps asking me to tell her over the telephone, but I won't," Punkin laughed. "I just love keeping her in suspense."

"You have been engaged for nearly a week and you haven't even told your best friend yet?" Mark sounded annoyed.

"Well, like I said, I wanted to tell her in person, and since I've been working all week and spending all of my extra time with you, I haven't had time to get over to her house to tell her."

"Oh, well, as soon as you accepted my proposal, I told all of my family and friends. I just assumed that you would be just as excited to tell your friends. I mean we're talking about an engagement," he huffed in an aggravated manner.

"Look, baby, just chill, because the news will get out today." She thought, *now, I know he is not trippin.* "I'll see you around seven, okay," she purred.

"All right, sweetie, I'll see you then."

Punkin hung up the telephone, as she pulled up in front of Dorothy's house. She climbed out of her car smiling. She couldn't wait to see Mark. It had been almost twenty-four hours since they'd seen each other, and ever since meeting him, she needed to see Mark everyday. She would go crazy if she didn't.

Punkin pranced straight into Dorothy's house without knocking, or ringing the doorbell, as usual. Whenever Punkin visited Dorothy, if the door was unlocked, she'd walk right in. She and Dorothy were cool like that. They were like sisters.

Dorothy was standing in front of the stove, stirring a skillet of something that smelled so good, it made Punkin's stomach growl.

"Dang, Dorothy what are you cooking up in here?" Punkin startled her friend who hadn't realized that she'd walked in.

Dorothy jumped and yelled out. "Cube steak and gravy, rice and green beans, and you better start knocking. One day you gon' walk up in here on the wrong thing."

Not even giving what Dorothy said any thought, Punkin continued, as if Dorothy had said nothing. "Damn, it smells good. When do we eat?"

Dorothy stood with her hands on her hips while staring at Punkin. "I don't remember passing out any invites," she huffed as she wiped her hands on her apron.

"Oh, you know I invites myself," Punkin said as she looked her friend up and down. Dorothy's skin seemed to be glowing, and her face and belly were starting to plump out. She was wearing an oversized housedress and her swollen feet were snugly fitting into a pair of clean, light blue house slippers. For a moment she turned back to stir her simmering skillet of cube steak and gravy. After dipping her spoon into the beans and rice for a taste test, she replaced the top and wobbled over to the table to sit down.

"Girl, look at you, I still can't believe that you're pregnant."

"I can't believe you got that big ole grin on your face," Dorothy said. "Mark surely has had some affect on you. Now quit playing, and come over here to tell me what you have to tell me. You know I'm about to explode with anticipation."

"He sure does, he has so much of an affect on me, I'd like to experience the feeling forever," Punkin smiled while talking to Dorothy, and thinking about Mark.

Punkin always gets all worked up about every new man who enters her life, Dorothy thought, never taking Punkin serious when she spoke to her about a man, because all the men she had would come and go so fast. Dorothy's thoughts must have been written all over her face

"I'm for real, Dorothy," while waving her left hand. "I plan on spending the rest of my life with Mark."

"I hear you," Dorothy answered, still not noticing the engagement ring that Punkin kept waving in her face. Punkin then walked over to the kitchen table and stood in front of Dorothy.

"Girl you hear what I said?" Punkin shoved her left hand into Dorothy's face and screamed, "I'm getting married."

Dorothy gasped as her eyes zoomed in on the ring. "Oh, my God, you're serious!"

"Damn right!" Punkin's gigantic smile spread from ear to ear.

"I am scared of you, Ms. Punkin. When did you get engaged?" Dorothy held on to Punkin's hand so she could get a good look at her ring.

"Last week."

"Did you set a date yet?"

"We're thinking about Valentine's Day, but the date is still tentative."

"Congratulations! Even the date is cool. That'll give me plenty of time to have the baby, and get the baby weight off, so that I can look good in one of those sleek dresses." Dorothy got up and pranced around the room with her hands on her hips. After stirring her gravy, Dorothy walked back to the table to join her friend.

"Are you positively sure that Mark is the one, Punkin?" Dorothy seemed concerned. "I'm just asking because you've only known him for what, a month or so, and you know how you are. You're in love one minute, and the next you don't want to be bothered. Marriage is hard work, and you can't get mad and want to quit as soon as Mark gets on your nerves."

"I'm sure, Dorothy," she yelled with happiness and excitement. "Mark is everything that I need in a man. He is caring, compassionate, he has his own business, saved, and has no children, and to top it all off, he knows how to make me *say his name, say his name,*" Punkin chanted. "Now how can I possibly go wrong with him? Mark's got a big dick and plenty energy. What more can a woman ask for?" Punkin laughed while getting up and dancing in front of her chair.

"How about some time to get to know him," Dorothy inquired.

"I know everything that I need to know," Punkin snapped back.

"I guess," Dorothy said while looking at her friend, and shaking her head. "And good God, when did you sleep with him?"

"The day he proposed. You know I had to try out what I'd be getting for the rest of my life. Brother Mark had me crying, Yes Lord,'" Punkin bragged.

"You know you are always going to be hot in the ass. Couldn't you have waited to give up that hot tail of yours," Dorothy fussed.

"Girl, please. Neither one of us can stay away from each other. I just got finished talking to him on my way over. I'm going to his house as soon as I leave here."

"See, that's exactly what I mean, marriage is about more than just having good sex. Have you thought about compatibility? Do you think you'll be able to live with the man, you know that's usually the more challenging part of the relationship. Great sex only last for so long."

"I know what I'm doing, Dorothy. Mark is the one," Punkin snapped.

"If you say so," Dorothy concluded, throwing her hands ups. "I've got your back no matter what, you know that."

"Cool," Punkin said. "Now how much longer is it going to take before that food is ready?"

"It should be ready in a few. I think I have enough to share with a freeloading friend," Dorothy laughed. "If you stop spending so much time screwing, you would probably have some time to fix yourself a decent meal." Punkin broke into laughter as she walked to the kitchen sink, to wash her hands.

CHAPTER 22

Andrea and Tim sat in the office of the clinic, waiting for Andrea's name to be called. The center was starting to fill with women of different ethnicities, but Andrea was fortunate to be one of the earlier one's to arrive. Besides Tim, there were only two other men sitting in the waiting room. It didn't seem to matter much to Tim, because he was there to support Andrea. He was as nervous as she about finding out if she was pregnant or not. Andrea had called him crying, the previous night, to let him know that she was going to the clinic, and needed him to go with her. She had missed her period. Andrea couldn't believe that she'd gotten herself into the same mess, a second time. She didn't know how she would approach her mother with the news, if the results were positive. She could hear her mother's voice talking to her. *I don't see why you want to keep getting pregnant for someone who hasn't married you.* Caroline would probably complain about how much of an embarrassment Andrea would be to her, once again. To avoid all the drama with her mother, Andrea figured she'd try to get her own place if the results were positive. After all, she had a good job now, and she also had Tim to support her.

Once her name was called, Andrea followed the nurse into a small room. The nurse handed Andrea a four-ounce plastic cup that had her name written in black marker. The nurse instructed her to go into the restroom, and fill it with as much urine as possible, then bring it back to her. When Andrea returned with the cup, the woman took a syringe, withdrew a portion of the urine from the cup, and expelled a stream onto the pregnancy test strip.

"We like to let everyone see their test being processed, so they won't complain about their results being mixed-up or confused with anyone else's. You can go and sit outside the door, in one of the chairs, and I'll call you once your results come back."

Andrea opened the door and stepped outside the examining room. Ten minutes passed before the woman called Andrea back into the office. She wasted no time delivering the news. "Your pregnancy test results are positive." The nurse slid the test from the table and passed it to Andrea. "What are you prepared to do now?" she asked

Andrea sat in silence for a moment, before she answered. "I think that I'll go ahead with the pregnancy. Since I just recently lost a child, I can't see getting rid of this one. Maybe this is God's way of giving me a second chance at motherhood."

The nurse's brow furrowed. She looked as if she wanted to ask Andrea how she had lost her first child, but she wasn't sure if the question was appropriate or not. "Do you have a family doctor or OB/Gyn who can start to see you on a regular basis?"

"No, but I do have insurance benefits that will take affect on the first of next month, so I have a few weeks to locate a good doctor."

Standing, the nurse walked to the other side of the small room. She grabbed a few brochures from the rack, and extended them toward Andrea. "Here are some listings of some clinics where you can find a reputable doctor. I'm guessing that you're about five weeks along, but the doctor can give you a more accurate estimate. Now, do you have any questions for me?"

Andrea shook her head no.

"Well, that'll be all for now." She then walked to the door and opened it, allowing Andrea to exit. She patted Andrea on the back and smiled. "Take care of yourself, honey."

After receiving directions to the accounting desk, where she could pay for services rendered, Andrea warmly smiled at the nurse. "I will. Thank you."

After paying her $10 co-pay, Andrea stepped through the door and waited for Tim to meet up with her. They exited the office together. "The results," she announced on their way out of the clinic, "were positive."

Tim didn't know what to say. Although he was confused and scared, he smiled and held on to his girlfriend's hand, as they exited the building.

CHAPTER 23

Rhenee clutched her briefcase, as the bell to the elevator door rang signaling its descent. She was on her way to her office, and was famished as a result of being in the courtroom all day. It was only the third day of trial, and she'd already felt worn out and tired. She waited for the two women to exit the elevator before she stepped in. As soon as the door closed, Rhenee leaned back against the wall, closed her eyes and exhaled. She still had a proposal that was due to be in the mail by the end of the day, and she had only written the first paragraph. Her professional reputation was on the line so she needed to get it together. Her downfall was that she didn't have a man. It seemed that whenever she was without a man, her professional life would be in shambles. A happy home life was what gave her the energy to go into the courtroom, and deal with the stressful challenges of being a criminal defense attorney. When she didn't have a man at home, to comfort her after a long day, it depressed her. Without a steady man in her life, Rhenee felt incomplete. She couldn't believe how Ray had called off their relationship, by telling her that he was tired of being unfaithful to his wife. He was treating her as if she was a one-night stand or something, not like someone who had risked her own marriage, by being caught for sleeping with him. Finally, the elevator stopped on the twelfth floor. Rhenee stepped out onto the marble floor and walked toward her office.

Finishing a full day's work, Rhenee decided to go to Flip's Sports Bar to hang out, and have a drink. Maybe a few shots of Patrone would help to relax her mind. Rhenee knew, however, that it would do nothing to ease her desperate yearning for the comfort of a man. It was nearly nine o'clock at night when Rhenee turned off the lights, and stepped out of her office. The cleaning staff had already come and gone, so she was probably the only one left at the office. As Rhenee moseyed toward the elevator, she took a deep sigh of relief and unfastened the buttons on her suit jacket. The liquor was calling her name, and her tongue was feigning for the smooth, soothing Tequila, which always seemed to wash away her problems. In the absence of a man, liquor was her comfort and pleasure. Besides sex, it allowed her to relax and think nothing but satisfying thoughts.

She stepped through the door of Flip's, and into the dimly lit room nearly filled with patrons. As she strolled toward the bar, Rhenee waved at a few familiar faces, who threw their hands in the air when she walked past. Taking a seat at one of the two available stools at the bar, she waited for the bartender to approach. When the short black woman stepped up and asked Rhenee if she wanted to order anything to drink, Rhenee smiled and replied, "A double shot of Patrone, on the rocks." Rhenee looked around to see if she recognized who she was looking for. There were several big named attorneys sitting around drinking. When she didn't see who she was looking for, she turned back toward the bar and waited for her drink to arrive. In the midst of all the music and background chatter, Rhenee heard a familiar laugh that caused her to turnaround. Her eyes roamed the room, and shuttered in surprise, when Ray came into view. She recognized his watermelon head right away. Ray was on the other side of the room, sitting with two of his colleagues from the firm. She couldn't help but to stare, hoping her eyes could capture his attention. When Ray looked up and saw her, he smiled and continued socializing. Rhenee's heart skipped a beat, because that was the most she gotten out of Ray in months.

Once the bartender returned with her drink, Rhenee asked her if she could order something from the kitchen. She hadn't eaten since lunch, and was starting to feel weak. Besides, she needed to put something on her stomach, since she was going to be drinking alcohol. The bartender reached for her cellular phone that graced her hip, and then back at Rhenee. "The kitchen doesn't close for thirty minutes," she yelled, over the mellow jazz track playing in the background.

"Cool, then I'll have the chicken Philly basket with fries and a coke. I'm willing to offer a generous tip for a speedy delivery. I'm starving."

"Sure thing," the woman said, as she smiled and walked away. Rhenee then raised her glass, turned it up, before sitting the empty glass back on the bar. She sighed, "Ahhh." It felt so good to be able to relax, finally. Now, all she needed was for Ray to follow her home so she could wake up in his arms. After a night with him, she'd be refreshed, relaxed and ready to take on the fight of the bull, the next day. The corner of her lips curled, when the thought of being with Ray vanished from her mind. Her eyes opened. When she looked over in Ray's direction again, he was gone. In a nervous frenzy, she sat straight up, as her eyes danced about the room, searching for her man. When she didn't see him, Rhenee panicked, but tried to calm her nerves, by telling herself that he'd probably gotten up to go to the restroom or something. With that thought, she chilled. Her food came out quickly and she inhaled the sandwich and fries along with two more shots of Patrone. After finishing her meal, Rhenee tossed a fifty-dollar-bill on the bar, and then she got up to leave. Apparently, Ray had taken off because her first time noticing him, was the last that she'd seen him.

Rhenee was awakened from her sleep at five o'clock in the morning. Her eyes fluttered, as she looked in the direction of where the cries were coming from. She wiped away the beads of perspiration covering her forehead, and climbed out of bed. She was so frightened; there was no way she was going back to bed. Since the accident, she'd never be able to sleep peacefully. It had been a long time since she'd had any nightmares, and for some strange reason, she'd had two within the past week. Rhenee decided to get dressed. She was going to leave for work early. Hopefully, being focused on her case would stop her from dwelling on why the nightmares were starting to re-occur.

That afternoon, she decided to have lunch at the Big Boy restaurant, since it was close to her job. It was a downtown location that she and her colleagues frequented on a regular basis, but today she wanted to eat alone. She chose Big Boy because it was within walking distance of her job and she needed some fresh air to clear her mind. Besides, she didn't want to deal with the lunch hour traffic.

She arrived at the restaurant and, luckily, she was seated immediately. Rhenee ordered the open-faced turkey sandwich, with a side order of mashed potatoes. As she waited, she sipped on her coffee, while looking through the daily newspaper. Coincidentally, when she glanced over the top of her paper, her ex-lover was stepping through the door of the restaurant. He stood at the hostess stand where he waited to be seated. Now, the place was so crowded, he'd be lucky to find a seat, and get his meal before his lunch break was over. Trying not to let him notice her, noticing him, Rhenee held up her newspaper to conceal her face.

A few minutes passed before a soft voice said, "Excuse me."

Rhenee quickly dropped the paper and turned to the woman standing beside her table.

"Ma'am, I am sorry to bother you, but the gentleman standing by the door, wanted to know if you would mind him sharing a table with you."

Rhenee looked in the direction of the pointing finger and noticed that the woman was speaking of Ray. Her heart raced like it was running a marathon. "Don't you all have any other available tables?" Rhenee griped.

"Well, we are quite busy, but the gentleman said that you all were colleagues and could possibly share a table, since there is about a thirty minute wait time for an available one."

Rhenee picked up her coffee cup and took a long sip. She hoped her nervousness wasn't so obvious. Placing the cup onto the saucer, "Tell him that I don't mind." She forced a noticeable fake grin.

"I will, Ma'am. Thank you."

"Finally, he is coming to his senses," Rhenee huffed as she waited for Ray to join her.

"Good, afternoon, counselor," he remarked when he walked up.

"Hi, Ray. Good to see you."

"I hope you don't mind my intruding, but I am starving, and didn't feel like waiting thirty minutes for a table." Ray took a seat. Rhenee remained silent while he looked over the menu. "What did you order?"

"The open-faced turkey sandwich, with mashed potatoes; I've had it before, and I enjoyed it."

"Sounds, great. I think I'll have the same thing then," Ray said, as his eyes scanned the room looking for the waitress.

"I miss you, Ray," Rhenee blurted.

Instead of answering, he turned to look out of the window.

"I wanted to talk to you the other night, but you took off before I could get around to it."

"Talk about what," he said in snide manner.

"Talk about us, Ray."

Ray looked away again. "Look, Rhenee," he spoke softly, while leaning on the table. "I already explained to you the way that things are between you and I, now why must we keep going over this? Friends, Rhenee, friends are all that we can be."

"Look in my eyes and tell me that you don't love me anymore," Rhenee begged, as the server walked up to the table.

"Good afternoon, Sir. My name is Cindy, and I'll be your server today. What may I get you to drink?"

"I'll have a cup of coffee and an ice water, and for my meal, I'll have the exact same thing that she ordered."

"Alright, then," Cindy said, after jotting down the order. "I'll be right back with your drinks, Sir." Cindy pranced off, and returned with Ray's drinks within a couple of minutes.

The lunch didn't accomplish anything for Rhenee. Ray refused to answer any questions concerning them being involved in anything besides a platonic relationship. Rhenee was so pissed with him, that she left the restaurant without even paying her bill. Ray was acting like a selfish asshole, so she left to avoid having a confrontation with him. She was so upset; she vowed to never have anything else to do with him, again.

CHAPTER 24

Punkin and her fiancé walked out of the clinic with smiles on their faces. They'd taken their blood tests, and had completed a two-hour marital counseling class, which was required in order to get their marriage license. Hand in hand, they strolled to Mark's car. After opening the door for her, Mark ran to the other side of the car and jumped in. Once inside, he reached over to embrace her with a long kiss.

"I love you, Charlotte Evans, and I can't wait until you become my wife," he mumbled softly in her ear. Punkin blushed. "I've never felt so fulfilled in my life."

"I love you too, baby," Punkin rebutted, as the car engine turned over. Mark looked over at his fiancé and smiled. Within minutes, the car was pulling out of the driveway, and onto the busy street. They rode down Fuller to Martin Luther King Park, located at the corner of Fuller and Franklin. Mark pulled his vehicle into an empty parking space, and cut off the engine. Punkin looked over at the recently built swimming pool that had what looked like a ten-foot long, spiral slide. *The renovation really helped to upgrade the park*, she thought. When her son Chalon was a small child, the pool was much different. The new construction of the pool gave the park an amusement park look. When she and her fiancé stepped out of the car, they headed for the swings, in the playground area. Mark told Punkin to get on a swing so he could push her. She was full of smiles, as she ran toward the steel swing set. Punkin climbed onto the swing, and Mark got behind her. He gave the big push, and Punkin was off. After a few pushes, she went higher and higher. Punkin felt like a little child.

"Higher, higher," she yelled to Mark.

After the swing, they played on the slides, and then the seesaw. They were having so much fun that Punkin wished the moment could last forever. Mark brought out the kid in her. He always went out of his way to make sure she was happy, and that's what she loved about him. After climbing off the seesaw, Mark pulled his fiancé into his arms, and delicately kissed her lips. Their union was interrupted by Mark's ringing telephone. He quickly pulled away from her.

"Uh, oh, looks like work is calling," Mark said, as he snapped the telephone from his hip, to look at the number on the display screen. Not recognizing the number, Mark pressed the voice mail key, and listened to the message that had been left. It was from a customer who had a question about a part that Mark had ordered for his fan. Mark needed to get over to the man's house to install a remote-controlled ceiling fan. After hanging up, Mark told Punkin that he needed to get going. He had taken nearly a three-hour break to handle his personal business, but now it was time to get back to the shop to pick up the part, and his work van.

"It's okay, boo," Punkin smiled. "I haven't had this much fun, on a day off, in a long time. I don't know what I'd do without you," she finished, as they walked back to Mark's car. Before getting out of the car, Punkin asked her fiancé if he still felt like riding out to see her son Chalon on the weekend. Mark said that he was looking forward to it. They embraced in a farewell kiss, and Punkin climbed out of the car. Mark pulled off.

She and Mark left her house, that Saturday morning, to visit with Chalon. He and Mark had never met before, but Punkin knew they would like each other. Chalon was a sweet, considerate, young man. They picked her son up from his father's house at a quarter of eleven. After Punkin introduced her son, and his father, to her fiancé, the three of them went to Longhorn Steakhouse for lunch. Chalon loved to eat steak, and Longhorn Steakhouse was his favorite place. On the way to the restaurant, Chalon seemed excited as he filled his mom in on all the happenings of his life, since they'd last seen each other. Mark remained quiet, letting his fiancé and his soon-to-be stepson, carry on in conversation.

Longhorn was unusually busy for an early Saturday afternoon. A long line of people waited to be seated, as Mark approached the hostess stand. She handed him what looked like a drink coaster, and said that it would light up when their table was ready. Since there was no available seating in the waiting area, Mark and his crew waited outside until their table was ready. It was unusually warm and sunny. The temperature hovered around sixty to sixty-five degrees. Mark and his party were finally seated thirty minutes later, at a booth in the back corner of the restaurant. The booth was in a location that had the lowest traffic and noise volume. Once they ordered their drinks and appetizers, Punkin listened to Mark and Chalon talk about sports. Chalon was a big fan of football and basketball, so he and Mark indulged in an interesting conversation that only they could relate. Punkin was full of smiles, and since she didn't know much about sports, she listened quietly, while marveling at all the cowboy memorabilia that lined the walls of Longhorn. There were large pictures of original cowboys on some of the pictures, and Punkin was surprised to see that black cowboys were being represented, since they were the originals.

Completely satisfied with their lunch, a stuffed to boot, Punkin rubbed her stomach and proclaimed, "Whew, I am full. I was planning on taking you shopping, but as full as I am, I don't know, Chalon," she joked.

"Naw, naw, Mama," Chalon rebutted. "You don't have to walk around in the mall if you don't want to. All you have to do is give me and Mark the money, and we will go shopping for the shoes I want. You can sit on the bench and wait for us. It won't even take us that long," he grinned.

Punkin shook her head as she stood waiting for Mark to open her door. "So, let me get this straight," she spoke jokingly. "You don't need me; you just need my money, huh?"

"Um, hum," he smirked with a devilish grin.

"Um, um, um," she huffed. "Where is the love?"

Inside the car, Chalon reached up into the front seat and gave his mother a big kiss, on her left cheek. "You know you will always be my favorite girl, Ma. I will always love you." He eased back into the backseat.

"Yeah, right," she huffed, as she turned to Mark, who'd just climbed behind the steering wheel.

"And I'll always love you too," Mark cosigned, as he reached over and kissed his fiancé on the lips.

"And I'll always love the both of you, too," Punkin subsequently, remarked. As the car backed out of the parking space, she kissed the tips of her fingers and blew a kiss toward her son, and then at Mark. "Well, let's go to the mall then," Punkin stated, as she leaned back comfortably into her seat.

They only shopped in two stores at the mall, and Chalon was in and out of both stores in no time. Punkin still ended up spending $282 on two outfits for Chalon. That didn't include the $150 that Mark spent on a pair of Michael Jordan gym shoes for the boy. When they left the mall, Punkin was scratching her head. She thought it was a good thing that Chalon's father did most of the buying for him because, if she had to do it, she would have to work two jobs, just to dress the boy.

To end the day, Punkin offered to take two favorite men to see the latest Tyler Perry movie, *Diary of a Mad Black Woman.* Leaving the movie in stitches, Punkin was a big fan of Tyler Perry's and she definitely felt that she'd gotten her money's worth. Chalon and Mark enjoyed it as well.

Before getting out of the car, Chalon told Mark that he was cool. "I guess you can marry my Ma, if you promise me that you'll take care of her, and never hurt her"

Mark promised that he would, and he and Chalon gave each other dap, to seal the deal. Mark waited in the car for Punkin to walk her son into the house. He definitely enjoyed spending the day with Punkin, and Chalon was a good kid. Mark was actually looking forward to getting to know Chalon a little better. He couldn't wait until the boy came to spend the weekend with them. Since he didn't have any children of his own, Mark was actually enthused on the idea of being a stepfather.

Before walking out the door, Punkin asked her son if he wanted to spend the night with her, but declined. Sadly, she reminded Chalon how much she loved him, even though she was disappointed that he didn't want to go with her. Whenever she asked Chalon why he didn't want to stay, he would shrug his shoulders. Punkin knew the reason he didn't want to go though. She'd heard that he didn't like staying at her place, because she treated him like a baby. Even though he was in high school, Chalon was still her baby. And, since he didn't live with her, she tried to smother him with as much love as she could, when she could.

"Don't forget to call me tomorrow," she yelled back at him, as he stood in the door, watching her walk back to Mark's car.

"Okay," Chalon answered, while waving. "And thank Mark again for the shoes." Punkin nodded her head, and trotted to the running automobile.

Mark drove Punkin by her house so that she could get a change of clothes. She'd planned on spending the night with her fiancé, so that they could get up and go to church the next morning.

At Mark's, they sat in the kitchen dining on their favorite meal, Popeyes chicken. "So tell me…what are some things you expect from me once we move in together?"

Punkin looked puzzled.

"I mean, we need to know what our likes and dislikes are, to avoid any conflict in our union." He reached over and kissed Punkin's greasy lips.

"Well," she cleared her mouth and stated, "I'm not a neat freak, but I ain't nasty. I don't cook everyday, and I can't stand it when guys forget to let the toilet seat down, after they use it, and I end up with wet butt after sitting in a puddle of cold water. I always end up yelling at Chalon for doing that when he comes over."

Mark burst into laughter the mental picture. "I promise not to leave the seat up, Sunshine," he smiled.

When they finished eating, Punkin and Mark showered together, and climbed into bed. They cuddled, and talked all night before falling to sleep in each other's arms.

Punkin waited in the church vestibule for Dorothy and her husband to come out of the sanctuary. As soon as she saw Dorothy, she had to go and rub her belly. "Do you know what it's going to be yet?"

"No, we have asked the doctor not to tell us. We want it to be a surprise," Dorothy answered.

"Oh, yeah, I forgot your butt was old fashioned," Punkin laughed.

"Whatever," Dorothy retaliated with a smile. "I have a doctor's appointment tomorrow."

"*We* have a doctor's appointment tomorrow," Sullivan happily interrupted. "We're going on six months now, and I can't wait to see the progress of our little one."

When Sullivan wasn't looking, Dorothy cut her eyes at Punkin. "I'm sorry, *we* have an appointment tomorrow," she replied in a jokingly sarcastic manner. The four of them broke into laughter, as the children stood around looking like they were ready to go, as usual. "Punkin, I need for you to come over and help me send out the invitations for the baby shower. You know that next month will be here before you know it."

"Okay, Dorothy, I will come over on my next day off," Punkin confirmed.

"Cool," Dorothy replied. "Well, let us get on home then. I have some stew simmering in a crock-pot at home, and I need to get there to see about it. You all know that you're more than welcome to stop by, if you'd like."

"No thanks, D, Mark has to get home. He's expecting a phone call from his mother in Carolina," Punkin remarked. "He's been telling her so much about me, she says she can't wait until the summer, so she can come down to spend some time with us. When Mark first told her that we were getting married, she asked him, how he was going to marry someone, whom his mother has never met. Since her health isn't so good, she won't be able to make it to the wedding. I've talked to her once and she's really nice. She said that she was looking forward to meeting her new daughter in law," Punkin bragged.

"We'll she's in for quite a surprise, then," Dorothy laughed, before waving and walking away. "Call me later."

"Alright," Punkin laughed, as Mark walked up with a strange look on his face. He looked as if he was aggravated by something. "What's wrong, Mark?"

"Nothing," Mark said quickly as he clutched Punkin's arm, and they exited the church.

Punkin was scheduled to work from noon to eight o'clock that Monday, but after waking up in Mark's bed, she knew that she needed to call in for work. She sat up in the bed, and ran her hands through her untamed mane. She looked over at her fiancé, who was still knocked out, and lying in the bed. She had intentions on going home, but Mark begged her to stay. They stayed up all night talking and laughing. Punkin learned so much about Mark, she felt like she'd known him for a lifetime. Punkin climbed out of bed and walked over to the telephone. Once he was on the line, she explained to her boss that she had been stricken with a sudden case of the twenty-four-hour flu. After asking forgiveness for her lie, Punkin climbed back into bed and cuddled under her man. When Mark opened his eyes, Punkin was the first one he saw.

"Good morning, baby."

"Good morning to you, too, my love." He reached over and wrapped his arms around her. "If I ask you something, would you promise to say yes?"

"That depends on what it is."

"If I asked you to marry me, will you say yes?"

"That's a silly question. I've already said yes to that, or did you go to sleep and wake up with amnesia? We're already engaged, fool," she joked.

"No, I mean, if I asked you to marry me today, would you?"

Punkin's mouth fell wide open, as a strange look came over her face. "What are you talking about, Mark?"

"I'm talking about you and me, getting married, today. Let's say we skip the waiting and planning, and just do it today. I mean we've already had our counseling and blood test that proves were no kin, so why wait any longer? I want to lie down with you every night, and wake up with you as my wife, every morning, not as my girlfriend. I love you, and you love me, so let's just do it. We can save our money and have a nice big reception in the summer."

Punkin didn't know what to say. She was in total awe.

"What do you say?"

She hesitated to answer. While contemplating her thoughts, Punkin stuck her finger into her mouth, and nervously nibbled on her nails. "I say, okay," she finally mouthed. Her face was covered in joyful tears. She couldn't believe that she was actually about to get married. "Yes," she shouted a second time, when she realized that Mark was for real. "Yes, Mark, I will marry you, today," she laughed while jumping up and down.

Mark got up from the bed and lifted her into the air. He kissed her lips. "Thank you."

"I can't wait to spend forever with you."

CHAPTER 25

Tim sat in his morning math class daydreaming. The professor was working out a problem on the blackboard while Tim was trying to work out the situation about the baby, in his head. What had he gotten himself in to? Tim wasn't exactly sure if he was ready to become a father, at this stage in his life. A baby was something that he wasn't prepared for. Tim wanted more than anything to prove to his parents that he deserved a second chance, by finishing college and starting his career in teaching. A baby was something that wasn't written in his plans for at least the next five to ten years, and Tim wasn't exactly sure, how to handle the situation at hand.

What would his parents say if they found out that Andrea was pregnant? Tim shook his head in frustration because he could hear his father's angry voice yelling in his ears. *"A baby is out of the question. We are spending lots of money to send you to school so that you can get your life on track, not so you can screw it up again."* His father's voice played clearly in his head. Tim's parent's had agreed to support him, only if he was being productive by trying to reestablish his life and having a baby, out of wedlock, before he finished college was definitely not what his father had in mind. He knew that his parents wouldn't hesitate to pay for Andrea to get rid of the baby, but Tim knew that Andrea planned on keeping the child.

Tim wondered how he could be there for Andrea and the baby, when he worked part-time, and was a full-time college student. Dwelling in his mind, was the thought to go ahead and take two extra classes each semester, so that he could finish early, and graduate ahead of schedule. If that were to happen, then he wouldn't have much extra time to spend with Andrea, and every since she'd been back in his life, he went crazy when he didn't get the opportunity to see her. Every other day he needed to be graced with her beautiful presence, to get him through the next couple of days. He loved Andrea very much, and wanted to spend the rest of his life with her. However, it wasn't the right time for them to start a family. He felt bad, for being a coward, when he considered all that Andrea had been through with their first daughter. If Andrea wanted to keep the baby, Tim had to be a permanent fixture in that child's life. Deep in thought, once he looked around the classroom and noticed that it had cleared of the students, and was starting to fill with students he'd never seen before, embarrassingly, he smiled and quickly gathered his book and notepad, and stuffed them into his backpack. He then quickly left the classroom. Luckily, Math 102 was his only class for the day. Since he'd been distracted and had missed the entire lesson, he'd have to call his friend Toby to find out what was due before class met again on Thursday.

That night, at the supper table, Tim slowly explained to his parents that he and Andrea were expecting a baby, and their plans to be married. His mother immediately shouted before his father could register what he'd heard.

"How could you let this happen again, son? I knew that you seeing that girl was not a good idea. She is nothing but trouble. You've only been back with her for nearly three months, and already she's caused you to loose your focus. Tim, you were doing so well," she cried with disappointment, as she got up from the table and walked away, wiping her eyes with her dinner napkin.

Tim's younger brother, Bobby, never took his eyes away from his plate. He was too busy trying to scarf his food down so that he could go back to his bedroom to tend to his PlayStation.

"But I love Andrea, Mom, and I want to marry her as soon as I graduate," Tim yelled to her, after she'd left the room.

His mother didn't respond, but his father did. After clearing his mouth, his father spoke in a soft voice. "Son, you'll be ruining your life if you think about starting a family while you're in the process of getting your degree. You'll have plenty of time to get married and have a child, but right now is not the right time. I think that you and Andrea should reconsider having a baby right now, and do the right thing," his father said hoping to sway his son from making the wrong decision.

"The right thing, ha," Tim commented as he got up and walked away, ending their conversation. "I've got to get some studying done, Dad," he rudely stated while heading to his bedroom. Once he got there, Tim stepped inside his room, slammed the door, and fell onto his bed. He needed some time to think.

The minute Caroline found out that her daughter was expecting another child, she felt like the Lord had answered her prayers. Although Caroline's baby making days were over, there was still hope of her having a chance to experience motherhood, once again, since Andrea was having a child. The baby would really be like her own, since Andrea and the baby would be living in her house. Normally, Caroline would object to her daughter having another child, out of wedlock, but Caroline couldn't be happier. Her sudden overzealous reaction even surprised Andrea. Andrea had been so afraid of what her mother would say about her being pregnant, that she didn't willingly tell her. If it hadn't been for Caroline walking into her daughters' bedroom, and seeing Andrea staring blankly at the form from the clinic, she probably would have never found out. Andrea told her mother that she'd planned on keeping the pregnancy a secret because she felt ashamed, and didn't want them to be disappointed in her. Reluctantly, and after being found out, Andrea told her mother that she was two months pregnant.

At first, Caroline threw her hands over her mouth and said nothing, but after a few silent moments, she gave her daughter a big hug. Caroline felt torn between mixed emotions of guilt, shame and pleasure, because she selfishly wanted her daughter to go ahead with the pregnancy, for personal reasons, but she sincerely didn't want Andrea to bare another child out of wedlock, to risk being alone like she was before. So, Caroline explained to Andrea how important it was that she and Tim consider getting married before the baby was born. By the end of their mother-daughter talk, Caroline and Andrea had amicably settled what would result in the up and coming months.

No sooner than the clock struck three, Andrea was on the telephone dialing Tim's cellular number. He had an afternoon class that ended at three and she wanted to see if he could meet her after she got off work. She had her first doctor's appointment coming up and she needed him to go with her. Tim didn't answer by the third ring, so Andrea hung up, before his voice mail picked up. She rushed to her locker to put her things away. Although she was pissed, she only had fifteen minutes before it was time for her to punch in for work. It seemed that since discovering her pregnancy, Tim had become distant. Whenever she wanted to see him, he was always studying or focused on something else other than her, when before, he would break his neck to spend time with her. Whenever she did reach him, he was always rushing off of the telephone stating that he was so busy;

he'd have to call her back. What was up with him? Had the thought of becoming a father scared him away? Was he not ready to commit to her and their child? Not knowing for sure what to think, Andrea tried to dismiss her personal thoughts and focus on working. Since she was a machine operator, she needed complete concentration, because even the slightest distraction from the machine at the wrong time, could result in the loss of a limb. She would simply have to deal with Tim later.

≈ ≈ ≈ ≈ ≈

Tim walked out of class behind Matt Krensky. They were discussing the notes that the instructor went over during class. Professor Conrad had given them all the answers to the questions that would be on the exam, he was giving the following week.

Matt said to Tim, "This biology exam is going to be the toughest one that I'll have this semester. I had a math and English exam last week and, a Liberal Arts exam yesterday, and I think I did pretty well on those, but I don't know about this one. I can't wait until Wednesday so that we can take the exam and breathe again. Dude, I can't wait to go on break." He strutted down the hall beside Tim.

"Yo, man, the last couple of weeks have been hectic for me too. I've been spending so much time studying, that I haven't even had time for my girl. I have one more exam tomorrow, and the biology one on Wednesday will be my last. Andrea is going to flip whenever I talk to her because I've been really putting her off so that I can stay focused. I don't plan on taking any classes over next semester."

"I know what you mean," Matt spoke as he and Tim reached the intersection of the hallway. Since Tim had to go one way and Matt the other, they exchanged handshakes. "Well, I'll see you on Wednesday, Dude. And good luck. Maybe after class next week we can go and have a few celebration drinks."

"We'll see," Tim said as Matt walked off. After parting ways with Matt, Tim finally whipped out his phone and powered it on. He had cut it off during class, but wanted to check and see if Andrea had called. After strolling through his missed calls list, Tim noticed that Andrea had called but hadn't left a message. As he exited the building, Tim dialed his girlfriend's cellular number. He knew that she was probably working and wouldn't be able to take his call, but Tim wanted to leave Andrea a message to let her know that he had family in town, and he and his parents were meeting up with them for dinner at five. The message was to let her know that he would be tied up for the night, and would get back with her the following day.

The professor announced that as soon as the students were finished with the exam they would be free to leave. Tim, who felt he'd done pretty well on the test, finished it in about thirty minutes and was out. He exited the school with a relieving smile on his face. The sun was shining, and a nice breeze was blowing. Tim inhaled a good whiff of fresh air and exhaled. Since he didn't have any other classes for the day, and it was a little after nine o'clock, he decided to stop by Andrea's before going home. He knew that she was upset with him because she left a message on his voice mail the night before saying so. Hopefully, stopping by would get him out of the doghouse.

When Tim pulled up in front of Andrea's, he excitedly jumped out of his car, and headed up the path to the door. He stepped onto the porch and dialed Andrea's number to wake her. When she didn't answer, he rang the doorbell. After a few minutes Tim heard footsteps. Andrea spoke in a raspy, morning voice. "Who is it?" she yelled from the other side of the door.

"Your baby's daddy," Tim answered. Andrea patted her hair, hoping it didn't look too crazy before she opened the door. Tim had a lot of nerve to dodge her all week and then show up without calling her first. One, she hated surprises and two she was still upset with him.

Finally, Andrea sprung open the front door. "Tim, why didn't you call me first? I haven't talked to you all week, and now you just pop over here, this early, unannounced."

Tim was already used to Andrea's grouchiness and mood swings and knew that in time they'd only amplify. He smiled while following Andrea upstairs to her bedroom. She climbed into her queen-sized bed and buried her head under her pillow. Tim took a seat on the bed beside her.

Tim broke the loud silence that hovered over the room. "So, you're just going to act like I'm not even here?"

"Why didn't you call first?" Andrea mumbled from under the pillow. "You should have known that I was still in bed. I am tired from working all night."

"Oh, Andrea, I haven't seen you all week, baby. I missed you, and I thought you would have missed me too. And I did call," he added. "You didn't answer the telephone."

"You've been avoiding all of my calls and giving me the cold shoulder. It seems that ever since I've been pregnant you've been acting funny."

"Avoiding you! Andrea, I've been studying hard and taking finals all week long."

Andrea pushed the pillow to the other side of the bed to reveal her face. "You never told me about any finals."

"Well, I have taken three so far, and I have one more on Wednesday. After that, I am all yours for the entire summer. I am also free right now," he smiled mischievously, while bending down to give her a kiss. Andrea smiled while puckering her lips.

"I missed you," Tim confessed again, as he stood up to undress.

Andrea sat up in the bed. "Why are you taking your clothes off?"

"Because I want to make love to you. Didn't you miss me?"

Andrea smiled and slowly pulled her gown over her head and waited for her fiancé to join her in the bed. Tim removed Andrea's underwear and glanced down at her naked body. Her belly was starting to protrude. First, he rubbed and kissed it, and then he zipped his tongue all the way up to her lips. He placed it in her mouth and climbed into the bed, on top of her. He kissed her again, and Andrea moaned, as he slid himself inside her. Compassionately, she stretched her arms out around Tim's neck, as he slowly stoked her with his love. She rocked her body with his and cried out with approval. Within minutes, his stiffness was rolling steadily in and out of her. She whispered in his ear, as her hips gyrated against his erect penis. Tim rolled his wet tongue behind her ear, and Andrea purred like a kitten. Tim's genius strokes sent chills through her body. Tears of perspiration draped them. Andrea wrapped her legs around Tim's back, and moved her body to his smooth rhythm. Up, and down, he stroked her; in and out, they rocked in a chorus. Suddenly, Tim breathed heavily as his body locked with hers. Thrusting, his body stroked her rapidly. Andrea threw her head back, closed her eyes, and moaned. Tim later collapsed on top of Andrea, as they each blurred moans of euphoric satisfaction. For a moment she lay there mesmerized. She felt very relieved, and was happy that Tim decided to stop by. Whatever her reasons were for being mad at him, had been stroked from her memory, with the sexual seduction he'd put on her. After getting dressed, they walked downstairs to the kitchen so Andrea could fix some breakfast.

Tim sat at the kitchen table, totally turned on by observance of his pregnant fiancé, standing in front of the stove, preparing a hearty breakfast of scrambled eggs, bacon and toast. He couldn't wait until they were married so that he could be graced by her presence everyday.

When Andrea finished with breakfast, she and Tim sat down and ate together. Andrea took a bite from her bacon. "I have my first doctor's appointment at twelve o'clock on Wednesday. I want you to go with me. What time do you get out of class on Wednesday?"

The sudden frown on his face caused her blood pressure to rise. "Wednesday I have my science exam. Normally class is from eleven to one, but I can leave as soon as I'm finished with my final."

"That'll probably be chancing it and I was looking forward to you being there, Tim. I really didn't want to go alone."

"Well, can you reschedule, because there is no way for me to make up the exam if I don't take it on Wednesday?"

"No, I can't reschedule," she quickly retaliated.

Tim looked puzzled. "Well, Andrea if you'd have asked me about my schedule before making the appointment, then we could have avoided this. If you can't reschedule, then I won't be able to go, Andrea."

Andrea quickly jumped up from her chair and walked over to the counter. She filled a glass with water and stood at the sink, drinking it. "Tim, I can't show up at my first doctor's appointment unmarried and alone. How can you leave me to do this alone?" she screamed.

"Andrea, honey, I'm not intentionally leaving you to do this alone. If this was that important to you, why didn't you advise me before scheduling the appointment? Don't you think I want to be there to support the mother of my child?"

"I had to schedule the appointment around my work schedule, or wasn't that even a consideration? Do you think that you are the only one who has things to do?" she asked in an angry tone.

"Look, Andrea, let's not argue about this," Tim said, as he got up and walked toward her. He reached out to give her a hug, but Andrea shoved him away, yelling.

"Tim, I don't want to argue either. I just want you to be there for your child and me."

"Andrea, I think that you are being inconsiderate. What do you expect me to do? I can't go to the professor and ask to take my final at another time so that I can go on a doctor's appointment with my girlfriend. I can see if it weren't a final, then I could easily make-up the test, but unfortunately, that's not the case. There is no way that I can miss the final without failing the class."

"Okay, Tim, I just want you to leave," Andrea demanded. "I am not feeling well, and I don't feel like arguing with you." She spoke vainly as she rubbed her stomach.

Tim shook his head, while looking dead into Andrea's watering eyes. He could not believe the way she was behaving. Again, he tried to give her a hug, but Andrea put up her hands, warning him off. Tim backed away and shook his head. "Okay, Andrea," he sadly responded. "I'll leave. Maybe tomorrow you'll feel a little bit better." Tim grabbed his keys from the table and headed for the door.

Andrea walked behind him without saying anything. After he stepped out the door, Andrea yelled to him. "Why would I expect you to be here to support me with this baby, when you were never there to support the first one?" Her tone was frigid, before slamming the door in his face. Andrea ran upstairs to her bedroom shouting, "Fuck you, Tim. I don't need your white ass." As soon as she reached her bedroom, she fell onto the bed, and wept into her pillow.

CHAPTER 26

Punkin's eyes popped up and shuttered repeatedly as they tried to focus. The morning sunlight was peeking through the seams of the off-white vertical blinds that covered the window. She lifted her head, wiped the sleep from the corners of her eyes, and looked over at her sleeping Bo. Mark was still dead to the world. Punkin smiled and leaned back into the arms of her King. She scooted in closer to Mark and relaxed her head on his chest. The fragrance of the Dolce & Cabana shower gel was still embedded in his skin. She sniffed and inhaled the lingering aroma of what seemed to be her man's signature scent. It smelled as if it were made to grace the remnants of his dark brown skin. Punkin marveled up at the ceiling of the honeymoon suite that her husband had carried her into, right after their private nuptial ceremony. Still not believing that it had all happened, Punkin felt delighted, as well as overwhelmed to be the first Mrs. Charlotte Woods.

Since she'd taken on her new title, she and her new husband had remained locked away in their suite making sweet, passionate love. Mark introduced Punkin to what being his Queen was all about. First of all, he had reserved a room at the most expensive, five-star hotel in town, The Grand Plaza. It was situated downtown, and their room, on the fifteenth floor, overlooked the Grand River.

Once they entered the room, Mark placed Punkin's feet on a bed of red rose petals. When Punkin looked around the room she noticed that the rose petals led to the king-sized bedroom suite, which was covered with the rose petals as well. Burning candles were sitting on each of the nightstands, beside the bed, and on the table in the dining area. Not knowing what to expect, she stood there wondering what Mark's next move would be.

He kissed her lips softly as they stood in the corridor of the room. In a melodious voice, while undressing her, Mark explained what he was about to do.

"After I undress you, I want to see your naked body strut into the bathroom. Tonight I am going to purify you, since it's official that you belong to me, and me only, now. I want you to join me in a bubble bath, where these hands will wash every part of your body. These juicy lips and strong tongue want to explore you from head to toe. Tonight, there is no place I won't go," he warned.

Punkin smiled bashfully, as she lifted her arms and allowed her husband to pull her dress over her head. To get a good look at her bareness, he paused for a few minutes. He unsnapped her bra, then kissed her nipple. It sent chills up her spine.

"First, I'll make love to you in the bubbling Jacuzzi," he paused as he kissed the other nipple, "and then I'll carry you, my Queen, to the bed where I will place your beautiful, wet body down on the satin sheets, and make sweet, sweet love to you again. I want to know what every part of you tastes like, what every part feels like. For so long, my Sunshine, I've wanted to make love to you until our bodies collapse from fatigue, and tonight, is the night," Mark said, as Punkin stepped out of her thong. He turned her body around and tapped her on the ass. As it jiggled, Mark's eyes lit up like the night skies on the Fourth of July. He quickly undressed. Punkin stood directly in front of him and gyrated her body into a sensual dance that made her butt bounce up and down. Mark's adrenaline pumped something fierce. He was sweating and his penis aimed directly at her.

"Damn, baby, don't do that," Mark said as he walked up to her. He wrapped his arms around her waist and pushed her toward the bathroom.

While the tub filled, Mark poured the champagne in the flutes that sat beside the tub. He handed her a glass, and after a toast, they each sipped a bit, and smiled. Mark continued to kiss his wife all over as she purred like a wild cat in heat. The two of them were so tired, after several rounds of lovemaking; they eventually collapsed in each other's arms.

The next two nights they spent at the hotel were very similar to the first. After night two, Punkin swore to Mark that he'd secretly taken some Viagra or something because he had so much energy. She begged him to stop wanting her.

"Baby, I think that I've taken all that I can take. One more round could result in me soaking this thang in some ice for the rest of the night. Please save some of your energy for after the honeymoon," she told him.

Mark smiled and promised that he'd try to make himself stop wanting her. "I can't help it that your stuff is so good," he stated as he lay down in the bed, next to her. The next thing Punkin heard from him was him snoring.

She and Mark were heading to church from the hotel. Punkin couldn't wait until after church so she could go to her place to get some of her things. Since it was nearing nine o'clock., and they had to be checked out of the room, and dressed for church by eleven, she figured she'd get up and get dressed, so that by the time Mark awakened, she would pretty much be ready to go. She eased out of the bed without waking her husband, when she heard a knock on the door.

Punkin rushed to the door, and looked out the peephole to see who it was. It was room service, with the breakfast that Mark had pre-ordered for them. Scattering around the room to find a robe, Punkin yelled, "hold on," as she found something to slip on. Within seconds, she slipped into her robe and headed for the door again. The attendant happily pushed the tray into the room, uncovered each dish, and then turned to leave. Punkin stopped him and gave him a $5 tip, and then she closed the door behind him. When she turned around, Mark was sitting up in the bed, trying to wake up.

"Breakfast has arrived, Baby." Punkin cheerfully stated.

Mark wiped his eyes with the back of his hand. "What do we have?"

"What you ordered," Punkin responded. "Bacon, smoked ham, scrambled eggs, hash browns, toast, fruit, and orange juice. Care to join your wife for breakfast?"

Mark slowly got out of bed and walked his naked body to the bathroom. Right away, Punkin fixed two plates. She picked up a piece of the crisp bacon and ate it. Mark soon joined her at the table. They ate quietly. After breakfast Mark headed for the shower.

They hadn't spoken to any friends or family since they'd gotten married. Punkin was so busy being wrapped up in bed with her new husband that the rest of the world didn't even exist. Mark had gotten several calls on his business phone, but he refused to answer any of them. All the business he had would be handled after his honeymoon was over. Punkin knew that everyone was going to flip as soon as they found out that she and Mark had eloped.

The Pastor dismissed the morning congregation and as soon as Dorothy was let out of the sanctuary, she maneuvered her way through the crowd to find her friend Punkin.

During service, she and Brother Woods announced that over the weekend they'd gotten married in a private wedding ceremony. Dorothy, amongst others, was shocked. She could not believe her best friend had married and hadn't even told her. Dorothy walked right up to Mrs. Woods, and grabbed her arm, leading her away from the couple that had stopped her and Mark to say congratulations.

"I can't believe that you went off and eloped. You are lucky that we are in this church or I would really give you a piece of my mind," Dorothy warned.

Punkin remained silent, but smiled as she stuck out her left hand to reveal her wedding band to Dorothy. "Can you believe it, Dorothy?" she asked. "I's married now," she joked, mocking Shug Avery from the movie, *The Color Purple*.

Dorothy couldn't suppress her laughter. She then reached over and hugged her friend. "No wonder I haven't been able to reach you all weekend, and where did this here wedding take place?" Dorothy's tone was speculative.

"We got married at the courthouse on Friday morning. I've been Mrs. Mark Woods for exactly three days now and, I'm loving every minute of it. After church, I am going to go to my apartment to pick up some of my things, since I'll be moving in with my husband."

There was a brief pause in their conversation. "Well, Mrs. Woods, I guess I'll have to send your invitation to the baby shower to your new address."

"That'll be just fine," Punkin proudly responded.

"Well, be looking out for it. Sullivan will be mailing them in a day or two. My sister is covering all expenses. She has rented a hall, and a caterer," Dorothy lastly stated, as she prepared to walk away, as their husbands walked up.

"Ready, baby?" Mark reached out to hug Dorothy. Sullivan and the children stood to the side waiting.

"Sure am," Punkin answered, after speaking to the children.

"Well, guys, congratulations again, and we hope to see the both of you next week," Sullivan said. Afterwards, he placed his arm around Dwayne's shoulder and walked with him toward the door. Dorothy and the others followed.

Mark took a good look at his wife standing next to him, looking extremely beautiful in her navy blue dress. He pulled her into his arms and gave her a long hug. During their embrace, he whispered something into her ear. Punkin's eyes lit up and the corners of her mouth turned, revealing her excitement. Soon, another member of the congregation walked up to them. Realizing that they were not alone in the room, the couple separated and quickly extended their hands to greet the brother. Brother Smith wished them a successful marriage. He also reminded them that if they kept God first, things would work out fine. Afterwards, he was quickly on his way.

Before exiting the church, Punkin asked Mark to hold up while she went to the ladies room. "Wait here," she instructed Mark. Afterwards, she quickly headed toward the bathroom, without waiting for her husband's comment. Mark shook his head, and walked over near the exit door so that he would be in his wife's view once she exited the bathroom.

Sister Sylvia Wilson noticed Brother Woods standing alone by the door, so she decided to go over and offer her congratulations while he was free. She'd attempted to tell him earlier, but someone else walked up.

Mark noticed Sylvia approaching him. His smile depleted. The smile she was carrying made him think she was up to one of her devious schemes. Sylvia was a very attractive slim, dark-skinned woman that Mark had taken a liking to right away, when he became a member of the church. She was Deacon Brown's niece.

"Good afternoon, Brother Woods." She paused in front of him.

"Sister Wilson," Mark remarked, hesitantly.

"I just thought that I would come over and wish you well in your marriage. I didn't even realize that you were dating anyone long enough to propose a marriage."

"Yeah, Sister Charlotte and I have a love like no other I've experienced. No other woman has fulfilled me the way she has. I had to marry her. I couldn't risk letting her get away," Mark happily bragged, hoping to make Sylvia jealous. "Our love is so genuine. I think we have a special connection," he commented. "I think that I have truly been blessed to find my soul mate."

Sister Wilson's nose turned up. She knew that this strange woman, who popped up out of the blue was not all that Mark was making her out to be. He couldn't have known that much about her, and relationships didn't develop into perfection over night. Sylvia knew that Mark was trying to make her jealous. Sister Wilson and Mark had dated for a short time, but after a while, Mark kindly told her that he didn't want to see her anymore. Sylvia didn't take it too well, though. During their short dating period, Mark found Sylvia to be too needy, in a gold digger kind of way, so he had to let her go. He found her to be the type of woman who would leap incredible bounds, if you were talking the right dollar amount. All you had to do was show her the dollars, and she was down for whatever. It was sad how she thought that attending church every Sunday would cleanse her of all the sins she committed throughout the week.

"I'm sorry that I can't stick around to meet this perfect woman," Sylvia snidely remarked," but I've got to go. I'm meeting someone for lunch, and I don't want to be late."

Mark's smile resurfaced. She was bad news and he'd tried hard to keep his distance since their break-up. He was more than delighted that she had a date. Even though it had been months since Mark broke things off with Sylvia, it didn't stop her from calling his phone anytime she didn't have anyone to cuddle up with at night.

"I hope your wife will accept you with your baggage," Sylvia lastly stated as she handed him a folded copy of the program from morning service.

With a peculiar look on his face, Mark accepted the program. He had no idea what Sylvia was up to, but from the looks of things, it wasn't good. In his own defense, he answered, "My wife accepts me just as I am," he smiled with glee, happy to have something to rub in her face.

Disgustingly, Sylvia shook her head and walked off. Before Mark could look to see what was inside the program, his wife emerged from the ladies' room. Punkin was headed his way with a huge smile on her face.

"I'm ready," Punkin smiled when she approached her husband. Nervously, Mark stuffed the program in his jacket, grabbed his wife's hand, and the two of them exited the church together.

Mark opened the car door and waited for Punkin to take her seat. She had her cell phone in her hand and was waiting for Chalon to pick up. With his mind a million miles away, he closed the passenger door and slowly eased to the other side of the car. Inconspicuously, Mark pulled out the program to see what Sylvia had stuck inside. He was sure that it wasn't the program that Sylvia was trying to get to him. Sylvia always had an ulterior motive, so Mark was nervous about what he would find inside. She was famous for expressing herself through words, so Mark figured it was another one of her love letters expressing how much she needed him in her life.

Inside the program was a small piece of folded white paper. The stationary was from some doctor's office. Inside the body of the letter stated: Results from HIV Antibodies Test. Immediately, his hands trembled as his eyes continued to scan the paper from top to bottom. Beads of sweat beads formed on his forehead, as the palms of his hands became moist. Mark's eyelids fluttered as the word *Positive* seemed to glow in his eyes like the rays from the morning sun. He suddenly became null and void as the thought of himself being possibly infected with the virus crossed his mind. How would he tell his wife that he had possibly contracted the HIV virus, and that she might be at risk? Shaking the thought away, Mark ran his hands through his head, and then he read over the document again. After reading it for the third time, he folded the paper into a small piece, and then stuck it back into his pocket. He tried to regain his composure by telling himself that he couldn't possibly be infected but that didn't work. He'd have to be tested before telling his wife. The blood test that they took prior to getting married, was to determine if they were kin, it wasn't to detect sexually transmitted diseases.

He took a quick glance inside the car to see if his wife was still on the telephone. He heard her saying goodbye, so without further ado, Mark climbed into the car with a smile. His wife immediately delivered the message sent by their son, Chalon.

"That was Chalon. He told me to tell you hi and congratulations. I told him that we got married and he was somewhat disappointed, although he still is happy for us and wishes us well."

"What a thoughtful young man," Mark eased out, in a distracted tone. His mind was still gone, although he tried not to make it seem obvious. He wanted to be able to concentrate on what his wife was saying, but the thought of dying overpowered his thoughts.

Punkin obviously had not sensed the distraction in his voice, nor had she noticed that he was deathly worried about something. She continued to go on and on about what she had promised to get for Chalon the next time they went to the mall. "All that boy ever thinks about is shopping," she continued.

As soon as they arrived home, Punkin went to the bedroom to change out of her Sunday clothes so that she could prepare an intimate dinner for them. She prepared the meal, and set the table, and then she headed for the bathroom to take a quick shower before they ate.

The minute Mark heard the running water he picked up the telephone and stepped outside. He quickly dialed Sylvia's telephone number and waited for her to answer the telephone. He was so nervous, gritted his teeth, his jaws flexing. He wanted to get Sylvia straight before his wife caught wind that something was going on. If the HIV scheme was another one of Sylvia's plots to get close to him, he didn't have time for it. She needed to go on with her life and leave him alone.

"Hello," she answered.

"Sylvia, this is Mark and I'm calling to let you know that the game you are playing is not funny," he huffed angrily.

"Oh, hey, Baby," she remarked when Mark let her get a word in.

"Look, Sylvia, I don't have time to play these childish games with you. Why in the world would you stoop so low as to get a fake HIV test? Do you actually think that's going to help you get me back? Don't you understand that I have gone on with my life? I didn't want you then, and I definitely don't want you now. What is wrong with you?" he yelled.

"Look, Mark, this is not a joke, and the paper was not a fake." She chuckled softly before becoming completely irate. "I was tested positive for HIV," she yelled, "and the paper that I gave you was the original that I got from the nurse at the clinic. The counselor advised me to contact all my previous sex partners so they can get tested. Since you refused to answer any of my calls, I had no other choice but to present to you what I had in writing. I knew you wouldn't believe me. If I hadn't gotten through to you then a nurse from the health department would have been paying you a visit. I called myself doing you a favor."

Mark was perspiring with sweat. His undershirt was starting to stick to him. "Well I'm not worried because I just took a blood test a couple weeks ago and the test results came back negative," he retaliated.

"Well, I don't know what type of blood test you took, but I'm warning you that you need to go down and have yourself checked. I have no idea who gave this mess to me, but I'm trying to look out for you by informing you. You can do what you want to do. The first time that I took the test it came up negative, but the second one was positive. Sometimes the virus can be in your system and not be detected in the early stages. I'm telling you this for your own good, Mark," Sylvia concluded.

Mark heard a sudden crack in Sylvia's voice. He could tell that she was crying.

"You need to tell your wife to get tested too, because I know you've been giving it to her, the way you used to give it to me." She paused. "I miss you Mark," she cried.

Mark tried to recall the times that he'd spent with Sylvia. They had dated during a course of about two months before he broke it off with her. They'd slept together numerous times during those few months, sometimes using protection and sometimes not. Although he hated to admit it, he could very well be at risk of having contracted the virus.

He could hear Sylvia sniffling and crying, and he actually felt sorry for her. She was only thirty-two years old, she had no children, and here she was discovering that her body was harboring a deadly disease. "Has anyone that you contacted tested positive yet?"

"No," she sniffled. "So far, I am the only one who has tested positive. I pray that your results are negative. I would hate to think of myself as being the one to hinder you from living a happy life with your new bride. And by the way, how will you break the news to her? Have you ever told her about us?"

"I thank you for sharing the information with me, Sylvia," Mark said, ignoring her question, "and I will be sure to get in touch with you when I get the results of my test back."

"All right," she cried. "I'm sorry Mark, and no matter how things turn out, I will always have a place in my heart for you." She then hung up.

As Mark stood in his front yard daydreaming, he wondered how he would tell Punkin about this, and how could he go into the house and make love to her, when he knew that is what she was inside preparing for. More so, how would he refrain from making love to his wife in the days to come? They were newlyweds. If he told Punkin, it would surely bring an end to their beautiful, new relationship, and he didn't want to risk that, he loved Punkin too much.

He walked back into the house and noticed that his wife hadn't made it back to the kitchen. While contemplating a plan, he paced the living room floor hoping to come up with an answer to his problem. He continued to pace the floor for about ten more minutes before a thought came to mind. To avoid having sex with her, he would suddenly fall sick, maybe an upset stomach that would at least buy him about a week. Then, he would secretly be tested without telling his wife. Should the test results come back positive, then, and only then, will he reveal anything to Punkin. In his heart, Mark felt bad about having to keep a secret from his wife, but he had to. He didn't want to get her all worked up without having some hard proof of what Sylvia was claiming. He'd never loved a woman the way that he loved Punkin, and he was afraid of losing her. For such a long time he'd been praying for someone like her, and now that God had finally answered his prayers, Mark's past was coming back to haunt him.

CHAPTER 27

Mark secretly went to the health department the day after Sylvia had given him the news. Since he had not informed his wife about taking the test, he couldn't help but to be on edge waiting to receive the test results. He hated to admit it, but ever since he left the clinic, Mark seemed to be irritated and more aggravated than usual; quick to lose his temper. Everything Punkin did bothered him. He didn't like the person that he was turning into, and it wasn't fair to her, that he was harboring such a secret. He knew it would not take long before Punkin would become suspicious of him not wanting to have sex. In a matter of days, Mark had gone from not being able to take his hands off of his wife, to not touching her at all. There was no way that he could let her know the real reason why he was wasn't being intimate with her.

That Friday, as Punkin busied herself in the bathroom mirror getting ready for Dorothy's baby shower, her husband walked into the bathroom to help her get a rush on things. "Are you ready yet?" he asked as he stood at the door.

Punkin took a spin and faced him with a smile on her face. "How do I look, baby?"

"Is that what you're wearing to the baby shower?" Mark questioned with a dissatisfying look on his face.

Punkin had on a pair of sleek black jeans, and a short sleeve pink and black shirt. Her smile faded as she looked at her husband, who didn't appear to be too happy. "What's wrong with what I have on?" she asked as Mark's eyes surveyed her body from head to toe.

"Well, for one, those jeans look two sizes too small. Have you forgotten that you are a married woman?"

Punkin was confused. "What does me being a married woman have to do with what I'm wearing?" Punkin was becoming irritated.

Mark didn't speak. Instead, he walked up close to his wife and pulled her into his arms. He gave her a big hug and gripped her backside. "I don't want anyone staring at all this. This is for your man's eyes only." His obvious jealously turned her on. Since Punkin and her husband had not had sex in almost a week, she was vulnerable. The slightest little touch by her husband set her body on fire.

"Baby, you ain't got nothin' to worry about. This is all yours" She planted a gigantic kiss on her husband's lips. "And you better quit grabbing me like that before we end up arriving a little late to the baby shower. Now, go, so that I can touch up my lipstick and then I'll be ready."

A few minutes passed before Punkin emerged from the bathroom with a smile on her face. "I'm ready."

As they walked toward the car, Mark commented, "I am going to have to take you on a shopping trip so that we can purchase you an entirely new wardrobe, because I can't have my wife walking around looking like an unmarried woman."

"Now how does an unmarried woman look?"

"She wears loose clothing; not clothing that clings to her body and reveals all of her curves."

"Well, Mark, I happen to be a curvaceous woman, and these curves are going to be revealed in anything that I wear. And, as I recall, it was these curves that caught your attention when I was an unmarried woman," she mouthed, while rolling her eyes. "Don't be a hypocrite." They climbed into the vehicle.

As they rode off down the street, Mark warned to his wife, "And that feistiness is another thing that we are gonna have to work on."

Punkin rolled her eyes and gazed out of the window. She wasn't giving any thought to what he was talking about, and she was not about to let him piss her off before she made it to the baby shower.

The shower was held at a reception hall on the corner of Franklin and Sheldon. Caroline had the event catered by a local barbeque restaurant. There were already lots of people there when Punkin and her husband arrived. The hall was decorated with the theme colors of yellow and blue. Streamers, balloons, and confetti were all over the place. The tables were covered with fancy white tablecloths, and some of the chairs had yellow and blue bows attached to the back of them. It was easy to tell that Dorothy had no input in what was going on. At the front of the hall sat a large table with two large chairs sitting behind it. It was the designated table for the parents to sit and open the gifts, and gifts were being brought in by everyone who walked through the door.

When Punkin and Mark walked in, Punkin headed toward Dorothy, who she located immediately amongst the room full of people.

After exchanging hugs, Dorothy pointed Punkin to her and Marks designated seats. Punkin was excited to see that Caroline had assigned their seats up front, near Dorothy's table. After she and Mark took their seats, Punkin surveyed the room to see if she noticed any familiar faces. She smiled and waved at the few people she did know. It surprised Punkin that so many men were there. If she had known, she would have left her cock-blocking husband at home so that she could let loose and be herself. She had no idea that Mark was such a jealous man.

Monet, her siblings, and her son all were seated at the table with Mark and Punkin, so when Caroline announced that it was time to eat, Monet followed Punkin up to the serving table. Monet looked over the buffet to see what her stomach was hungry for. There were so many choices; she didn't know what to decide on. The table was displayed with buffet pans of BBQ chicken, pork ribs, potato salad, mixed greens, fruit salad, and a medley of steamed vegetables. For dessert there was chocolate and lemon cake, banana pudding, and peach cobbler. Caroline, as usual, went all out. Since Dorothy was having her fifth child, and never had a baby shower, Caroline said that she wanted the shower to be the best one her sister had ever had. Monet decided to sample a little bit of everything she could get on her plate. What she didn't put on her plate, she placed on Deshawn's.

It didn't take long for guests to get their plates and start eating. Later, the hired help collected the soiled dinnerware, and the games started shortly afterwards. Caroline had come up with fun and interesting games that all the ladies, and even the guys enjoyed. Once everyone got wind of the nice gifts that Caroline was giving out, they all wanted to get in. Monet won the "guess the weight of the mother game" and the prize was a $50 BP gas card. She was so excited when she went up to collect her prize that one would think that she'd won a car.

Dorothy and Sullivan could not believe how many gifts they had to open, but they opened each gift with Christmas excitement. They felt so blessed to have so many people who cared for them and the baby.

"Thank, you," Dorothy kept saying after she would pull the last strip of paper away from the concealed gift. She was so happy, that she cried tears of joy. Every other pregnancy for her was a long and lonely one. But finally, she was experiencing the essence of having a new baby. When she was pregnant with Monet, she was alone because she was naive a teenager who'd made the mistake of letting a boy talk her out of her virginity. She ended up pregnant and alone, because Tony had gotten what he wanted and had moved on to the next girl who would give it up like she had. Sadly, every time that she got pregnant with either of Delvin's children, her ex-husband, Delvin had been in jail for some reason or another. This was the first pregnancy that she was truly experiencing joy. This time she didn't have to worry about how the bills were going to get paid while she was down for her six weeks. When she was pregnant with her daughters, Tonya and Keisha, she had to return to work four weeks after giving birth. Times were so hard then, she had no other choice. It was either return to work or ask Caroline for a loan, and before she had to kiss her sister's butt to get a few dollars, Dorothy gave in and headed back to work. Monet was her support system because, without her to baby-sit, Dorothy didn't know what she would have done. Thinking about how far she'd come, and how much she'd accomplished made Dorothy shed more tears than she wanted to. She cried for every child that she had brought into the world under those horrible circumstances. She always prayed that God would one day make a better way, and her life was living proof of His miracles. An unplanned and unwanted pregnancy was turning out to be her best childbearing experience.

As the party came to a close, Dorothy and her husband stood at the door thanking the guests as they exited. Dorothy looked around the room and noticed Punkin giggling with some guy on the other side of the room. Her husband Mark was sitting at the table, drinking on his drink, but he never took his eyes off of her. Dorothy knew Punkin like the back of her hand, and although she was married, and it had only been for a short period of time, people didn't change overnight. Dorothy soon maneuvered her way over to

Punkin and the man to make their conversation not seem as intimate as it looked. Punkin, who was, as usual, very friendly with the men, was so indulged in a conversation with some man, that she didn't even notice Dorothy walk up. And, even though it could have very well been an innocent conversation, it didn't look that way, and Dorothy knew that she had to do something, because the way Mark was glaring over at them, he wasn't liking what he was seeing. Dorothy didn't want there to be any mess with the newlyweds at her baby shower.

Dwayne, Sullivan, and Thomas carried the gifts to the car as the women straightened up the place. The hired help had cleared all the tables but hadn't wiped them down, so Punkin tried to lend a hand with the clean up. Caroline absolutely refused. Punkin was a guest of the party and wasn't allowed to lift a finger to do anything.

"Girl, please, we've got plenty of help. Andrea and the rest of them girls are going to take care of cleaning these tables. You go on home, and we sho' 'preciate you comin."

Punkin hesitated for a minute. "Well, I guess I'll see you later then, Big Mama." She was teasing Dorothy. "Call me in the morning," Punkin said lastly with a wave. "Bye, y'all," she concluded on her way to the door."

"I will," Dorothy answered. "And your behind is wider than mine, and you ain't even pregnant," she retaliated. "Na." She stuck her tongue out at Punkin who had no comment.

In return, Punkin gave Dorothy the finger, and she and Mark exited the building.

Mark asked Punkin if she could drive home because he wasn't in the mood for driving, and besides he had been drinking. Punkin probably would have been drinking had she not been up in some man's face, running her mouth all night.

The car veered onto the highway and Punkin slowly eased her way into the middle lane and coasted. Mark was laid back in his seat. He hadn't said much since they'd left the party, and she hoped that he wasn't still mad about her not wanting to change her outfit before they left home. To make sure that he wasn't mad, she turned down the radio and said, "Don't be over there looking like you are tired. You know you have to put in some work once we get home. I don't know why you've been holding out on me lately, but I can't take it anymore. I'm ready."

Mark didn't answer right away. He sat up straight in his seat. He looked over at Punkin with rage in his eyes. He spoke in an angry tone.

"I see now that I can't take you nowhere without you acting like a ho. I need to get you trained right away, on how to conduct yourself as a respectful woman, because every time I looked around tonight, you were up in some man's face giggling and shit. I knew you put on those tight ass jeans for a reason. You just ain't showed me no respect," Mark argued. "I bet you wished I hadn't even come tonight. I bet I blocked a lot of your action."

Her eyes squinted as her thoughts recalculated what her ears heard. Punkin's neck jerked backwards. Her tongue was frozen. For a moment, she tried to figure out if her husband had said what she thought she'd heard. "WHAT?" she finally gasped, her eyes now stolen from the road and focused on the stranger occupying the passenger seat.

"You can act like you don't know what I'm talking about if you want to. I saw how you were all up in those men's faces at the party. You were caring on as if I weren't even there."

"Look, Mark," she yelled. "We're going to have to get some shit straight, right here and damn now. Just because you're my husband, don't mean that you are going to get away with talking to me fucking crazy. I ain't the one. If your jealous ass can't accept the fact that I AM going to talk to other guys, then you might as well walk away right now, because I am going to talk to whoever the fuck I feel like talking to, when I get ready to talk to them." Although she tried to hold back, the old Punkin had emerged. The car was rolling about eighty miles an hour down the highway. Punkin's neck was busy swaying from side to side, as she cursed her husband. She was so mad she felt like pulling his car over to the side and walking the rest of the way to her apartment. Here she was not even completely moved in with Mark, and he was already tripping. Her finger rose into the air as Punkin continued yelling.

"And furthermore, I ain't never had no man talk to me any kind of way, and I ain't about to start. Husband or no mother-fucking husband, I will leave your black ass, and won't think nothin' of it. Don't play with me," she warned.

"I know one thing. That mouth is going to get you into a lot of trouble. You better practice learning how to talk to me with respect, and without raising your damn voice," Mark threatened. "I ain't going to have you talking to me like I'm your child."

"Whatever, Mark. You sound like a foo–"

Before she could finish her sentence, SMACK went the back of Mark's hand into the side of her face. The tips of his finger stung her lip. She heard the flesh separating when his fingernail cut through it. For a moment, she saw vivid darkness, and then she felt a stinging sensation penetrating the right side of her face. It went numb. A trickle of blood dripped from her bottom lip, and fell onto her shirt. Out the corner of her eye, she could see Mark nodding his head with a satisfying look on his face. She snapped out of her trance and grabbed her face. The car was veering in and out of traffic.

"Now keep on talking," he sneered. "I'm gon' have to show you better than I can tell you."

As he let the last word pass, Punkin's right fist crushed into the left side of Mark's face. "Are you crazy?" she yelled with satisfaction.

Once Mark realized what had taken place, he lifted his fist and punched Punkin. Punkin, in return, swung as many licks as she could while trying to stay focused on the road. The car continued swerving in and out of lanes. While trying to protect herself by dodging fists, Punkin tried to maneuver the car to the side of the road. She tried to block as many of his punches as she could while still driving, but that didn't prove to be effective. Mark's fists were packed with power and the only way that Punkin could defend herself was to stop the car, dead in the middle of the street. Other commuters passed them blowing their horns, but Punkin could've cared less. She eventually was able to maneuver the car to the shoulder of the highway, and put it into park.

Immediately, she unfastened her seatbelt. "You could have made me run off of the road, you crazy motherfucker," she yelled. "Are you trying to kill me?"

Mark grabbed Punkin and pinned her to her seat, then he continued punching her in her face. She could not believe that he was swinging powerful man punches at her. Punkin's hair was wild, and her light-colored skin was bruising purples and blacks. As she felt her lip swelling, Punkin swallowed the blood that was surfacing in her mouth and continued fighting off her attacker. When her hand was able to maneuver the car door open, Punkin finally jumped out and ran around the car screaming. She hoped that someone would stop to rescue her from her deranged, and soon to be ex-husband. Her face was covered in blood and tears, her body was aching, and her heart was broken. She could not believe that Mark had turned into a totally different person so fast. Cars whipped past them staring and honking.

"I want a divorce," Punkin cried. "I can't believe that you put your hands on me Mark. I thought that you loved me. Now I know that you ain't shit, just like the rest of the men. I wish I would have never married you."

"Come here, Charlotte," Mark demanded from the other side of the car.

"Don't call my name," she screamed. "Don't call my name never again, you psycho. I can't believe you did this," she cried.

"Come on and get in the car," Mark begged. His angry tone had turned into a concerned caring one.

"Fuck, you," Punkin shouted at him.

Mark spat and rubbed his hands through his hair. His face was covered in scratches. He also had a cut under his eyes that was stinging. He huffed and puffed trying to catch his breath. As he looked over at his distressed and abused wife, he now regretted hitting her. He couldn't believe that he'd lost control and lashed out on his wife the way he had. He didn't know what had come over him.

"Come on, Punkin, get in the car," he huffed after spitting a second time.

"I ain't going nowhere with you. I will walk before I get in the car with your psycho ass." Tears of frustration continued to pour from her eyes. "How could you do this to me, Mark?" Punkin looked down at her ripped blouse. "It ain't supposed to be like this," she bawled.

Mark wiped the sweat from his face, and then he quickly took off toward Punkin. She saw him coming, and she ran around to the front of the car, but Mark quickly caught up to her. He grabbed Punkin and threw her on top of the car. She threw her hands in the air, to block Mark from hitting her in her face again. Out the corner of her eyes she saw red and blue lights flashing and knew that God had finally sent someone to her rescue. Mark immediately froze and threw his hands up in the air, as instructed by the officer when he jumped out of his vehicle with his gun drawn.

"Now, slowly step away from the car, and turn away from me, but keep your hands up where I can see them," the very tall officer demanded. Cautiously, he approached the couple. He pulled out his handcuffs. "I got a call from someone who rode past here and observed you all fighting."

"Officer, we just came from a party and I was driving. He was beating me while I was driving so I pulled over and jumped out of the car. He was acting crazy, and I was trying to get away from him. Look at my face," Punkin cried.

Mark said nothing.

The officer didn't appear to be pleased with Mark, although his face bared a few battle scars. The officer placed his gun in his holster and asked Mark to place his hands behind his back.

Mark complied.

After placing the cuffs on his hands, the officer searched Mark's pockets. Since he was clean, the officer turned Mark around and asked him to stand against the car. Punkin was still standing by the front of the vehicle. She didn't want to stand too close to the police car because the lights were bright and she didn't want anyone passing by to recognize her. She waited while Mark told his side of the story to the police. The officer wrote down everything, afterwards determining that Mark was under arrest for domestic violence, and disorderly conduct. To her shocking surprise, after the officer placed Mark under arrest, he then asked Punkin to place her hands behind her back, because she was being placed under arrest and charged, right along with her husband.

"What the hell," Punkin lashed out at the officer. "Why am I being arrested?"

"Ma'am, I got a call that a couple was fighting, and when I pulled up, you guys were swinging at each other. I also observe wounds on your husband as well as on you, so I have to place the both of you under arrest. Since I'm unable to search you, and I don't have a female officer in the area, I'll restrain you in cuffs and you can be searched at the precinct."

Punkin cursed all the way to the back of the officer's car as they were driven away to the station together. She promised the officer that she would have his badge as soon as she was released. "I can't believe you're arresting me, the victim," she scowled.

Even though Mark kept repeating how sorry he was, Punkin remained with her head turned. She never wanted to hear his voice, never in life. Punkin cried. She could not believe that she'd been jumped on by her supposed-to-be, loving husband. She hadn't even been married a month yet, and already the marriage was over. There was no way that she was going back to Mark after what he'd done to her. Tonight, he'd shown his true self.

With obvious sympathy for Punkin, the officer peered in the back seat at Punkin's bruised face and let out a long sigh, while shaking his head. "Mr. Woods, you really should be ashamed of yourself."

Punkin glanced over at her husband as her drizzles of tears suddenly turned into a pouring storm. She had never been hit by a man, so Punkin was in total shock. She couldn't believe how bizarre the events of the day had played out. Her lip felt like it was three sizes larger and her right eye was so sore, that keeping it closed lessoned the pain. She had no clue what to do, because, officially, she was still a newlywed.

CHAPTER 28

Rhenee finished up her last set of dictations, before shutting down her computer and preparing to leave work for the evening. She peered out her office window and noticed that the day had turned into night while she'd been busy working. It was 9:20 PM., and she had arrived at the law firm a little after eight that morning. She couldn't wait to get home and soak her tired body in a hot bath. Rhenee slid her feet into her size eight-and-a-half pumps and rose from her seat. When her computer turned off, she grabbed her briefcase from the side of her desk and unlocked the clutch. She placed folders, from her desk, along with her hand held recorder, inside of the briefcase, in case she got in the mood for more work after she got home. She was grateful that Friday had come to end her work week.

Before exiting her office, she took one last look around to see if she was forgetting anything, before hitting the light switch and heading out, closing the door behind her. During the course of one week, Rhenee had worked nearly seventy hours, and her mind, body and soul was due for a break. Monday was the start of a new case for her, so she definitely could use the two days off to rejuvenate. As she strutted down the hallway, Rhenee pondered. *Working this much is the very reason that I'm without a man, now.* She shook her head disgustingly and resumed her thought, *Shit, when I did have a man, I worked so much, that I never had time to spend with him.* "I can't win for losing," she mouthed silently, as she pressed the button for the elevator, and stood in front of the stainless steel door, waiting for it to arrive.

As soon as the door slid open, Rhenee stepped into the twelve-by-twelve box and closed her eyes when the door closed. "Ooh, we," she yawned. "What a day, what a day." Rhenee hadn't had twenty hours of sleep, all week, and she could feel the bags starting to form under her eyes. Her body was so tired that she was contemplating giving the hot bath a rain check. She was so fatigued that all she could think about was hitting the bed. It was a relief that no one else was riding the elevator with her, because she didn't feel like seeing, or having to talk to anyone about law.

On the 8th floor, the elevator came to a halt, so Rhenee immediately fixed her clothes and put on a working smile. The door opened, and in stepped an attractive gentleman. Rhenee smiled at the thought of testosterone is her presence. She'd been sexually deprived for so long, that being in the attendance of a good-looking brother caused her clitoris to dance.

The gentleman stepped in and looked directly at her. She'd seen that look before. His eyes were asking her if it was okay to do her, right there in the elevator. Trying not to appear desperate, Rhenee moved in closer to him, hoping his body would do what his mind was imaging. Before she could place her briefcase on the floor, his tongue was down her throat. Her lips wrapped around his as his hands slipped under her skirt.

"I missed you so much, Rhenee," he whispered in her ear.

"I missed you too, baby," she mumbled through locked lips.

"I know that I've been a bad boy, treating you the way that I have lately, but you can punish me by inviting me over to make it all up to you," Ray said, as his hand came from under her skirt and wrapped around her waist.

"Oh," she exhaled, with her mouth wide open, saddened that his hand had stopped massaging her clit. Rhenee knew it wouldn't take long for him to come to his senses. "What about your wife," she asked, as he continued kissing her face and neck.

"She's back in Philadelphia."

"Again!" she quizzed.

"Her mother had a set back. They don't think that she is going to make it. Celeste told me that she'd be gone for at least a month."

"What happens to us, once she returns?"

"We'll cross that bridge once we get to it."

"How long will it take you to get to my house?"

"I can be right behind you," Ray answered separating his lips from hers.

"Okay," Rhenee happily answered, as the elevator door opened. Once they stepped out of the elevator, Rhenee told Ray that she'd meet him on the corner, right outside of the parking deck.

As Rhenee walked to her car, a smile as wide as Lake Michigan spread across her face. She hadn't had sex in over three months, and she knew Ray was going to give it to her the way she wanted it. She'd been patiently waiting for him to realize that he couldn't live without her, and now she was about to be rewarded for her endurance. The thought of knowing that she was about to get some was nearing her to a climax. Once she was in her car, and on the way out of the parking deck, she got a call from Ray. He was calling to see if she had any wine at her place. Rhenee told him that she didn't, so Ray said that he would stop at a Sprits shop to pick up a bottle, and he would meet her back at her place.

"All right," Rhenee agreed, before hanging up. Her face lit up like the morning sunshine. Today had to be her lucky day. Rhenee always knew that on paper, Ray was married to Celeste, but in essence, she was his wife. It sometimes bothered her that Ray wouldn't go ahead and leave the woman, but Rhenee was a firm believer in the saying "good things come to those who wait." Hell, if Ray wasn't acting like he was married to Celeste, then why should she? She didn't owe his wife anything. If wifey was smart she'd go ahead and divorce Ray, and then move back to Philadelphia to take care of her dying mother. He'd never been faithful to her anyway. Although Ray would never admit it, Rhenee knew that he didn't marry Celeste for love, because if he had, there was no way that he'd keep running back to her every chance that he got.

As soon as Rhenee made it home, she rushed into her apartment, threw down her briefcase, kicked off her shoes, and ran around the apartment gathering up all the outfits she'd worn throughout the week, to throw them into the closet. Next, she hurried into the kitchen to throw away all the empty food containers sitting around. She scurried through the apartment collecting soiled dishes to load them into the dishwasher. She didn't want Ray to see what a slob she really was. Rhenee simply didn't have time to clean up.

After Rhenee got the place to looking somewhat presentable, she hurried into the bathroom to get the jets going in her whirlpool tub. She filled the tub with bath beads, rose petals, and bubble bath, and then she grabbed a washcloth and rushed to the sink to freshen up before her date arrived. Back in the bedroom, Rhenee pulled out a sexy nighty and slipped into it. After Ray arrived, she would escort him straight to the bathroom where they could have a few glasses of wine in the Jacuzzi, and make plenty good love.

Ray walked in the door with a brown paper bag in his hand. He exhaled and immediately loosened his tie. His mouth fell wide open upon gazing at Rhenee in her two-piece nighty. The top half consisted of two spaghetti straps, attached to a couple of black, glittering pasties that barely covered her nipples, let alone her breasts. The bottom half of the outfit was a slinky g-string that revealed everything, and left nothing to the imagination. Rhenee was also wearing a shiny pair of five inch, black patented leather pumps. Her hair was swept into an up-do that tied in the back, and her make-up was flawless. Ray couldn't take his eyes off of her. "I don't know where you want this bag, but I know where I want you," he flirted.

Rhenee smiled, and turned away from Ray and switched seductively toward the kitchen. "You can bring the bag into the kitchen, and I have a fruit tray and some glasses out on the counter. And Counselor," she added, "you can have me anywhere you want me," she teased as she pursed her lips to kiss his.

Ray pulled her body in close to his, so close she could feel his aroused penis rubbing up against her. He reached around Rhenee's waist and gripped her behind.

"You better stop," she chided, as she pulled away from Ray and reached for the fruit tray on the counter. When she turned back toward him he was nearly naked. She smiled wickedly, and raised her brow. "Get the glasses and follow mama," she advised.

Without hesitation, Ray grabbed the wine and glasses, and followed Rhenee into her bathroom suite. Ray immediately jumped into the bubbling bath and invited Rhenee to join him. She slowly pranced over to the side of the tub with a whipped cream dipped strawberry in her hand. She knelt down beside him. He slid her g-string to the side, then took his finger and surveyed the slit of her center. One finger, than two, and then four finally entered her. Rhenee continued to stuff the strawberries into Ray's mouth. They both moaned systematically. "Ummh!"

She placed the tray of fruit onto the ledge of the tub, and grabbed another piece. Ray stood up in the water, and slid her panties over her hips and down her long silky legs. As they dropped to the floor, Rhenee stuck the fruit into her mouth and moaned. *Ooh*, as his magic fingers continued to dazzle her.

Ray's tongue gently slid across her semi-shaved patch of love, which caused Rhenee to flinch. "Ooh, I missed this thang right here," he moaned, as his tongue traveled up her stomach. His hand pulled back the pasty to reveal the full breast. He sucked her nipple into his mouth and held it there momentarily. "Come on, get in. What are you waiting for?"

Rhenee smiled while slipping out of her heels. With her hand wrapped around his, she slowly climbed in, joining Ray in the hot bubbling water. They wasted no time locking lips with each other. While taking brief breather breaks, Rhenee told Ray over and over how much she needed and missed him.

"I missed you too, baby," Ray told her as he suddenly gripped her waist and pulled her body from the water. Ray, still in the tub, got onto his knees as Rhenee sat on the ledge right above him. She had bubbles dripping from the area he was trying to get to. Wasting no time to give him what he wanted, Rhenee cocked her leg, gripped Ray's head, and then she drove his face right between her thighs.

His tongue quickly dug into the wet womb. His head moved back and forth inside her. With slow, easy thrusts, Ray eased his finger in and moved it out, simultaneously with his sopping wet tongue. Rhenee cried out with blissful pleasure. Ray was satisfying, a yearning that had been hoarding for way too long. After being pleased by Index, Pointer and Mr. Tongue, Rhenee was no longer able to restrain herself from dropping down onto the long stiff pole peeking up out of the bubbling water. She slowly slid down on the pole, rocking and maneuvering until all of Ray was inside her. He gripped her butt and waded in and out of her inviting tunnel of love.

She purred like Cat Woman, and in the heat of passion, she asked, "Is this pussy good enough to make you stay here with me? Is it good enough to make you leave her?"

"Yes, Yes, yes," Ray answered, as he rocked with her rhythmic flow. When his words slurred, Rhenee rode faster and with more thrusts. She knew that Ray was about to climax and she wanted it to be a joint conclusion, so Rhenee threw her head back and closed her eyes. She imagined being with him forever. He cried out, as his biological fluids released. His body stiffened. Rhenee's satisfying climax reached its peak. She gripped Ray's shoulders and jerked her body until her few seconds of euphoric pleasure came and went.

Resting her head against his chest, she exhaled. "When?"

"When, what," Ray panted.

"When can I look forward to you being here with me permanently?"

Ray pushed her off of him, and then he stood up and climbed out of the tub. "Now, why would you want to ruin a good time by bringing up something that you know I don't have a definite answer to?" he fussed.

Surprised at how quickly his demeanor had changed, Rhenee climbed out of the tub and mean-faced Ray. Without saying another word, she grabbed a drying towel and stormed off to her bedroom. She fell onto her bed and buried her face in the sheets. She felt like a fool. She wished she had never brought it up. Even though she was speaking what was on her mind, Rhenee didn't want to upset Ray so that he would want to leave. She didn't want to sleep alone, and she regretted saying anything to kill their good vibe. Rhenee didn't think it was fair for Ray to risk his marriage, by sneaking around to be with her, only to show up and have to argue about why he couldn't stay permanently. "Who wants a complaining mistress? Rhenee mumbled to herself. What she needed to do was be a patient woman. If she couldn't have Ray when she wanted him, the least she could do was try not to upset him, during the time they did have to enjoy each other.

Rhenee crawled over to him and apologized for upsetting him. Ray turned to Rhenee with open arms, and she gladly fell into them. They laid in silence for a few minutes until Ray rolled over on top of her and made love to her again, before they fell asleep in each other's arms.

"RHENEE, WAKE UP, WAKE UP. It's only a dream," Ray said as he continued shaking his mistress out of her apparent nightmare. "It's only a dream, Rhenee. Once you wake up, it'll all go away," he assured her.

Once she snapped out of her nightmare, Rhenee opened her eyes and wiped the tears from her face. She quickly looked in all directions to see if she was in deed in her own bed with Ray. Rhenee reached out and asked Ray to hold her. After their embrace, she hurried into the bathroom, closing the door behind her. She grabbed a washcloth, held it under the running cold water and wiped her face. *What a night for them to come back*, she thought, as she lowered the lid on the toilet, and took a seat.

Engrossed in tears for at least fifteen minutes before Ray called out, "Are you okay?"

"Yes," she cried out.

Standing at the door, Ray finally pushed it open. "Can I come in?" Rhenee quickly wiped away her tears, before he saw her face. "What's going on with you? This isn't about me leaving my wife, is it?"

"No," she sniffed without raising her head.

"Well, I know that it has got to be more than a bad dream that has kept you in this bathroom crying for twenty minutes. What's going on, Rhenee?"

"It hasn't been that long," Rhenee laughed, trying to sound happier than she felt.

"Well, I'm prepared to sit here and listen to you confess to me, about what it is that's bothering you, if it takes all night," Ray told her. Ray reached out for Rhenee. They walked back into the bedroom together.

Since she felt like she could trust him, Rhenee decided that she would tell Ray about what was bothering her. "Ray, I just want you to know that what I have done, I am not proud of."

He looked confused, not sure where the conversation was going.

"I have done a very bad thing that has come back to haunt me."

Still not sure what Rhenee was talking about, Ray continued to listen. Slowly, and as accurate as she could remember, she told her story while she and Ray sat on the edge of her bed. As Rhenee revealed the sordid details of the accident, Ray looked at her as if she was the worst kind of person that he'd encountered. In the end, Ray was so taken back, that all he could do was get dressed. He left abruptly. He never said bye or when he'd see her again, he just left.

Rhenee didn't know what to think. She had not expected Ray to react the way that he did. After he left, she called his cell but he didn't answer. The next day she tried him again, and got the same response. She didn't know if he was so upset that he never wanted to see her again, or what. She hoped Ray wasn't so mad that he'd expose her secret.

CHAPTER 29

Monet was counting down the days until her boyfriend, Malcolm, would be returning home from college, for summer vacation. In exactly eleven days she would be able to see her fiancé whom she had not seen in almost a year. With eleven days left, Monet's nights had been sleepless with anticipation of him coming home. She and Malcolm would have nearly three months to spend together and she couldn't wait. Malcolm's mother phoned and asked Monet if she could pick Malcolm up from the airport and drive him over to her house. Dr. Maddox said that she'd planned a surprise party, in her backyard, for her son's homecoming. She explained her plans for that day and, Monet enthusiastically told her soon-to-be-mother-in-law that she had no problem picking up Malcolm.

Monet really did like Malcolm's parents, especially his mother. When she and Malcolm first started dating, Monet thought his parents wouldn't like her because she was a teenage mother and Malcolm was a star player on the football team and had a promising future ahead of him. Since the Maddox's were an affluent, middle class family, Monet thought they would find her inadequate to be with Malcolm, but that was totally not the case at all. His parents were cool, and from day one, they didn't seem to pass judgment on her. After getting to know her, they probably figured that as long as Malcolm loved Monet, she was worthy of their love as well. That night when Malcolm called her, Monet was happy to tell him that she would be there to pick him up. He was equally as excited as she was.

Monet was out of school, on summer break and she was delighted with the idea of sleeping in, although she'd be starting a new job the following week. She'd been hired on as an intern at the hospital. She could use a few extra dollars in her pocket. "Only one more year to go," she mouthed, as she lay in bed thinking about her up and coming school year at a glance. She'd still be cutting corners to keep up on all her bills, but her earnings from the full-time job would definitely help. Her rent was the only bill that she paid in full, on a monthly basis, only because her landlord would not accept partial payments. If she didn't have the full $400 rent money, on the first of every month, she would be back at her parent's house living out of a room, so Monet always made sure to have all her rent money. She loved her independence too much. Going back home was absolutely not a part of her plans. Even though her parents were willing to help Monet out with making ends meet, she hated to ask them for money. She didn't want them thinking that she couldn't take care of herself and her son.

After graduating from college, she would no longer have to worry about struggling to make ends meet. Once she found a job working as a Physical Therapist, and she and Malcolm were married, they'd definitely have enough money to splurge with. Even with paying back student loans, they would have steady income to pay bills, and some extra money to put to the side for a rainy day.

She couldn't wait until child support enforcement caught up with Derrick. If she got a steady child support check from him, that would make things a little easier too. The last time that Derrick gave her anything to contribute to the well being of their child, was about two months prior. He stopped over, gave her $200 and told her to buy Deshawn shoes and an outfit. Instead, Monet used the two hundred to pay the remaining balance on her electric, and telephone bill. To this day, she still couldn't figure what she was thinking by being interested in Derrick.

The day that her fiancé was scheduled to arrive in town, Monet was at the airport almost two hours early. She didn't mind hanging out at the airport waiting for Malcolm to arrive. She was so anxious, she couldn't sit at home another minute without driving herself into a nervous frenzy. When the on-time arrival of Malcolm's flight was announced, Monet and Deshawn were the first two in line at the Delta Terminal. Her smile was wide and bright. She was so excited about her man's arrival that Monet flinched and straightened her clothes as the first class passengers exited the plane. She'd spent over two hours picking out the perfect outfit to wear, and another hour getting dressed and making sure that her hair was right. Monet was wearing her favorite pair of black Baby Phat jeans, and a short-sleeved, baby blue blouse. Her hair was flat-ironed silky straight, and it graced the middle of her back. With Deshawn attached tightly to her right hand, they continued waiting for Malcolm amongst the crowd of unloading passengers.

She recognized that cool walk anywhere. As her man strutted down the narrow hallway, sporting his red and black Atlanta Falcons jersey, Monet smiled as his slow-paced steps brought him closer into her view. Malcolm looked as if he'd gained about ten or fifteen pounds, but he was still fine. His hair was freshly cut, and his goatee was trimmed to perfection, making him appear a couple years older. He looked more masculine now, more like a man. When she could no longer resist, Monet took off toward her man. She pardoned and excused her way through the large crowd of people until she was within arms reach of Malcolm. She jumped into his arms, as he opened them to accept her embrace. Malcolm's duffle bag hit the floor, as he wrapped his arms around the only girl he'd ever loved. He missed her so much.

After he and Monet parted, Malcolm looked down at Deshawn, who looked as if he'd grown three inches taller. He rubbed the top of the boy's head and said, "I see you have gotten taller, Lil' Man. In a few more years you'll be almost as tall as I am," Malcolm exclaimed. "Give me five!" Deshawn held his hand out, palm side up as Malcolm slapped him five. "Have you been good?" Malcolm asked.

Deshawn nodded his head yes. Finally, the three of them walked through the airport toward baggage claim.

The car pulled up about three houses down from Malcolm's parents' house. After realizing this was the closest parking spot to the house, Monet turned off her car and pulled the key from the ignition.

"I can't believe that we have to park all the way back here. Somebody must be having a party. Look at all these cars out here," Malcolm said.

Since he was unaware that it was his party, Monet smiled and said. "I know that food smells real good. My nose can smell barbeque a mile away."

"I haven't had a home cooked meal in so long, I might pay my neighbor's a little visit. Maybe we'll just pop up to the party and blend in with the rest of the people. I can be a distant cousin," Malcolm joked. He and Monet laughed together as they climbed out of the car.

Deshawn had fallen asleep in the back seat, so Monet had to shake him a few times until his eyes popped open. After getting out, Monet reached into the backseat of the car and reached for him. "Come on mama's big man," Monet cooed. Deshawn climbed out of the back seat wiping his eyes. Once his vision was 20/20 he grabbed a hold of his mother's hand and walked with her and Malcolm down the street toward his parent's house.

Once they approached the private fenced backyard, Malcolm looked to Monet with a quizzical expression on his face. "I guess Ma is the one having the party. Look's like we made it right on time." It was apparent that he still had no clue as to what was going on. His mother had phoned Monet about ten minutes prior asking their whereabouts, and Monet inconspicuously explained that they were about ten minutes away from the house. Mrs. Maddox wanted to get everyone ready for the big surprise welcome they would yell as soon as Malcolm stepped through the door.

"Surprise!" The family yelled, when Malcolm pushed open the door of the fence. He gasped, as his eyes scanned the backyard and noticed all his cousins, friends, aunts and uncles.

"What is this, a Family Reunion?"

"No, son, it's a welcome home party," his mother spoke as she danced her way over to him. She and Malcolm hugged. and then she kissed the side of his face. "I knew you'd want a home cooked meal as soon as you got here, so I invited over a few friends and some kinfolk, so that we can all feast and party together."

Malcolm looked at Monet, who didn't seem to be surprised at all. "So you knew all about this ha?"

"You'll have to forgive me, boo, but I was sworn to secrecy." She gave him a big hug and promised not to keep anything from him again. Malcolm then tracked across the yard toward the food table. Not stopping, he greeted a few folks on his way. He was so hungry, he had to eat first, and then get his party on later.

After everyone finished stuffing their bellies, the D.J pumped up the volume on the music and told everyone that they needed to get up and dance off all the food they'd eaten.

"Come on everybody, up on yo feet. It's time to par..taay," Uncle Jeff yelled into the mic. One by one, they all got up and headed to the designated dance area of the yard. Monet nearly drug Malcolm out to where the crowd was establishing in the middle of the yard. Even though Malcolm was bashful, and couldn't stand dancing, he followed his fiancé's lead. Within minutes, he and Monet were bopping along with everyone else who was doing The Electric Slide. When he looked over at his father, Malcolm laughed, because his dad was in the front line of electric sliders, and he was the stiffest of them all.

You couldn't tell him that he wasn't jamming though. Mr. Maddox was so off beat that no one else could watch him without getting thrown off beat themselves. Even though Malcolm wasn't the best dancer, he did at least know how to keep up with the beat. He figured he must have inherited his rhythm from his mother.

The celebration came to a closing once the day turned to dusk. It seemed that everyone had enjoyed themselves, and they'd partied peacefully. Malcolm's mother, her two sisters, and a couple of the other women all helped get the backyard cleaned up. While some of them picked up trash around the yard, the others helped fold up the tables, and put away the left over food. Monet offered to lend a hand, but Dr. Maddox wouldn't hear of it, so she and Malcolm prepared to leave, since Deshawn was starting to show signs of sleepiness. Malcolm told his parents that he'd be over the next afternoon to spend some time with them. Before he and Monet left, Malcolm thanked everyone for coming.

Monet unlocked the door to her apartment, while Malcolm waited with a sleeping Deshawn collapsed over his shoulder. He had fallen asleep in the car. She stepped aside and directed Malcolm to lie Deshawn down on the sofa, until she got his pajamas ready. In minutes, she returned with the wet towel and sleepwear. Malcolm remained on the edge of the couch watching Deshawn. He was afraid that if he got up before Monet returned, the boy would roll over and fall on the floor. Monet shook her head and smiled.

Once she took a seat, Malcolm jumped up immediately and asked where the bathroom was.

"It's the first door on the left," Monet directed as she proceeded to undressing her son and wiping him down with the soapy washcloth. Once she finished dressing him, Monet took the pillows off the couch so that she could pull out the sleeper bed inside. She laid Deshawn on top of two of the pillows before she left the room to go and get some clean linen. As she was walking back into the living room with the clean sheets, Malcolm was exiting the bathroom.

"I need to take a shower," he smiled. "Where do I get the washcloths, Baby?"

"They're in that closet right there." Monet pointed to the linen closet.

"Well, I need to go to the car to grab my bags. Where are your keys?" he whispered, not wanting to wake Deshawn. She grabbed her keys from the coffee table and handed them to Malcolm.

"Don't be too long, I might start missing you too much," she kidded.

While Malcolm went out to the car, Monet hurried into her room to find a cute nightgown to put on because she sure didn't have anything sexy.

After showering, Monet and Malcolm settled down in her bedroom, in front of the television. While in bed, Monet expressed to her man how much she missed him. Within minutes, his hands, his lips, and every part of him, was all over her. She became overwhelmed with passion. His touch took her breath away. Malcolm's soft hands caressed her face as his tongue dove in and out of her mouth. The urgency of obsession raced through her like a bolt of lightning. His soothing hands finally parted her legs and made their way up her nightgown. Her head fell back, her eyes closed. Sweat beads welled up all over her body. His muscular frame rested on top of hers. Monet moaned pleasingly. She'd missed him so much, being in his arms turned her fire into desire.

Malcolm lifted her nightgown over her head, and slid his hand all the way up to her breast. He gently groped one before sucking it into his mouth. He inhaled the gentle scent of baby oil all over her.

"Umh," he mumbled, while kissing her lips. "I love y…" A sudden knock at the door interrupted his words. Malcolm froze as Monet's head popped up like a popcorn kernel in hot grease. "Who is that?" Malcolm asked in an aggravated voice.

"I don't know."

Malcolm quickly rose to his feet, and grabbed his t-shirt, as Monet slid back into her gown. The knocking continued. This time they were longer and stronger. If Deshawn wasn't asleep in the living room, Monet would have ignored the knocking, but her fiancé seemed to be anticipating the uninvited visitor.

Monet's first thought was that her mother had to be in labor, but she quickly dismissed the idea knowing that Sullivan would have definitely called before stopping by her place. After slipping into her robe, she walked into the living room, with Malcolm close on her trail. She was pissed now, because whoever it was would wake her son if they didn't stop knocking like someone was after them. She flipped the light switch on and crept up to the front door. She pulled back the curtain to reveal the face of the person who was about to be tongue lashed for showing up at her house so late, and unannounced. She could not believe who was standing on the other side of the door. Her only reaction was, "What are you doing showing up at my house, and beating on my door like you're crazy?" she fussed.

"Monet, please let me in, I need to talk to you. This is an emergency for real," Jamil yelled through the door.

Monet looked at Malcolm, whose facial expression was begging to know what was going on.

"Let me handle this, it's Derrick's friend, Jamil."

Malcolm shook his head and walked back to the living room to sit down. He didn't say anything. Monet hoped there wasn't anything wrong with her baby's daddy although, Derrick definitely didn't deserve the title. She inhaled, exhaled, and unlocked the front door.

A frantic Jamil stepped into the apartment and stood to the side. He had worry written all over his face.

"This better be worth you knocking on my door at nearly two in the morning. Make it quick, and keep your voice down because my son is sleeping."

"Look, Monet," he huffed. "Yo boy just got vamped on by the police while we were up on the block. They took him down for possession, but he gave them a fake name 'cause he got a warrant. He can be released on a quick bond out, for $2,500, and Derrick wants to bail out before they book him and run his fingerprints, to find out he ain't really who he say he is. If they do, they gon' keep him for the warrant they got on him."

Monet's eyes were rolling in the back of her head. She was so pissed that she could have slapped the dog shit out of Jamil, for disturbing her groove with some bullshit about Derrick. As long as he wasn't dead, she could care less about what happened to him. Through a frown, she exclaimed, "So what does this have to do with me?"

"Derrick asked me to come by here to see if you could help me out with the $300 that I don't have. I only have $2,200, but Derrick says that as soon as he gets out, he'd bring the three hundred back to you right away."

Was stupid written all her forehead? Did Derrick actually think that she had an extra $300 to give him on bail, when she was struggling to raise and provide for *their* child on her own?

She shook her head and rolled her neck. "Jamil, would you please tell Derrick that I don't have no damn $300 to get him out of jail. And, if I did have some extra money, I would take it and spend it on his son, who he doesn't take care of. Better yet, you tell him that the day I pay some money to get him out of jail, will be the day when he goes down to The Friend of the Court to pay me all the back child support he owes me and his son. I wish I would take some of my hard-earned money to get his ass out of jail. He better call one of those hoes that he's always laying up with 'cause I ain't the one."

Jamil shook his head with disappointment. "Man, Monet, you shouldn't even be like that."

She approached the door. "Whatever, Jamil. I'm about to go to bed. Tell Derrick that I can't do nothin' for him."

"Man, that's cold blooded, Monet." Jamil sighed as he turned to walk out.

"Whatever," Monet huffed. She watched him walk back to his car. Afterwards, she slammed her front door and turned off her porch light. She huffed, "The nerve of him."

Malcolm, who was sitting on the edge of the couch hearing everything, stood with disgust written all over his face. He threw his arms around Monet and said, "Who cares about those punks? Let's get back to what we started." He smiled as he and Monet eased back into the bedroom. Deshawn remained sound asleep.

CHAPTER 30

Dorothy could not believe it when her friend Punkin called her collect saying she and her husband had been arrested for fighting on the side of the highway. Dorothy was pissed because of having to get up out of her bed to go down to the police station to bail her friend out. She'd gotten into a good sleep when she got the call from Punkin.

Punkin and Mark had been charged with disorderly conduct and domestic disturbance. "I can't believe this foolishness," Dorothy kept repeating to Punkin, as they left the police station together. As Punkin continued venting and tongue lashing her husband, who wasn't there, Dorothy shamefully shook her head and listened. Punkin kept hollering about having the officer who arrested them fired, because he'd arrested her, after her husband lost his mind and beat her up.

"Since when do you get arrested for getting the shit beat out of you? Look at my face, Dorothy. That police has got to be stupid, and I can't believe that I've caught a case fucking with this psycho ass motherfucker. Girl, that punk put his hands on me once, but it won't happen again, I promise you." From one subject to the next, she continued venting. The raspy pitch in her voice revealed her pain and hurt. "I'ma' need to stay wit you until I can get a place of my own. Lord knows I don't want to have to kill that man," Punkin fussed.

Dorothy begged Punkin to let her take her to the hospital, but Punkin refused. Punkin was to embarrassed to go to the hospital after being beat up by her husband. "In the morning, I'm going to get all my belongings so that I won't have any connections to that crazy bastard. It's not too late for an annulment is it?"

Since Punkin didn't want to go to the hospital, Dorothy ran to the bathroom, grabbed her first aid kit and clean wet towels, once they arrived at her house. Dorothy returned with the peroxide, towels, and bandages. She really tried to convince Punkin to go to the hospital because the cut over her eye was deep enough to need a few stitches. Again, Punkin refused. The only thing she wanted to do was tell Dorothy how the man, who was supposed to love her forever, nearly killed her. She cried while telling Dorothy exactly what happened. Dorothy remained silent, while rubbing her belly and shaking her head in disbelief.

"You know that you are welcome to stay here as long as you need to Punkin, but what are you and Mark going to do?"

"I am divorcing his ass, that's what I'm going to do," Punkin confessed. "That man is crazy Dorothy. I can't believe how he flipped out on me. I never saw that one coming. You should have seen how his entire demeanor changed."

Dorothy didn't want to say, I told you so, but she had warned Punkin. It wasn't that she didn't want Punkin to marry Mark; she only wanted her to give it some time, so that she could get to know him, to avoid situations like the one Punkin was in. Although, Dorothy did know that the man was looking pretty upset when he and Punkin left the baby shower, there was no way that Mark should have put his hands on Punkin. If he had taken time to get to know Punkin, then he would have known how flirtatious she was. But, the way that Punkin described his sudden change in behavior, and judging the way that her face looked, Mark had completely lost his mind. Since Mark didn't have any family in town, and he and Sullivan were church brothers, Sullivan bailed him out, although he definitely had to scold Mark for his disrespect to his wife.

Punkin stayed with Dorothy and Sullivan for nearly two weeks before Punkin finally decided to go back home to her husband. After a few counseling sessions with the Pastor, Punkin and Mark decided to try and work out their marital issues. Dorothy loved Punkin dearly, but was glad to see her go. She had simply worn Dorothy out with all that she was going through. She'd brought so much drama in the two weeks that she stayed, she made Dorothy's stomach hurt. Even though Dorothy was ready for her friend to go, she didn't want to push her off on Mark, if Punkin wasn't ready. After all, he had flipped the script once and there was no telling if that was a one-time episode, or if the dude was crazy for real. Punkin was still her girl though, so if Mark put his hands on her again, Dorothy would pay a hood boy to whoop up on him.

From time to time, she'd been experiencing light contractions, but Dorothy was adamant about not going to the hospital until it was time for the baby to come for sure. She'd had four children and could pretty much tell the difference in false contractions and labor. If Sullivan would be around when she'd happen to have a slight jolt of pain he'd ask, "Are you okay sweetie, would you like for me to call the doctor, or do you want me to take you straight to the hospital?" There was no doubt in her mind that Sullivan wouldn't have their baby spoiled rotten.

After Sullivan left for work that Wednesday, Dorothy quickly dressed. Monet would be picking her up at one o'clock. They were going to have lunch with Malcolm and his mother, Hallema. The four of them were going to meet to start plans for Monet and Malcolm's wedding. Soon, the two would be graduating from college, and the wedding would take place one month afterwards, so they needed to get going with the planning. Dorothy was happy that Monet's wedding would be coming soon. That would give her motivation to get the baby weight off, once the baby was born.

They all agreed to meet up at a popular seafood place in town. Malcolm loved seafood, and picked the spot. When Dorothy and Monet arrived at the restaurant, they noticed that Malcolm and his mother had not yet arrived. When they finally arrived, Hallema's bright smile entered the restaurant before she did. Dorothy slowly stood up to hug Hallema and Malcolm. After they greeted, the hostess escorted the group to their table. This was Dorothy and Malcolm's mother second time meeting, so they had plenty to talk about before their children took that leap. Over lunch, the couple decided on an official date for the wedding, August 12, a month and a half after their graduations. The chosen theme colors were ivory and peach. The wedding would be held at Malcolm's home church, and the reception at the Ann Street Complex Hall. Of all six halls Monet inquired about, the Ann Street Complex was the only one that would allow them to choose their own caterers. Hallema had a good friend, Sylvia, who'd agreed to cater the reception, as a favor. Sylvia had her own catering business, and was a great cook.

Since Malcolm's parents decided to cover the cost of the wedding and reception, Dorothy agreed that she and her husband would cover the honeymoon expenses. It could be their wedding gift to the newlyweds, who'd settled on Mexico as their destination of choice. Mexican food was Monet's favorite dish and she couldn't wait to taste it in authentic form. Both Monet and Hallema took brief notes; putting ideas to paper would make it easier to convey to the wedding planner Hallema planned to hire. When they left the restaurant, Dorothy asked Monet if she could run her by the grocery store. She needed to grab a few items, and since she couldn't drive herself, she wanted to go while she had the opportunity. For the last couple of days, Dorothy had been experiencing periodic contractions, but she was sticking to her plan. There was no way she was going to the hospital until it was time.

As Monet turned into the parking lot of the grocery store, she quickly spotted an empty space and pulled into it. She got out of the car telling her mom how overwhelmed she was about her wedding approaching. While Monet unfastened her son's booster seat, Dorothy said, "Rest your nerves child. You have plenty of time before you have to start worrying," as she sat sideways, with her feet resting on the ground.

"Are you okay, Mom?" Monet asked.

Dorothy sat there, shaking her head back and forth, while rocking. "I can't make it any further. This baby is ready to come out."

Monet panicked. "What are we gonna do?"

Dorothy looked at Monet as if she was crazy. The girl almost made her curse. "We've got to get to the hospital, Monet. Get the baby back in the car. I'm going to call Sullivan."

Monet quickly picked her son up and strapped him in his car seat. "Do you need help putting your feet inside, Mom?"

"I got it," Dorothy answered after she'd forced her feet back into the car.

Monet started the car and backed out of the parking space expeditiously.

"Mommy, Mommy," Deshawn yelled. "You didn't close my door." Monet hit the brakes, the tires screeched and the car door slammed shut. "It's closed now, Mommy." The car continued racing out of the parking lot.

Sullivan answered his phone on the second ring. "It's coming baby! The baby is coming. I'm in the car with Monet, and we're in route to the hospital right now."

"I'm on my way," her husband huffed. He then hung up.

Dorothy was sweating and hyperventilating. She kept breathing in and out, to ease the pain, and calm her nerves. She hadn't gone through child labor in a long time; she almost forgot how unbearable those contractions could be.

Sullivan grabbed his jacket, and dashed out of his office. He'd call later to tell someone what was going on. His child was about to be born, and he couldn't believe it was true. He'd waited so long. It had taken him over forty years to become a father and now that the time was here, he didn't know how to act.

Dorothy dialed the number to her sister's job. When the woman answered, Dorothy asked her if she could tell Caroline that her sister was on her way to the emergency room. Gene said she would deliver the message ASAP. Caroline would know exactly what that meant.

Monet was driving like a bat out of hell. It was no wonder Dorothy didn't give birth in the car. When the car pulled up to the emergency room door, Monet jumped out yelling, "I need some help. My mother is going into labor." Two EMS workers helped Dorothy out of the car and into a wheel chair. Monet jumped in afterwards and zoomed off. She had to park the car before they took her mom back into the delivery room. With Deshawn's hand wrapped around hers, Monet raced into the hospital in search of her mother. Deshawn was crying and scared. He had no idea what was going on.

Since Dorothy had dilated seven centimeters, she was immediately rushed into the birthing room. The nurse assisting her said her baby would probably be coming within the hour. Dorothy had been in labor for quite sometime and hadn't even noticed. Her water burst on the way to the delivery room. Dorothy tried to remain as calm as she could, for Deshawn's sake although she was in tremendous pain. Every five minutes, or so, she would look up to see if her husband was walking thru the door. She was worried that he wouldn't get there in time for the birth. This was the one thing she didn't want Sullivan to miss.

At approximately, 2:51 PM., Dorothy and Sullivan welcomed into the world their new son, Sullivan Michael Edwards, Jr. Dorothy was only in delivery one hour before she pushed out her eight pound, three-ounce baby boy. Monet, Sullivan, and Caroline were in tears. Fortunately, Deshawn had slept through the whole delivery. Dorothy was somewhat exhausted, but not more than she was happy. She could not believe how handsome her second son was. She had been praying for a boy, although she told everyone it didn't really matter.

Once baby Sullivan was cleaned, he was brought into the room and placed in Sullivan's arms. He had a smile on his face wider than the Pacific Ocean. The moment he'd been waiting for all his life, had finally come. Dorothy had made him a father. His first-born was nestled in his arms and it still seemed like a mirage. The feelings he felt were so overwhelming, they were indescribable. He held the baby tight in his arms, never wanting to let him go. Looking over at his fatigued wife staring at him and their newborn, he whispered, "Thank you." Dorothy smiled and closed her eyes. Sullivan couldn't wait to get his son home so he could stay up all night talking to him and telling him about the thing called life. He had millions of things planned for him and his son. Although he loved Dwayne and the rest of their children with all his heart, he felt a different kind of love, now that he had his own. He couldn't wait to call his family and tell them that he'd had a healthy new son.

Around four o'clock, Monet decided to leave the hospital to pick up her younger siblings and bring them back to see the baby. After she dropped them off, she'd start home. She was planning to cook dinner and her man would be coming though later that evening.

Dorothy called Punkin that night to spread the news about the baby. She and Mark came up the next day with more balloons and flowers. So many people had come up to see the baby. They all brought flowers, balloons, and gifts. As always, Caroline had gone overboard and bought three of the largest "It's A Boy" balloons Dorothy had seen, not to mention the three outfits she also bought. A couple of Caroline's friends even visited. Sullivan needed to take some of the gifts home, because Dorothy's hospital room looked like the end results of a baby shower. Her husband had invited everyone from his office to come see the baby. All nineteen of his office buddies showed up and congratulated the couple on their blessing.

The first thing out of Punkin's mouth, after she stepped into the room was, "Where's my nephew? I want to see how much he looks like me."

Dorothy shook her head at the loud mouth girl and told her to lower her voice. "He's in the nursery, girl."

While the guys were exchanging handshakes, Punkin reached over and hugged her friend. She told her that she loved her. "How you feeling, 'cause you damn sho' look like shit." While talking, Punkin rubbed her hands through Dorothy's messed up do.

"I know, I was thinking about getting my hair braided, but the baby came before I could get around to it."

Sullivan interrupted. "Baby, Mark and I are about to walk down to the nursery to see our son." He had a big smile stretched across her face. He couldn't wait to show off his baby to Mark. Dorothy smiled and shook her head as the guys exited the room. Punkin took a seat in the chair on the side of her friend's bed.

"How are things going since you've been back at home?"

"He's trying hard Dorothy, kissing my ass big time," Punkin chided. "I told him that we will be cool, as long as he keeps his hands to himself. He told me that the day we got into it, he had been frustrated because Sylvia from church had recently delivered him some bad news. She told him that she was HIV positive, and since the two of them had a relationship, that he failed to inform me about, he was upset about possibly being infected. Girl, who would have known that stankin' slut Sylvia had been with my man. I knew that trick wasn't as holy as she claimed to be. She's lucky that his test came back negative," Punkin continued. "Besides that though, Mark said that his dad use to beat on his mother. I guess he must have been vicariously his daddy the day he whooped my ass."

Dorothy was surprised to find out about Sylvia and Mark creeping, but she was more shocked about the girl being HIV positive. Dorothy felt sorry for Sylvia.

"He promised me that he was gone try real hard to do right by me. I also found out that he was married before, for three years. He said that he and his wife divorced after he jumped on her one time and broke her ribs. You'd never be able to tell that he could be that insecure and controlling. Overall, Mark's a real nice guy, and I love him. If he loves me, he'll change 'cause I can't take no ass whoopings."

"Y'all will be alright. Just take it one day at a time. With prayer things will get better. Besides, I like Mark," Dorothy confessed.

Punkin changed the subject. "Girl I still can't believe that your over forty-year-old ass done had a damn baby. What is the world coming to when grandma-ma's are having babies?"

She and Dorothy fell out into laughter.

CHAPTER 31

After Punkin and her husband left the hospital, they decided to go out to eat dinner, since it had gotten so late. In the car, Mark went on and on about how happy the new baby had made Sullivan. Sullivan had told him that from the moment his son entered the world, he'd gained a whole new outlook on life, bringing so much worth to his life. Punkin rolled her eyes as she looked out the window. She was happy that Dorothy and Sullivan had a healthy new addition to their family, but Mark was definitely a little too enthused about the baby.

She was never happier to see a Houlahan's Steakhouse in her life. The car wasn't in park for thirty seconds before she jumped out, straightened her clothes and walked toward the door.

Mark climbed out of the car. "What's the rush?"

"Oh, I have to use the restroom, Baby," Punkin announced.

Mark hurried after her, so he could open the door before she got to it. He opened the door of the restaurant and stepped inside after his wife. Punkin headed straight to the restroom, while Mark reserved the table. By the time she came out, the hostess was ready to seat them. They sat down, ordered drinks, and looked over the menus while their waitress gave them a few minutes to decide. Punkin ordered an appetizer with her meal. When it arrived, she and her husband shared the spicy chicken nacho salad, while waiting for the main course to be served.

The food came quick, and it was delicious. After the waitress cleared the table of all dinner items, she offered the couple dessert. Punkin ordered French Vanilla ice cream with a turtle brownie and caramel on top. Mark ordered an Apple Pie A-la-mode.

While they waited for their dessert, Mark reached across the table and grabbed his wife's hand, and kissed it. "I want you to know that I truly love you, Punkin." She blushed and batted her eyes at him. She was melting. "I think that we should do like Dorothy and Sullivan and have a child of our own. I mean, now that we're married, what else could make it more complete than to have a child of our own."

Punkin snatched her hand back to her side of the table. Looking into Mark's eyes, his face was sincere. How would she tell him that there was no way that she was about to have any children, without him being offended. Punkin didn't plan on having anymore children, at all, whatsoever. Her son was almost grown, and she thanked God his father had decided to raise him, and teach him to be a man. There was no way she planned on doing it all over again. She and Dorothy were two different people. If Dorothy chose to have another child, after all the time that had passed, that was her business.

"Mark, I don't plan on having any children, sweetie. I am more than happy with our life the way it is now. Why don't we just take time to enjoy, and get to know each other?"

"What more do we need to know about each other," he snapped. "We've promised to spend the rest of our lives together, so whatever we don't know about one another thus far, we're sure to find out along the way." His voice was escalating, and his demeanor had changed for the worst.

She looked around embarrassingly. "Honey, can you please lower your voice. We can talk about this another time."

"What more do we need to talk about? What we need to talk about is why I married your sorry ass if you don't think I'm good enough for you to have my kids?"

Punkin got up from the table, and walked away. She was not going to sit around and continue to be disrespected by the closet psycho. Mark jumped up and grabbed her arm. "Let me go," she warned.

"Where are you going?"

"Let go of my arm, Mark! I'm getting the hell away from you. You're creating a scene."

"Well, go the fuck on then," he cursed as he released her arm. Punkin hurried out the door, hoping that he wasn't walking behind her.

The people at the surrounding tables stared as Mark sat back down. The waitress came over quickly with the check. Mark threw the money on the table, and walked out. He wasn't finished with this discussion, and they would finish it at home, whether Punkin wanted to or not.

By the time he made it outside the restaurant, his wife was nowhere in sight. He drove around the whole parking lot and found her sitting on the curb behind the building. When he pulled up and told her to get in the car, she wouldn't budge. He asked again, this time he was saying it while getting out of the car and walking around the car toward her. "Don't make me force you into this car, girl. Now I said get in before you make me do something I regret."

Punkin burst into tears, as Mark approached. She stood up because she didn't want him to catch her off guard. As he approached, she stepped about three feet backwards. He stopped, rubbed his hands through his head, and paced back and forth.

"I can't do this, Mark. I can't keep going through this. I think that you have some serious issues to work out with yourself. I don't know what it is, but you need some help, and I am not getting in the car with you."

"Why do you have to be so complicated?" he yelled. "All I said is that I wanted us to have a child. You are the one who's acting like I'm not good enough for you. You had a child for Ralph, and he didn't even marry you. At least I had enough decency to marry you before I asked you to have my child."

A couple was walking to their car, so Punkin looked away from her husband as if they weren't even together. She was happy to see somebody because she was afraid of what Mark would do next.

"Ralph has nothing to do with this. We can't even get this relationship right and you're talking about having kids. We've only been married two months, and so far it hasn't been working out. I don't know who you are at times, and I don't even know if I have the energy for this relationship. Maybe this marriage was a mistake, Mark."

"Oh, now you want to just give up on me?"

Although she wanted her marriage to work, it didn't seem like it was going to. Still newlyweds and already they'd had a physical fight. Punkin couldn't believe that after he had begged her to drop the domestic violence charge on him, and after he begged her to come back home, Mark had disrespected her in public. She was afraid to get in the car because she didn't know what tricks he had up his sleeve. She told him to go on, and she would catch a cab home. Mark said he wasn't going home without her, so they continued standing outside of Mark's running car.

For nearly forty-five minutes they went back and forth arguing before Mark finally said, "Charlotte, will you please get in this car. I'm not going to hurt you. I'm sorry for the way I acted in the restaurant. I don't know what came over me. Sometimes I can't control my anger, Punkin. Let's just go home and talk about this. I don't want to argue with you any more. I love you." He stretched his arms out to hug her, but Punkin walked around him and climbed into the car. By now, she was tired and her feet hurt. Unfortunately, she'd left her cell phone at home, and Mark wouldn't allow her to go back inside to call a cab. She was so ready to go home, so she prayed that God would keep her safe. After she got home, she would figure out what to do about getting away from her crazy husband.

The couple rode home in silence. Punkin had all sorts of thoughts running through her head. Indeed, she did love Mark, but the relationship was not a healthy one. He really wasn't making things easy for her. Drama was the main reason that Punkin had remained single for so long. She didn't have time for all the issues. She loved living her life happy and carefree and ironically, she hadn't done that since she'd been married. That wasn't the way things were supposed to go.

When they arrived home, Mark cut the car off and sat in silence. So did his wife. She wanted to take her time getting out. This was a situation she truly didn't know how to handle. Usually, when she got into it with one of her male friends she'd send him packing. But, this time it was different. Mark was her husband. This time she'd actually had to go inside and work this matter out. The only thing she could think to do was to go inside and call Dorothy. Her friend would know exactly how to handle a situation like this, and if anyone had patients to deal with a man, it would be Dorothy.

After Mark got out, so did Punkin. She slowly drug in behind him wondering what he could possibly say that would convince her that he wasn't a crazy motherfucker. All she knew was that she didn't feel like arguing. He could argue with himself. She'd get in her car and leave; she wasn't fool enough to stand around arguing with a person with an unstable mind. If he put his hands on her again, she'd have to kill him dead.

Punkin walked into the living room and plopped down on the sofa. She hoped her husband would go lie down in the bedroom, but of course, he didn't. Instead, Mark sat right on the end of the sofa and rubbed her back.

"Did I tell you that you were the best thing that ever happened to me?"

Punkin rolled her eyes. *Oh, now he wants to play lovey-dovey*, she thought to herself.

"Look, baby I—"

Punkin jumped up from the couch and headed toward the bedroom. She was nowhere near being ready to forgive him for the way he spoke to her in the restaurant. "Save all your words for the Pastor, 'cause that's who'll need to hear it. You have issues that you need to ask God to help you with."

"Damn," he snapped. "Can't you even give me a chance to apologize?"

"You apologized after you hit me. What difference did that make? You go right on, not even a week after that, and disrespect me in a restaurant full of people. What's next, Mark? I mean it's never a dull moment with you. You just never cease to amaze me. What type of outburst shall I expect next?" Punkin continued down the hallway to their bedroom, as her husband stormed after her. "I'm leaving you, Mark."

Mark was right on her heels. As soon as she threw her purse down on the bed and turned around, there he was. Mark pushed her down onto the bed and fell on top of her. He kissed her lips and her face, then her neck. "I love you baby. Please don't leave me. I'm sorry."

She tossed her head from side to side, trying to refuse his kisses, as tears fell from the corners of her eyes. Mark overpowered her with his weight. "Stop Mark," she cried. "Get off of me."

He licked the tears as they fell from her eyes, then he forced his tongue between her closed lips. "Let me make it up to you, baby. Don't cry. I love you." With one hand, he held her arms, and with the other, he unzipped his pants. Her squirming back and forth made it difficult for Mark to get her out of her jeans, but eventually he succeeded his goal. He didn't have time to go through what he went through trying to take off her jeans so he ripped his wife's underwear off. He forcefully dug his two fingers inside her and probed her womb. Through tears, she continued squirming. As if in a trance, Mark pulled his fingers from her and licked them. There was so much pleasure in his eyes. It was scary. Mark kissed her again, and then yanked one of her breasts from her bra. He placed the nipple into his mouth and sucked hard on it. He stuck his free hand, back inside her. It felt so good; she ironically felt herself relaxing. His fingers were pleasing her, as they never had before. Mark seemed more in tuned than before.

She yelled, "Stop," as her legs proceeded to spread apart. When he kissed her again, she wasn't so resistant. Feeling his long, thick, piece of muscle against her leg, made her yearn for his grand entrance. Once the python entered her, she could no longer fake the funk. She wrapped her arms around his neck and her legs around his waist.

As he chimed, "I love you," in her ear, she moaned and rocked in concert with him, as tears continued to drop from her eyes. Why she was crying when he was pleasing her so well was boggling to her, but Punkin went along with what felt right. She and Mark made love like they were afraid they'd never get the opportunity again. On top of him, she reached her ecstasy before falling on top of his chest. She was breathless, speechless, relieved, and crazy in love.

CHAPTER 32

Andrea hung up the telephone after speaking with Tim. She wore a smile so wide; it stretched across her entire face. She couldn't wait to go upstairs and tell her mother that the Doberson's had invited them to dinner on Saturday. Tim told Andrea that his parents wanted to meet with her family, in a more formal setting. It only made since to get to know each other better, since Andrea and Tim were having a baby, and planning to get married.

Andrea crept up the stairs slowly. She called out to her mother as soon as she reached the top. "Mom, I have something to tell you," she yelled.

Caroline was in her bedroom preparing for her weekly pamper session. She had a private masseuse come out to the house every Friday evening at eight to give her a full body, therapeutic massage, a deep tissue, steam facial, a paraffin manicure and a pedicure. Caroline claimed she had to have this service every Friday, to take away the stress of the week. Andrea thought it was outrageously ridiculous for her mother to spend nearly $300 a week, for someone to come and give her a massage. Caroline always sat in her hot tub hours before the masseuse even performed any services. Andrea tapped on the door of her parent's bedroom before she pushed it open and walked in.

"Mom," she called out again.

Caroline sat down her genuine crystal flute, and shouted in an aggravated tone. "What?"

"Mom, the Doberson's have invited us for dinner on Saturday. Tim said they'd like to get to know you all better."

"Damn, Andrea," Caroline cursed while removing her eye pads from her eyes. "Couldn't you wait to tell me that? You're coming up in here, during my hour of tranquility and meditation, to tell me that somebody invited me to dinner. Can you please spare me the details until after U'sante leaves? I am trying to get some me time, if you don't mind, sweetheart. I will be happy to discuss everything later, so can you please close the door on your way out?"

After she turned and walked away, Andrea rolled her eyes and mumbled, "She's just rude for no reason."

That Saturday, Andrea dressed up real pretty. She wanted to make a good impression on her soon-to-be in-laws, so she put on a brand new pair of denim maternity pants, with a nice black cotton blouse. To make her outfit appear more dressy-casual, Andrea wore a pair of black two inch heels. Since her hair was braided, she quickly pulled it back into a ponytail and was ready to go.

Caroline had been complaining, and coming up with excuses why she didn't want to meet up with the Dobersons every since Andrea informed her of the invite, but she took two hours getting dressed on the day of. In the car, Caroline continued her fussing and cursing as her family pretended to listen.

"I can't believe these people claim they want to get to know us so bad, and they invite us to dinner at a damn restaurant. Now, either Tim's mother doesn't know how to cook, or they just don't want all of our black asses over to their house."

Andrea continued rolling her eyes behind her mother's back. She was praying that her mom didn't embarrass her once they arrived at Olive Garden.

"I wanna know what they want to know about us anyway. I mean, it ain't like they gon' find out no more about us from eating dinner with us, than they already know. Or do they just want to know how we act."

"And I hope that you show them the dignified you, and not the real thing," Andrea commented. "If you do, they're bound to think that my baby is going to come out crazy."

"Yeah, Sweetie, just chill," Thomas consented while rubbing the back of his

wife's hand.

Caroline looked at him, and then she turned to Andrea. "Yeah, I'm going to chill, but I'll tell you both right now. Nobody better say shit to piss me off, 'cause you know I don't hold my tongue for nobody."

"We know, dear. We hope they don't piss you off either," Thomas concluded. He of all people knew that his wife could get beside herself. He was a witness to her having absolutely no self-control. After the fight with Sheila, he didn't speak to his wife for three days, because he was so appalled. Tonight he hoped she could tame the alter ego of the wild ghetto woman inside her.

The restaurant's lounge area was crowded. Andrea made her way up to the hostess and asked if the Doberson's had arrived. The young hostess was dressed in a black skirt and white blouse. She looked down at her reservations list, and then back at Andrea.

"Yes, they've been seated and were awaiting your arrival. If you'll follow me right this way, I'll escort you to your table." Andrea called for the rest of her family, and they moseyed their way up to the podium. They walked behind Andrea as the hostess led them to their table.

The Doberson's rose to greet the Smith's, when they walked up behind the hostess. Tim hugged and kissed Andrea, before pulling her chair out from the table. The Doberson's were dressed up like they were going to church. When Caroline noticed this, she looked at her husband and mumbled, "I guess they don' put you to shame." Thomas wore a pair of brown slacks, and a beige cotton shirt, and Tim, his dad, and his brother were all wearing suits and ties. Mrs. Doberson was wearing an old, flowered rayon top, with a long black skirt that ended at her ankles. Caroline, who was dressed in a $300 Anne Klein evening dress, didn't feel intimidated at all.

The two families were relaxed by the time the appetizers arrived. By then they had all been formally introduced, and were finding out what each other did for a living, and so forth. In the beginning, everyone except Caroline was sharing. It took her two glasses of Chardonnay to take her nose out the air. Being the pessimistic person that she was, she walked into the restaurant with a bad taste in her mouth. She wasn't expecting Tim's family to be as receptive as they were. So, after seeing everyone else getting along, Caroline dropped her guard and mingled as well.

When the time came to order dessert, everyone was complaining about being full, but still each person at the table ordered something. Taylor and Tim's little brother dug into their ice cream while the adults slowly picked at theirs. Mrs. Doberson nodded when the waitress came to the table with a quarter-sheet, decorated cake.

Caroline wanted to know what was going on, so, she asked, "What are we celebrating?"

Tim looked at his parents with a smile on his face. After wiping his mouth with his napkin, he announced that he had a surprise. While his mom did the honors of slicing the cake, Tim rose from the table. Andrea's entire family was awaiting the surprise.

Tim stood in front of Andrea and asked for her hand. She became nervous as he got down on bended knee. Mr. Doberson rose from the table and pulled a small jewelry box from his pocket. He handed it to Tim. Caroline's eyes almost popped out of her head when Tim finally presented Andrea with her engagement ring and asked her if she would kindly do him the honor of becoming his wife.

Thomas immediately rose from the table and clapped when Andrea answered yes. Andrea's face was covered in tears, as she rose from the table and kissed her fiancé. She could not believe how sly Tim was. She had absolutely no clue that he'd invited her to dinner to present her with a ring.

"Congratulations, dear," Mrs. Doberson cried out as Andrea embraced her soon-to-be father-in-law, and her parents. Even Caroline had tears in her eyes. She had no idea what the Doberson's were up to by suddenly inviting them to dinner, but now she knew. After sizing up her daughter's ring, and coming to the conclusion that it was a one karat, class two, diamond solitaire, Caroline finally came to the conclusion that the Doberson's were all right.

As they all took their seats, Mrs. Doberson proclaimed, "I want you to know, Andrea, that as long as Tim is in school, Mr. Doberson and myself will do everything that we can to see to it that all your needs are met. We don't want you to have worry about anything accept carrying and delivering us a healthy grandbaby."

"I agree," Thomas added.

"So, when is it all to take place?" Caroline inquired.

Tim looked at Andrea. "Well, Andrea and I still have to discuss the details. You guys will be the first to know when we've decided on a date."

"I think we should do it before the baby is born,"

"Andrea, you want to have a belly when you walk down the aisle?" Caroline quizzed.

"That doesn't matter," Andrea smirked. "I think it's more important that our child be born to married parents. That's the way I've always wanted it to be."

Everyone fell silent, trying to finish dessert, because it was getting late. When the evening came to an end, The Doberson's accepted the check and said their farewells to

Andrea and her family. There was a lot of planning to be made since Andrea wanted to get married right away.

Andrea told her mother that she wanted a small, simple wedding; mostly friends and family, so that following week, Caroline almost ran herself crazy, trying to plan her daughter's wedding. Andrea had set her wedding date for August 19. It was right before Tim went back to school, that way they could have time for a short honeymoon right after the wedding. Although she hadn't informed Tim on the day that she selected, she knew that as long as it was during his summer break, he wouldn't have any objections. Caroline totally took matters into her own hands. The way she was making plans and hiring people, you would have thought it was her wedding. First, she made sure that the pastor of her church would marry them, and then she placed a $1,000 deposit on a reception hall. She thought it was a good price, since the hall decorating was included. She spent nearly three hours in David's Bridal picking out a selection of dresses that she liked. She and Andrea would be able to see her chosen selections via the Internet. Since it was nearly seven o'clock when she left the bridal store, Caroline rushed to the print shop where she ordered fancy wedding invitations, which cost her nearly $400. She also went to a nearby bakery and ordered her favorite, a rum cake with whipped butter cream frosting. By the time she tallied up the purchases, she'd spent nearly $4,000 and she still hadn't hired a caterer or a DJ.

Andrea was extremely happy to be getting married. She couldn't wait until she and Tim were as one, and living on their own. Since she'd been working and didn't have to pay any bills, she'd saved up a little over $6,000. She was saving up for a down payment on new home. Andrea planned on moving out of her parent's house shortly after she was married. Hopefully, she and Tim would be able to choose and close on a house no longer than ninety days after their nuptials.

After work, Andrea jumped in her car and headed straight to her Aunt Dorothy's. Dorothy had promised to fix Andrea's favorite meal, and she couldn't wait to get to it. Her stomach was growling. She couldn't wait to dig into that baked lasagna that no one fixed better than her Aunt Dorothy.

To her surprise, Monet and her fiancé were also at Dorothy's when she got there. "I hope you didn't touch that Lasagna that my Auntie made for me."

"I know we did," Monet joked as she walked up to her cousin with her arms wide open. "Give me a hug," she insisted. After their embrace, Monet introduced Andrea to her fiancé Malcolm. The two greeted one another. Before Andrea could say anything else, Monet blabbed, "And when did you get this big rock on your finger?"

Andrea quickly hushed her older cousin. "Girl, be quiet. You'll find out everything after dinner."

Monet snidely stared at Andrea, as she headed for the kitchen where her auntie was setting the table.

When Dorothy called out that dinner was ready, everyone scrambled to the table to grab a seat. Sullivan was working late, so the family dug in to the feast without him. Tonya had put Sullivan Jr. down for a nap, but as soon as Dorothy sat down good to eat, the baby gave an encore performance. Dorothy pushed her chair away from the table and headed into the bedroom to get him. She looked at Andrea and said, "You might as well get ready because you'll be going through this in a few more months."

Monet chuckled.

Andrea looked up at her and said, "What are you laughing at? I give you and Malcolm a year after the wedding to be dropping your next load."

"I don't think so. My next load won't be coming for some years."

Malcolm didn't say a word. He was too busy stuffing his mouth with the delicious lasagna that Dorothy had prepared.

Dorothy returned with the baby in her arms. She sat down and laid him across her lap. She hoped she could get through her meal without Sullivan Jr. interrupting her again. About two good bites into her meal, the telephone rang. Dorothy rolled her eyes, cradled the baby in her arms and jumped up from the table, since no one else bothered to. She caught the phone on the forth ring. It was her sister. "You would be the second one to interrupt my dinner, wouldn't you?" Dorothy barked into the phone before even saying hello. She saw her sister's number pop up on the caller ID and felt no need for the formal greeting.

"Dorothy, is Andrea still over there?"

"Yes she is; we're having dinner."

"Good, I was hoping to catch her before she left so that I could tell her to bring me a plate."

"Bring you a plate of what?"

"A plate of that lasagna, and whatever else you cooked. I know you still have some left."

"And what if I do, who said I was sending some to you?"

"Please don't make me beg, Dorothy, I'm not good at it."

When Dorothy shifted the baby from one arm to the other, he turned up his face and whined, as tears poured down his cheeks. "Okay, that's my cue. I got to go. I guess I can scrape up some scraps to send to you. I'll call you back when Andrea gets ready to leave."

"Okay." Seeing that her sister was rushing her off the line, Caroline quickly managed to get one last word in before being disconnected. "How you like the ring?"

"What ring?"

That's when Caroline paused, because she realized that Andrea probably hadn't told her aunt about her proposal yet.

"Never mind," she muffled and quickly hung up.

Dorothy disregarded her comment and hung up the telephone. She walked back to the table and said to her niece, "It was your worrisome mother. She wants you to bring her a plate home."

Andrea nodded, and continued digging into her food.

Dorothy sat down at the table and rocked her baby. As soon as he fell off to sleep, she placed him in his basinet. Now, everyone else was finishing their dinner. Somewhat peeved, Dorothy grabbed her plate and headed to the microwave. She nuked her lasagna for one minute, and returned to the table to eat before her son woke up again. What was once crisp, buttery garlic bread was now a soggy mess in the microwave. Slowly, her irritation was beginning to escalate. "Andrea, can you pass the plate of bread, baby?" Unaware that she was showing off her sparkling new engagement ring, Andrea lifted the plate from the table. The twinkling diamond immediately caught Dorothy's eye.

Dorothy screamed, and demanded answers. "Andrea, are you getting married?"

Andrea blushed and looked toward Monet.

"What? I didn't tell her," her cousin gawked.

"Did my mom tell you?"

"No, she didn't," Dorothy stuttered, trying to cover for her sister. Now it had dawned on her, what her big mouth sister almost told. "Your bling bling is about to blind me," Dorothy finally exclaimed.

Andrea blushed. "Yes, Aunt Dorothy, your niece is about to get married."

"When, Andrea, when is the big day?"

"Next month."

"Girl please, when were you going to tell me?"

"Today! I just got the ring Saturday. I'm surprised my mom didn't tell it. You know she can't hold water," Andrea remarked.

"She didn't tell me anything," Dorothy repeated.

"I wanna be in your wedding," Keisha volunteered.

Nominating himself, Dwayne added, "I can be your ring barer." He smiled while getting up from the table with his empty plate.

"Boy, what you need to be volunteering for is to get upstairs and take a bath. Before you know it, you'll be sleep."

"But, Mom, I took a bath last night," Dwayne whined.

"Boy, if you don't go get upstairs, I'ma hurt you," Dorothy shouted as Dwayne quickly got out of sight.

"My mom is making all the plans for the impromptu wedding. If you need to know anything, just ask her. Otherwise, you all will have to wait until she sends the invitations. They should be ready soon."

Dorothy wiped her hands on the towel, draped it over her shoulder, and pushed her chair away from the table. She walked over to give her oldest niece a hug. "I can't believe this. I'll be attending two weddings in one year," Dorothy concluded, while shaking her head back and forth. "I guess if I can be a grandmother, and a mother of a newborn, anything is possible."

Within seconds of her pulling away from her aunt's house, Andrea passed her uncle Sullivan, who was heading home. She honked her horn, as their vehicles passed. She was full, and ready to go home and fall in her bed. Tim was supposed to return home from vacation the following day, and she wanted to be well rested so she wouldn't be in a bad mood once she saw him. When he called the day before, he admitted to missing her, and couldn't wait to see her. Andrea was equally anxious to see him. She couldn't wait to tell him how her mother nearly had the entire wedding planned, in the short length of time that he'd been away.

The Doberson's arrived home from there vacation to Indiana on Sunday. They were on vacation for seven days. Tim called Andrea as soon as he got to his bedroom. Not only had he missed hearing her feisty fuss, he couldn't wait to see her. He'd thought about her and the baby the entire length of his trip. During the trip, his parents suggested possible ideas to see to it that Tim wouldn't be distracted from school, while still attending to his obligations to Andrea and the baby. They kept reminding their son that they only wanted what was best for them. They kept reiterating to Tim how much things would change once he became a husband and father. Tim was tired of hearing their boring speeches. As if he didn't have enough pressure on him already, they were making him extremely nervous about getting married. In the course of a few months, Tim had gone from worrying about passing his finals, to discovering that he was going to be a father, and a husband.

Since she hadn't seen her man all week, Andrea called in from work on Monday morning. She and Tim had plans to spend the entire day together. That would give them the opportunity to discuss their wedding plans. Tim picked Andrea up around eleven thirty. They were going to have lunch, and then take a ride through some neighborhoods to do a little house hunting. Andrea wanted to check out specific neighborhoods before they contacted a realtor.

The couple had lunch at a nearby steakhouse. As they waited for their order to arrive, the couple held hands across the table. She loved how soft his skin was. Andrea had a different sparkle in her eye when Tim was around.

"Who'd have thought we'd come this far, in retrospect to where we were a couple years ago?"

"I don't want to even think about the past. All I want to talk about is the present," Tim said. "Let's talk about the future we'll have together."

Andrea smiled. "Okay then, lets talk about the wedding. I can't believe that it will take place in only a month. More so, I can't fathom being Mrs. Tim Doberson."

Tim's smile quickly dissipated. "One month," he muffled, with quizzical eyes.

"Yeah, that's one of the things I wanted to talk with you about. I've decided that I want this thing done and over with as soon as possible, so my mom and I have started making plans for our wedding to take place next month."

Tim's head fell. Hearing Andrea's plans only disappointed him. He didn't quite know how to break the news to Andrea, but he had to. When his face resurfaced, his sad eyes told Andrea that he had something on his mind.

"Well, Andrea, I kinda thought we should wait until after the baby before getting married."

Andrea's neck jerked. She was ready to unleash the venom. "I thought I told you that I wanted to get married before we had the baby, Tim. Do you remember us discussing that?" Her voice was escalating and anger covered her face.

"I do, and I know what you said, however, I think and agree with advice I got from my parents. They think we should wait until after I graduate, and after you have the baby before we get married." Tim was speaking in a slow hushed voice.

Andrea sensed that there was something wrong, but she continued to sit, impatiently, while waiting for Tim to finish talking.

"You see, part of the reason for our trip to Indiana was for me to get transferred and enrolled into school. I will be attending Wayne State College this fall. I'm going to be moving down there to stay with my aunt and uncle until I finish my last year of college."

Andrea wiggled uncomfortably in her seat.

Tim continued. "My parents and I think that transferring from community college, to a University, would look better on my resume. Graduating from a university will lead to better paying job offers, which is what I need, starting out fresh with a family and all. I'll only be away for a year tops. Afterwards, I can come home to you and the baby, and we can become one happy family."

Andrea felt deceived and humiliated, as tears poured from her eyes. "When were you going to tell me all this, Tim? I'm your fiancé, and I'm the last to find out about your plans to move out of town and leave me and your child hanging. How dare you, Tim?" Andrea yelled as she picked up her water glass and flung the water in his face. Dropping the glass, she jumped up from the table and stormed away.

Tim rushed behind Andrea out the door. Why didn't she understand that he was doing what was best for them?

"Take me home," she screamed as he approached his car. "How dare you do this to me? I hate you, Tim. I hate you," she cried.

As he walked up to wrap his arms around her, she backed away. "Please, Andrea, don't do this. Let's talk about this."

"I don't want to talk about anything, just take me home. Better yet," she paused as she scrambled through her purse for her cellular phone, "I'll call my mother to come and get me. I don't want to talk to you, I don't want to marry you, and as of right now I no longer even want to have your baby." Andrea pounded her finger into the keypad of her phone. Tim stood off to the side wondering what he could do to resolve the situation. Andrea placed the telephone up to her ear and waited. She waited and waited. After about the tenth ring Andrea hung up and slammed her phone back into her purse. She tried to dial her mother, but after getting no answer, she realized that Carolyn never carried her cell phone into the plant while she worked.

"Andrea, please, let's talk about this."

Andrea pulled on the door handle of Tim's car, demanding for him to take her home. Tim ran to her door while nervously fumbling for his keys. Finally, he got the car door unlocked, and pulled it open for Andrea. She climbed inside and slammed the door. Tim ran to the other side, jumped in, and turned on the engine. Andrea remained quiet throughout the entire trip. When the car pulled up in front of her house, she jumped out without saying even a thank you. Andrea ran up the pathway to the house.

He didn't follow. Instead, Tim pounded his fists into the steering wheel. He could not believe that he'd messed up the best thing that ever happened to him. He sat out in front of the Smith's place for a good thirty minutes before he decided to call inside. Andrea knew it was him because she picked up the telephone and immediately slammed it back down in his ear. Sadly, Tim started his car and pulled off. He couldn't wait to get home to tell his parents how they'd helped ruin his life.

CHAPTER 33

Rhenee stormed out of Ray's office, slamming the door as hard as she could behind her. Almost tripping over the cleaning lady, Carla, who was right behind the door, Rhenee stared furiously at the woman and propped her hand on her hip. She knew that Carla had overheard her conversation with Ray. Carla's nervous demeanor and confused expression on her face told Rhenee that her ears had heard too much. Rhenee walked straight up to the little Hispanic woman and pointed her finger so close in Carla's face, that if Carla were to move, Rhenee's fingernail would poke her in the eye.

"I don't know how much of my conversation you eavesdropped on but, I can promise you one thing. If you so much as mumble a word of what you heard to anybody, I will make sure that your stay here in America will come to an abrupt ending. You try me, my dear, and you will never work another day in this town," Rhenee scolded.

"I hear nothing, I promise, Madam," the frantic Carla mumbled in broken English. "I was jus…"

"You were just what?" Rhenee interrupted.

"I was just dusting when you walk out here," the woman said, shaking nervously.

Rhenee looked the woman up and down as if she was trash. "Do you think that you're smarter than me?"

The woman didn't comment. She continued to stand in silence while staring closely at Rhenee. She had no clue of what was about to transpire. All she knew is that a lunatic came storming out of the office, obviously upset about something she thought Carla had heard. Carla had no idea what the woman was in such a rage about, but she didn't want any trouble.

"Fuck with me, and I'll have your green card revoked faster than you can get your immigrant ass to the bus stop." After chastising the woman, Rhenee walked off. She wasn't the least bit worried about Carla.

The fierce Rhenee strutted through the parking lot toward her car. She was frustrated, nervous, and upset. She had so much going on in her life that her nerves were soaring out of control. Now, two people knew her secret, and the situation was taking a much different turn than she planned.

She approached her vehicle, and disarmed the alarm before opening the door and collapsing behind the steering wheel. She tossed her briefcase to the back seat, and turned on the engine. Moments later, the car pulled out of the parking space and sped out into the traffic. As she drove the sports vehicle down the street, Rhenee unfastened her suit jacket and pounded the steering wheel. What would she do if the cleaning lady were to tell what she'd heard? Although the woman claimed that she didn't hear anything, that didn't stop Rhenee from being in doubt.

"Damn it," she yelled, pouncing her hands on the steering wheel. "I don't have time for this shit." She was defending a client, whose trial would end on Monday, and she didn't have time to loose her focus. The trial was becoming much more stressful than she imagined, now that the prosecutors had thrown in unsuspected evidence. A Xanax, a valium, and a stiff drink would do her good. Out of the thirty-six cases she'd defended, she'd lost only one, and that was her second case, which she'd lost on a technicality. She didn't have time to be distracted by something that was so unimportant. The strategy to win her case would be to have a closing statement that was well prepared and thought out. She was at the peak of her game. Rhenee was earning nearly $400,000 annually, and was still trying to climb her way up the success ladder. Her plan was to become senior partner within the next two years at the firm, where she was employed. If she wasn't given the position she felt she more than deserved, Rhenee was walking. Her long-term goal was to start her own practice, and eventually she would. She had enough money saved up to live off of for the first two years it would take to get established.

At first, Rhenee thought she could erase the last few months of her life from her memory, but now there was interference. She couldn't believe that Ray was acting like her rival, instead of her supporting lover. After all the deceitfulness they'd committed together, how dare he now have a conscious? She would have to keep a close eye on him from now on. She didn't know if she could trust him or not. She was in a Catch 22. How could the man she was so deeply in love with be her adversary?

Rhenee retrieved her cell phone from her purse and answered it on the fourth ring. It was Ray. "I sure hope I didn't piss you off. The last time I did that, you cut off my supply of kitty-kitty and I don't know what I would do if I couldn't have that."

She was instantly soothed. Her face lit up like the morning sun. "I'm on my way home. I'll have a glass of wine chilling, and you can meet me in the hot tub," she seductively cooed.

"I'll be there in half an hour," Ray confirmed before hanging up.

Rhenee hung up the phone and sped thru traffic like a Nascar driver. She needed to get to her house to freshen up before Ray made it there. After the way she'd stormed out on him, she was certain that what they'd had was over. The impromptu phone call from him reassured everything was okay. Now that Ray was coming over, she knew she'd be able to get some good loving and a good nights rest. Rhenee had complications sleeping when she didn't have Ray lying next to her. When he was home with his wife, she had to take sleeping pills.

She didn't know why she always gave into Ray so easily; didn't know why she loved him so much, but she did. Here she was this cold blooded attorney who was notoriously known for being aggressive and dominating, to anyone who stepped in her path, but when it came down to Ray, she was powerless. She went out of her way to please him, and yearned for his affection, which is why she accepted him whenever she could have him. Even though Ray belonged to someone else, when he spent time with her, he always made her feel so good. Ray made her feel as if no other woman in the world existed but her. She knew where his heart was. Rhenee knew that Ray couldn't possibly love his wife more than he loved her. With her, Ray had the full package: a powerful, strong and successful woman, a best friend, a colleague, and a lover. She felt she could always be open and honest with him. He was easy to talk to, and was about the only one who could tame her wild streak, which is what Rhenee lusted for most. A strong, powerful man, who was able to keep her in line, she'd been in love with Ray even when she was married to Sullivan, which was the reason her marriage ended. For some reason, she wasn't able to tame her lust for Ray. She thought about that man from the time her eyes opened in the morning, until they exhausted to sleep at the end of the day.

When she pulled up into her driveway, to her surprise, her King was already there. His car was the first thing she noticed. She smiled and continued to pull her vehicle into an empty parking space. After gathering up her briefcase, purse, and the bag she'd gotten from the store, Rhenee climbed out of her car. Ray got out his BMW and stepped in her direction. He appeared to be on the phone. Once he disconnected the caller, Rhenee smiled and reached up to kiss him. Afterwards, she handed Ray the bag and her briefcase, and they walked toward the building together.

"I was expecting to walk in and be ready to step right in to a hot tub of bubbles, and you," he flirted.

She blushed while sliding her key card through the slot on the door. "After I hung up the telephone, I realized that I didn't have any wine, so I ran to the store. You're going to need something to cool you off after I get finished with you."

The lobby was quiet. Rhenee walked up to the elevator and pushed the up button. While waiting for the elevator, she turned to Ray. "How about you have me for dessert, then we can relax in the hot tub while sipping wine."

Ray smiled, as their lips met. Rhenee was half way out of her blouse by the time they made it to her floor. She had to pull Ray's hand away from her when the elevator stopped on her floor. As soon as she unlocked the door to her condo, Rhenee dropped her clothing to the floor and was all over her man. She pinned Ray up against the wall, as his hands groped her buttocks. First, Rhenee undressed him, and then she jumped into his arms. He stuck himself inside her. Rhenee rode him. About three minutes into their lovemaking Ray fell back onto the wall screaming. His legs became weak, as his hardness quickly faded. Rhenee yelled out his name when she reached her ecstasy, before climbing down off of him.

"Whew," she panted, as she walked slowly into her bathroom. Ray went into the kitchen to get the wine glasses. On the way back toward the bedroom, Ray picked up the wine from the floor by the door, and headed toward the room after Rhenee. She was standing around the tub pouring bubble bath under the running water. She was still butt naked. Ray smiled as he sat the glasses down and proceeded to opening the wine bottle. Once the bath was ready, Rhenee and her man stepped in and cuddled in the relaxing hot water. They sipped their wine and talked about the up and coming week. Rhenee told him about the gun the prosecutors presented, which had fingerprints belonging to her client.

"All this time, Alan had me convinced that he was the victim. Even after the weapon was presented, Alan still claimed he had nothing to do with the drive-by shooting. I can't tell if he's telling me the truth, or not, and how can I properly represent him if he's not telling me the truth," she fussed.

Ray told Rhenee to focus on them and not think about her job. He wanted her to enjoy the time they were spending together. She was going on way too long about her case, and he wanted to relax and get intimate. He reached over and buried a juicy kiss on her lips. Instantly, Rhenee was silenced.

They got out of the tub and sat in the living room waiting on take-out Rhenee had ordered. They ate in front of the fireplace. After pouring up the wine, Rhenee and her man made love again. Later, they fell asleep in each other's arms.

After Ray left the next morning, Rhenee showered, fixed lunch, and worked on her closing statement for the last day of the trial. Although she had no doubts she would lose, she wanted to be well prepared for the case. Rhenee was one of the finest litigators at the firm and had a long list of credentials to prove it. Even though a curve ball had been thrown her way, they hadn't heard the last from her. Somehow, she had to make the jurors see that her client was the victim, whether she knew if he was or not.

Her client, Alan, had pleaded not guilty to the accessory to murder case that was pending against him. He continued to stick to his story, claiming to be barbequing on the day of the murder. Supposedly, a friend offered him a ride, but said he had to make a quick stop first. Alan, the back seat passenger, had no idea that the guys, he was riding with, were about to drive by on Willie Smooth to blast him, until it happened. In court, that Friday, the prosecutors revealed evidence that stated a second set of fingerprints were found on the murder weapon. The passenger seat driver, Sean Blakely had already been charged and sentenced for the murder. He took a plea for fifteen years. The driver of the car, James Smith, got off with a ten-year sentence. In order for Rhenee to be pleased, her client had to walk. She hadn't decided her strategy, but she was going to get him off.

As she paced the floor of her condo, she chewed on her fingernails. Rhenee prowled her mind for ways to evade the jury in some way. She looked over all the notes she had from the Blakely and Smith's cases to see what she looked over before, that would help her out now. She also looked at the forensics file to see what evidence they'd collected. Anything she could find would help her. If it took her all weekend, come Monday morning, she would have a dynamite closing argument that would result in her client walking as a free man.

CHAPTER 34

Rhenee stepped inside the courtroom on Monday morning, both rejuvenated and happy. Over the weekend, she had compiled some persuasive evidence that the prosecutors never bothered to investigate. She had absolutely no doubts about her win, and Rhenee told her client so, when she took her seat beside him in the courtroom. After the bailiff asked everyone to stand, Rhenee whispered to her client, "You have nothing to worry about."

Alan smiled as he flipped the collar of his black Sean Jean suit. Behind them sat Alan's family, and the girl who'd come to Rhenee's office and paid the retainer. Alan's mother looked worried as she sat with a white napkin in her hand. Today would seal the fate of her son, and she looked as if she was ready to get the whole thing over with.

Rhenee rose from her chair, and walked over to the jurors to begin delivering her closing statement. "Ladies and gentlemen of the jury, I ask that you take a close look at my client, Mr. Alan Shapen, and see that he is not a cold blooded killer, nor an accomplice to any murder, as he's being accused of. Now, I want you all to think long and hard about all the evidence that has been presented to you by the prosecutor. In all this legal maneuvering, let's seek out what we know about this case, the truth, or shall we say, the known facts. In the eyes of the law, we have a duty, under God, to seek the truth, without prejudice." Rhenee looked straight into the eyes of the jurors as she spoke.

"Today, I want you all to recap all the evidence presented to you. You will see that the information against my client has been fabricated, and he, in fact, is an innocent man. If you all find my client anything besides not guilty, then I'm afraid that you all will be simply sending an innocent man to prison."

Rhenee paced back and forth, in front of the twelve jurors. With great confidence, poise, and cleverness, she broke down the case how she saw it.

"Let us go back to the day in questioning. Say we start right where the defendant got into the car with his friends, and the car in question is, a two door 1976 Cutlass. My client, Mr. Shapen was the back seat passenger. Now these three men leave the defendants house, headed to the store. My client has no knowledge, whatsoever, that the driver and passenger, who we know to have already pled guilty, and have been found guilty, and sentenced in a court of law, were about to commit a drive-by shooting, in broad day light. All my client knew was that the driver, Mr. James Smith, had to make a quick stop before taking him to the store. Now, at the crime scene, where police collected over fifteen witness statements saying that the gunshots fired at the victim came from the passenger riding in the front seat of the car. Now fifteen people, who were at the scene, on the day of the murder, all stated that they saw shots coming from the front seat of the 1976 Cutlass. We all know that my client was a back seat passenger, because when arrested only two blocks away from the scene of the crime, officers pulled my client, Mr. Alan Shapen from the back seat of the vehicle. These, ladies and gentlemen, are the facts that the prosecution knew, and never failed to tell you."

She took a deep breath, paused. "Now, let's talk forensics. During the trial, forensics evidence showed us that the victim was shot by bullets being fired from a northeast angle of the vehicle. Now wouldn't it almost be impossible for my client, the backseat passenger of the vehicle, to shoot out of the moving vehicle, traveling at what forensics estimated to be at least sixty-five miles per hour, without shooting the front seat passenger, who he was seated behind in the car? Doesn't this raise an obvious question in your minds, ladies and gentlemen, of the jury? How in the world was it possible at all?"

"The real question, ladies and gentleman, is why my client is even here. Why is he being charged with a crime we know he didn't commit? All throughout this trial, prosecutors have tried to make my client look like the bad guy. My client has committed no crime. My client has hurt no one. Yes, we know that he is a twenty-six-year-old black man who still lives at home with his mom, but is that a crime? Yes, my client hasn't found a suitable place of employment for the last year or so, but I ask again, is that a crime?" Rhenee continued pacing back and forth, in front of the jury, while she spat questions at them.

"My client is simply a victim of naivety, I admit. When my client's friend asked him to open the duffle bag sitting next to him in the backseat of the car, he was a fool for taking the gun from the duffle bag and holding it. It was immature of him to place his fingerprints on a weapon while admiring the beauty of the remarkable piece. It wasn't even wise when my client passed the weapon to his friend, who which then proceeded to wave it out the window and spraying bullets into another human being. But, I say again, ladies and gentleman of the jury; my client has committed no crime. Does holding a gun make him a murderer? No, ladies and gentlemen, I'm telling you, that my client, Mr. Shapen, is the victim here. Now one may ask what is he a victim of. Well, I'll tell you. My client is a victim of asking for a ride to the store, and should he pay for that with the rest of his life?" Rhenee stared intently into each juror's eyes.

As Rhenee prepared to close her statement, she concluded, "I say again, ladies and gentleman, since I've presented you with the facts, I ask that you all do the right and just thing, which is to find my client, Mr. Alan Shapen, not guilty." Afterwards, Rhenee smiled, and turned to walk back to her seat, before confirming, "The defense rests."

Silence blanketed the courtroom.

The judge looked up from his notes and said, "Court will stand adjourned until the jury comes back with a verdict." He slammed the gavel down on the wooded plate and dismissed everyone.

The jury deliberated for almost two hours before coming back to read the verdict of not guilty. Roars came from all over the courtroom. Rhenee smiled as her client thanked her. Alan was so happy; he lifted Rhenee off her feet, and spun her around. When her feet touched the floor, he shook her hand and said, "Thank you, Rhenee. You really saved a brothers life. I owe you the world. I will have the rest of your money in your office on Friday."

Rhenee smiled while closing her briefcase. "I'll be looking forward to it!" She was ecstatic about her win, even though she'd known all along what the verdict would be. She always won.

Rhenee was in a rush to get by all the press because she was trying to make it to the restaurant where she was meeting Ray. He had called her earlier while the jury was out, to tell her that he had some important information to share with her. She couldn't wait to get to the restaurant and hear him tell her that he'd left his wife and was moving in with her. That would really be a fairytale ending to what had already been a good day, she pondered.

Although she'd hoped to, Rhenee didn't make it out of the courtroom without doing two press interviews. On camera, she boasted about how she was never worried about getting her client off. For her last camera comment, she reiterated a phrase she'd used during her closing statement. "My job from the beginning was to seek the truth that would free my client, and that's simply what I did." Afterwards, she eased away to get to Ray as soon as she could.

When she arrived at Dudley's, Rhenee pulled up to valet and jumped out of her freshly restored, Porsche. Dudley's was an upscale restaurant tucked away downtown. The atmosphere was cozy and private. You had to have advance reservations, if you wanted a seat, nearly any night of the week. Dudley's was always packed with upscale business buppies. They served delicious food, and the finest wines. Dudley's was certainly considered as the number one upscale, fine dining restaurant. There wasn't an entrée on their menu under $50.

The hostess escorted Rhenee through the crowded restaurant to the table where Ray was waiting for her. When he noticed her approaching, Ray stood to greet her with a kiss. He smiled, to cover up the hurt he was hiding. After greeting his date, he took a seat.

Rhenee sat down at the table full of smiles. "I guess you heard about your girl winning her case," she bragged as she opened the menu handed to her by the hostess.

Seeing somewhat disinterested, Ray nodded, then took a sip from his drink. "I did," he finally commented.

"Am I bad or what?" Rhenee continued to revel in her own success.

"You are," he huffed, nonchalantly. "I always knew you'd win the jury over. You are one of the finest attorney's I know."

"Did you order any appetizers? I'm starving." She unfolded her napkin and placed it on her lap. "After all that brilliance, I think I'm mentally drained. I've worked up quite an appetite."

"I can't make my mind up about what I want," Ray answered sadly. "Or at least, that's what I've been told." Rhenee's eyes looked up over the menu to stare at Ray. She wasn't sure where he was going with the conversation.

"I'm sorry," she exclaimed.

"Celeste knows about us. She called me today from Philadelphia saying she has known about our affair for quite sometime, and since I can't make up my mind about who I want to be with, she's leaving me. She said that she was going to stay in Philly to take care of her mother. She's going to send movers for her things." He exhaled. "Can you believe she's leaving me?"

Rhenee didn't know whether to jump for joy, or be sympathetic about Ray's wife leaving him. Although it was the best news she'd heard all year, she didn't want to show her true feelings. She wasn't sure what to say. Her mouth hung open with astonishment. "Oh, Ray," she finally spoke.

"Oh, Ray, my ass," Ray shouted. "Celeste wants me to agree to pay her $5,000 a month, alimony, or she'll take me to court for half of everything."

Rhenee didn't know what to say.

"I can't believe this shit," Ray cursed as he drank the last of his drink in one gulp. "I don't even have an appetite," he fussed while flagging for the waitress. As soon as the waitress arrived at the table, Ray asked the woman to get him another Scotch on the rocks.

"Right away," the woman answered, as she left the table.

"Look, Ray, if you don't feel up to this, why don't we order our food to go, and take it to my place? Maybe there you can relax."

"No, I don't want to ruin your good day. Let's celebrate your big win. I don't feel like dealing with my problems right now."

Rhenee smiled as the waitress came back to the table with Ray's drink. "I'm ready to order," Rhenee told the woman. Both Rhenee and Ray ordered from the menu. After their meal, they skipped dessert and decided to go back to Rhenee's place.

At her condo, Rhenee headed straight to the kitchen and took a frozen turtle ice cream cake from the freezer. She cut two slices and placed them on saucers. Ray walked into the kitchen wearing only his boxers. Rhenee sat the two saucers on the counter and pulled out two bar stools. They sat down and enjoyed their desserts in silence. Finally, she'd gotten her man. Rhenee quickly finished her dessert in what seemed like three bites. She rinsed her saucer in the sink, and then placed it inside the dishwasher. She walked over to Ray and rubbed her hand across his bare back.

"I can tell this whole thing is really bothering you, but I want you to know that I'm here for you, always."

He turned to her and embraced her with a comforting hug. He looked directly into her brown eyes. "I appreciate that, Rhenee. You know we've been through a lot together.

This is nothing," he confessed. Rhenee sadly held her head down. "What's the matter, why the sad face?"

Rhenee hesitated before answering. "It's nothing. I'm just tired from a long day."

Ray lifted her head. "I love you."

Rhenee blushed and pushed away from him. "Come in the bedroom and show me how much you love me," she cooed.

Ray climbed down from the barstool and took Rhenee's hand, and she escorted him to her bedroom where they climbed into bed and made love. Their passionate lovemaking ceased all their problems from the rest of the world.

The next morning, was Tuesday. Ray was going into the office late, and Rhenee wasn't going in at all, so they spent the rest of the morning in bed. When her eyes noticed daylight, Rhenee got up and decided to fix breakfast for Ray. Although the reason was beyond her, her man was going through some rough times, and she wanted to comfort him in any way she could. After all, his wife was divorcing him, so Rhenee could finally have Ray to herself, which was a cause for celebration. She needed to get used to catering to her man, on a regular basis. She was thankful that her prayers were finally answered. As Ray slept, Rhenee proceeded into the kitchen to start his breakfast. If he hadn't awakened before she finished cooking, she'd have to serve it to him in bed.

Ironically, on her way to the kitchen, the doorbell rang. Rhenee never had any company besides Ray, so she was hesitant about opening the front door. As she tied the belt around her robe, Rhenee proceeded to the door with caution. What if it was Celeste? What if Celeste had followed Ray to her place? "Damn," Rhenee cursed. What was she going to do? She looked toward the bedroom to see if Ray had been awakened by the doorbell. He was still sleeping, so she crept to the front door. When she peeked threw the peek hole Rhenee was surprised to see that her visitor wasn't who she'd expected. Instead of worrying about Celeste, Rhenee was confronted by a couple of officers.

Her heart stopped. "Oh, Lord," she cried. "What do they want?"

The doorbell sounded again. This time it was preceded by a knock.

"Who is it?" she asked in a sleepy voice.

"Kent County Police, Ma'am. We need to talk to you."

"Just a minute," Rhenee stated. I need to get dressed." She was so scared she didn't know what to do. She stuck her hands into her mouth and screamed silently. *Were they coming to arrest her*, she thought. Frantically, Rhenee ran to the bedroom and woke Ray.

"Ray," she called, while shaking him. "Ray, wake up, the police are here."

Ray's eye's fluttered open slowly as he wiped his vision clear with the back of his hand. "Ray, the police are here," Rhenee said again. The doorbell rang, again.

Quickly, Ray jumped up from the bed and grabbed his pants, while wondering what was going on. He jumped into them while following Rhenee to the front door. She looked thru the peek whole again. They were still there. With Ray standing at her side, Rhenee finally turned the locked and pulled open her front door.

"Are you a Ms. Rhenee Edwards?" the officer asked.

When Rhenee answered yes, the officer immediately read Rhenee her rights. One of the officers informed Rhenee that she was being taken down for the hit and run accident that occurred nearly a year ago. Rhenee cooperated and went with the officers willingly. She cried profusely as the two police officers escorted her away. She never thought she'd see the day when she had to be taken downtown like a criminal, but today was her day. It was the day, when all her luck had finally ran out.

CHAPTER 35

When Dorothy finally got Sullivan Jr. down for a nap, she quickly went into the kitchen to continue preparing the dinner she was cooking. It was a quarter to twelve, and Dorothy liked to have her dinner ready by three when her husband and children got home. After placing her meatloaf in the oven, Dorothy stirred her pinto beans and walked into the living room to turn on the television. If she were lucky, she'd be able to watch the twelve o'clock news, and the first part of The Young and the Restless in peace.

At only four months old, Sullivan Jr. was spoiled rotten. Dorothy wasn't able to maneuver as much with him as she had been with her other children. Even her grandson, Deshawn was a calm mannered baby, compared to her son. Whenever Sullivan was home, he held the baby. Dorothy had been getting on her husband about holding their son so much, especially while he was sleeping, but for Sullivan that went in one ear and out the other. He loved that baby to death. Dorothy loved him also, but all of the constant fussing he did was starting to get on her nerves. She had to break her son now before his hip-riding habit got out of control.

After flipping the channel to ABC, Dorothy sat down on the sofa. A commercial was on, so she threw her head back and exhaled. It was only nine more minutes before the opening seen of her soap opera. Dorothy was anxious. "Oh, come on with it," she lashed out at the television as soon one commercial went off, and another one immediately followed. It was a special news report. Aggravated, she rolled her eyes. She wished the dark haired news reporter would hurry up and tell her story, so they could get back to the scheduled program. When Sullivan's ex-wife's mug shot appeared on screen, Dorothy quickly turned up the volume on the television, and impatiently waited to see what was going on.

Rhenee's picture popped onto the upper thirds of the television screen and then disappeared. A series of graphic pictures from a car accident site appeared next, soon after, the news reporter, Sally O'Brian reported her story..

"Today, exactly one year after the fatal, hit and run accident that took the life of a young toddler, and injured several members of her family, police have finally arrested a suspect," Sally reported.

A pre-recorded video of Rhenee being escorted by police, into the police department, appeared on the screen. Dorothy was speechless as she continued to listen.

"Ms. Rhenee Edwards, a local defense attorney, is accused of hitting the victims as they crossed the street, and leaving the scene of the crime. Today Ms. Edwards was arrested in her home after an anonymous tip put detectives on to her. Ms. Edwards is being charged with several charges, we're told, one being vehicular homicide. At this time, we're still gathering information on this story. We'll have the full report at six."

Tears streamed down Dorothy's face. She could not believe what she was hearing. Never in a million years would she have thought Rhenee was the vicious killer of her niece. *Rhenee. Oh, no,* she thought. Dorothy wondered if Rhenee was aiming to kill her, as her hands trembled. She jumped up from the couch and raced for the telephone. Her hands trembled, but she steadied them momentarily, in order to dial the number to her husband's job. When Sullivan answered, she immediately poured out her discovery to him. "It was Rhenee, baby. It was Rhenee who hit us that day and took Timya away from us. Baby, it was your ex-wife who tried to kill us."

For a short time, Sullivan was voiceless. It took a couple seconds for him to decipher what his wife was trying to tell him. On the phone, Dorothy was panting, and crying uncontrollably.

"Sweetheart, can you calm down and try to calmly explain to me what you're talking about?"

Dorothy sniffed really hard slightly gained her composure enough to tell her story from the beginning. "Sullivan, I just saw Rhenee on the news being taken into the police station. They said that she was the one who hit us and drove away. The news reporter said she was being held on vehicular homicide charges."

Sullivan tried hard to believe that Dorothy had somehow gotten the wrong information. He truly did not want to believe that Rhenee could be so treacherous as to try to kill his wife.

"Rhenee was out to hurt me, and Timya was the one who suffered. Lord it was supposed to be me, not the baby," she cried.

"Dorothy, I'm on my way home," Sullivan told her. "Just calm down and I'll be right there."

"Okay," she cried over the phone.

Her husband hung up and raced out of his office. In his car, Sullivan dialed the number of the detective who was working on the case, then proceeded to drive his car onto the street. When the operator asked, "How may I direct your call?"

"Detective Beason," Sullivan answered. There was a few seconds pause, and then the detective picked up.

"This is Detective Beason."

"Detective Beason, this is Sullivan Edwards. My wife got some disturbing information from a news briefing about the car accident. Can you please tell me what's going on?"

"I'm sorry, Mr. Edwards, that the press got a hold of the story before I had the chance to contact you all, but you'll be happy to know that we have the accused suspect in custody. It appears that the person who we arrested is your ex-wife."

"So it is true," he mumbled inaudibly.

"She is in an interrogation session now. We have reason to believe that this whole ordeal could have been premeditated. Ms. Edwards already has council to defend her, so she'll probably go for a preliminary hearing in a couple days. The minute I find out more, you'll know," the detective told Sullivan.

Sullivan was speechless. He couldn't believe what he was hearing. Why would Rhenee deliberately try to kill his wife? Then it suddenly hit him. His thoughts took him back to a particular day when Rhenee appeared at his job saying she wanted to see him. As his reflections appeared clearer, Sullivan could visibly recall the day when Rhenee showed up for a spontaneous visit to his job. It was the exact same day of the fatal car accident. He should have known something was wrong. Rhenee had never stopped by his job, unexpectedly, not even when they were married.

"Oh my goodness," Sullivan huffed. Although he tried to focus on driving, his mind kept wandering back to the situation at hand. "It was going to be a long day."

CHAPTER 36

On the day of Rhenee's trial, Dorothy, Sullivan, Andrea, Monet and Caroline sat in the courtroom silently waiting for the jury to return with the verdict. Besides the press, there weren't many people in the courtroom. While the jury was deliberating, everyone else sat around making small talk. Rhenee's parents were situated in the first row behind their daughter. Caroline and her family sat on the opposite side of the courtroom, in the same row as Rhenee's parents. Throughout the entire trial, Caroline had kept a close eye on Rhenee. When the subject of her drinking during the time of the accident, was brought up, Caroline wanted to jump up, and pull Rhenee out of the chair by her hair, and beat her down to the floor. At no point during the trial did Caroline see any signs of remorse on Rhenee's face. Rhenee was such a cold-hearted bitch. Caroline hoped the jury would convict her to serve time for the rest of her life. She'd taken the life of her granddaughter and had continued on with her life as if it were flawless. How could she live with herself knowing that she'd taken the life of an innocent child?

Dorothy was such an emotional person, she cried throughout the entire trial. The bizarre turn of events had sent her right back into a state of depression. Monet was at her side, assuring her mother that everything was going to be okay. Dorothy was on an emotional trip because the trial brought back her issues of guilt that she'd felt in the beginning. She felt like it was somehow still her fault that Timya was gone. Her family reassured her that there was no way she could have prevented the accident. As she wiped her face with the Kleenex given to her by her husband, Dorothy sat back when she noticed the bailiff and the jurors entering the courtroom.

After the judge's eyes scanned the verdict, written on the paper handed to him by the bailiff, the bailiff handed it back to Juror Number One. Dorothy's family held hands, and Dorothy closed her eyes as Rhenee was read her verdict.

"We the jury, find the defendant, Rhenee Sullivan, **GUILTY** of the charge of manslaughter," said Juror Number One.

The rumble of chattering voices rang out in the courtroom.

"Order in the court, order in the court," the judge yelled, while slamming the gavel onto the wood plate.

Rhenee's head jerked back in disbelief. She actually looked shocked. Dorothy's family jumped to their feet after the judge assigned a sentencing day for Rhenee. It was scheduled the following week. When court was dismissed, Caroline ran up to Rhenee who was being escorted out of the courtroom by an armed officer, and spat in her face. "I hope all your days are of suffering."

Chatter rang about in the courtroom, as Rhenee's mother ran toward Caroline, yelling. Dorothy quickly grabbed her sister by the waist and pushed her out of the courtroom, before she ended up sharing a cell with Rhenee. Rhenee stood expressionless and somber. Her thoughts were so far gone, she hadn't even responded after Caroline violated her. It was as if she had drifted off into a world of her own. The officer handed Rhenee a napkin to wipe her face, then he walked her out of the courtroom. Her parents stood around, until their daughter disappeared behind the wooden doors.

Respectfully, Sullivan walked up and hugged Rhenee's parents as they exited the courtroom. They, like him, could still not believe that Rhenee was capable of such a crime. All of the incriminating evidence the prosecution laid out during his testimony had proven everything. Why Rhenee would trust, a two-bit hustler, no one could never figure out. For some reason, she'd told Crip Lee, all the gruesome details of the accident, which Crip Lee happened to have the entire conversation captured on a security camera tape, from inside his body shop. Charles Lee had given the tape to the police as hard, physical, evidence to incriminate Rhenee, and exonerate himself. The police viewed the tapes, and observed the transpiring of all the illegal activity, in which they suspected, going on inside of Lee's chop shop. It also captured the disassembling of stolen vehicles inside the establishment. Lee had no idea that all his hi- tech, video equipment he'd invested in would be used to prosecute him.

As the two families parted ways, Dorothy commented out of the blue, "One down, two to go." Quizzically, Monet sighed.

"Ha!"

"One trial down, and two to go," Dorothy repeated again. "After the sentencing next week, there will also follow a civil law suit. Andrea, Caroline and I have decided to sue Rhenee for the pain we've suffered."

Monet smiled. "That's right, Mama, get that cunt for everything she's got." They all laughed and continued heading toward the exit.

That following week, Dorothy's family sat in court as the judge sentenced Rhenee to seven years in a private women's prison, and he announced that her license to practice law had been permanently revoked.

Dorothy couldn't believe it. "That's it?" she yelled. "For taking the life of my niece, all she receives is seven years. With good behavior, she'll be out in five and a half." Dorothy yelled before her husband quickly sat her back in her seat and asked her to please remain calm. Dorothy was totally ecstatic.

After the verdict, Sullivan sadly held his head down and left the courtroom. Although Dorothy didn't feel they received justice in the criminal court, the $300,000 she was awarded in her civil case, nine months later, made it all seem better. Andrea and Caroline were awarded $500,000 for the losses that they'd suffered as well.

In May, Andrea gave birth to another baby girl she and Tim named Grace Marie Doberson. Unlike the birth of their first child, Tim was there to welcome Grace into the world. Andrea was all smiles. The following month, Andrea and Tim finally tied the knot. Since it was summer, they were married in a small ceremony, in the Doberson's backyard. During the reception, Caroline actually walked up to Tim and addressed him as her son-in-law, and congratulated him on his vow of love to her daughter forever. Andrea was elated. She and Tim weren't able to go on a honeymoon, but a few weeks after their wedding, they moved into their very own home. Tim found a job right away and supported his wife's ideas of being a stay at home mother.

Dorothy wished to have her settlement money by the time her daughter's wedding came around that July, because she was going to cancel all their previous plans, to give Monet a fairytale wedding, but the money didn't come through that soon. So, the ceremony, as planned, was held at Malcolm's family church, and Monet couldn't have looked prettier. The day after, Monet and Malcolm would head to Mexico for their honeymoon, compliments of Dorothy and Sullivan.

THE END

EPILOGUE

Punkin sat irritated while Malcolm and Monet exchanged wedding vows. She wept. Even though Monet and Malcolm seemed to have a genuine love for one another, and would probably have a long beautiful marriage, Punkin was glad it was Monet saying "I do," instead of her. She was glad to be free. Marriage just wasn't for her, and although it wasn't that long ago when she and Mark were married, she was happy to be single again. Punkin had tried to work things out with Mark, but her choice to leave was what seemed to bring the peace back in her life. Mark was crazy and abusive, and she wasn't the one to be walking around making up lies for why she had a black eye or busted lip. Even after the counseling sessions with the pastor, there was still no change in Mark, and to avoid having to go to jail for killing him, Punkin chose to go her own way. After the episode in the grocery store, where he snatched her neck, because he said she was using her eyes to flirt with another man, Punkin couldn't take anymore. Never in her wildest of dreams did she think a simple "Hello," to a man in the grocery store, would have her husband's fingers wrapped around her neck. He nearly choked her breathless, until someone interfered and threatened to call the police. The next day, she moved, and into her own place. Even though he begged her to come back, she simply didn't want to be a victim anymore. Mark needed major counseling to work out his issues, and Punkin wasn't sticking for regular ass beatings, until he pulled his act together. After their divorce was final, she decided not to get back into the dating game for a while. Punkin simply wanted to take time to enjoy the freedom that she'd given up to be in a dysfunctional marriage, with an insecure psycho.

During the ceremony, Mark reached over and placed his arm around her shoulders. She quickly jumped up and ran out of the sanctuary. She hated that the two of them had been placed in seats right next to each other, and since they were still married when the wedding planner made the seating arrangements, it was too late to change. *Why was he here anyway*, she thought, as she stood in the bathroom, waiting for the ceremony to end. She would stick around to apologize to Monet for leaving in the middle of the ceremony, but she didn't want to be in the same proximity as her ex-husband. Even though she'd taken out a restraining order for him to stay away from her, that didn't stop Mark from stalking her and begging her to take him back

When she heard footsteps entering the bathroom, Punkin turned on the water in the sink, and pretended to be washing her hands. To her surprise, when she looked into the mirror, it was Mark. Quickly, she turned the water off and backed into the wall.

"What do you want, Mark? Don't you know that you're not supposed to be anywhere near me. Why can't you just leave me alone?"

Mark slowly ambled toward her. He had an evil, deranged grin on his face, and his hand was hidden behind his suit jacket. "I want you," he said, enunciating every word, as his hand resurfaced holding a small black firearm, "and if I can't have you, then no one will," he declared.

Ever since Mark had been calling and threatening her, Punkin had purchased a 32-caliber pistol for protection. Even though she'd taken the proper precautions to keep him away from her, the reality was that a restraining order didn't mean that the police were going to watch her twenty-four hours a day, so she had to protect herself, but, her purse was sitting on the counter.

As he continued his approach, Punkin quickly reached for her purse. When Mark noticed what she was doing, he tried to snatch the Coach bag from the counter before she could get it, but he failed. Punkin grabbed her purse, quickly reached inside, and situated her hand around the cold piece of steel. Mark aimed his gun at her, just as she whipped hers from her purse and waved it at his head. Two clips clicked, and two guns fired, nearly in unison.

BOOK DICUSSION QUESTIONS

1.Early on in the novel we can see that Caroline's character has not changed much from the first book. Do you think that Andrea's having a second child, whom Caroline was so proud of, will change her for the better?

2.Do you think that Caroline's reaction to her husband riding with Sheila was justifiable. (b) Do you think her actions will affect Thomas' relationship with Sheila and Thomas Jr. (c) If you were Sheila would you feel comfortable letting your child go back over to his father's house, after the fight she had with Caroline?

3.Do you think that Punkin and her husband's relationship would have worked out differently if she and Mark had taken more time to get to know one another before jumping into a marriage?

4.Rhenee was a sucker for Ray, and even though he always treated her as a rebound, she considered what they had to be a relationship. If she had not gone to jail in the end, do you believe Ray would have been in an exclusive relationship with her after his wife left him?

5.Caroline, Punkin, and Rhenee all seemed to be searching for something that each of their lives lacked. Discuss what you think each woman was on a quest for.

6.Since Sheila's date, Cameron was never mentioned again, do you think she ever went out with him again?

CONTEST!!!

DO YOU WANT TO WIN SOME MONEY, MONEY, MONEY???

From the Epilogue

What do you think happened in the end?

Unscramble the words and fill in the blanks to find the answer. Email your answer to www.maseyree.com to win $50

The person who emails me the correct answer will receive the money

Fill in the blanks with the words provided

Y B R U A S D M T L F O O Y E I T N T H H T S E E

— — — — — — — — — — —   — — — — — — —   — — — — — —

DON'T FORGET! LOG ON TO WWW.MASEYREE.COM TO CLAIM YOUR PRIZE!!!

BOOK/ ORDER FORM

To purchase *Only Time Will Tell*, by Maseyree please make check or money order out to
Tongue Untied Publishing
P.O BOX 822 Jackson, GA 30233.

For Purchase of book *Only Time Will Tell*   **$14.00 per book**

Book Quantity_____   **Total Enclosed $**_____

Name_____

Address_____

Phone/optional _____ Email _____

Book autographed to _____

Thanks for supporting my vision,

Maseyree- **President**

ALSO BY MASEYREE

It Just Gets Better with Time

For more information log on to

www.maseyree.com